The TWISTED ROAD *to* YOU

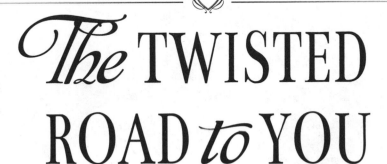

The TWISTED ROAD to YOU

A LOVE FROM THE HEARTLAND NOVEL

Barbara Longley

Montlake
Romance

Text copyright © 2015 Barbara Longley

Published by Montlake Romance, Seattle
www.apub.com

Amazon, the Amazon logo, and Montlake Romance are trademarks of Amazon.com, Inc., or its affiliates.

ISBN-13: 9781503948242
ISBN-10: 1503948242

Cover design by Shasti O'Leary-Soudant / SOS CREATIVE LLC

Printed in the United States of America

Nanci, Chris, Jim and Mary: thank you for your unwavering support and enthusiasm.

CHAPTER ONE

WESLEY SET HIS BROOM ASIDE and checked the wall clock. Almost the end of his shift. As soon as Langford & Lovejoy's day crew arrived, he'd head to the Perfect Diner for his daily dose of Carlie, the diner's pretty assistant manager. The food wasn't bad, either. Anticipation thrummed through him, bringing a grin to his face.

"You do that every morning," Ken grumbled. "It's creepy."

Wes's smile widened. Ken was always grumpy at the end of his shift. He ought to know, since he'd been supervising the overnight crew of furniture finishers here in the small town of Perfect, Indiana, for a year and a half now. "Grinning is creepy?"

"It is when you do it every single morning at *exactly* the same time," Ken groused. "Makes me think you're up to something."

"Naw, bro. It's not creepy. That's just your paranoia talkin'." Miguel slapped Ken on the shoulder. "Wes is just smiling 'cause he's gonna go see his girl soon."

Wes walked over to his dog's bed and scratched the old German shepherd behind the ears. Rex had already had his trip outside. He'd be fine here for a while. "I don't have a girl."

"Right. Have it your way." Miguel chuckled and shook his head. "It takes a woman to put that stupid smile on most men's faces. But I guess for you all it takes is eggs and bacon. How about I join you for breakfast this morning?"

"Sure, but won't your wife be upset when you don't come home for the breakfast she'll have waiting for you?"

"Good point." Miguel patted his flat belly. "Nobody cooks like my Celia. Guess I'll head home after all."

The back door swung wide, letting in a blast of early November air. "Morning," Ted Lovejoy said, holding the door open for his fiancée, Cory.

"Hey, Ted, Cory." Wes did his customary once-over on Cory to make sure everything was good with her. Her radiant expression said it all. She was doing well and continuing to heal from the trauma she'd suffered at the hands of her staff sergeant a couple of years ago.

He and Cory had grown up in the same trailer park on the south side of Evansville, and he'd always looked out for her. She and his youngest sister were best friends and had been since the day Cory and her mother moved into the park. "How are the wedding plans coming along?"

"I'm glad you brought it up," she said, taking him by the arm. "Come with me. I have a favor to ask."

His stomach rumbled, but this was Cory. Hunger could wait. She led him to the storefront, dropped his arm and fished around inside the purse she carried slung over her shoulder.

Pulling out a thick, butter-colored envelope, she turned a hopeful look his way. "This is your invitation to our wedding. I've talked it over with my mom, and she agrees. You're like a brother to me, Bunny," she said, reverting to his childhood nickname. "You're the reason I have my job here. If it weren't for you, Ted and I wouldn't have met. I don't know what I would've done without you in my life." Her voice quavered. "Will you walk me down the aisle?" She handed him the invitation.

"Whoa, Squirrel. Didn't see that coming." Warmth spread through his chest. "I'd be honored." He stared at the fancy script on the front of the envelope. Wesley Holt . . . and guest.

"Good." Cory patted his forearm. "One more thing."

"What's that?" He raised his gaze to hers.

"Bring a date."

"Uh . . . no. I don't think so." He rubbed his forehead and shifted his weight, edging toward escape. "I'm not—"

"Ask Carlie. We'd like her to be there, but we don't know her well enough to invite her." Cory's chin angled up a determined notch. "You and Carlie have chemistry. Neither one of you can keep your eyes off the other when you're at the diner." She poked him in the chest. "Ask her."

Memories swamped him—an e-mail sent by his wife, now his ex, while he was deployed. Two short paragraphs. That's all she wrote, but those two paragraphs had plunged him into a deep, dark well of misery and rage the night before a mission. His throat tightened, and a familiar image flashed into his brain. Wes forced the image of the young Marine's face back into the far recesses of his mind, but then the anger and betrayal living in his gut like a parasitic worm raised its ugly head. He inhaled and exhaled slowly, while visualizing himself stomping the worm into the rocky desert with his Blackhawk Desert Ops combat boots.

He no longer risked getting involved. Who needed that kind of pain? Not him. His heart was no longer up for grabs. Coping with his PTSD was about all he could handle, thank you very much.

"It's time, Wes." Cory's brown eyes filled with concern as she peered up at him. "Just because your heart was broken once doesn't mean the same thing is going to happen again."

It had been a struggle, a constant uphill climb, but he was content with his life and somewhat at peace. Admiring Carlie from a distance was all he could handle. What did he know about her, anyway? Sure, he lusted after her, but . . . nope. Not worth it. The dreams he'd had for a family of his own were long dead. Besides, he was almost forty—too late for a do-over. He'd gotten into the habit of sleeping during the day, because he had fewer nightmares then, and even though he'd come a long way in the past year and a half, he still experienced the occasional flashback. Irritability and paranoia still got the best of him sometimes, and he never could predict what might trigger a reaction. What kind of parent and partner would he make? "I'll think about it." *No, I won't.*

"Good." Cory nodded. "Think about it all the way down the street to the diner, and then ask her."

He raised the invitation. "Consider me RSVP'd. I'd be honored to walk you down the aisle."

"Thanks, Bunny." Cory's voice went shaky again. "My dad was a Marine, too, you know? Having you stand in his place means the world to me."

The next thing he knew, she had him in a hammerlock hug. His heart melted, and he hugged her back. "Me, too," he mumbled before disentangling himself. "Get to work, Squirrel. I've got to go get something to eat."

"All right." She glanced at him, her eyes bright. "While you're at the diner, don't forget to ask Carlie to be your date for our wedding."

"Humph. Think I'll head on out to the truck stop for breakfast this morning," he teased.

Cory's laughter brought his smile back. He handed her the invitation. "Put this in my in-box in the production room, would you? I'll grab it when I get back." His smile once more firmly fixed, Wesley headed the two blocks down the street to the local diner. Pancakes sounded mighty good this morning, or french toast with a side of thick-cut bacon and extra-crispy hash browns with onions.

Half a block away from the diner, the air carried the scent of sausage, bacon and onions. He salivated, and not just for food. The sight of Carlie Stewart bustling around the retro fifties diner in her snug black jeans, equally snug white T-shirt and red apron did that to him.

In the summer, she'd worn shorts, giving him an eyeful of her shapely legs. Even better.

The small bell chimed as he opened the door. He looked around . . . and frowned. Someone was sitting at *his* corner table—the table Carlie always reserved for him. She was nowhere to be found. Disappointment fogged his brain.

Jenny Maurer, the diner's owner, approached. "Good morning, Wes." She motioned him toward a different table.

He didn't budge. "Where's Carlie?" Since he'd moved to Perfect, he'd never known her to miss work. His gaze roamed the interior of the diner, even though he knew he wouldn't find her there. Her absence was a tangible force pressing him back against the wall. *Overreact much?* Nothing more than his PTSD acting up. *Slow inhale. Slow exhale.*

"We don't know. She didn't show up for work this morning, and she hasn't called." Jenny's brow creased with worry.

That brought him up short. A prickle of unease raised the fine hairs at the back of his neck. "Did you call her?"

Jenny nodded. "Several times. She's not answering."

Twenty years of finely honed combat instincts flared to life. Something was wrong. He hadn't overreacted. Images of Carlie trapped in the wreckage of her car somewhere along the highway flashed through his mind. What if she was unconscious in her house from a fall or a carbon monoxide leak? "Where does she live?"

"Do you know the McCurdy farm?" Jenny asked. "It's about ten minutes west of Perfect. Carlie rents the little white house about a mile down the road from there. It's the only other house on that stretch of road."

"No." He shook his head. "But if you have an address, I can put it in my GPS."

"I don't. You know how it is when you've lived your entire life in the same small town. I know where everything is, but I couldn't give

BARBARA LONGLEY

you more than a handful of addresses." Jenny moved to the cash register. "Harlen, hand me a piece of paper and a pen. I'll draw a map."

"Way ahead of you, honey." Harlen glanced at Wes. "I was about to head out to check on Carlie myself, but that would leave Jenny even more shorthanded here at the diner." He handed Wes a piece of paper. "I drew a map while you two were talking. Sheriff Taylor's personal cell phone number is at the bottom. I was going to give him a call just as you walked in. I still will, though at this point there's no real reason to send him out to Carlie's. Would you mind heading out that way to check on her?"

"No, I don't mind. I have the time." Wes caught something in Harlen's expression as he took the map. The older man knew something he didn't. Harlen was also a veteran. He'd been in the military police during the Vietnam War, plus he'd been sheriff of Warrick County for twenty-five years before he retired. Wes pulled out his cell phone and entered the sheriff's number into his contacts before folding the map and stuffing it into his back pocket. "What do I need to know, Harlen?"

"Carlie has . . . history." The retired sheriff glanced at his wife. Jenny nodded slightly. "It could be that her past has come looking for her. Then again, her absence might be nothing at all. Maybe she had car trouble this morning, and she's on her way right now. She could have misplaced her cell phone, or her son might be sick." He crossed his arms over his chest. "We'd appreciate your willingness to give her a hand if she needs one."

Wesley frowned. He had a feeling her absence wasn't as simple as a lost cell phone or a sick kid. Adrenaline flooded his system and he tensed, battle ready. "On my way."

"Wait a minute," Jenny called as she disappeared into the kitchen.

He didn't want to wait. Worry for Carlie twisted his gut. "What kind of *history* are we talking here, Harlen?" he asked. Carlie was divorced and had a son named Tyler, that much he knew.

"I'm most concerned about her physically abusive ex-husband." Harlen's voice dropped to barely audible. "All we know about him is that he's a real piece of work with a criminal record."

Wes nodded. A bully he could handle. He rolled his shoulders and turned his head from side to side to loosen up, forcing himself to remain where he was until Jenny reappeared. She came back to the register, holding a white paper bag in one hand and a to-go coffee in the other.

"On the house," she said, handing him the bag and the cup. "It's a fried egg, bacon and cheese sandwich, and the coffee is just the way you like it. You can eat on the way."

"Thanks." He took the bag and the coffee from her. "I'll call you when I find out what's going on with Carlie." In its current knotted state, his stomach couldn't take food, but Rex would appreciate the treat. Sucking down the coffee on the fly, he hurried back to L&L.

Three sets of eyes turned to him the minute he burst through the back door. His boss, Noah Langford, glanced at the clock, and Ryan Malloy, L&L's design genius, raised an eyebrow. Wes took the egg sandwich from the bag, unwrapped it and tossed it to Rex. The dog caught it midair and devoured the treat in seconds flat. The empty coffee cup and paper bag Wes tossed into the trash bin.

Ted Lovejoy, co-owner and business manager of L&L, straightened up from whatever furniture design the three of them were studying. "You're back fast. Is everything OK at the diner? Is my aunt Jenny—"

"Jenny's fine." Not wanting to waste any more time, Wes took the stairs two at a time to his third-floor apartment. Once he was inside, he headed for the closet in his living room where he kept his handgun in a locked metal box. He unlocked the box and took out the handgun, its cold weight fitting against his palm familiar. Too familiar.

He loaded the M9 Beretta, put on the safety and shoved it into the back of his belt. Years of training and experience took over, and he went through the mental steps preparing himself for the job ahead. Rescue and protection. Carlie and her son, Tyler, were his mission. If her bully of an ex-husband had anything to do with her absence, he'd set the man straight. As he ran back down the stairs, he planned how he'd go about getting the job done. He crossed to the hooks on the wall where he kept one of Rex's leashes.

"Why the gun, Wes?" Ryan followed him and blocked the back door.

Grabbing Rex's leash from its hook, Wes shook his head. "We'll talk later. Might be nothing."

"Do you *feel* like it's nothing?" Noah studied him.

Shortly after retiring from active service, Wes had met Noah through the VA center in Evansville. They'd gotten to talking, and the next thing Wes knew, he'd been offered a job in a growing furniture business that only hired veterans. Plus, Noah had offered him a place to live in the small, quiet town of Perfect.

If anyone understood the way battle-honed instincts acted upon a veteran, it would be Noah. They had both commanded a platoon during their military careers. They were both haunted by the loss of good soldiers under their command. Ever since that first meeting, they'd been in the same PTSD support group, along with Ryan Malloy and a couple of the other L&L employees.

"Carlie didn't show up for work this morning." Wes's grip tightened on the leather leash. "Harlen and Jenny are worried. She never misses work, and she's not answering her phone. They asked if I'd check it out, offer her a hand if she needs one. Harlen is worried her abusive ex-husband might have something to do with her absence. The gun is just a precaution."

"You want backup?" Ryan asked.

"No, but thanks. Harlen already called Sheriff Taylor. He's on standby."

"All right." Noah straightened. "Be careful, and call us if you need anything."

"Roger that." Wesley clipped the leash onto Rex's collar and commanded the three-legged dog to heel. Pulling Harlen's map out of his back pocket, he strode to his SUV. Rex's right hind leg had been shattered beyond fixing by mortar fire in Afghanistan, and jumping into Wes's vehicle was no longer easy for the retired explosives-detection dog. Like all military dogs, he'd undergone two trainings—explosives detection and bite-to-capture. Wes had been required to learn what the dog's training entailed before he could adopt him. He needed to know the commands in order to avoid inadvertently causing Rex to go into attack mode around other people. He lifted the dog and placed him on the front seat. "Time to work, buddy."

Rex's tail thumped, and his ears stood up at full alert. Wesley ruffled the fur around the dog's head for a second before circling around to the driver's side and climbing in. He studied the map. Not too complicated. Not a whole lot of chance for error when it came to the few rural roads he'd have to navigate. He started his car, pulled out of his space and headed west.

Scanning the side of the two-lane road, he searched for any sign of a car accident. Relieved at not finding Carlie's car in a ditch, he searched the side of the road for the green fire marker with the number Harlen had written down. There it was—the intersection with an oak tree on the west side, a winter-wheat field on the east and the McCurdys' farmhouse set back at the end of the long gravel driveway. He turned left onto the narrow road. Carlie's house would be a mile down on the right.

Trees and brush grew alongside the lane, and leaves still clung to some of the branches. Good. Cover was good. About a quarter of a mile from the small white house, he pulled over and parked his Chevy in the dry grass beside a gnarled blackberry thicket. If Carlie was in trouble, he didn't want the bad guy to see him coming.

Carlie's old Ford Escape was parked in the driveway, alongside a late-model sedan. Now he knew for certain she wasn't alone. He gripped the steering wheel, and his mouth went dry. *What if she's with a lover and just forgot to set her alarm clock?* His chest tightened, and the familiar burn of betrayal scorched him. *What? Let it go.* He had no business putting that on her. Carlie had every right to see whomever she wanted. It wasn't like *he'd* ever made a move on her or even asked her out for coffee. Nope. Their association started and ended in the diner.

Wes helped his dog down and gripped the leash. Keeping close to the side of the road, taking cover where he could, he moved slowly toward the house. Once he was within range, he pulled out his cell phone, snapped a picture of the unfamiliar car and license plate and sent them in a text to Sheriff Taylor's cell phone number. Just in case.

Using the parked vehicles for cover, he crouched low and made his way to the corner of the house. Then he crept along the foundation until he reached the bay window to the right of the front door. He heard an angry male voice on a rant.

Man, what he'd give right now for some of the high-tech surveillance gear he'd had access to while deployed. Holding his breath, he rose slowly and peered through the window. What he saw stopped his heart cold. Carlie and her little boy sat huddled together on the couch. A man paced in front of them, waving a wicked-looking combat knife in the air. Carlie's right eye had swollen shut, and her lower lip bled where it had been split. Wes dropped back down, swore under his breath and focused on listening.

"You and the kid belong to me, Kara. We're a family. You had no right to take my son from me. No. Right. You and Tyler can either come with me today or I end you now. After what you did to me, I *should* end you. Worthless bitch, with or without you, I'm not leaving this hellhole without my boy. You hear me? I'm taking my son."

Kara?

Carlie responded. Her voice was too low for him to hear what she said, but he could detect the note of pleading. Rage exploded in his chest. What kind of man beat a woman, threatened to *end them* and terrorized their kid?

Wesley unleashed Rex, gave him the hand signal to heel and circled around to the back of the house. He prayed he'd find the back door unlocked. Folks in Perfect rarely locked their houses, especially out in the country. If he was lucky, he could sneak in and capture the enemy before the guy even knew he and Rex were there.

Slowly, he pulled the screen door open and checked. *Not* his lucky day. *Damn.* The back door had been locked, probably by the asswipe terrorizing Carlie and her son. Stepping back, he drew his gun, undid the safety and sized up the door. One kick, and a resounding crack filled the air. The wood frame splintered around the piece-of-crap dead bolt, and the door swung wide.

"Get 'em, Rex," he commanded. Growling, his dog shot through the house. Wes followed. "Drop your weapon," he shouted, gun raised. Rex slipped on the polished wood floor. The dog went down and scrabbled to recover. The slip gave the bad guy the seconds he needed to sprint out the front door. Rex followed on his heels, and Wesley ran out after them. The guy managed to slide into his car, but Rex had him by the ankle, and he wasn't letting go. The car started. The man put the sedan in reverse and gunned the engine, dragging Rex alongside the vehicle.

"Rex, *out*," Wes called, aiming his Beretta. He didn't want Rex getting caught under the tires—or by a bullet. Rex let go, and Wesley fired. He missed the tire, and the bullet pinged against the hubcap. He fired again—and missed. The car door slammed shut, and the car peeled off in a wave of gravel and dust.

"Heel," Wes called. Rex trotted toward him, stiff legged, with his ruff still standing on end. His heart hammering against his rib cage, Wes put the Beretta's safety back on and shoved the gun back into his belt. "Good dog," he crooned, scratching the dog behind his ears, giving Rex the reward he sought for a job well done. The shepherd's ruff settled, and his tail wagged. Wes snatched his cell phone from his pocket and called Sheriff Taylor. "This is Wesley Holt—"

"I ran the license plate. The vehicle is stolen," Taylor said without preamble.

"Figures." Wesley ran a hand over his buzz cut. "A man had Carlie and her son at knifepoint. He's gone now. Took off in the stolen car. She's been beat up, and I overheard the guy threaten to kill her and take her son." He turned back to stare at the house.

"On my way," Sheriff Taylor said. "I'll put out an all-points bulletin with the vehicle description. Will you remain on site until I arrive?"

"Hell, yes." Wesley eyed the open front door. "I'm not leaving." For now, Carlie and her son were safe. Wesley planned to see that they stayed that way, no matter what it took. He and Rex headed for the house. He had no idea how to comfort Carlie and her boy after such a trauma, but he'd do his best. He just hoped his best was enough.

"Rex, drop." The dog plopped to his belly on the rug inside the front door, his ears pricked up for any sign of danger. Wes couldn't bear the hurt and fear he saw in Carlie's pretty blue eyes, and seeing her lovely face so battered and bruised turned him inside out. His hands curled into fists. He wanted to inflict the same damage and worse on the scumbag who'd split her lip and put that frozen-in-fear look on her little boy's face.

"Sheriff Taylor is on his way. I'll be right back." He went to the kitchen, opened the freezer and snatched a bag of frozen corn. He returned to the living room and handed it to her. "That man . . . he's your ex?" Her eyes filled, and his gut tied itself into a painful twist.

Carlie nodded. She pressed the bag of frozen corn to her face and drew her son closer to her side with her free arm. "You saved my life, Wesley. If . . . if you hadn't—"

"Glad to help." Wes crouched down in front of the two of them, eye level with the kid. "Hey, I'm Wesley Holt, a friend of your mom's. You OK there, buddy?" The little guy's face had lost all color, and his eyes didn't seem to focus until he spoke to him.

The boy glanced at Carlie and then at Wes. "I"—his chin quivered—"I had a accident." Color rushed back into his face.

Wes patted the kid's knee. "Happens to the best of us." He reached out to touch Carlie's cheek but stopped himself. He wanted to gather her up and hold her until she stopped trembling, until she knew she was safe in his arms, but they weren't on a touching basis. Instead, he placed his hands on the couch on either side of the two, encircling them as closely as he dared. He met her eyes. "You OK?"

She shook her head. "No, but I will be, thanks to you. Come on, Tyler. Let's get you cleaned up."

Wes rose and reached down to help her up. She dropped the bag of corn on the couch and placed her hand in his. His breath hitched, and a frisson of heat coursed through him at the skin-on-skin contact. He steadied her once she was on her feet. Her tears had started in earnest, and helpless frustration stirred him to a froth. He needed something to *do* with his hands—something that would keep him from wrapping his arms around the woman who tugged at the ragged edges of his soul the way she did.

"You have accidents?" Tyler stared up at Wes, saucer eyed.

Grateful for the distraction, Wes nodded. "I've had one or two, sure. It's natural to be afraid when you're being threatened, and sometimes that fear causes a man to lose control." The child's face relaxed a little, and Wesley's heart turned over in his chest.

"You coming with me and my mom to my room, Mr. Holt?" Tyler's gaze turned to the shadowy hallway between the living room and the kitchen.

"You can call me Wes." He peered down at the little boy whose blue eyes were so much like his mother's. Tyler gripped Carlie's hand with double-fisted tenacity, like he was afraid she might disappear if he let her go.

"I thought I'd stay here in the living room and keep an eye on things," he told the kid.

Tyler's face went pale again, and his eyes filled with panic. He couldn't even imagine what it must be like for Carlie's son right now.

He'd seen his mom get beaten up, and the little guy had heard his dad say he planned to end his mother's life. Wes's jaw tightened, and a lump clogged his throat. Not right. Not right at all.

Wes backpedaled. "On second thought, how about I stick close to you and your mom? You and I would make a pretty good team, don't you think?"

Tyler nodded, and his shoulders unbunched a fraction. Wes followed the two down the hall to Tyler's bedroom. Dark blue walls with glow-in-the-dark planets and stars appliquéd all over the surface greeted him. A matching bedspread covered the twin bed of the cozy, little-boy bedroom. He stood at the door so that he could keep the two of them in his sights.

"Get what you need, Ty. I'm going to go fill the tub." Carlie gently pushed her son toward the dresser, and then she left for the bathroom.

Wes couldn't tear his eyes from her. Petite and curvy, she was dressed in her snug black jeans—the best part of the uniform she wore for work—and a long-sleeved white T-shirt. He hated seeing her shoulders so slumped and defeated. He hated that her ex had stolen the smile from her pretty face and the light from those heart-stopping blue eyes of hers. The need to protect her had him itching once again to drag her into his arms.

Shoving his hands into his back pockets, he turned his attention back to Tyler's room. A wide bookshelf crammed full with books and toys caught his eye. He imagined Carlie reading to her son at bedtime. Wesley's mom had never read to him or his brothers and sisters. By the time she finished her day cleaning other people's houses, she was exhausted. It was the same with his dad, who worked at a tool and die company.

His parents had worked long, hard hours to keep their large family afloat. They were good people, and he never doubted their love for each other, or for their six children, but it had never been easy. Still, as tough as it was, neither of his parents had ever raised a hand in anger against each other or their children. They'd always been a close, loving family, and he counted his blessings where they were concerned. As the oldest, Wes had been the one to read to his brothers and sisters, help with homework, clean and bandage scraped knees and dole out the PB&J sandwiches for lunch.

Tyler opened dresser drawers, pulled out clean jeans and a pair of briefs with some kind of superhero printed on them. Wes's chest took on a whole new ache, this one churning with anger. The little guy's sense of safety and security had been ripped to shreds. No child should have to live in fear, and when the source of that fear is one of the people you should be able to trust the most? Well, that just made it a thousand times worse. "All set?"

"Yeah."

"Let's go, partner." He took the bundle of clean clothes from the boy and held out his hand. Tyler tucked his small hand in his, and again Wesley's heart wrenched.

The sound of a siren grew close—Sheriff Taylor, no doubt. Carlie met Wesley and Tyler outside the bathroom. "That will be the sheriff." He squeezed the little boy's hand. "I have to go meet the sheriff, but I'll be back." He handed Carlie the clothes and left Tyler with his mother. Then he walked through the house and out the front door to wait.

The sheriff's SUV raced down the country road, lights pulsing and the siren breaking the peace and quiet of the autumn rural landscape. The incongruence brought a frown to his face. The sound of a siren and the sight of flashing lights didn't happen very often in Perfect, Indiana, and when they did, it was usually due to a car accident or some act of stupidity on the part of the local adolescents. Wes crossed his arms over his chest and leaned against Carlie's Ford.

The vehicle barreled down the gravel driveway, coming to a sudden halt a scant few yards away from where he stood. Paul Taylor, the sheriff of Warrick County, climbed out, clipboard in hand. He shook Wesley's hand. "Hey, Wes, I appreciate your help. Is everything secure here?"

"For now." Wesley gave him a description of Carlie's ex and filled him in on the details of what he'd witnessed and heard. When he finished, the two of them walked toward the house together. They found Carlie waiting for them, with her son stuck to her side like he'd been fastened there with Velcro. Rex's head came up from his paws, looking to him for direction. He motioned for him to stay, and the dog let out a long sigh and dropped his head to his paws again, clearly disappointed by the lack of action.

"Jared violated the restraining order I have against him," Carlie said, slipping a legal-looking document from the manila folder she held against her chest. She handed it to the sheriff. "I . . . he shouldn't be out of prison yet. He . . . he's not eligible. No one notified me that he was out. They were supposed to let me know." Her voice held an edge of fear.

Sheriff Taylor gestured toward the couch. "Let's sit down, Ms. Stewart. We can start from the beginning."

Nodding, Carlie and her boy moved to the couch. The sheriff took the chair in the corner, and Wes remained standing. *Prison?* Her ex had called her Kara. Was she in some kind of witness protection program or something? "So, violating a restraining order, assault with a weapon and car theft—if he is on parole, he's pretty much blown it, right?" Wesley arched a brow in question.

"I have my deputies out looking for the stolen vehicle, and hopefully he'll still be in it. I've also notified the neighboring counties. Now that I know who he is, we can issue a warrant, though I suspect there may already be one outstanding."

Sheriff Taylor and Carlie got down to business, and Wesley scanned the yard from where he stood, looking for any movement in the surrounding fields and forest that might indicate the bad guy had circled back. The thought that Carlie's ex might be out there watching and waiting sent a chill down his spine. Her place was too damned isolated—too far from help should she need it.

"Thank you for the picture, Ms. Stewart. This will help. I have everything I need for now." The sheriff rose from his chair. "We'll have a deputy parked in your yard tonight in case your ex returns."

"Thank you. I appreciate it." Carlie set the folder down on the couch and rose with the sheriff, walking with him to the door. "I didn't have my house locked. I'll keep both doors locked from now on—and the windows."

Wes shook his head. "I wrecked the back door." He pulled out his cell phone. "I'll see that it's replaced today, along with a better dead bolt than the one you had before. Do you have a tape measure?"

"I do," Carlie said before heading down the hall.

The minute his mom left the room, Tyler moved to Wes's side and reached for his hand. Wes took it and gave him a reassuring squeeze. "I've got it covered here, Sheriff. I'll bring Carlie and Tyler with me when I go for a new door. They won't be alone, and her ex knows I'm armed. I took a couple of shots at his tires." He shrugged. "I'm out of practice. Missed both times." He'd have to make a point to get to a shooting range to practice.

"I'm going to assume you have a permit for that handgun." The sheriff's brow lowered.

"Of course I do."

"This is the moment where I have to tell you *officially* to stay out of police matters. *Unofficially*, though, the Warrick County sheriff's department is undermanned and lacking resources. We don't even have our own SWAT team anymore. I have to call on Evansville to have their team come out when we need it. I can't really spare the manpower to keep a deputy here around the clock. I appreciate your willingness to keep an eye on Ms. Stewart and her son. Just don't turn any more vigilante than you already have today. Got it?"

"Got it." Not really. If Carlie's ex crossed his path, he'd do what needed to be done to render the guy senseless until the sheriff could come and haul the piece of human garbage away.

The sheriff attached his pen to the clipboard. "I'll be in touch." He opened the door. "I'll have a deputy parked in her drive by the time you get back. Call me on my cell if you catch sight of Carlie's ex."

"Will do." Paul left, and Wes hit speed dial one-handed for L&L. Tyler still clung to him, and he wasn't about to let go of the kid.

"Langford & Lovejoy," Paige Malloy answered. "What can we build for you today?"

"Hey, Paige. This is Wes. I need to talk to Noah."

"I heard Carlie is missing. Is everything all right?"

"For now." He frowned. "Man, news travels fast in Perfect. How'd you hear?"

"Jenny called to talk to Noah. I just happened to be the one who answered the phone. She didn't say much, only that Carlie was missing from work this morning and you were checking things out. We figured something might be wrong when the sheriff raced through town with his siren blasting."

He glanced at the folder Carlie had set on the couch. "I need to talk to Noah—or Ted, if your brother isn't available."

"What's going on? Did you find Carlie and her son?"

"I did. They're fine for now, but I need some help with—"

"You've got it. I'll get my brother. Hold on."

Carlie returned to the living room with the tape measure. With the phone pressed between his ear and his shoulder, and Tyler's hand in his, Wes headed for the door he'd busted. Noah came on the line, and Wes gave him the short version of what had happened. "I need to install a new door and dead bolt at Carlie's, and I could use a hand."

"I'll help," Noah said. "Do we need a new frame?"

Wesley eyed the mess he'd made. "Afraid so, and I don't want to go the prehung route. The door she had on here before kicked in way too easily. I'd like to do some reinforcing with a new door and a good solid frame."

"Hmm. We can come up with a plan for something sturdier. Measurements?"

"On it. Hold on." He let go of Tyler and handed the phone to Carlie, trading it for the tape measure. "Tyler and I will measure; you relay the information to Noah. All right with you, partner?" He peered down at the boy.

The hint of a smile lit Tyler's face, and he nodded. Carlie went to one of the kitchen drawers and pulled out a small pad of paper and a pen.

"OK." He put the end of the tape measure on the outside of the broken frame. "Hold it here for me, Tyler." It would've been much easier and faster to do the task himself, but he wanted to take the kid's mind off the scary stuff. The two of them measured and gave the dimensions to Carlie, who wrote them down and relayed the information to Noah.

Once the task was completed, he took the phone back. "What do I need to get?" He listened while Noah gave him a list of supplies. "Got it. I'll call you back when we have everything together. Later." He hit End Call and took the pad and pen from Carlie to make a list. "Get jackets. We're heading to Home Depot. You can call Jenny and Harlen on the way."

"No, Wes." Carlie averted her gaze. "I owe you an explanation first. You have a right to know what you've stepped into."

"No. I don't." A fresh surge of adrenaline fired up his nerves, sending his pulse skyrocketing. He sandbagged his heart and hunkered down behind the barricade. Knowing stuff about Carlie meant getting close. Too close. Too personal. "You don't owe me a thing."

CHAPTER TWO

CARLIE STOOD IN THE MIDDLE of her kitchen, dying a little inside. How had Jared found her? For the past two years, she'd clung to the notion that she and Tyler could have a normal life in Perfect. *Guess not.* And Wesley. Her stomach dropped, and shame burned through her. After seeing her like this, he'd never look at her the same way again. *That* was far worse than the black eye and split lip she'd suffered at her ex's hands. "Why are you even here, Wesley? How did you—"

"I stopped by the diner like I always do, and you weren't there." His gaze strayed to the yard outside the shattered back door. "The Maurers were worried. Harlen was about to head out here himself, but that would've left Jenny and the diner in a pinch." His eyes came back to her. "I offered to check up on you and lend a hand if need be."

"You have no idea how glad I am you did." Her chest tightened, and she had to force herself to take a deep breath. "Tyler, get your tablet and headphones. You can watch a movie or play a game while Mr. Holt and I talk." Her son cast her a look that said he didn't want to miss the adult conversation, but he went back to the living room and did what he was told. She and Wesley followed.

Once Tyler was settled on the floor with his headphones in place and the tablet on his lap, Carlie gestured for Wesley to sit on the couch. She loved the way he moved—so sure, so confident. Powerful, but in a good way. She didn't sense any meanness in Wes the way she did with some people. With her history, she'd developed an instinct when it came to judging a person's character.

Her insides fluttered. Hearing the back door burst open, seeing Wesley with his gun drawn and charging after Jared—that was a sight she'd remember for the rest of her life. Her ex would've killed her and taken Tyler; she harbored no doubts about that. He'd certainly come close enough in the past—more than once. She ran her tongue over her lower lip, wincing from the sting.

After today, things would be awkward between her and Wesley, to say the least. He'd probably find somewhere else to have his breakfast. What must he think of her? The retired Marine had no idea his visits to the Perfect Diner were the high point of her days.

Since the first moment he'd walked into the diner, she'd been drawn to him. She hadn't been able to take her eyes off the big guy with his broad shoulders and solemn hazel eyes. He just seemed so . . . solid. Safe. Six feet tall, built like a tank, quiet, kind . . . What would he think if he knew she'd created an entire fantasy world around him?

She'd known all along nothing could ever come of her attraction to the big Marine. After her ex, she didn't want to chance letting another man into her life, or her son's. Another disappointment in the daddy department would shatter her boy, not to mention the devastation she'd suffer. Instead, she fantasized. The dreams had given her something to look forward to, like his daily visits to the diner. Regret stole her breath, and more tears filled her eyes.

Picking up the folder from the couch, she took a seat beside him. "I was born Kara Hague. Before I moved to Perfect, I had my name legally changed to Carlie Stewart. Stewart is my grandmother's maiden name. I had Tyler's last name changed, too."

"OK." Wes slapped his thighs and stood up. "Good to know. Let's go."

He didn't want to hear it, didn't want to know anything about her. Her chest ached—an all-too-familiar sensation since her heart had been broken a least a thousand times in the past two decades. It was a wonder the thing still beat. She rose from the couch and walked to the door. "I get it, and I don't blame you."

Wesley's dog hadn't moved. The German shepherd raised his head from his paws to peer at her, his tail thumping on the rug. Carlie stepped around him. "I can't even begin to tell you how grateful I am for your help this morning." Gritting her teeth to keep from sobbing, she opened the door. "I'll call my landlord about the back door. It's not your responsibility."

Color flooded his face, and he stared at his dog. Perhaps he wasn't quite as solid as she'd thought. She'd built him up in her head, imagined he was as drawn to her as she was to him . . . from a safe distance, of course. "It's OK, Wesley. You can go. Sheriff Taylor is sending a deputy, and I'm sure they'll have my ex back in custody before the day is over."

"I'm not leaving." He widened his stance, crossed his arms and shook his head. "It's not that I don't *want* to hear your story, Carlie. It's just that . . . I'm just not good at . . ." He shrugged his big shoulders. "It's your personal business." His gaze met hers, and his expression seemed to beg for understanding.

"And you don't want to get . . . personal," she muttered. "It's all right. I don't want to get personal, either, but I can't accept your help without telling you. I *won't* accept help from you unless you know what you're getting into. Don't ask me to explain why that is, because I can't."

She gripped the doorknob so hard her hand hurt. "I just . . . it's there, you know? My past." She glanced at Tyler. He followed what was going on between them, his eyes huge. "I know I'm not making any sense. Please, just go. It's best you don't get tangled up in my problems anyway."

Wesley heaved a huge sigh, walked back to the couch and sat down. He picked up her folder and held it out to her. "I'm not leaving. If that means you need me to listen while you spill your guts, then that's what I'll do." He made a hand sign to his dog. Rex got up, moved to Tyler's side and lay down, his tail thumping again. Her son's face lit up, and he turned his attention to petting the dog.

Walking back to the couch, she almost smiled. Wesley looked like a man facing his execution. "You don't have to stay, Wes. We'll be all right."

His brow rose. "Which part of 'I'm not leaving' did you not get?"

A nervous laugh escaped. *Here goes everything—another dream bites the dust.* It was for the best. No more fantasies. She didn't want Wesley, or anyone else for that matter, entangled in Jared's sticky web. Her ex was a jealous and violent man. Wes needed to know what the danger was before he decided whether or not to take another step toward her heap of trouble.

"Harlen and Jenny are the only ones in Perfect who know my story—some of it, anyway." She took the folder from him and sat down. "I have . . . kind of a troubled past." She glanced at Tyler, relieved to see he was still more interested in Rex than he was in listening to her. The dog had rolled onto his back, so Tyler could scratch his belly.

Carlie drew in a long breath and began. "I ran away from home when I was sixteen. I had a serious drug addiction by then, and I pretty much lived on the streets until I was picked up by the cops just before my eighteenth birthday." She stared at her hands. "I'm a recovering narcotics addict, but I've been clean and straight for seventeen years now."

Wesley leaned forward. Propping his elbows on his knees, he stared straight ahead with his chin propped on his fists.

She hated admitting even that small bit of truth to Wes. He'd think less of her. How could he not? What would he do if she blurted out the horrible things she'd done back then to get her hands on the cash she needed to buy drugs? Bile rose to burn the back of her throat. She couldn't do it.

The burden of her past was always there, hanging over her like a cloud of poisonous gas. The sordid details of her poor choices separated her from life in the present and made a liar out of her. She was weary to the bone of living in the shadow that cloud cast. The poison affected every aspect of her life, and she longed to step out from under the darkness—just not today. *Coward.*

"Being arrested was the best thing that ever happened to me. Since I was still a minor, the judge was pretty lenient. Probation. Treatment." She brought the folder to her knees. "I got straight, got my GED and started taking classes at a community college." She sat a little straighter. At least she'd managed to get an education and get herself on the right track—until Jared came along.

Wesley hadn't moved, but he'd started pulling on his lower lip with his thumb and forefinger as if in deep thought. Her bad judgment and the choices she'd made would kill any interest he might have had, and it was best she let him go—not that she'd ever really had him.

Letting him go shouldn't matter—she hardly knew him—but it did. It mattered a lot.

"Jared and I met in a narcotics anonymous group five years after my arrest. We weren't supposed to get involved with group members, but he and I dated. I saw signs of his temper, but he swept me off my feet, and I ignored the red flags. By then I was halfway through working on my degree in hospitality. I had a pretty decent job as a waitress at a nice restaurant in town, and he operated a forklift in a warehouse.

"We married a couple of years later, after I finished my degree. Things went fine for a while. We had fights, of course, and a couple of times he shoved me around, but he always apologized and swore he'd never do it again. I should've left him the first time that happened, but I didn't. I forgave him." Bad judgment, the hallmark of her life. She kept her gaze fixed upon the folder on her lap.

"When the economy went into a recession, Jared lost his job. I was pregnant with Tyler at the time, and the pressure and stress got to Jared. He couldn't handle it. He blamed me for everything wrong with his life, and the shoves turned into slaps and then punches. He'd feel so bad about what he'd done, he'd break down, swear he loved me and promise never to do it again. Then the cycle would begin all over again." Her life had become an unpredictable living hell during those years.

"He tried to get another job, but after a year of being unemployed, he gave up and started dealing drugs. Nothing too serious at first, but after a while, it wasn't enough for him. His dealing soon morphed into drug trafficking on a larger scale." She shuddered. "I feared for my life, for my son's life. Jared insisted I quit working and stay home with our son. To keep the peace, I did what he wanted me to do, and we lived on his drug money."

She opened the folder and pulled out the picture that was taken after her husband had beaten her so badly he'd put her in the hospital. She recoiled from the memories the picture evoked. He'd broken her jaw and three ribs that day. Her face was one massive swollen mess. She handed it to Wes. He took it, studied the eight-by-ten for a minute, then handed it back without a word.

"I realize now that separating me from my job and from my friends was another way he had to control me. After this beating," she said, running her finger over the photo, "I was desperate to find a way out, because I knew I'd die at my husband's hands if I stayed much longer. Jared had already threatened to kill me more than once." She swallowed the lump forming in her throat.

"If I had died, where would that have left my son? I didn't want him to become a monster like his father. I pressed charges for the beating. Jared was already in the system, and he was on the DEA's radar by that time. Two agents came to me when I was in the hospital, and I agreed to cooperate with their investigation. I gave them more than enough information about Jared's drug dealings to put him and a few of his contacts away for a long time." She sucked in a breath. "Jared Baumann is a dangerous man, and the people he associates with are even worse."

Glancing at her son, she continued, "He went to prison. I divorced him, got full custody of Tyler and had my ex's parental rights terminated. That was four years ago. I lived with my mom and grandmother for a while, worked, saved money and changed my name in the hopes that Jared wouldn't be able to find us." Carlie put the photo back into the folder. "The rest you know. Two years ago, I moved here to work for Jenny at the diner." She waited and watched. Wes pulled at his bottom lip again.

"Why Perfect?" he asked, casting her a questioning look.

"My grandmother is from here. She and Jenny are distant cousins. Gran contacted Jenny and asked her for help on my behalf. Gran also knows Harlen Maurer. She knew I'd have some support here in Perfect."

Her throat closed up as memories of that time in her life flooded through her. "Things just fell into place. Jenny wanted to cut back on her hours at the diner, and she was looking for someone to take over some of the management duties at the diner."

"Makes sense." He nodded.

"That's it? Out of that entire sordid tale, all you want to know is 'why Perfect?'" She raked her fingers through her hair. "I'm a recovering drug addict. Don't you have anything to say about that?" she whispered.

"Nope. Like you said, you've been straight for a long time, and I'm in no position to judge." He rose from the couch. "As far as I'm concerned, you're one hell of a strong woman. You pulled your life together under the very worst circumstances imaginable—more than once." Wes stared into her eyes. His were filled with resolve. "Pack some stuff for you and Tyler. You aren't safe here."

She huffed out a strangled laugh. "Where is it you think Tyler and I can go where we *will* be safe? I changed my name and moved to a small town in the middle of nowhere, and Jared still managed to find us."

"The two of you are going to stay with me until your ex is back behind bars. I live on the third floor of L&L in a three-bedroom apartment. The building has a state-of-the-art security system." When he'd agreed to take on the job of building security for L&L, along with his other supervisory responsibilities, he'd insisted on the alarm system. Given where they were located, it was definitely PTSD overkill, but he'd still insisted, and Noah had backed him on the issue.

"There's plenty of room, and I'm always there to protect the two of you. I have friends and coworkers who are also veterans. They'll help. The building is hardly ever without staff on site, and other than Paige Malloy and Ted Lovejoy, every single one of our employees are stand-up veterans with combat experience—male and female. You and Tyler will be protected around the clock close to where you work, which is a far sight better than what the sheriff's department can provide."

"Five minutes ago you didn't want to get *personal*. Now you're telling me Tyler and I should move in with you? I can't do that! What will people think?" She blinked at him, her mind spinning from the unexpected turn their conversation had taken. "What will they say?"

"They will say that under the circumstances, you're making a smart move." His gaze bored into hers. "Besides, you won't be *moving in* with me, Carlie. You'll be staying in my apartment as my guest in your own room until your ex is apprehended and put back behind bars."

He motioned for Tyler to take off his headphones. "I work nights and sleep during the day. You'll have the place pretty much to yourselves. I'll walk you to work in the mornings, take Tyler to school, and I'll be there to walk you home and pick him up from school in the afternoons."

"School!" She shot up off the couch and went for her purse. "I have to call Tyler's school . . . and Jenny. I have to—"

"Pack," Wes commanded. "You can make your call to the school once we're on the road, and I'll call Jenny and Harlen while you're getting your stuff together." He pulled out his cell again. "Tyler, you and your mom are going to come stay with me and Rex for a while. Is that all right with you, partner?"

Her son's enthusiastic nod weakened her defenses. She frowned. Living under the same roof with the object of her desire was not a good idea, especially now with her ex on the loose. Doing so would send Jared into a jealous rage. He'd be even more dangerous. "Wesley, I didn't agree—"

"It's not open for debate. I want to keep the two of you safe. L&L's third floor is the best place for you and your son right now." He held out his hand to Tyler. "Come on, buddy. Let's go get some of your stuff together, enough for the next few days, and then you can help me nail that back door shut." He shot her a look that said *don't argue.* "We can come back for more of your stuff as needed."

She caved, and her knees went weak with relief. What would it be like to feel safe, to have someone in her corner, protecting her and Tyler? She'd almost been lulled into believing she *was* safe, until this morning. "Only until my ex is behind bars again."

"Exactly," Wes said, heading down the hall with her son's small hand in his.

Studying the circle of wetness the bag of corn had made on her couch and the matching circle of wetness caused by her son, she struggled to pull her thoughts together. Her lip still stung, and the entire left side of her face throbbed. Until today, she'd managed to keep her past a secret from everyone except the Maurers, and they knew only a small portion. Now, everyone in Perfect would hear about her ex. No way could she hide her bruised face, and news of the manhunt would get around. It was only a matter of time before they found out about the rest. Grabbing the thawing bag of corn, she stood up. Once Jared was back in prison, she'd start looking for a new job somewhere else— somewhere out of state.

She opened the door of her freezer and tossed the corn back inside. Tears clogged her throat and her eyes brimmed as she reached under the sink for something to clean up Tyler's accident. A truckload of grief pressed into her from all sides. She'd been wrong to think she could find peace here in Perfect. Would she ever be free from her past? Would she ever find a safe place where she could put down roots and make a permanent home for herself and her son?

That's all she'd ever yearned for, and once again her dreams had slipped beyond her grasp.

Carlie ended her call with Ty's school just as Wesley pulled out of Home Depot's lot. Everything they needed to repair the back door had been tied to the rack on top of his SUV, and her stuff filled the cargo space. "Tyler's school needs a copy of the restraining order and documentation that Jared's parental rights were terminated in our divorce. Otherwise, they said they can't deny him access to his son. I want to take care of that as soon as possible. When we drop the door stuff at my house, I'll get my car and head over there with Tyler."

Glancing at her, Wes shook his head. "We'll go together. You have the folder with you, right? We'll head there now—just tell me where it's located."

"Wesley—"

"I'll likely be picking Tyler up and dropping him off for the next few days. It would be good to show my face there so they'll know me."

"That's another thing I haven't agreed to." She was beginning to chafe at the control he wanted to exert over her life, no matter how well-intentioned it might be. She'd had more than enough of that with Jared. No man was ever going to put her into a box like that again.

"How has Tyler been getting to and from school up to now?" Wes asked, glancing at her again. "You start at the diner pretty early, way before the buses pick up the locals."

"I've been dropping him off with Jenny's niece, Ceejay. She has kids in the same school, and they all ride the bus together. Their oldest, Lucinda, keeps an eye on Tyler for me." She turned to check on her son. He was sound asleep with one hand resting on Rex's back. Poor little guy was worn out from the fright he'd suffered. "I'm off about the same time school is out, so I pick him up."

"I'm not comfortable with that arrangement." Wes checked on Tyler in his rearview mirror. "There are too many holes—too many opportunities for your ex to grab him."

A chill crept down her spine. Jared would take Tyler if he could. Hadn't he said with or without her he wasn't leaving without his boy? Somehow he'd managed to slip away from the federal facility in Terre Haute where he'd been held. Sheriff Taylor had contacted Wes with that information. As the sheriff had suspected, a warrant had already been issued. Jared wouldn't be free long enough to snatch Tyler. Would he?

"With more than one warrant out for his arrest, don't you think he's fled the area by now?" Grasping at straws, she chose that hope to hold onto. "He has to know the sheriff has everyone in Warrick and the surrounding counties looking for him and so does the state."

"I heard what your ex said to you, Carlie. I heard his threats. Do *you* think he's gone?" Wesley shot her an incredulous look. "Are you willing to risk your life and Tyler's while Jared is still on the loose?" He shook his head. "I'm not."

Her hand came up to touch the tender, swollen places on her face. "It's just that . . . you've already done so much. I can't ask you to rearrange your life for us." Her throat closed, and she couldn't catch her breath. "I don't want—"

"My help?" The muscle in his jaw twitched. "You didn't ask, but I'm giving it to you all the same." His grip on the steering wheel tightened. "Trust me, Carlie."

"Yeah, well . . . that's not as easy as it sounds." She choked out a laugh and pointed to her swollen face. "You can see what happened with the last guy I *trusted*."

"I understand," he said, his voice gruff. "I haven't been so lucky in the trust-placing department myself." His mouth tightened into a hard line, and his Adam's apple bobbed again. "But you can trust *me*, Carlie. I swear that I will do *everything* in my power to keep you and Tyler safe. You can take that to the bank."

What did *everything* entail? He glanced sideways at her, and her heart seized at the absolute determination she read in his hardened expression. He was a Marine, an experienced soldier sworn to serve and protect, and she'd just caught a glimpse of what that meant. "Why?" Her eyes stung again. "Why would you do so much for me, when we hardly know each other?"

"You've always been good to me." He shrugged. "I appreciate the way you reserve that table in the corner of the diner for me every morning." One side of his mouth tugged up in a wry grin. "I need to have my back against the wall. I have to face the door when I'm at the diner. You figured that out without a word from me. I"—he cleared his throat—"I enjoy seeing your smiling face every morning, Carlie. Makes my day," he said, his face coloring. "I sleep better after my visits to the diner."

Wow. Just . . . wow. Who'd have thought such a big, tough guy like Wesley Holt could be so sensitive? Who broke this wonderful man's trust? What would she give to be loved by someone like Wesley Holt? She'd never be so lucky or worthy.

Drawing in a much-needed breath, Carlie focused on where they were headed. She pointed to the sign for the next county road. "Take the next exit and head east for Tyler's school." Shoring up her battered nerves, she turned to face him. "You have no idea how much your help means to me. What can I do to thank you?"

"Let me and the crew at L&L help you and your boy." His eyes met hers. Warmth and concern shone from their depths. "Just stay safe. That will be thanks enough."

She nodded, unable to speak. Would all of his willingness to help disappear if he knew the rest of her sordid tale? Once he found out what she'd done to get drugs while living on the street, surely he'd turn away in disgust.

Wes pulled into the large parking lot of Tyler's school and parked in one of the spots reserved for guests located near the front door. Carlie's gut filled with dread. She climbed out of the SUV and went to the back, where she'd tucked the legal folder into the laundry basket holding some of her clothes. By the time she had the folder, Wes had Tyler in his arms. Her son rested his head on Wes's shoulder, still half-asleep.

She marched through the front door, holding it open for Wes, and then headed for the office. The three of them walked through the double glass doors and up to the counter. "We need to talk to Principal Halverson and my son's teacher, Ms. Hoff. Is there someone who can cover her classroom for a half hour or so?"

The school secretary's eyes widened at the sight of Carlie's swollen face. "If you'll have a seat, I'll see what I can do."

Carlie nodded, moved to the bank of chairs against the opposite wall and sat down. Wes's presence beside her was the only thing holding her together. She hated this. The busy office teemed with people. Teachers' aides working at the copier, a woman putting things in the bank of mailboxes against the wall, other parents—they all stared her way, their expressions filling with pity and shock before they quickly turned away. Yep. Time to move.

CHAPTER THREE

WESLEY SCANNED THE AREA AROUND the school, checking for any sign of Jared's stolen car on the road or in the parking lot. Tyler walked between him and Carlie. He placed his hand on the boy's shoulder and guided the two back to his Chevy Suburban.

Sunny Hollow Elementary School now had a copy of Carlie's restraining order and documentation proving she'd had her ex's parental rights terminated in the divorce. Carlie also provided the office staff and Tyler's teacher with a short list of people allowed to pick Tyler up at the end of the day. Wes made sure he was at the top of that list.

One look at Carlie's face, and the principal, assistant principal and Ty's teacher had rallied around her, swearing to keep her son safe. No information would be given out about his whereabouts over the phone, no matter whom the caller claimed to be. The assistant principal swore he'd stick by Tyler's side once school was out until Wes, Carlie or the Maurers arrived to take him home.

Wes opened the back door of his SUV and positioned himself behind Carlie and her son, blocking the two from view. Carlie fastened her son into the booster seat they'd taken from her car, and Wes continued to hover until she was settled into the front with the door shut and locked. Only then did he circle around and climb into the driver's side.

His eyes burned with weariness, and his stomach rumbled. He needed food and rest, and he was starting to get edgy. "Do you mind stopping by the diner before we drop your stuff off at my apartment? It's close to lunchtime, and I skipped breakfast." He glanced at her.

"No, I don't mind. I'd like to see Harlen and Jenny anyway." She twisted around to look at Tyler. "I'll bet you're hungry, too, aren't you, buddy?"

"Yeah," Tyler answered with an enthusiastic nod.

"Good." Wes started his SUV and headed toward town. "Lunch first and then we'll drop your stuff off at L&L. Noah and I will head out to your house to replace the back door once you're settled." He'd nailed the broken door closed as best he could, but if anyone wanted to get in, it wouldn't take much to break it down again. Coffee. He needed buckets of the stuff, because it was going to be a while before he could sleep.

An hour and a half later, fed and dosed with unhealthy amounts of caffeine, Wesley pulled into his parking spot behind L&L. Carlie had brought Jenny and Harlen up-to-date on everything that had happened, and he'd called Sheriff Taylor to let him know there was no need for a deputy to park outside Carlie's place. He'd also talked to Ted, filling him in on everything that had happened and letting him know that Carlie and her son were going to stay with him for a while.

He climbed out, unloaded Rex and scanned the alley. Once he was certain the perimeter was secure, he opened the back cargo area of his SUV. Carlie got Tyler out of his booster seat, and the two of them came around to join him.

"Can you manage this?" He handed Tyler a small cardboard box containing toys, his tablet, headphones and electrical cords. Tyler nodded and took the load from his hands. The back doors to L&L opened. Noah and Kyle joined them.

Kyle got to them first. His gaze settled on Carlie's swollen face, then flicked to the pile of stuff in the back of Wes's Chevy. "What do you need?"

"I'm assuming everyone knows what's going on," Wes asked, reaching into the back of his SUV for a large laundry basket holding Carlie's things.

"We do." Kyle reached out to take the basket from him.

As soon as Kyle took the load from Wes, Noah leaned into the truck and hauled out a couple of beat-up suitcases.

"Carlie and her son are going to stay here until her ex is caught," Wes told them. "I'd appreciate it if you guys would look out for her and Tyler while Noah and I head out to her place to fix the doors."

"Done," Kyle said, heading for the door with his hands full.

His dog didn't behave as if anyone lurked in the shadows. Rex meandered to the corner of their building and sniffed around for any new pee-mail on the narrow strip of dry grass. He relieved himself against the bricks, then he trotted back to Wes's side like he didn't have a care in the world.

Still, Wes couldn't shake the feeling that they were being watched. Shouldn't surprise him. Most likely a PTSD reaction to the day's events. Exhaustion mixed with an overload of caffeine probably didn't help the paranoia. He yawned, and his jaw made a cracking sound inside his head. *Fix door, and then sleep.*

Wes grabbed the last box, looked around the alley one more time, took up the rear and trailed the rest of the staff into L&L. His friends surrounded Carlie and Tyler as they entered the production area, keeping them in the center—the safety zone.

"Oh, my God, Carlie!" Paige cried. "Are you all right?"

"I'm fine," Carlie muttered.

"Come on, let's get you two settled." Paige walked toward the elevator. "Cory and I put fresh linens on the beds in the spare rooms of Wes's apartment, and Ryan is up there now, making sure all the windows are locked and the blinds are down. We use the two extra bedrooms to photograph our furniture samples, and the last beds we photographed are still there. You and Tyler will be sleeping in style."

Carlie's face reddened. "Tyler and I appreciate having a safe place to land for a while."

Wes looked around the room. "Speaking of Cory, where is she? Where's Ted?"

"They left to run an errand, and then they're picking up sandwiches for everyone. We're staying put for lunch today." Paige hit the Up button on the freight elevator. "The guys and I will get Carlie and Tyler squared away. I know you have a door to fix. You and Noah can go."

"Is that OK with you, Carlie?" Wes studied her. He could see being the center of so much attention made her uncomfortable, and he didn't like the idea of leaving her.

"Sure." She nodded. "We'll be fine. Thanks, everybody. I'm just feeling a bit . . . overwhelmed right now. Tyler and I aren't used to having so much help."

The freight elevator thunked into place on the first floor, and Paige unlatched the iron gate. "You might as well get used to it." She gestured to Carlie and Tyler to get in. "You go to school with my brother's kids, Lucinda and Toby, don't you? How old are you, Tyler?"

"I'm six," Tyler said, clutching the box to his chest. "Mommy said I could stay home with her today. That's why I'm not at school. I'm in the first grade. Toby's only in kindergarten, but he's my friend. We take the bus to school together, and I get to play at his house sometimes."

"That's good. I have a little boy who just turned one," Paige chattered on as she stepped into the elevator. "I'll bet Sean would enjoy playing with you, too." Paige glanced at Carlie. "I'll bring him by soon."

"That would be great. I haven't seen him since the last time you brought him into the diner, and that's been a few months. I'll bet he's grown a lot since then." Carlie smiled, but then grimaced and touched her lip. "Ouch."

The guys put their loads down in the elevator, and Kyle got on, reaching for the box Wes carried. Wes handed it over, and then he and Noah headed for the door. "Make yourself at home, Carlie. I'll be back in a few hours."

Once they were on the road, he breathed freely for the first time all day. "Carlie's ex can't get to her on the third floor of L&L. He'd have to get past the security system and the crew, and the guys won't let that happen."

Noah shot him a sideways look. "Who are you trying to convince, me or you?"

"Me." He shot him a sheepish look. "I'd feel better if we kept a gun handy on the first floor production area, just until the guy is back behind bars." He shifted in his seat. "Carlie's ex threatened to kill her."

"She told you that?"

Wes shook his head. "I heard him. He held Carlie and her boy at knifepoint, and you can see what he did to her face. After the sheriff left, Carlie showed me a picture of her ex's handiwork." A sick feeling lodged in his gut. "That asswipe beat her so bad he put her in the hospital." He huffed out a breath. "I don't get it, Noah. I can't wrap my brain around how he could do that. How can a man hurt his wife so badly he breaks her bones, and then tell her he *loves* her?"

"I don't understand it, either," Noah said. "We won't let him get to her, Wes."

His phone rang through his car's syncing system, and he hit the phone icon on the dash. "Hey, Paul," he greeted the sheriff. "Tell me you have him."

"I wish I could. I called to let you know he's ditched the stolen car. We found it on the side of the highway a few miles west of the turnoff to Carlie's place. We don't know if he's on foot, if he's stolen another vehicle, hitched a ride or even which direction he's heading."

"Damn." Wes smacked the steering wheel. "He could be anywhere."

"I'll keep you updated," the sheriff said. "We're looking for him, and so are the surrounding counties. He may have hightailed it out of the area."

"It's possible, but my instinct tells me he's still close. Noah and I are almost to Carlie's house now." He took the left turn, surveying the surrounding area for places where Jared might hide. The woods near a tributary to the Ohio River looked likely. "We'll scope out the grounds for any tracks before we fix the door."

"Let me know if you find anything," Paul said.

"I will, Paul. Talk to you later." He ended the call and glanced at Noah. "Unless Carlie's ex has help, he can't have much money or gear. He's going to have to surface eventually."

"And when he does?" Noah's gaze shot to him. "What then?"

Wesley's jaw tightened. "When he does, I'll be ready."

"To do what?" Noah's eyes narrowed. "It's best to leave this to the sheriff."

"Oh, I plan to—so long as Jared doesn't get anywhere near Carlie or Tyler."

🐑 🐑 🐑

A delicious aroma woke him from a dead sleep. Wesley's mouth watered, and for a few seconds, the smell confused him, but then it all came back to him. *Carlie.* He scrubbed at his face with both hands before checking his alarm clock. Six p.m. He'd only had a few hours of sleep, and he didn't start work until ten. He thought about closing his eyes again, but the scent of something home cooked compelled him to get out of bed.

He could manage to make a few basic meals, enough to keep himself fed, but nothing that smelled as good as what was wafting into his bedroom right now. Swinging his legs over the side of his bed, he sat up and struggled to come fully awake. The second shift would be downstairs now, and he was sure Ted or Noah would've filled them in about Carlie and her son.

Yawning, he stood up, stretched and moved to the master bathroom. He took care of business, splashed water on his face and brushed his teeth. A shower could wait. He had a woman in his kitchen, and the wonderful smells filling his apartment hinted that said woman could cook. He pulled on a pair of sweatpants and a T-shirt and headed down the hall.

The sight that greeted him sent his heart into a tumble worthy of the Olympics. Carlie stood at the stove, stirring the contents of a large pot. Tyler worked on homework at the kitchen table, and Rex was stretched out by the boy's feet. For the first time ever, his apartment looked and felt like a home. Plus the place smelled like heaven.

Carlie smiled at him over her shoulder, and his insides mustered to attention. Even with her eye blackened and her lip swollen, she was so damn pretty she took his breath away. Knowing she was under his roof where he could protect her sent a surge of heat through him. It felt right, like somehow she was supposed to be there.

No! Carlie was a threat to the fragile peace he'd managed to scrape together out of the ruins of his life. If having her there felt right, if he got used to her presence, his heart would break for good when she left, and she was bound to leave. This was temporary. He'd best not get used to it. Too much had happened to him over the years. He wasn't fit for cohabitation. What if he had a flashback or a nightmare with Carlie or Tyler nearby? Would he hurt them? He'd heard about veterans who'd attacked the people they cared about while in the throes of a flashback, and he didn't want to be that guy.

Still, it didn't mean he couldn't appreciate a good meal. "What smells so good?"

"I made smoked-ham-and-split-pea soup. I also made biscuits. I hope you're hungry."

"When did you go grocery shopping?" He frowned. "Tell me you didn't go by yourself."

"I didn't go by myself." She turned off the flame under the soup and moved to her purse where it hung on one of the pegs by the door leading to the back stairs. Pulling out a small leather-clad canister, she held it in the air for him to see. "Ted and Cory bought this for me today. It's a combination of pepper spray and Mace. Cory carries one, too. They also took me and Tyler to the grocery store. We weren't alone, Wes."

"Good." He ambled over to the coffeemaker and got things ready to start a pot brewing. This was his morning, after all. "What are you working on, Tyler?"

"Spelling," he said, sparing a glance for him. "Ms. Hoff says if we all get at least eight out of ten correct on our next spelling test, we're gonna have a popcorn and games party next Friday." He sat a little straighter. "I already do better than that on all my spelling tests."

"It's a good thing we stopped at your school and picked up your assignments today. I wouldn't want you to fall behind." Wes chuckled and tousled Tyler's sandy-blond mop of hair. "I'm not surprised you do so well in school, partner. I knew from the get-go you were a smart kid. Do you have any other homework?"

"Yep. Reading and math." He beamed. "I already did it." He turned back to his spelling practice. "Math is my favorite."

Rex got up to greet Wesley with a cold nose nudged into his palm. He scratched the dog behind the ears while grinning like a fool. Silly, really, but he was proud of Tyler. Carlie was one hell of a mom, and she did it all on her own.

"Dinner is ready." Carlie opened the oven door, pot holders in hand, and pulled out a cookie sheet filled with golden-brown biscuits. "Put your homework away, Tyler, and go wash your hands."

"What can I do?" he asked.

"Wash your hands and set the table."

"Yes, ma'am. Rex, rug," he commanded. The dog went to the rug by his food and water bowls and circled around a few times before dropping to his belly.

She shook her head. "I'm sorry. I'm so used to talking to Tyler like that. I—"

"No worries. I don't mind." Wes washed his hands at the kitchen sink, and then he set the table as ordered.

Carlie ladled out three bowls of soup and brought them to the table. Then she filled a plate with the biscuits and put them in the center, along with butter, strawberry jam and honey. His mouth watered. He poured himself a large mug of coffee and headed to the fridge for cream. "What do you two want to drink?"

"Tyler will have a glass of milk, and I made sweet tea." She shrugged. "I know it's not summer anymore, but I drink the stuff all year long." She took off the apron she'd been wearing, hung it on a hook on the wall and called for Tyler. "He starts playing in the sink and forgets what he's supposed to be doing."

"Yeah, my younger brothers and sisters used to do the same thing. I hear Toby does that, too. It's no wonder Tyler gets along with Noah's son." Wes set Tyler's milk on the table and returned to the counter to pour Carlie's tea.

"How many siblings do you have?" she asked, peering up at him.

Wes placed her beverage down and took his seat. His stomach made an embarrassing rumbling noise. "Five. I'm the oldest, so I ended up taking care of them. A lot."

"Ah. That explains why you're so good with Tyler."

Another surge of warmth washed through him, this time sending color to his face. "You think I'm good with him?"

"I do. You helped Tyler today by making him feel important. You gave him tasks to do so he felt included, and you distracted him from his fear. You'd make a great dad." Her eyes met his for a second, then darted away. "I'm surprised you don't have a family of your own."

His mouth went dry, but then Tyler returned to the kitchen with his hair dripping wet. A good thing, too, because Wes had no intention of touching upon the subject of his lack of family. "How'd your head get so wet washing your hands?" he asked with a mock scowl.

Tyler shrugged his skinny shoulders and slid onto his chair. "I don't know."

Carlie laughed, and Wesley shot her a grin. "In what state did you leave my bathroom, I wonder?"

"Indiana." Tyler's face scrunched with confusion. "Right, Mom?"

"That's right, kiddo." Carlie grinned.

Wes barked out a laugh. "Well, that's good."

Tyler's gaze shot to his mom. "Can I play video games after supper?"

"We'll see," she answered, splitting a biscuit and placing it on her son's bread plate. "Eat. The food is getting cold."

Wes took a biscuit and settled into his meal in earnest. He was on his second bowl of the hearty soup, and on his third biscuit slathered with butter and jam, before he came up for air. "I don't remember the last time I ate so well. This is by far the best split-pea soup I have ever had." He leaned back and patted his full stomach. "My compliments to the cook. To show my gratitude, I'll do the dishes."

Stuffing half the biscuit into his mouth, he was gratified to see Carlie's face light up. She looked mighty pleased with his praise. If praise led to more meals like the one he'd just inhaled, he'd lay it on as thick as the strawberry jam he'd spread on the warm, buttery biscuits.

"How do you usually spend your evenings?" she asked, rising from her place. "The only time I ever see you is early in the morning after your shift."

"Hmm." Wes began gathering the dirty dishes. "Generally I go for a run, or head to Boonville to the gym where I work out. Then I hang out with friends, read or watch TV before work. I go to a PTSD support group with Noah, Ryan and Kyle on Thursday evenings. It used to be on Tuesdays, but we had to change it to accommodate Noah's kids' after-school activities and schedules." He stood up and took the dishes to the sink.

"What's PTSD?" Tyler asked, slipping from his place at the table. He grabbed his silverware and empty glass and carried them to the counter by the sink.

"PTSD stands for post-traumatic stress disorder. Severe trauma can change a person's brain chemistry, and those of us who have PTSD need to learn how to cope."

"Oh." The kid's face fell. "Do you think I'm gonna have it? You know, because of what happened . . ." His mouth turned down and his blue eyes grew huge and bright.

"You know what?" Wes crouched down in front of him. "You're going to be all right, Ty, but I don't think we ever get too big for a hug now and then. Do you?"

Tyler shrugged his shoulders again, and a lump formed in Wes's throat. He held out his arms, and the little boy kind of collapsed into him. He hugged him close and ran his hands up and down Tyler's back. "It's going to be OK, partner. Me and the other guys here at Langford & Lovejoy are going to make sure you and your mom stay safe. You have my word; I won't let anything happen to either of you." Tyler sniffed, and Wes's T-shirt felt damp where the kid burrowed his face against his shoulder.

"If you want, Rex can sleep with you on your bed." He looked to Carlie for permission. Her own eyes had grown bright with the sheen of tears, and she nodded. "Rex is a retired military dog," Wes said. "He's a soldier, just like me. Did you know that?"

Tyler sucked in a few gulps of air and shook his head. "Do you think he'd do that—sleep on the bed, I mean?"

"I'm sure he would. I never let him on my bed, so sleeping on yours would be a special treat." Wes gave the kid one more hug and let him go. He stood up and ran his hand over Tyler's head. "Feel better?"

"Yeah." He swiped at his eyes. "Can I play video games *now*, Mom?"

"On your tablet," Carlie told him. "That's all we have with us for now."

Tyler patted his hand against his thigh. "Come on, Rex." The dog's ears went up, and his tail wagged.

"Go ahead, boy," Wes said to his dog. The two new friends ran together down the hall to the room Tyler had chosen. It hadn't surprised Wes at all when he'd learned Tyler had taken the room between the master bedroom and the third bedroom at the end of the hall. Tyler had placed himself between the two adults. For safety.

"Wesley," Carlie said, a telltale quiver to her voice.

"Hmm?"

"Thank you."

"No thanks needed." He squirted dish soap into the plastic tub in the sink and started the water. The kitchen had a dishwasher, but he preferred to do his dishes by hand.

"There must be something I can do to repay your kindness."

"Well"—he shot her a hopeful look—"I sure wouldn't mind if you wanted to make a few more dinners for me. I'm not much of a cook myself."

Her expression softened. "It would be my pleasure." Carlie picked up a dish towel and came to stand next to him. "You wash and rinse. I'll dry the dishes and put them away."

A simple task, domestic, yet it filled him with a pleasure he'd rarely known before. *Dangerous.* He'd just managed to shake himself out of his reverie when her arm brushed against his as she reached for a bowl to dry. His pulse leaped. "You smell good." He stifled a groan. He should not have said that out loud.

"It's the dryer sheets I use for the laundry." Carlie grinned at him. "I'm not wearing any perfume."

"Oh." He nodded, wondering what brand she used, so he could get the same kind.

"I don't like the idea that my car is still out at my place. I wouldn't put it past my ex to steal it," she said, breaking his train of thought.

"Give me the keys, and I'll have one of the guys head out there with me tonight on our break. I'll drive it here and park it out back."

She caught his gaze and held it, sending his heart into a thumpfest in his chest.

"That would be great." She nudged him with her shoulder. "What do you want for supper tomorrow night?"

"Do you make meat loaf? My mom used to make this meat loaf recipe with ketchup and brown sugar on the bottom of the loaf pan. I haven't had it for years, but boy, I sure did like that recipe."

Carlie laughed. "I don't have the ingredients to fix it for tomorrow, or the recipe, but I'm pretty sure I can find something similar on the Internet. You're easy to please, Wes. I like that about you. You have no idea what a relief it is, and I don't think the words exist for me to tell you how much I appreciate your help."

"Hearing you laugh is enough, Carlie. I like the sound of your laughter." The temperature in his kitchen rose a few degrees, and the little bit of space between them thrummed and arced with the magnetic pull of sexual attraction. Did she feel it, too? *Probably not.* Wes concentrated on washing the few remaining dishes. "You want to put that soup in a plastic container so I can wash the pot?"

"Hmm?" Carlie blinked up at him, her face flushed and her pupils slightly dilated. "Oh, the soup. Sure." So it wasn't just him. She wiped her hands on the towel, put it on the counter and looked at the cabinets. "Where do you keep things for storage?"

"Last cabinet underneath the counter." The sweatpants he had on weren't doing much to hide the effect she had on him. He moved closer to the counter and forced his thoughts to other things, like how he'd like to pummel Carlie's ex into the ground. He needed to keep his focus on the task at hand—keeping Carlie and Tyler safe. Once Carlie's ex was back behind bars, his life could return to normal. Between the two of them, he and Carlie had enough issues as it was. Neither of them needed to add sexual tension into the mix.

❦   ❦   ❦

Wes heard footsteps and Tyler's voice coming down the back stairs. He glanced at the clock. He'd already made arrangements with Noah to start and end his shift a little earlier so that he could walk Carlie to the diner at six in the morning and then take Tyler to school when it was time.

Tyler jumped down the last two steps. He already had on his jacket, and his school backpack hung from a shoulder. Rex trailed behind him.

"Hey, little dude," Miguel said, giving Tyler a high five. "Good morning, Carlie. You're looking . . . umm . . . a little less . . . swollen this morning."

Ken grunted. "Subtle, Miguel. Real subtle."

"Thanks, Miguel." Carlie smiled and nodded to Ken and the other two guys on the night crew.

"You and I are going to walk your mom to work, Tyler," Wes said. "We're going to hang out there for a while, have breakfast, visit with Jenny and Harlen, and then I'll take you to school. Is that all right with you, partner?"

"Sure. Can Rex come?"

"Not this time," Carlie said, running her hand over a cowlick in her son's unruly hair. "We don't allow dogs in the diner unless they're service dogs."

"What's a service dog?" Tyler's face took on the scrunched-with-curiosity look already familiar to Wes.

Tyler had an inquisitive nature. He asked a lot of questions, a sign that his brain was always working. Wes grabbed his jacket from the back of his chair and slid his arms into the sleeves. "It means a dog that has been specially trained to help individuals who have disabilities, like a Seeing Eye dog."

"Oh." The scrunched look remained. "Rex is especially trained, too. He helps me."

"He can't come to the diner with us, partner, but you can help me take him outside before we go."

"OK." Tyler's shoulders dropped in defeat for a second, but then squared up again. "Can I hold his leash?"

"If you want." Wesley reached for the leash and hooked it onto Rex's collar. He handed the looped end to Tyler.

"I think I'll come along to help." Carlie joined her son by the back door.

The three of them walked out of the building together. Dawn was just beginning to show on the horizon, and the day promised to be clear. Wesley sucked in a deep breath of the autumn crispness chilling the air. He turned Tyler toward the patch of grass, just as Carlie gasped.

"What is it?" He swiveled around to see what had her spooked. She pointed, and he couldn't help but notice the way her hand trembled. Tension tightened his muscles, and he automatically went into fight mode. A note had been placed under her windshield wiper. She started toward her car. He reached for her hand and stopped her. "Don't touch it, Carlie."

He fished into his jacket pocket and took out the roll of small plastic bags he used to pick up after his dog. "I'll get the note. You stay with Tyler and Rex." He searched the shadows, rooftops and windows for any sign of Jared as he made his way to Carlie's Ford. He tore off a bag, and using the flimsy plastic like a latex glove, he tugged the note from under the wiper. Then he moved under the security light mounted above L&L's loading dock doors. Using the baggie, he opened the folded note as if it might be an IED about to explode in his face. He read the handwritten words scrawled onto the white surface.

I'll get to you and Tyler, Kara. Don't think I won't.

Wesley pulled the flimsy plastic up over the note until it was securely enclosed. Evidence. Jared had abandoned the stolen car. How was he getting around? He raised his eyes to find Carlie staring intently at the biodegradable green baggie in his hand.

His jaw clenched, and he seethed. Asshole didn't know who he was messing with. No way was he going let that punk get past him. Jared was never going to hurt or terrorize Carlie and Tyler again. Not on *his* watch.

Even in the dimness thrown by the fluorescent security light, he could see Carlie shaking. Keeping his distance be damned. He strode across the alley and pulled her into his arms. Her breaths were shallow puffs of warm air against his throat, and she trembled from head to foot. Keeping his eye on Tyler and Rex, he tightened his hold around her and rested his chin on the top of her head. "He's nothing—just a coward trying to bully and scare you into compliance." He rocked her back and forth. "I've got your six. I'm not going to let that man get anywhere near you or Tyler."

"My . . . six?"

"Yeah, your back. I've got you covered."

She nodded and leaned into him, and he tightened his hold around her slight frame. He liked the feel of her in his arms. A lot. Too much.

"Rex pooped," Tyler crowed, blissfully unaware of the drama unfolding behind him. "It's a big one, too!"

Carlie huffed out a nervous laugh and stepped out of his arms. That part he didn't like so much. "Good, since you're in charge, you get to pick it up," Wes told him.

"Gross!" Tyler's gaze shot to him. Despite calling the task gross, his eyes lit with excitement.

"Yeah, it's gross, but you get used to it." Wes stuffed the note into his back pocket. Then he pulled out another bag from the roll he kept handy. He studied the pile on the grass and then Tyler's small hands. "This time, I'll show you how it's done, but next time you'll have to man up to the task if you want to share responsibility for Rex."

"OK," the kid said, watching intently as Wes slipped the plastic over his hand and leaned over to pick up the mess. He tied the bag shut and dropped it into L&L's dumpster.

Once the dog was squared away and back inside L&L, Wes reached for Carlie's hand. She held her son's, and the three of them walked between L&L and the building next door, taking the shortcut to the sidewalk on the main street through Perfect. He kept the two of them next to the businesses they passed, while he took the point-guard position on the outside.

"What did the note say?" Carlie whispered, keeping her eyes on the sidewalk.

"Nothing new, just that he's not giving up." He shrugged. "Once Tyler is in school, I'll get the note to the sheriff." He put his arm around her shoulders and tucked her close to his side. "He's a coward and a punk. *I'm* a Marine. You've got nothing to worry about."

"I wanna be a Marine when I grow up." Tyler puffed out his chest and lifted his chin. "Just like you." His face scrunched again. "Wes, what *is* a Marine, anyway?"

Wesley's chest expanded a few inches, and so did his heart. "A soldier. I'm a retired Marine, an elite branch of the US military. I'd be mighty proud if you followed that path, Tyler, but you have a lot of years to go before you decide."

"I'm gonna be seven next July. How old do I gotta be before I decide, Mom?"

The three of them had reached the diner. Carlie fished around inside her bag for her key. "You have to be eighteen before you can join the Marines, Tyler."

Wes leaned close and whispered, "I was only seventeen when I joined." He liked the way she shivered and tilted her head in response. Once all of this mess with Jared was over, he might have to have a good sit-down-and-think session with himself. Maybe Cory was right, and it was time to move on. Could he let go of the past and take another chance with his heart? What if he did, and . . .

A wave of panic crashed over him, and the ghosts of combat missions past sent spectral images dancing through his head. *OK, maybe not.* Not if even thinking about opening himself up again sent him into a tailspin. Either way, it didn't matter. He clamped down on the panic. One thing at a time, and right now, protecting Carlie and her son had to come first. His shit would still be there once the threat to Carlie was long gone.

CHAPTER FOUR

ONCE SHE SETTLED HER SON at a table, Carlie tied on her work apron. Jared wasn't giving up. No surprise there. The familiar surroundings of the diner acted like a balm on her raw nerves. The cooks were working away in the kitchen, and the Maurers would arrive any minute.

She wasn't alone—that centered her even more. She glanced at her son, and her insides knotted with worry. The toughest part would be watching Tyler leave for school without her. He'd be out of her sight and out of her reach.

At least Wes would be taking him to school. Her ex wouldn't dare try anything while Wesley was with Tyler. Would he? *No. Jared is a coward.* She repeated that to herself a few times until it sank in. *He's nothing but a bully and a coward.* Yes, but bullies could be dangerous, and they did stupid things. Especially Jared.

She touched the healing split on her lip with her tongue and moved behind the counter to begin her setup tasks for the day. The sound of vegetables being chopped by the cooks reverberated through the diner. The smell of fresh onions, peppers, frying bacon and sausage filled the diner. Fitting a wire basket filled with a paper filter and freshly ground coffee into the large commercial urn, she flipped the On switch. Then she did the same for the decaf side. "Coffee's on. As soon as it's done, I'll bring you a cup, Wes. What kind of juice do you want this morning, Ty?"

"Apple." He looked up from the kids' paper place mat he was coloring.

"Apple it is." Carlie reached into the refrigerator under the counter for the covered plastic pitcher. Once she had Tyler's juice in front of him, she began filling the sugar caddies. Next she'd fill and set out the salt and pepper shakers that had been run through the dishwasher yesterday. Keeping busy was good. Focusing on something other than the danger facing her was even better. "Speaking of service dogs," she said, continuing their conversation from earlier, "were you Rex's handler? Is that why you have him now?"

"No." Wes propped his elbows on the table, his expression grim. "We often had a couple of handlers and their TEDDs assigned to our platoon, though. Dogs and their handlers move around a lot. It's a tough job. They're pretty much on their own."

"What's a TEDD, Wes?" Tyler stopped coloring to stare at his hero.

"TEDD stands for tactical explosives-detection dog." Wes glanced at Tyler. "About a decade ago, my unit was on mission, and we had a handler and his dog with us. We took a lot of fire that day, and the handler and his dog got hit by an RPG. Corporal Reid feared for his dog. I stayed with Reid until he was loaded into the medevac helicopter." His jaw muscle twitched, and he averted his gaze. "He was pretty bad off, but his primary concern was for his four-legged partner. I didn't have the heart to tell him the dog had already died. He was agitated . . . the man needed peace, so I promised I'd adopt his dog in his honor if . . . if anything happened to him." His mouth thinned to a straight, tight line.

Carlie swallowed against the sudden lump forming in her own throat. The dog's handler hadn't made it, either, that much was clear. She wanted to wrap her arms around Wes's shoulders; instead, she busied herself with placing the filled salt and pepper shakers on all the tables. "So how'd you come by Rex?"

"I told a buddy of mine, a mustang like me who was involved with the dog-training program, about the promise I'd made to Corporal Reid. A year before I retired, he told me about Rex." Wes grunted. "Adopting Rex involved months of waiting and lots of red tape, but I'd made a promise to a dying man, and one way or another, I meant to honor Corporal Reid and his dog." His eyes sought hers, his stare so intense he reached places deep inside her she'd long ago shut down. "I keep my promises, Carlie."

"What's a mustang, Wes?" Tyler stopped coloring, his attention focused on Wes.

"A mustang is an enlisted man who rises through the ranks and goes on to become a commissioned officer." He grinned at her son's confused expression and tousled Tyler's hair. "None of that means a thing to a six-year-old, does it? Ask me when you're older, partner."

"OK, Wes." Tyler went back to coloring.

The front door opened, sending the bell above it chiming. Carlie startled and her hand rose to cover her pounding heart. "Harlen, Jenny," she said, her voice shaky. "Whew, you startled me."

"We do come in by the front door at the same time every morning." Jenny stashed her purse under the register.

"Still a little jumpy, I see." Harlen hung his jacket on the coatrack in the corner. Then he walked over and sat at the table with Wes and Tyler. "Keep the front door locked until we get here, Carlie. We have keys."

"I will, but with Wes here, there didn't seem to be a need. It's just my nerves." She smiled. "Coffee's ready." She gathered mugs and began to pour coffee for everyone. Fixing Wes's with cream and no sugar.

"Guess what, Mr. Maurer?" Tyler rose to his knees on the chair. "Me and Mommy are staying with Wes and his dog, Rex."

"Are you now?" Harlen's eyes widened, and he shot Wes a questioning look.

"On your pockets, Ty," Carlie said. He sat for a few seconds, but then he got up on his knees again.

"My place is on the third floor, and we always have a crew on site." Wes shrugged. "It's the safest place for them right now. I only use a portion of that apartment anyway. There's plenty of room."

"Sounds like a good idea to me," Jenny said, tying on her apron. "Especially with the security system and Rex there as well."

"I'm hungry, Mommy," Tyler said, still on his knees.

Carlie glanced at the wall clock. Twenty minutes until they opened. "Bill," she called back to the kitchen. "Are you guys about ready to go? We could all use some breakfast before Wes and Ty leave for school."

Bill's familiar grin filled the window to the kitchen. "Sure. What'll it be?"

"French toast and bacon, please," Tyler piped.

"That sounds good, partner. I'll have the same, and throw in some extra-crispy hash browns with onions." Wes lifted Tyler like he weighed nothing and settled him down with his bottom once again safely planted on the chair. "You want to share some hash browns, Ty?"

"Sure, Wes."

Harlen chuckled. "You two are on a first-name basis, I see."

"We're partners," Tyler chortled, rising to his knees again.

Wes shook his head, his expression stern. Tyler sat right back down. A flutter tickled Carlie's insides, and Wes's words about misplacing his trust in the past came back to her in a rush. Had his trust been broken by a woman, a girlfriend from his past? If so, that woman was a fool. Men like Wesley Holt were rare—rare and unobtainable to someone with a history like hers.

Once Wes and Tyler had been fed and they'd left for Tyler's school, things settled into the familiar rhythm of a busy Wednesday at the diner. Carlie was grateful for the distraction. Regulars filed in, men carrying their newspapers and wearing John Deere baseball caps pulled low over their foreheads, friends getting together over breakfast, locals on their way to work. Old men sat at the same spots at the counter where they always did, bantering with one another and with her as she poured their coffee and took their orders. Carlie hustled through her day, too occupied to think much about Jared.

Working at the Perfect Diner was such a blessing. She loved the place and the constant stream of people. Leaving was going to tear her apart, but she had to have a plan B. Once Jared was back behind bars, she might have to find a new place to hide, somewhere farther away and harder to find. She'd cross that bridge when the time came.

"Hey, Carlie." George, a retired farmer and a lunchtime regular, took a seat on one of the stools at the counter. He studied her face. "Whoa. What'd you run into, young lady?"

Anger burst into flame within her. "My ex-husband," she snapped.

George's eyes grew wide, and his mouth opened and closed, like he didn't know how to respond. Who could blame him? Blurting out that little factoid was a real conversation stopper. She'd answered the same question at least a hundred times already today. She saw no reason to prevaricate, since the news would be all over town anyway.

"Sorry, George. Didn't mean to snap at you. I'm just a little testy, I guess." Carlie turned over a ceramic cup on its saucer and slid it in front of him. "Coffee?"

"Uh, sure. Thanks." George grabbed the menu from the counter and studied the laminated card stock.

"The lunch special today is shepherd's pie with a small salad. I'll be back to take your order in a few minutes." She poured his coffee, and then she walked away.

After an early supper, Wes had left for his workout at the gym in Boonville, and Carlie savored having the place to herself. Sinking back into the plush couch, she channel surfed the TV while listening to Tyler hold a one-sided conversation with Rex about the merits of Legos versus Tinkertoys. The dog's ears stood at attention as he listened raptly to her son's rambling.

Relaxed and feeling safe for the moment, Carlie stretched. Wes had a nice place. The hardwood floors had been recently refinished, and the dining room had a gorgeous built-in buffet of oak, but the room was empty of any furniture. Wesley had pointed out that, since he lived alone, he had no need for a dining room table and chairs. The table in his kitchen was all he needed.

His apartment held an old-timey charm, but with all the modern amenities. Wes had told her Paige and Ryan Malloy had lived there before they built their house, and they were responsible for bringing the place up to date.

A knock on the door sent her heart racing. She stilled, listening. Rex's tail wagged—a good sign. *Note to self: once this is over, get a dog.* A German shepherd or a Rottweiler—some kind of big, scary breed. After the second knock, she got up and crossed the room to the door. The fact that the apartment had two doors—one leading to the rear stairwell from the kitchen, and the other off the living room leading to the front stairway—bothered her. She kept both doors locked and all the blinds on the windows closed. "Who is it?" she called.

"It's Cory and Paige," Paige called back.

All the tension left her. She undid the dead bolt and opened the door. "Hey." She gestured them in. "What brings you two by?"

"We've come to whisk you away for a girls' night out." Cory grinned. "An evening out with a specific purpose in mind."

Paige nodded. "We're signed up for a self-defense class in Boonville, and we want you to come with us."

"I can't leave Tyler," Carlie said. "I'd love to join you. I . . . I need to learn a few moves, but—"

"It's all been arranged," Paige told her. "Ceejay is coming with us, and we're going to drop your son, my son and Ryan off at the Langfords' on our way to pick her up. We won't stay out long. The class starts at seven, and it only lasts an hour."

"Noah and Ryan will both be at the Langfords'?"

"Yep. The men are watching the children, and Wesley's gym is practically next door to the mixed martial arts studio where we're taking our class. If anything feels threatening, we'll text him."

"He knows about this?" Her brow rose. "Why didn't he say anything? Why didn't you say anything earlier?"

"We made our plans weeks ago." Cory shrugged, her expression apologetic. "Bringing you along is a spur-of-the-moment thing. We texted Wes about it on the way over, and he's on board. I'm sorry we didn't include you from the start, Carlie."

"That's OK." She turned toward her son. "With my hours, and being a single mom, I haven't really been very social. If it weren't for my current situation, you'd have no reason to include me." Sadly, that was the truth. Since moving to Perfect, she'd isolated herself. Ashamed of her past and still suffering from the trauma that had led her to move to Perfect in the first place, she'd crawled into her cave and hadn't come out. Even forming friendships had seemed too great a risk to her bruised heart. She hadn't reached out to anyone, nor had anyone reached out to her—other than Harlen and Jenny, that is. "Ty, how'd you like to go play with Toby and Lucinda for a while?"

"Yeah." He started throwing his Legos back into their plastic tub. "Can Rex come?"

"Do you think we could bring the dog along?" Carlie asked Paige. "Ty feels safer having Rex with him. He's even asked to bring him to the diner and school."

"I'm sure it would be fine. I'll ask to be sure." Paige pulled out her phone and began to text. Paige's phone pinged almost immediately. "Ceejay says Rex is welcome." She slid her phone back into her purse. "Looks like you're already dressed for the class. Let's go."

Carlie glanced down at her sweatpants. "I guess I am. I'll go get my shoes. Tyler, get Rex's leash from the kitchen," she called before heading to her room for sneakers.

A few years ago, she'd been too busy working, saving and caring for her toddler to take self-defense classes, but the thought had always been there in the back of her mind. She didn't like being defenseless—not a good position to be in at all. It was about time she learned to fight back. "I'm not a doormat," she muttered to herself as she pulled a pair of athletic shoes from the closet.

Hadn't Jared learned that when she'd filed charges against him and sent him to prison? The jerk must have a serious learning disability. Excitement thrummed through her. If this class went well, she'd find a way to continue. Jenny and Harlen had volunteered to watch Tyler more than once, but Carlie had never taken them up on the offer. Now she would.

She returned to the living room, fetched jackets from the coat closet and bundled her son into his. "Thanks for including me," she said, smiling at the two women waiting patiently for her. "I'm really looking forward to this."

Ryan sat in the driver's side of Paige's minivan, which was parked in front of L&L. He got out and put Rex into the back while they all piled in. Tyler sat next to Sean, and he did a great job of keeping the toddler entertained on the short drive to Noah and Ceejay's house. Toby and Lucinda were waiting for them on the front veranda with the bright porch light illuminating both of them and their monster dog, Sweet Pea.

Toby held a couple of action figures in his hands, and when he caught sight of Tyler, he jumped up and down. "Tyler, you wanna play Transformers wif me?" he shouted before they were even out of the van.

"Sure," Tyler called, scampering off ahead of Carlie the second his feet hit the ground. Once he reached the porch, he stopped and turned back. "Rex," he called, patting his thighs. "Come."

Ryan had just lifted the dog out of the back. Rex squirmed and whined to get free, and once his paws hit the ground, he raced to Tyler's side, only marginally interested in Sweet Pea. In a flurry of arms and legs, the children and dogs disappeared into the house. Carlie followed the other adults to the front door. Ryan held his fussing son in his arms.

Noah and Ceejay greeted them in the foyer. Micah, their younger son, clung to his dad's jeans-clad thigh, and Grace, the Langford's toddler, studied the incoming adults with a somber expression and a thumb planted firmly in her mouth. With reddish-gold ringlets and big blue eyes, Grace was the spitting image of her mother.

"Hey, Gracie." Paige touched her niece's nose. "Look who we brought for you to play with."

Ryan approached with Sean now straining to get down. Grace's thumb popped out of her mouth, and a huge grin lit her chubby face. She reached out a hand toward her cousin.

Carlie soaked it all in, the sense of family, community and love filling the Langford house. Good people. A pang stole the smile from her face. She wanted so badly to give Tyler a life like the one the Langford and Malloy children had. Cousins, siblings, aunties and uncles . . . She hadn't even spoken to her brother since the day she was arrested, and her relationship with her mother and grandmother still held a lot of strain. She'd hurt them all so much. She blinked against the sudden sting in her eyes.

"Ryan and I will keep a close eye on Tyler." Noah came to stand in front of her. "You don't have to look so worried."

"Hmm?" She jerked back to the present. "Oh. I know you will."

"Any word from the sheriff?"

"None." She sighed. "Thanks for watching Tyler. With you, Ryan and the two dogs, I'm not worried. My mind was drifting, that's all."

"Let's go, ladies," Paige said, herding them to the door. "We're going to be late if we don't hit the road."

Paige and Ceejay kept up a constant stream of conversation about their children on the short drive to Boonville, and Carlie settled back, content to listen. They pulled into a small parking lot beside a squat redbrick building with a large glass window in front. She followed the women into the building, taking it all in.

The Warriors' Den offered a variety of martial arts classes, including self-defense for women. Carlie read the schedule posted on the wall. Kickboxing sounded like fun. The studio consisted of one large room with rubberized floor mats and a number of movable pieces of equipment pushed into a corner. Mirrors covered one wall, and several women were already there, standing alone or in small groups. A few were stretching, loosening up for the class.

"This is Lee Greenwood, the owner." Cory introduced her to the instructor, a short, balding man without an ounce of flab on him. He looked like he might be in his fifties, yet he was in amazing shape. "Lee is going to be our instructor tonight," Cory added. "Lee, this is Carlie Stewart. Thanks for letting us add her at the last minute."

"Welcome to the Warriors' Den," Lee said, holding out his hand to shake hers. "The first three lessons are free," he told her. "If you decide you want to continue after that, I have a brochure listing all of the options." His eyes settled on her healing lip and blackened eye for a second. "I'm glad you've decided to join us." He rubbed his hands together. "You can fill out the paperwork after you've put your things away."

"Thanks." Heat crept up her neck to fill her face. Yeah, it was obvious to all she needed to be here.

"Come on, Carlie. The locker room is back this way," Ceejay said, tugging on Carlie's jacket sleeve. "I'm so out of shape," she grumbled. "I hope I can keep up."

"Is this your first lesson?" Carlie's eyes widened. She'd assumed the group had been coming for a while.

"All of us are first timers," Ceejay informed her. "Cory has a leg up because of her military training, though."

"Not really." Cory opened the door to the locker room and ushered them into a concrete-floored room holding a few wooden benches and two rows of lockers. "I haven't done much in the way of exercise in months, and I have to look good in a wedding gown soon. I'm counting on these classes to help me regain some much-needed muscle tone."

"Oh, that's right. When's the big day?" Carlie asked while stuffing her purse and jacket into a tiny locker.

"December nineteenth. Ted and I are spending Christmas and New Year's Eve on a two-week cruise to the Bahamas," she said with a dreamy sigh. "Brenda, my maid of honor, would be here tonight, but she had to work. She'll join us for the next lesson. She's Wesley's younger sister. Have you met her?"

"Not formally. She's been at the diner with Kyle several times, though."

"She and Kyle are dating," Cory said with a grin. "They met around the same time Ted and I did. She's helped me out a lot with the theme and decorations for our wedding."

Once they'd all stowed their belongings, Carlie followed the three women back to the studio area. She filled out a form and then lined up as the instructor began the class.

An hour later, her muscles were protesting, and sweat covered Carlie's face. "Oh, I'm going to hurt tomorrow," Paige groaned as the instructor ended the class. "Who knew kicking butt would be so hard?"

Cory rolled her shoulders. "We should practice together this week so we're ready for our next lesson."

"Good idea." Ceejay plopped down on one of the benches. "Anybody up for going out? I'm not ready to end my child-free evening yet."

"I don't drink." Carlie glanced at her. "But I'd be happy to be the designated driver."

"Who said anything about drinking?" Ceejay asked. "I was thinking ice cream."

Paige shut her locker door, her coat and purse in hand. "I'm in."

"No ice cream for me. I'll drink tea." Cory shook her head. "I have a size-six wedding dress to get into soon."

"Me, too." Three sets of eyes swung her way, and heat once again flooded Carlie's face. "I mean I'm in for ice cream, not that I have a wedding dress to fit into."

"You and Wesley should join us for poker night next Friday. Ryan and I are hosting," Paige said, her eyes lighting up. "It's a lot of fun."

"I don't know how to play poker, and besides, I've heard that's kind of a couples' thing in Perfect. Wes and I are not a couple. He's just helping me out until my ex is caught."

"Actually, it's a community thing." Ceejay led the way out of the locker room. "Gail Offermeyer and I started poker night a few years ago. We did it to get the younger adults in Perfect together. The older folks play bridge, and we wanted to start something similar but more contemporary. Anyone is welcome, whether single or involved."

Paige slung her purse over her shoulder. "You wouldn't be the only single person there, believe me. It's a great way to get to know everyone, and we'd love to have you. Wesley, too, if he's interested. You don't have to know how to play. It's easy enough to pick up as you go, and we'll all help. We alternate our get-togethers with the older generation's bridge night."

"Why's that?" Carlie blinked in confusion.

"Who do you think watches our kids while we play?" Paige snorted. "Cory's soon-to-be in-laws watch Sean for me, since Jenny and Harlen take care of Ceejay's brood."

"Oh." If Jenny and Harlen babysat for Ceejay, who could she find to watch Tyler? "It sounds like fun," she said. "I'll think about it."

A large figure hovered outside the front door of the Warriors' Den. She'd recognize those broad shoulders anywhere. Her pulse raced, and a smile burst free. *Wesley.* She moved ahead, wanting to be the first to greet him. Cold air bathed her overheated face as she opened the door and walked out to the sidewalk.

His eyes sought hers, and he pushed himself off the wall he'd been leaning against. "How did it go?"

Carlie opened her mouth to reply, but Cory beat her to it. "She did great, Bunny. Do you want to come with us for ice cream?"

"Sure, Squirrel. Carlie and I will follow in my car."

Carlie laughed. She couldn't help it. She'd heard the two use their ridiculous nicknames before, so it wasn't just that. Wes's brow rose in question. How could she explain? Doing something positive on her own behalf made her happy. Going out with the girls was a new experience for her in Perfect, one she thoroughly enjoyed, and seeing Wesley hovering protectively outside the door was the capper to her perfect evening. "I plan to continue." She jabbed at the air with her fists. "I'm thinking about taking up kickboxing." The look of approval in Wesley's eyes sent her heart gyrating.

"Sounds like a great idea." He placed his hand at the small of her back, slung his gym bag over his shoulder and walked with her to the minivan. "I'd be happy to watch Tyler while you take classes. The two of us can come with you. While you're learning how to kick butt, Tyler and I can head over to McDonald's for a Happy Meal. There's one down the road a few blocks that has an inside playground. That'll keep us busy while you take your class."

Her breath hitched. "You'd do that for me?"

"I'll support anything that will help keep you and Tyler safe," he said, his voice hoarse. "Kickboxing, karate . . . the shooting range . . . whatever you need, Carlie, you just let me know, and I'm your man."

My man. She knew he meant he'd watch Tyler and help in any way he could, but hearing him say the words sent all kinds of crazy yearning racing through her. Months of fantasizing about him were to blame, no doubt. Oh, how she wished he really could be her man.

"You and Carlie should come to poker night, Wes. It's at our house next Friday." Paige looked at Wes over her shoulder. "It's a lot of fun. If you do decide to join us, let me know. I've hired one of Ceejay's cousins to babysit Sean, and she can watch Tyler, too."

"Maybe." Wes ran his hand over his buzz cut. "We'll see. If Carlie's ex is still on the loose, I don't want anyone else's home on his radar. He left a note on Carlie's car this morning. I suspect he's stolen another vehicle, and he's sticking around."

Carlie's bubble of happiness popped, and a cold dose of reality chilled her. She searched the shadows between the buildings for any sign that someone might be lurking there. Was Jared watching her right now? If so, seeing Wesley place his hand at the small of her back would send him into a rage. She didn't want Wesley or anyone else in danger. "I think I'll pass on poker for now. Maybe once Jared has been caught . . ."

Once he was behind bars again, she'd be looking for a new place to call her temporary home. A new place where she could hide her true identity, along with her past. Her heart aching, she climbed into Wes's SUV and stared out the window. By the time they pulled up to the ice cream parlor, she'd lost her appetite.

Carlie placed an order on the cooks' wheel and picked up the coffeepot resting on the burners. Circulating around the diner, she topped off coffee mugs in her section and checked on tables.

No news is good news. That's what she told herself, anyway, and she was desperate enough to cling to that hope. Her ex had showed up at her place on Tuesday morning, left the note on her car on Wednesday, and today was Friday.

She hadn't seen or heard a word from her ex or the sheriff since the note. Had Jared figured out he couldn't get through the safety net Perfect's residents had thrown up around her and Tyler? Had he given up and left, or was that too much to hope for?

The lunch rush was winding down enough that she could think. If she didn't hear Jared had been caught soon, she'd have to head out to her house for more of her things. Tyler missed his books, and he wanted more of his favorite toys. They both needed more clothes, too, so she could wash the few they'd brought with them.

Her cell phone vibrated in her back pocket, along with the Sunny Hollow's ringtone. Moving back behind the counter, she put the coffeepot down and reached for her phone. Ty had complained of a stomachache that morning, but he hadn't had a fever. Probably stress, or he was angling to stay at Wesley's apartment all day with Rex. "Hello?"

"Ms. Stewart, this is Amy Hoff. Tyler is safe, but . . ."

Carlie's lungs seized, and her grip tightened around her phone. Ty's teacher had never called her before. She'd never had to. "What has happened?"

"I don't want you to worry. Tyler is here, and he's safe, but your ex-husband attempted to take him while we were out at recess. Tyler is upset, and he's asking for you. He's in the office. Sheriff Taylor will be here any second. I have someone covering my class, and I'll stay with your son until you get here."

"I'm on my way," Carlie choked out. Her hands shaking, she slid her phone back into her pocket. As calmly as possible, she made her way to Jenny, who was saying good-bye to a group of women by the front door. Though she wanted to run like hell, she forced herself to walk. Tyler was safe. "I have to go. Jared tried to kidnap Tyler from school." She tried to breathe, but tension held her in its steely grip. As she reached for her purse under the register, her mind reeled. "The sheriff is on his way to Sunny Hollow. Tyler is in the office. He's OK, but—"

"I'll drive you." Harlen rose from his stool. "Will you be all right on your own, Jenny?"

"I'll be fine. The rush is over, Sally's still here to take care of the few remaining tables, and the cooks can help out." Jenny gave Carlie's shoulders a squeeze, her eyes filled with worry. "Go get Tyler."

Her hands were ice-cold, and she couldn't think straight. Harlen handed her jacket to her. She slipped it on and followed him out the front door to the diner's small parking lot. It had been sleeting that morning when she, Wes and Tyler had come to the diner. They'd taken her car rather than have Tyler get soaking wet on the walk over, and then Wes jogged back to L&L.

"Here," she said, taking her keys from her jacket pocket and handing the Harlen. "Let's take my car. Tyler needs his booster seat. He's . . . he's so little." She pressed her hand against her mouth, and tears filled her eyes.

Harlen took her keys, and she scrambled into the front seat and buckled up. The sleet had turned to rain as the day wore on, and the sound of the windshield wipers had a hypnotic effect on her. "Tyler's OK," she murmured.

"He is," Harlen agreed, turning onto the main road out of Perfect.

"Thank you, Harlen." She held out her trembling hands. "As you can see, I'm in no shape to drive."

"Don't mention it. Under the circumstances, I don't think it's a good idea for you to go anywhere alone, at least not until Jared is back in custody."

Why hadn't they caught her ex yet? She nodded and stared out at the corn and wheat fields that were just stalks now. A quarter mile before the turnoff to Ty's school, a *POP, POP* rent the air. Something pinged against the passenger door. "What was that?" She looked back. A cluster of trees, a large boulder and brush formed an island in the middle of the field they'd just passed.

Harlen cursed under his breath, but he didn't alter his course or slow down. If anything, he sped up.

"Oh, God. Those were gunshots, weren't they? Jared has a gun."

"Now, we don't know that. Might've been a stray shot from some hunter."

"What hunters?" Her heart raced, and her mouth had gone so dry, she could hardly get the words out. "Is this even hunting season?"

"Sure it is, Carlie. It's always hunting season for some form of game or another. Right now it's coyotes, raccoons and a variety of game birds, like ruffled grouse. Deer season opens next week. Might be some fool decided he couldn't wait until it's legal to hunt deer." He patted her knee. "Don't go thinking the worst."

They pulled up to the front entrance of the school, and Harlen parked her car behind the sheriff's vehicle. Carlie shot out of her Ford and raced into the building, leaving Harlen to follow. She hurried into the office. There she found her son, sitting in a chair, his eyes wide and tear filled, with the sheriff, the assistant principal and Ms. Hoff surrounding him.

"Mommy!" Tyler scrambled off the chair and ran into her arms.

She lifted him, and he clung to her, burying his face against her neck. "It's OK, Ty," she soothed, hugging him tight. "I've got you."

Harlen had followed her into the office and gestured to the sheriff. The two of them stood off to the side in deep conversation. "We'll be right back." Harlen tipped his head toward the bank of chairs against the wall. "Have a seat for a minute, Carlie."

She knew. Harlen and Sheriff Taylor were going to look at the bullet hole in her car door. Had Jared shot at her? Had his attempt to take their son been nothing but a ploy to get her out in the open?

No, that didn't make sense. If he'd had a gun, he would've used it against her the morning he showed up. He was on the run, an escaped convict without resources. Where and how would he have gotten a gun? Harlen had said more than likely they'd been caught by a hunter's stray bullet, and she wanted to believe that, too. Harlen and the sheriff were just being thorough, that's all.

"I w-wanna g-go home," Tyler stammered. "C-can we go h-home n-now, Mommy?"

Her heart squeezed painfully. *Home.* She might not be living on the streets anymore, but somehow she was still homeless, still adrift in choppy waters, and she had no idea how to change the direction the current was taking her.

Hadn't she paid the price for her past already? Would it *never* end? Her throat closed up, and her ears rang from the pounding in her chest. "As soon as Mr. Maurer and Sheriff Taylor come back, we'll head to Wesley's. Rex sure will be glad to see you, won't he, Ty? That dog misses you something fierce while you're in school."

"Y-yeah." His little arms tightened around her, and he hiccupped. "I'll sure b-be g-glad to see him, too."

"Carlie"—Ty's teacher approached them—"after what happened today, I've made arrangements for Tyler to choose a couple of friends and have indoor recess for the foreseeable future. I hope that's all right with you."

"Absolutely, Amy. I appreciate it." She needed to find a way to stop drifting—find a place where her ex couldn't get to them. Then she'd put down roots and make a permanent home for herself and her son. The *how* and *where* eluded her, but she'd figure it out. She had to.

CHAPTER FIVE

WESLEY'S CELL PHONE ON THE bathroom counter buzzed away in an insistent tone. Not yet sufficiently awake, he shut off the stream of steaming-hot water he stood under, grabbed a towel from the rack and stepped out of the shower. By the time he'd wrapped the terry cloth around his waist, the buzzing had ceased. He checked his recent calls. The sheriff. Hitting call back, he brought it up to his ear and waited. "Hey, Paul, sorry I missed your call. What's up?"

"Have you spoken to Carlie?"

"No. I just got up a few minutes ago." He hadn't seen her yet, but the delicious smells coming from his kitchen let him know she was there. "Why?"

"She had a rough day." Paul grunted. "To say the least. Mind if I head over? I have news, and I think it would be best to share it while you're with her."

Hadn't all her days been rough since Jared's sudden and unwanted appearance? What now? His chest tightened. "OK. Have you eaten?" He'd heard through the town grapevine that Paul had recently gone through a divorce, and Wes knew firsthand what the bachelor life was like. The guy would probably appreciate a meal that didn't come frozen in a cardboard box.

"Uh, no. I haven't."

"Plan to, then. Carlie's one hell of a cook."

"I don't know, Wes. The news I have to share isn't good. Carlie's ex tried to nab her kid today. She might not be in the mood for company." Paul cleared his throat. "Maybe you should talk to her first before inviting me to dinner?"

Damn. Rage exploded inside him. Wes pinched the bridge of his nose, and his jaw clenched. "Regardless of what the news might be, she cooks enough to feed a squadron, even though it's just me and Ty. You're going to be here anyway. I'm sure she won't mind."

"All right. Thanks. I'll be over in about twenty minutes."

"Good. See you then." Wes ended the call, dried off and pulled on his clothes in record time. He needed to know that Carlie and Ty were all right. Shoving his phone into the back pocket of his jeans, he strode to the kitchen. The pressure in his chest eased some once he laid eyes on the two of them.

Rex's dog bed had been moved to the spot between the kid's chair and the cabinets. His dog got up, stretched and made his way over to him for a pat on the head. He obliged his three-legged friend while eyeing Tyler. "Hey, partner, I hear you and your mom had a rough day."

Tyler had a couple of toys, crayons and a coloring book in front of him. His eyes widened, and he nodded. "I almost got *napped.*"

"Kidnapped," Carlie corrected, her eyes riveted on her son. The corners of her mouth tightened and turned down. "Jared showed up at Sunny Hollow while the children were out at recess." She leaned against the kitchen counter and wrapped her arms around herself. "He tried to get to Tyler. Thank God there were adults looking out for my son, or . . ."

She lifted her gaze to his, and his heart turned to lead in his chest. Her eyes were a study in misery, but they also held a deep resolve, like she'd come to a difficult decision. What was going on in that head of hers? "Paul is on his way over," he told her. "He has news. Do you mind if he eats with us while he's here?"

"No, of course not. I made the meat loaf you asked for the other day." She turned back to the stove, and her shoulders slumped forward. "We're also having garlic smashed potatoes and fresh green beans." She sighed. "I like to cook. It relaxes me."

He moved behind her and put his arms around her waist. Pulling her against him, he held her close. "It's going to be all right."

"So you keep saying," she said, her tone flat. "Someone shot at my car on the way to Ty's school," she whispered. "Harlen said it was probably some hunter's stray bullet, but I'm pretty sure it was my ex."

Guilt washed through him. He should've been there with her, guarding her. His phone rang. "Probably the sheriff," he told her, pulling it from his pocket. "Hello?"

"It's Paul. I'm parked in the alley."

"Knock on the loading dock doors. The crew will let you in and show you the way up." Wes ended the call and crossed the room. He opened the door to the corridor and glanced at the freight elevator and the storage rooms across the hall from his apartment. Then he checked the narrow hall in both directions and listened to the sound of the sheriff's footsteps on the back stairway.

Out of uniform, Paul wore jeans, a plaid flannel shirt and a leather jacket. Even while off duty, the man gave up his free time to come talk to them, and that made him a stand-up guy in Wes's book.

"Come on in." Wes opened the door wider. "Thanks for stopping by."

"No problem. Sure smells good in here, Carlie." Paul's head bobbed in Carlie's direction as he slid out of his jacket. "I apologize for barging in on your suppertime."

"There's no need to apologize." She brought an extra place setting to the kitchen table. "We have plenty, and you're more than welcome to join us."

Words like *we* and *us* coming from Carlie while she bustled around in his kitchen caused a rush of conflicting emotions. A heady mix of pride and possessiveness, salted with alarm, chased around inside him like a dog after its own tail. He and Carlie weren't a "we." He knew that's not how she meant it, but he couldn't help the way he reacted. "Let's eat, and after supper we can talk," Wes said in a low tone.

Paul nodded. He hung his jacket on one of the pegs by the door and took a seat at the table.

"Tyler, time to put your things away and wash up for supper." Carlie lifted four plates down from the cabinet. "Try not to splash water all over the bathroom while you're at it."

"OK," Ty said. He slipped from his chair and grinned at Wes before running down the hall to the bathroom.

Once Ty came back, they settled in to their meal and made small talk about the weather and what was going on in Perfect and Boonville. "This meat loaf is even better than my mom's," Wes said, scraping up the last morsel from his plate.

"Excellent." Paul leaned back and patted his stomach. "Thank you, Carlie."

"You're welcome." Carlie's pleased smile lit up the room, stealing his breath. Her lip had healed, and the bruises around her eye were beginning to fade. He glanced at the sheriff. Wes couldn't help but notice the appreciative glint in the other man's eyes as Paul watched Carlie rise from her place.

Wes pushed his chair back so that it made a scraping noise against the ceramic tile floor, drawing the sheriff's attention. He got up and put his arm around Carlie's waist, shooting a sideways look the sheriff's way for good measure. "I'll take care of clearing the table. Why don't you get Tyler and Rex settled in his bedroom?"

"All right. Come on, Ty. You can play games on your tablet or finish coloring the picture you were working on before dinner. No school tomorrow, and I'm off. We can sleep in."

"Can I watch a movie?"

"Sure." She ushered her son out of the kitchen with Rex tagging along behind.

Wes moved to the counter, the last of the dinner dishes in his hands. "You want a beer or a cup of coffee, Paul?"

"Coffee would be great, thanks."

Wes was just filling a couple of mugs when Carlie returned. "Should we move to the living room?" he asked her.

"No, I'd rather talk in here." She helped herself to another glass of sweet tea. "There's less chance that Tyler will listen in or overhear things I'd rather he didn't."

Wesley placed a mug of coffee in front of the sheriff. "What can you tell us?" he asked, pulling Carlie's chair out for her before taking a seat himself.

"Our boy has been busy." Paul frowned and gripped his mug. "At least I'm pretty certain it's our guy. Late this afternoon, we got a report of a break-in on the east side of town. A hunting rifle, ammunition, cash and a credit card were stolen from the house. The theft happened while the homeowners were at work, and they didn't know about it until they returned home."

Carlie paled. "Jared is armed. That bullet hole in my car door . . . it happened while we were driving to school after he tried to grab my son. Jared shot at me. I know it was him."

"It's possible." Paul nodded. "Harlen and I pried the bullet out of your door. It's a fit for the Browning semiautomatic rifle that was stolen."

"Great. Now everyone who associates with me is in danger." Her expression tightened with worry. "What if . . . what if he walks into the diner with that rifle?"

Not good. Not good at all. Jared was armed, and the stakes had just been raised. Wes placed his hand over hers. "We'll make sure Harlen keeps a handgun on the premises. He was a sheriff for twenty-five years, Carlie. He knows how to handle situations like that."

She nodded, but he could see she wasn't convinced, and she wouldn't make eye contact.

Paul shifted in his chair. "While the homeowner was at work, he got a call about suspicious activity on his credit card. Someone used it at a sporting goods store in Evansville. Whoever stole the card purchased a lot of camping gear and more ammunition." He shook his head. "Then we got a call about another stolen vehicle abandoned on a rural road—another old-model car that's not worth much. I believe Jared is stealing junkers to keep a low profile, and because they're not likely to have GPS or other tracking devices. He abandons them before we can catch up with him, and then he steals another."

Wesley's jaw clenched. "What's the plan?"

"Jared is an escaped convict, and today he attempted to kidnap your son. The Associated Press has picked up the story. It's on the news. That's going to make it a whole lot tougher for your ex to get around, Carlie." Paul glanced her way, then brought his gaze back to Wes.

"We're doing a manhunt tomorrow. Neighboring counties are lending us some manpower. The SWAT team from Evansville is joining us, and they're bringing in a K9 unit and a helicopter with an infrared heat detector. I believe he's camping somewhere near Carlie's house. We'll find him. By tomorrow afternoon Jared Baumann will be back in custody, and if he's not, the US Marshals will be here by Monday."

"US Marshals?" Carlie's eyes widened.

"He's committed new crimes and broken out of a federal prison. He's a fugitive." Paul nodded. "We've been in contact with a number of other agencies to let them know what Jared has been up to in Warrick County. If we don't get him tomorrow, the US Marshals will lead the search once they're here, and we'll assist however we can."

Carlie's expression lightened at that bit of news. Restless energy coursed through Wes, like it always did before a mission. "I want to help in the manhunt."

"No civilians." Paul cast Wes an apologetic look. "Help by sticking close to Carlie and Tyler."

"Tomorrow is Saturday. There won't be a crew downstairs, Wes." Carlie turned his way, her eyes filled with worry. "Once Jared figures out there's a manhunt going on, he's going to be desperate. He knows Tyler and I are here, and this is where he'll head."

"This place is a fortress," Wes reminded her. "If you don't feel that's enough, I'll invite a couple of the guys over. There's got to be some kind of sport we can watch on TV tomorrow."

A mulish look suffused her face, and once again he wondered what was going through her mind. "Or, if you'd prefer, the three of us can go on an outing tomorrow, stay somewhere else for the night. Once we get the all clear from the sheriff, we can head back."

Then she'd pack up her stuff, head back to her house, and his life would return to normal. His heart wrenched at the thought. He didn't find the prospect of life returning to normal nearly as satisfying as he ought to.

No. He wanted things back to the way they had been. The predictability and routine he'd mapped out for his days provided him with the structure he needed to cope with his PTSD. Everything had gone to hell since Carlie's ex had appeared, and adjusting was a wearing struggle.

"If we went somewhere else, Jared would find a way to follow." Carlie propped her elbows on the table and buried her face in her hands. She groaned. "We'd be sitting ducks."

"I could park nearby in an unmarked car," Paul said. "If your ex *did* follow, I'd be on his tail. Your leaving might flush him out. We could position a squad car or two just outside of town in the direction you plan to go. Set up a roadblock and—"

"Absolutely not," Wesley snapped. "I didn't suggest we leave so that Carlie and Tyler could be used as bait. Jared is armed. I'm not about to allow you to place the two of them anywhere near a possible shoot-out. We'll stay here."

"You're right. Of course it's best if the three of you stay put." Paul pushed his mug away and rose. "Thanks again for the fine meal, Carlie. I've got to be going. Rest assured, if Jared's out there tomorrow, we'll get him."

Wes got up and walked with the sheriff to the door. "I'd appreciate it if you'd keep us in the loop tomorrow."

"Count on it. I'll call you when I know something." Paul held out his hand, and they shook.

Wes handed the sheriff his jacket and saw him out the door. He turned back to find Carlie starting the dishes. "That can wait. You cooked. I'll clean up later, after you and Tyler are in bed."

She shook her head. "I need to keep busy, or . . ."

"Or what?" She'd looked close to the breaking point while they'd talked about Jared, and it killed him to see her so worried. Carlie shrugged her shoulders, and that small gesture of defeat went straight through him. He crossed the kitchen, turned her around and pulled her into his arms. "Carlie . . ."

"I've been doing a lot of thinking since the morning my ex showed up." She rested her damp palms on his chest. "Jared is cunning. They aren't going to catch him tomorrow. I know they aren't, and I can't bear the thought of anyone in Perfect getting hurt because of me." She sucked in a shaky breath and raised her eyes to his. "I'd never forgive myself if Jared hurt you or anyone else in Perfect, and I can't let him take Tyler. I can't. I think it would be best if I left. If Tyler and I are not here, there's no reason for Jared to stay."

She's leaving me. A buzzing started at the back of his brain, and all the buried hurt, the sense of betrayal simmering below the surface, surged through him. *No. Not rational.* Carlie wasn't his, so technically, she couldn't leave him. Still, the buzzing increased and his vision blurred.

I'm going to lose her. More rational, maybe, but no less jarring. He swallowed and scrambled to form a coherent argument to keep her in Perfect. She was still talking, and he'd missed a lot of what she'd said. Somehow he managed to pull himself together and tune back in to her stream of words.

"Ty and I will disappear, go somewhere where Jared can't find us. I'll leave the state," she murmured. "Find a better place to hide—"

"You think a geographical fix is the answer?" He flashed her his best skeptical look. "If Jared sends you running, he's won. Is that what you want, Carlie? Are you going to let that dirtbag dictate the rest of your life?"

"No!" she snapped. "But I don't know what else to do." Her hands curled into fists against him. "I thought changing my name and moving away would put an end to the Jared chapter of my life. How did he manage to find me?"

She looked so lost, it broke his heart. How could he protect her if she left? The need to convince her to stay overrode everything else. Wesley tightened his arms around her. "You were married to him. You and he have a son together. I suspect he still has your Social Security numbers. You filed joint taxes at some point. He has to have stuff like that stored somewhere, right?"

He rubbed her back. "It's easy enough to find someone if you have the right information. If he could get into the right database, he'd be able to find out where Tyler was registered for school, or where you're working. The rest is easy."

"I didn't even think of that." She groaned. "I . . . I'm not equipped to deal with any of this."

"That's where I come in." Relief swept through him. Her decision to leave was nothing more than a knee-jerk reaction to stress and fear. "Running would be a serious tactical error on your part. You have a support network here in Perfect. If you leave, you'll be cutting yourself off from the herd." He raised an eyebrow. "Easy prey."

"You're right. I know you're right, but Jared is dangerous. Not just to me and Tyler, but to anyone close to us. You have no idea how jealous and possessive he is. He's out there watching, and he knows Tyler and I are living in your apartment. I'm sure he's seen us together."

Her eyes filled. A single tear traced down her cheek. Wes caught it with his thumb. Man, her skin was soft.

"Jared once threatened to kill a man at the grocery store, just because he thought I was flirting with him. The first time I told him I wanted a divorce, he threatened to kill me. He said if he couldn't have me, nobody could." She blinked, and another heartrending tear followed the first. "He's going to come after *you*, Wes."

"I'm counting on it." He couldn't help himself, couldn't stop the force compelling him forward. His lips brushed hers. She didn't back away. Nope. Instead, she leaned into the contact, sending hot currents of need racing through him—straight to his groin.

"You don't mean that," she whispered against his mouth.

"Yes, I do." She was so close, so sweet and soft in his arms. What else could he do but go in for more—not a full-out assault with tongue, but definitely a bit of mouth-on-mouth action, a recon mission of sorts. Would she leap away, or . . . She kissed him back. His pulse amped up, and he forgot how to breathe. Her palms smoothed over his chest, then over his shoulders, inciting a riot in his pants. Did she even realize what she was doing?

She broke the kiss. "I can't bear the thought of anything happening to you." She caught and held his gaze. "Why, Wes? Why would you put your life at risk for me?"

She searched his face with such intensity it sent his heart ping-ponging against his rib cage. He struggled to bring his pulse rate and breathing back to normal. He *should* be offering comfort, not wishing like hell he could get her naked and press her up against the nearest wall. He *should* back off, but he couldn't seem to let go of her. He ran his fingers through her curls, something he'd wanted to do since the first time he'd laid eyes on her. They were every bit as soft and silky as he'd imagined.

He had to think of something else, anything to take his mind off the lust threatening to overwhelm him. He pictured himself taking his Beretta apart to clean, and then he mentally went through the step-by-step process of putting the handgun back together again. It helped. Some.

"I've always had a problem with bullies," he said. "Can't stand 'em, and it makes no difference whether they're the playground type, the international terrorist kind or the wife and kid beaters."

His hands settled on her slender waist, and he placed his forehead against hers. "I don't discriminate when it comes to an intense dislike for the group as a whole." Lord, she smelled good. "Jared messed with you and Tyler, and *that* messed with me. I can't allow that, Carlie."

"Were you picked on as a kid?" She backed out of his arms and returned to the dishes waiting in the sink. "Is that why you're so protective of others?"

"Naw. Not me." Fighting the urge to drag her back into his arms, Wes picked up a dish towel and began to dry the already washed and rinsed dishes. "Nobody bothered me because of my size, but you get to a certain saturation point, and you lose your tolerance." Surely his childhood experiences had shaped him—to some degree, anyway.

"I spent a lot of time defending my siblings and the other kids in our neighborhood. We grew up in a trailer park on the south side of Evansville. Trailer trash—that's what everyone called us." He huffed out a laugh devoid of any trace of humor.

"Is that why you joined the Marines?" she asked, handing him another dish to dry. "To protect and defend on a larger scale?"

"Partly, but I also wanted to make something of myself, get an education, see the world."

"Did you? Get an education and see the world, I mean."

"Sure. I have a degree in business from the Citadel Military College in South Carolina. And once I had my degree, I went through OCS training and got my commission. I retired as a major." He shrugged. "I could've stayed in the Marines for another ten years or so, climbed the ranks and gone on to become a lieutenant colonel, maybe even colonel, but . . ."

Images flooded his mind: the faces of the Marines under his command who never made it home, their empty combat boots, guns and helmets set up as shrines in whatever FOB he and his troops were occupying at the time. The sound of RPGs, heavy gunfire, and the smell of burning flesh overtook him. He was lost, caught off guard and trapped in the experiences that had ravaged his soul and altered his psyche.

"Wesley." Carlie called him back, placing her hand on his arm. "Are you OK? You've gone pale."

"Yeah." He ran his hand over the stubble on his jaw. He'd been in such a hurry to make sure Carlie and Tyler were OK, he hadn't taken the time to shave. "Yeah, I'm fine. Promise me you won't do anything rash, Carlie. Promise me you'll stay where you know you have protection and people who care about you. Jared doesn't stand a chance against a full-blown manhunt with K9s and a helicopter equipped with infrared. You'll see. By tomorrow, he'll be back in custody, and this time he won't escape."

"It's getting late." She wiped her hands on a towel. "I'm going to go put Tyler to bed."

"I want your promise first."

"I promise to wait and see what happens tomorrow." Her chin came up a stubborn notch. "That's the best I can do."

Not enough. Not nearly enough, but he knew better than to push her any further. She walked out of the kitchen, leaving him with his insides a mess. Now he knew what the look of resolve he'd seen earlier meant. Carlie intended to run for it, leaving herself and her son open and unprotected. She believed doing so was the right thing to do in order to keep him and everyone else in her circle safe. He shook his head.

Now, more than ever, he needed to stick close by her side.

Wesley glanced at the clock. Only eleven. The rest of the night stretched out before him, and he had nothing to do. Weekends were tough. He focused on the book in his hands, but found himself reading the same paragraph over and over while his mind replayed his kiss with Carlie. She and Tyler were slowly worming their way into his heart and into his life. He wasn't sure that was a good thing.

Protecting them was the right thing to do, that much he knew for certain, but he'd better reinforce his defenses and maintain his distance. Otherwise he and Carlie were going to end up in bed together. Not a good idea. He'd never been casual like other guys when it came to sex. Where his dick went, his heart followed. So, no. Not a good idea. But man, he wanted her in the worst way.

Setting the book aside, he checked to see if there might be a movie on cable he hadn't already seen five times or more. He needed to get his mind off Carlie. Keeping the volume on low, he searched for something to watch. A door opened down the hall, and the soft pad of little feet headed his way. Tyler came into the living room. He wore pajamas with friendly looking dinosaurs printed all over them.

"Do you need to use the bathroom, Ty?" Wes dropped the remote on the couch, ready to get up if need be. The kid didn't even look like he was awake. His face was blank, and he stood in the middle of the room, staring at nothing, shivering.

Finally, Ty shook his head, walked over to the couch and climbed up beside him. He snuggled up to Wes's side and let out a shaky sigh. "I had a bad dream," he said in a small voice.

"Hmm. Understandable under the circumstances." Wesley wrapped his arm around the boy and hugged his shoulders. "Want to talk about it?"

Tyler shook his head again and leaned against him. They sat in silence. It must be what the kid needed, because he felt the tension leach out of the little boy bit by bit.

"I dreamed about *him*," Tyler said, breaking the silence. "About the man who *used* to be my daddy." He played with the hem of his pajama shirt. "Mommy said he lost the right to be my daddy, because he wasn't fit for the job." The little guy's chin quivered, and he took in a gulp of air. Wesley hugged him close and kept his mouth shut.

"Toby and Micah have a good daddy. All the kids in my class have good daddies, too." He lifted tear-filled eyes to Wes, effectively cracking his heart wide-open. "How come my daddy didn't love me and Mommy enough to be a good daddy like the other kids have?"

"It has nothing to do with you, partner. I know that much for sure. Any dad I know would be proud to have a son like you."

"Would *you* be proud to have a son like me, Wes?"

Tyler's big blue eyes looked up at him with such longing and hope that Wes could hardly speak past the lump that had formed in his throat. "Hell, yes . . . and don't tell your mother I said *hell* in front of you." He hugged Ty again. "You know what, partner? I'm proud as can be just to know you. I can't be your daddy, but I have five younger brothers and sisters. I'm pretty sure I can take on one more. How about it, Ty? You want to be my little brother, sibling number six?"

Tyler nodded, swiped at his eyes, and the rest of his tension melted away. He curled into Wesley's side, yawned and closed his eyes. Wesley tucked him up closer and grabbed the throw from the back of the couch to cover him.

Right then and there he made a promise to himself to look after Tyler. He was committed. He'd be there for Tyler, no ifs, ands or buts about it—from here on in, they were brothers.

He lifted the remote control, found something stupid to watch and stared blindly at the screen. Warmth spread through him where the little boy leaned against his side. A sense of peace stole over Wes, like something inside him had settled.

He had another reason to keep Carlie close. He'd vowed to look after Tyler, to be there for him, and he meant to do just that. He'd make his promise to Tyler clear to Carlie, and she'd have to stay—if not for him, then for her son.

CHAPTER SIX

Carlie ladled nacho dip out of the Crock-Pot and into a ceramic serving dish. The sounds of the football game the guys were watching drifted into the kitchen, and the occasional shouts of the armchair coaches brought a smile to her face. Having Wes's friends over was nice. She and Tyler were protected, but even more significant, it felt . . . normal, and that was a new experience for her, like going out with the girls had been. If she ever got the chance, she could get used to normal.

She tore open the bag of tortilla chips and dumped them into a plastic bowl. Her mind went back to the night before. Wesley had kissed her. She loved being held in his strong arms. His desire had awakened a passion inside her she'd thought she'd never again experience. Her insides quivered just thinking about it. She wanted him.

Shaking herself free of the notion, Carlie turned back to the chips and dip. Wes had been coming to the diner for over a year, and he'd never asked her out. *She* had fantasized about him, not the other way around. When he'd kissed her, he'd probably been caught up in the moment, attempting to offer comfort or distraction, nothing more.

Besides, once he knew the rest of her sorry history, the heat she'd seen in his eyes would quickly turn to revulsion. Letting things go any further without telling him what she'd done while living on the streets would be wrong, and *wrong* wasn't something she could do to him. Wesley Holt deserved better.

Curiosity about his past, wanting to know how and who had broken his trust filled her thoughts. Did she dare pry? He'd certainly insinuated himself into her life. For someone who claimed he wasn't any good at getting personal, he'd sure proved himself wrong. Grabbing the chips and dip, she headed for the living room.

They'd set up a card table for snacks in a corner of the living room. Carlie placed the chips and dip next to the chicken wings and the fruit she'd cut up into a salad of sorts. "Chips and nacho dip," she announced. It was the best she could do on such short notice. Wesley hadn't wanted to leave the apartment to make a trip to the grocery store. They'd both heard the sound of the helicopter as it made a pass over the west end of town early that morning, and she hadn't wanted to step foot outside, either. For all she knew, the surveillance helicopter had driven her ex away from the surrounding fields and into town.

"Thanks." Kyle got up from his place on the couch. "The wings are great."

"Come join us, Carlie." Wes patted the space beside him on the couch.

"Thanks for feeding us." Ken got up to join Kyle by the food. "You didn't have to, you know, but I'm glad you did. We would've come anyway."

"I like feeding people." Carlie sank down on the couch next to Wes. He slung his arm across the back of the couch behind her, setting her insides aquiver again. "Ty, aren't you going to get something to eat? It's past lunchtime."

Tyler and Rex were on the rug surrounded with toys. "I had some wings and fruit already."

Her son glanced at her. BBQ sauce smeared the corners of his mouth. "I can see that," she said. The scene brought a lump to her throat. The only people to come over to their rented duplex when she and Jared were still married were drug dealers and criminals. Jared hadn't allowed her to have friends of her own. She glanced at the clock sitting on the bookshelves. Almost one in the afternoon, and they hadn't heard anything from the sheriff.

"You should eat something," Wes whispered into her ear.

"I can't." She studied her hands where they rested on her lap. "Too nervous."

His arm dropped from the couch to her shoulders, and she found herself drawn closer to his side. She heaved a sigh and leaned into his strength.

Kenneth took his place on the couch and settled his plate on his lap. "If they don't get the guy today, I think *we*—as in those of us with combat experience—ought to get together and plan a special ops mission of our own."

"What do you have in mind?" Wes eyed his friend.

"Stealth." Ken's expression sharpened. "The sheriff and his posse are going about this all wrong. When cops go after criminals with their sirens blaring, their lights flashing and helicopters flying overhead, they give themselves *and* their location away. We could—"

"Can we talk about something else?" Carlie tipped her head in Tyler's direction. Just then, the sound of the helicopter skimming the edge of town registered again. Carlie's stomach lurched, and so did her heart. "I could make muffins, or . . ." She started to rise, but Kyle motioned her back down as he took his seat.

"No need." Kyle grinned. "You've made more than enough already." He glanced at his watch. "I have to leave in an hour anyway. I gave Brenda a ride to work this morning, and she'll be done around three."

Wesley's phone started to buzz and vibrate on the coffee table. Adrenaline hit Carlie's bloodstream, and her mouth went dry.

Wes picked it up. "Hello?" He listened intently.

Carlie strained to hear what was being said and studied Wes's face for clues.

"OK. Thanks for the update, Paul. Talk to you later." He glanced at her and ran his hand up and down her arm. "They found his campsite in a field about a quarter of a mile from your house. It's clear Jared left in a big hurry. The K9s have his scent. They're on his trail."

Blowing out a huge breath, she forced herself to relax. "That's good, isn't it?"

"Sure. If it really was your ex's campsite, and not some hunter's." Ken shrugged. "And even if it was Jared's site, then it's only good *if* the guy is stupid enough to be caught on foot, or *if* he's even still in the area."

"That's a lot of ifs." She bit her lip. Jared wasn't stupid. She hoped he had been the one camping so close to her house and that he was currently without a car.

The afternoon dragged on, and they didn't get any more calls from the sheriff. Kyle left, and after the football game ended, they moved to pay-per-view and chose an animated movie for Tyler to watch. She couldn't take much more sitting, and the sound of the TV grated on her nerves. By six o'clock, she'd had enough. Carlie got up to clear the mess left over from their snacks.

Ken stood up right after she did. He stretched and yawned. "You all right if I head out, Wes? I have plans this evening."

"Sure. We're good." Wes rose from his place and walked to the door with Ken. "Thanks for hanging out with us today."

"My pleasure." Ken grabbed his jacket from the closet. "I'll see you at work tomorrow night. Thanks for feeding me, Carlie. Wes is a lucky man."

What did he mean by that? "You're welcome." An awkward silence filled the space Ken left behind. Carlie gathered the plates and bowls and took them to the kitchen. She set things down on the counter and moved to the window over the sink. Lifting the blinds, she surveyed the alley below. The search for Jared was probably coming to an end now that the sun had gone down. In this case, no news was not good news.

The need to get out of the apartment overcame her. Restless and edgy, her mind went around and around about what to do. Was it too late to run? No. She could still throw her son and her stuff into her car and hit the road. Staring out the window into the gathering darkness, Carlie wondered what her life would be like today if she hadn't taken that first step down the path toward trouble so many years ago.

"Hey." Wes came up behind her. "I don't know about you, but I'm a little stir-crazy." He took her hand in his, and the blinds dropped back into place. Turning her around, he drew her close. "You OK?"

"I'm anxious." How could one man smell so good? Her heart raced and desire coiled through her. Being in his arms was the only time she felt safe. Where she and Tyler were concerned, this big strong man was a gentle giant, and that turned her on like crazy. She had to force her mind off what she wanted to do to Wes and back to the here and now. "Waiting to hear is driving me a little nuts."

"It's been a long day without any physical activity." He ran his hands up and down her back. "We can't go for a walk, but we could practice the self-defense moves you've learned so far. I can teach you a few new things while we're at it."

She could hardly breathe as it was. How could she practice self-defense when being so close to him stole her breath and melted her insides? All she wanted to do was put her arms around his waist and press up against him. Naked. That thought elicited a throbbing between her thighs. Carlie stepped away from him. "Let me clean up first, and—"

He drew her back into his arms. "Oh, no you don't." He chuckled. "You aren't the maid, Carlie. You're my guest. Don't think I haven't noticed how dust-free and tidy my place has become since you moved in. You don't have to cook and clean for me. You know that, right?"

He made her breathless and wanting. Did he feel the same, or was he just one of those people who liked to hug? He had a lot of siblings, and he'd pretty much raised them. More than likely he'd always been affectionate, and she shouldn't read more into it than what it was.

Wesley Holt was one of those genuinely nice guys who gave out help and hugs to any in need. She swallowed. She was just an "any in need" to him, and nothing more, and the sooner she drilled that into her head, the better. "Cooking and cleaning are my way of saying thank you."

"I know, and I appreciate it, but the chore will give me something to do after you and Ty go to bed." He hugged her once more and let her go. "Come on. Tyler can join us. We'll do some training. The activity will do us all some good."

What the heck. He was probably right. A little exercise couldn't hurt. She followed him out of the kitchen and through the dining room. "Tyler, Wesley and I are going to practice self-defense. Do you want to join us?"

"You mean like Ninja Turtles?" Tyler looked up at her, then at Wesley. "Yeah." His eyes lit up.

The rumble of Wes's laughter behind her caused her heart to flutter again. "Let's clean up your toys first." She walked to the rug where he was playing, grabbed the plastic tub on the floor and started tossing action figures into it. Tyler helped, Rex supervised and Wesley took care of putting the card table away.

"We'll use the dining room," Wes said. "There's lots of space to move around. Take off your socks so we don't slip around on the wood floor."

Wes had them stand side by side. "Demonstrate what you've learned so far, Carlie, and we'll practice each move a few times. Ty, walk through the movements with your mom."

For the next half hour she practiced the motions of slamming the base of her palm into Wes's nose, kicking his kneecap and kneeing him in the groin. She pretended her pepper spray was in her hands, with her thumb on the nozzle and her arms straight out in front of her. Tyler imitated her, for the most part, but he was tiring fast and getting silly. Putting him to bed wasn't going to be easy after so much stimulation.

"Hi-ya!" Tyler went into a Ninja Turtle karate pose. He kicked out a few times, then charged. He wrapped his arms around Wesley's legs and tried to wrestle him down. Wesley feigned defeat, falling to the floor, taking her son down with him while tickling Ty in the ribs. In a fit of giggles, Tyler tried to tickle back and pounced on top of Wesley's chest, and then Rex trotted over and started licking Wes's face.

"Yuck! I surrender," Wes cried, wiping the slobber from his face. "You and Rex got me, ninja. You win."

Carlie laughed, but then Wes's phone buzzed. All three of them looked toward the living room and froze. Wes was the first to move. He leaped up, taking Tyler with him. He set her son on his feet before hurrying to the living room, where his phone sat on the coffee table. He snatched it up and answered. "Hey, Paul."

Carlie's heart pounded. Tyler walked to her side and slipped his hand into hers. After this was all over, she'd have to see about getting some counseling for the both of them. She didn't want Tyler to be permanently scarred.

Wes's jaw tightened as he listened to the sheriff. "Right. Will do." He placed his phone back on the table and shook his head. "They *failed* to apprehend . . ." His eyes settled on Tyler. "Looks like I get to keep the two of you here awhile longer. I hope that's all right with you, partner."

Tyler let go of her hand and ran to Wes. He scooped her son into his arms. Tyler clung to Wesley and buried his face against his shoulder. Wes's eyes met and held hers, his expression grim and his jaw clenched.

She stood in the middle of the living room, her chest too tight to breathe, and her eyes stung. Hadn't she said as much? Hadn't she known all along they wouldn't catch Jared? He'd go into a rage now. He'd grow more bold in his attempts to get at them, and he had a rifle. Panic clogged her throat. Staying in his apartment put Wesley in danger. Jared would focus on Wes, seeing him as the obstacle in his way to her and Ty.

"Carlie." Wesley moved toward her. "Don't go there."

Numb with fear, she shook her head and stared at Wes through a sheen of tears. He drew her to him. Wesley held her and Tyler. She couldn't bear the thought of this beautiful man getting hurt because of her. She would die if anything happened to Wes or Tyler. She put her arms around them and held on to the two people who meant the most to her in the whole world, wondering what she could do to protect them both.

❦ ❦ ❦

Carlie couldn't sleep. Since climbing into bed, her mind had been in turmoil. The sheriff had told them he believed her ex had fled the area. *Ha.* Not for long—not if she knew anything about Jared Baumann. No, he'd wait until he believed things cooled down in Perfect, then he'd be back with a vengeance.

Two US Marshals were arriving the day after tomorrow. Monday. Hopefully they'd bring a new bag of tricks with them, because the local authorities had used up all of theirs, not that they were giving up, according to Paul Taylor, anyway.

A noise caught her attention, and she stilled to listen. Ty had been having nightmares since Jared's reappearance, and he was probably having another one. She turned on the lamp beside her. There it was again, louder this time. Wesley, not her son. She slid out of bed, crossed the room and opened her door. Light from the living room illuminated the hallway. Grabbing her robe from the hook on the back of the door, she slid her arms into the sleeves and tiptoed down the hall.

She knew veterans with PTSD often suffered from nightmares. Wes hadn't slept much the day before. He'd gotten up at eleven in the morning to be with her, and because Kyle and Ken were coming over. She found Wesley asleep on the couch with the TV on.

He moaned, and his arms thrashed. "Get down! Now!"

Should she wake him? She walked to his side, picked up the remote control and shut off the TV. Wes moaned again. He was clearly trapped in a nightmare. If waking him would free him . . . But she'd also heard stories about veterans who put their hands around their spouse's necks while in the throes of a bad dream. Well, hadn't she learned a move for that? Carlie crept closer to the couch, sat down beside him and shook his arm. "Wesley, wake up."

He pulled her down and flung himself over her. "Drop," he commanded, pressing her into the cushions with his full weight. "Stay down."

"Wes, wake up. You're dreaming." She had trouble breathing with his full weight on top of her. Squirming, she tried to slide out from under him. He responded by holding her in place tighter. She pinched his waist. Being held as she was, it was the only part of him she could get to. "Wake up!"

"Ow," he muttered in an accusatory tone. His eyes opened; he lifted himself slightly and stared down at her in confusion. "You pinched me. Why did you pinch me?"

"You were having a bad dream, and I—"

"How'd you get . . . under me?" His expression changed from confusion to heated, and he pressed his hips against her.

"I . . . you—"

"Aw, who cares?" He nuzzled her neck and tangled his fingers in her hair. "You always smell so damn good . . . feel so good . . . Carlie . . . want you so much," he whispered into her ear before taking her earlobe between his teeth.

A shiver of pleasure tickled its way down her spine. He wasn't fully awake, that much was clear. Still, all kinds of erotic sensations coursed through her. "Wes, wake up."

He raised his head and stared down at her with such intensity her lungs seized. His gaze roamed over her face and settled on her mouth.

"I am awake. Now, anyway." He propped himself on his elbows, trapping her arms by her sides. Then he lowered his head and kissed her.

His tongue traced the seam of her lips, and she opened for him. She lost herself in the heady sensation of the hottest kiss of her life—demanding, sensual, with just the right amount of pressure, moisture and warmth. Wesley Holt thrilled her to the very center of her being. Need ignited her blood. The sound of his heavy breathing and the feel of his erection pressing against her plunged her into a frenzy of need.

Tugging at the hem of his shirt, she sought bare skin. *His* bare skin. She ran her hands over his back. So hot, smooth. Bulging muscles rippled under her palms, and he groaned against her mouth. A rush of heat and a throbbing ache filled her. She lifted her hips, seeking relief.

How long had it been since anyone had wanted her? Even more important, how long had it been since she'd desired a man the way she burned for Wesley Holt? *Never.*

He untied the belt of her robe and slid his hand under her T-shirt. His chest heaved, and his hips ground into her. She nearly came when his hand covered a breast, pinching and rolling the hardened nipple.

"Carlie," he whispered before kissing her jawline and down her neck.

It would be so easy—wouldn't it?—to let go. Why not give in to what they both wanted?

Because of my sordid past, that's why. Shame sluiced through her, bringing a tiny shred of sanity following in its wake. She couldn't do this to him, not with the secret she still held between them. Sucking in a breath, she brought her hands to his chest and pushed. "Stop. We have to stop."

He groaned again, but this time the sound held more frustration than desire. "You're right. I don't have protection anyway." He removed his hand from her breast and slid it down to her waist. Pressing his forehead against hers, he murmured, "I'm sorry, Carlie. I had no right." He raised himself off her, and they both sat up. Rubbing his hands over his face, he took a couple of deep breaths and leaned his head back on the couch. "Forgive me. I didn't mean to—"

"You don't have anything to be sorry about, and there's nothing to forgive." She shook her head and retied her robe. "I was every bit as caught up as you were, believe me. I . . . we have to talk."

"Sure." He let out a strangled chuckle. "Let's talk."

Her heart pounded, and mortification stole her breath. "You only know part of my history. If you knew the rest—"

"Then what? I'd walk away? Is that what you think?" He dropped his hands and scowled at her.

She nodded. "You wouldn't want anything to do with me."

"You're wrong. I already know the rest, I'm still here, and I still want you."

"What do you mean by *the rest*?" Her heart skipped a beat. "What did the Maurers tell you?"

"They didn't tell me anything. I figured it out on my own."

"What . . . what do you believe you figured out?" She drew the edges of her robe together at her throat, as if that would shield her somehow. He couldn't know. Carlie racked her brain, trying to remember what she'd told him the morning he'd saved her life. She hadn't said *what* she'd been arrested for, only that she'd been picked up by the police. An image came to her—Wesley with his elbows propped on his knees with a look of deep concentration on his face as she told him her story. Part of it, anyway. Had he pieced it all together that first day?

He snorted. "Don't you think I can put two and two together?" He reached for her hand, twined their fingers and brought it to his knee. "I've been all over the world, and some of the places where I was stationed were ravaged by war and poverty. Desperate people do desperate things. Under the right circumstances, we humans will do whatever it takes to get what we need, and that's a fact. You were young, alone and addicted to narcotics. There aren't too many ways in that messed-up scenario to earn money. It's not like you could've held a job, what with no address and being high all the time. What else besides your body did you have to offer in exchange for currency or drugs?" He shot her a searching look. "Thieving and prostitution were your only options. Am I right?"

His words were blunt, his gaze direct and his expression a mask she couldn't read. No matter how hard she searched for the judgment she was certain she'd find, she couldn't tell what he was thinking. Adrenaline and mortification scorched every one of her nerve endings, obliterating her ability to think. Completely exposed and burning with shame, all she could do was stare into his hazel eyes. Her secret wasn't a secret after all, and she had no idea how to respond.

His grip on her hand tightened. "What I want to know is this: Where the *hell* were your parents when you needed them the most?"

The anger in his tone jerked her loose from the shock his revelation had caused, and she ran a shaky hand through her hair. "Don't . . . don't blame my mom."

"All right. Tell me, then." He grunted. "Who *is* to blame, because *you* were just a kid. That's the story I want, Carlie."

Next thing she knew, she was on his lap again. His warmth and strength permeated every black-and-blue corner of her bruised heart. Laying her head on his solid shoulder, she succumbed to his soothing touch. Freed from the bondage of her secrets, she just let herself . . . be.

"Tell me," he urged.

"It's nobody's fault. I was just a kid with too little adult supervision and too much time on my hands." She shrugged. "I fell in with the wrong crowd. You know how it is. If you hang around garbage long enough, you're going to start to stink. Nobody in my family knew enough about what I was doing to stop me. If they had, they would've."

"Why the lack of supervision?" He stroked her hair.

There were no demands in the way her held her, no expectation of something in return. He hadn't judged her for the things she'd done. Instead of turning away from her in disgust, he'd defended her. Sighing, she snuggled closer. "Mom and Dad divorced when I was fourteen. Dad moved to California, and my mom went back to school so she could get a better job to support us."

She lifted her head to look at him. "Being a single mom with two kids while going to school wasn't easy. She also had to work. It was a tough time for her, and she did her best. It was a tough time for all of us. My mom had to start over. We moved in with my grandparents, but by then my grandfather had already had his first stroke. Grandma had her hands full taking care of him. Plus, she wasn't real savvy when it came to figuring out what kind of trouble I was getting into." She played with the loose ends of her belt. "I don't blame anyone for the choices I made, and neither should you."

"What about your dad?"

"What about him?"

"Were the two of you close before the divorce?"

"My father left us for another woman. I haven't seen him since he moved to California with his new family. He used to send birthday cards, signing them with, 'love, Dad,' and he included the occasional Christmas check, but it sure didn't feel much like love to me." She raised her chin. "Enough about me. It's your turn."

"Yes, ma'am." One side of his mouth quirked up. "What do you want to know?"

"What were you dreaming about?"

"Ah." He rubbed his forehead. "I work nights and sleep days, because for some reason I don't have the nightmares as much during the daytime. I was dreaming about a young Marine who died during a mission we were on. His death was entirely my fault."

"Did you cause an accident?"

He shook his head. "It's a long story."

"I've got the time, and I can't sleep." She heaved a sigh and settled against him.

"A lot on your mind?" He shot her a wry look.

"Yep, and I find focusing on *you* helps keep my mind off of *me*." She returned his wry look with one of her own. "It's only fair. For someone who claimed he didn't want to get personal, you've certainly managed to uncover my most personal secrets. Without sharing any of your own, I might add."

"I never said I didn't want to get personal, Carlie." He brushed his lips against her temple. "I said I wasn't any good at it. There's a difference."

"Oh." She went boneless on his lap and struggled to keep her hands to herself. "Tell me about your nightmare."

Wesley let out a groan. "I was stationed at Camp Leatherneck in the Helmand province of Afghanistan. My platoon had been given a mission to clear out an insurgent compound in the Jowzjan province. The Taliban had a narcotics-processing factory there." He huffed out a breath. "At least that's what intel told us."

"*Your* platoon?"

He nodded. "Yeah, back then I was a platoon sergeant. It was a long time ago." He huffed out another breath of air, and she could feel his heart hammering away inside his chest. "The afternoon before our mission, I got an e-mail from my wife."

"Wait." She straightened so she could look him in the eye. "You were married?"

He nodded. "To my high school *sweetheart*," he said, his voice filled with bitterness. "Tina and I got hitched shortly after I went through basic, and then we lived on base while I was stationed at Camp Geiger in North Carolina while I trained for combat. While I was deployed, she'd head home to Evansville to stay with her folks."

"OK. So the afternoon before your mission she sent you an e-mail. What did she have to say?"

"My lovely wife e-mailed to tell me that she no longer wanted to be married to me." His Adam's apple bobbed a few times. "And that she was pregnant."

"You have a child?" Her eyes went even wider.

"No. I don't. I hadn't been stateside in ten months." The muscle in his jaw twitched. "After the e-mail, I heard from friends and family. Seems everyone but me knew she was running around. I was the last to know."

Misplaced trust—now it all made sense. Carlie threw her arms around his neck and hugged him close. "I'm so sorry, Wes. I can't imagine what you went through."

"You want to know what the real pisser was?" His voice came out a hoarse rasp. "I wanted a family in the worst way. Tina refused to even consider getting pregnant until I had a cushy desk job stateside. Fool that I was, I was working my ass off to make that happen for us."

What could she say to make him feel better? She couldn't fathom how anyone could do such a thing to a soldier deployed in an active combat zone. How heartless and self-centered did you have to be to do something like that?

He cleared his throat. "I was . . . distracted the next day. When we got to the insurgents' compound early the next morning, we destroyed the building intel had identified, but we didn't find any indication of a drug-processing operation. We did find a cache of hollowed-out artillery shells to be used for IEDs, though, so it wasn't a total waste."

He leaned his head back against the couch and closed his eyes. "We were in a hilly area at the bottom of the bowl. Not a good position to be in. Our Humvees were parked along a dirt road, and we were starting to pull out. If I hadn't been so distracted, I would've cautioned my troops. I knew the Taliban would strike back. We'd destroyed a building, and they couldn't let our presence go without retaliation."

"What happened?"

"Did you know that a bullet can travel faster than the speed of sound?" He swallowed a few times before continuing. "There was this kid, just nineteen, still wet behind the ears and fresh out of combat training. He'd just joined Golf Company the week before. He was walking down the middle of the dirt road toward me with this big cocky grin on his face. It was his first mission, and he was feeling pretty revved up." He exhaled a shaky breath. "I saw the damned hole in the middle of his forehead before I heard the shot. I'll never forget the stunned look on his face before he collapsed."

He pressed the base of his thumbs against his eyes as if trying to push out the images haunting him. "I should've told him to take cover, not to strut down the middle of the road like he ruled the desert. I knew we were in a vulnerable position, and I did nothing. I was too damned preoccupied with my own petty problems, and I let my troops down."

A shudder racked him. "All hell broke loose after that. We were in a bad situation with fire coming at us from the surrounding hills. One of our Humvees was hit by an RPG, and it exploded into flames with four Marines inside. We managed to put out the fire, but none of the Marines inside survived. I'll never forget the smell." Another shudder went through him.

"I called for air support. Helicopters made a Hellfire strike. They got the building where most of the fire came from, but the Taliban had snipers and grenade launchers scattered throughout the surrounding hills. The only cover we had were our trucks, and those were easy targets." He pulled his hands away from his face, and the bleakness in his expression stole her breath.

"We went into the hills after the enemy and lost two more Marines. My job was to keep my platoon safe, to prepare my troops for every possible contingency. I didn't do my job as well as I could have. I was distracted by my own personal problems, and because of that, seven Marines made the ultimate sacrifice that day."

"You can't blame yourself for what happened. You weren't the one who put your troops in that situation, and nothing you could've done would have prevented the losses your unit suffered." Her heart bled for him. "Even if you had made sure your Marines took cover while you were pulling out, you said yourself the Taliban were targeting the trucks. More troops might have been lost if they had used the trucks for cover."

"Like you can't blame yourself for the direction your life took when you were just a kid." He shot her a hard look. "The adults who should've been taking care of you failed to do their duty."

"I made choices. It's not the same thing at all." She slid off his lap.

"I don't see it that way." He leaned forward, placing his elbows on his knees and holding his head in his hands. "Carlie, I have PTSD. I can't sleep at night like a normal person, and I have . . . issues. I'm not good at . . . I'm not partner material, but don't think for a minute that your past makes you any less in my eyes. You're amazing. You've overcome so much, and you're a terrific mom, not to mention you're hot as hell."

He shot her a lopsided grin. "I'm not going to pretend that I don't want you, because I do." He shook his head. "But I just don't have it in me to—"

"Get personal?" She choked out a laugh and stood up. "We both have issues, Wes. I have lousy judgment when it comes to relationships, and I'm not sure I'll ever be able to trust a man with my heart again. Plus, I have a son to consider. I'm not sure I can allow another man into our lives again, not after what Tyler and I have been through with Jared. I don't even know if I want to stay in Perfect after my ex is caught. I love it here, but I can't stand the thought of everyone knowing about my past, or the way gossip travels around town."

She scrambled to hold it together. Wesley Holt was everything she'd ever wanted in a man, but way too many obstacles stood between them. Could they get through them? Was it worth the possibility of devastation to even try? "I'm not going to pretend, either. We're obviously attracted to each other, but if we take that next step, it means getting involved, and I'm not sure either of us want that."

She studied him. "Would it be better if I stayed somewhere else while Jared is on the loose? Because it's obvious where things are headed, and I don't want it to become awkward between us. I don't see any other outcome *but* awkward if we continue to stay under the same roof without agreeing on where we're going with this."

He opened his mouth to respond, and she shook her head. "I don't want to talk about this anymore right now. I'm tired, and so are you. Don't say anything until we've both had a chance to think."

"All right." Wes's gaze met and held hers. "If that's the way you want it, we'll leave it for now."

"Good night, Wes." How did she want him to respond to her questions? She didn't even know what her own answer would be, and what about Tyler? She could not allow her son to be let down by another man in his life, and honestly, she'd already allowed Wesley in too deep. Had she once again used poor judgment when she'd agreed to stay with him in his apartment? Of course she had. The longer they stayed, the more her son would be hurt when they left—the more she would be hurt.

Would she never learn? Her heart aching, Carlie went back to bed, more aware than ever how empty her life would be once things returned to the way they had been. It wasn't just Jared's sudden appearance causing all the upheaval. Wesley Holt had turned her life upside down and inside out.

CHAPTER SEVEN

WESLEY YAWNED AS HE APPLIED the last coat of varnish to the end table before him. After the past few drama-filled days, being at L&L felt more like a break than work. He hadn't reached this level of exhaustion since his last deployment, not to mention the degree of sexual frustration plaguing him. With all the worry he carried for Carlie and Ty, he held more coils than a box spring mattress. "I sure will be glad when things return to normal," he muttered to no one in particular.

"You're kidding, right? You don't really believe things are going to go back to the way they were." Ken snorted. "Do you?"

"Why wouldn't they?" After the talk he'd had with Carlie Saturday night, he planned to make it clear that he'd keep his hands to himself. No involvement and no awkwardness. That way, she could continue to stay safe in his apartment. Eventually Jared would be caught. Then she and Tyler would return to their own house, and he'd go back to his predictable routine.

"Yeah, bro. I gotta agree with Kenny on this one." Miguel shook his head. "You didn't think it through before you moved Carlie and her boy into your place. Things are never going to be the same for you."

"*Everything* will go back to the way it was once this is over." Except for his commitment to Tyler, but right now he didn't want to think about how he'd manage that. Ty was one thing, Carlie another. He glared at his crew, daring them to contradict him. All four pelted him with snorts of incredulity.

"Don't count on it." Ken shot him a pity-filled look. "Before all of this started, you didn't know Carlie and her boy. Now you do. The three of you have a *relationship*, and there's no use pretending otherwise."

"I'm not pretending anything. Carlie needed help. I'm helping. We're *all* helping, and that's all there is to it." Wes focused on the piece of furniture in front of him, sliding his brush over the grain. "We're friends, and friends help each other."

"You can fool yourself all you want." Ken shrugged. "But the rest of us know better."

"What do you think you know better?" Wes challenged.

"Do you really believe you can go back to square one after living under the same roof with Carlie, like you two never shared the same space?" Ken shook his head. "That's not how it works. You can't go from being that intimate with a woman to being mere acquaintances again. Especially not with a woman you look at the way you do Carlie. We've all seen *the look*, Wes. We've all *worn* the look at one time or another."

"He's right. Besides, you're irritable as hell, and we all know why, bro," Miguel chimed in. "You got it bad for Carlie, and that's a fact."

"Yep." TreVonne smirked. "He's got that right. Man, I'll bet your balls are blue by now. Unless you and Carlie are already—"

"That's enough," Wesley snapped. "Carlie is my guest until her ex is back behind bars. You are all reading way too much into the situation."

"Ha! Irritable *and* in denial. It's just a matter of time, Wes. Just a matter of time." Ken glanced around the production area. "Hey, if any of you are interested, I'm starting a pool. It'll cost you a five spot per square to get in. I'll make up the calendar on my break. Whoever calls it closest to the day Wes caves, wins. Who's in?"

Laughter and predictions about how long it would be before he and Carlie had sex and were officially a couple filled the room. Heat flooded Wes's face. "Rex needs to go out." He slid varnish over the last corner and put down his brush.

"Rex is snoring." Miguel chuckled. "That dog doesn't need a thing."

"Well, then I need to go out," Wes muttered.

"Cold air is not going to cure what ails you. What you need is a cold shower." David, their newest addition to the graveyard shift, took out his wallet and turned to Ken. He handed him a five-dollar bill. "Put me down for November eighteenth. I give it a week, tops. Be sure to include the first and second shifts in the pool so I win a nice big pot."

More laughter erupted. Wesley growled and stomped across the room. "Rex," he called, reaching for the dog's leash. "Come." Rex raised his head and thumped his tail a time or two. Then he yawned and put his muzzle back down on his paws. Wes would've sworn the dog shrugged at him. At least he didn't flip him the paw for his attempt to use him as an excuse to leave the room.

"Fine. Stay." Wes hung the leash back on the hook. He strode out the door into the cold night air. The chill cooled his overheated face. He scanned his surroundings, checking the rooftops, windows and shadows for signs of danger. He leaned against the bricks. As much as he wanted things in his life to go back to the way they had been, the guys were right. He and Carlie had gotten to know each other. They'd shared things. Deeply personal things, dammit, and that couldn't be undone.

The crew was wrong about one thing, though. His balls weren't blue. They were purple. He'd touched her. Blood rushed to his groin and his breath hitched at the memory of the way her skin had felt against his palm. He thumped his head against the bricks and groaned.

No doubt about it. If he and Carlie continued to stay under the same roof, they were headed for bed. Hadn't she said as much when she'd issued her ultimatum? *Are we getting involved, or should I go somewhere else to stay?* That's what she'd boiled it down to, and he wasn't about to leave her unprotected while Jared was still on the loose. Talk about being in a bind. His apartment really was the safest place for her and her son. So where did that leave him?

With all the PTSD and trust issues between the two of them, did he and Carlie have any real shot at a future together? The thought of not having her and Ty in his life left him feeling as hollowed out as a spent artillery shell. He wanted her with a desperation that defied reason.

Wait. What about a friends-with-benefits arrangement? Could he manage that? Could they form an agreement of sorts—one where they remained close friends, involved, but living separately? Involved, but with limits and boundaries . . . that *could* work. It would have to be exclusive. Plus, he'd made a promise to Carlie's son, and Tyler had to factor in when it came to any decisions he and Carlie might make. At least it would give them something to consider, something that would keep them together.

Wes thunked his head against the bricks again. What the hell was he thinking? Carlie would never agree to such an arrangement. Why would she? He'd really gone and done it this time. He was caught like a fly in a drop of honey—sweet but deadly. One thing was for sure, he and Carlie had to talk—and soon.

🐏 🐏 🐏

Wesley held Tyler's hand as the two of them walked into the Perfect Diner. The sheriff had made arrangements for Wes and Carlie to meet the two US Marshals at the Warrick County sheriff's office in Boonville that afternoon after Carlie's shift. "Hey, Harlen." Wes nodded a greeting to the older man.

"Hey, you two." Harlen grinned. "Carlie's in back. She'll be out in a minute."

Jenny approached. "And you get to come to our house, Tyler. We're going to make cookies. How does that sound?"

"What kind?" Tyler's grip on Wes's fingers tightened.

"Why, chocolate chip, of course. Your mom said they're your favorite." Jenny retrieved her things from under the register. "Wes's dog is coming with us."

"He is?" Ty flashed Wes a questioning look.

"That's why Rex is in my car, partner," Wes told him. "Harlen, the three of us will follow you to your place, and Carlie and I will head to Boonville from there."

Harlen agreed just as Carlie appeared. Wesley's heart did its familiar calisthenics routine. She was just so damned pretty. Their eyes met, and his knees nearly folded on him from the hit. He smiled. "Ready?"

"Yes."

Worry lines creased her brow, and the need to touch her overwhelmed him. Wes placed his free hand at the small of her back as they followed the Maurers out of the diner. He and Harlen kept an eye on their surroundings while Carlie locked up, and then they moved in a tight, protective group to the parking lot.

Once Tyler and Rex were settled at the Maurers' house, he and Carlie headed east through town for the drive to Boonville. Carlie sighed heavily. "You OK?" he asked.

"Sure." She turned away to stare out the window and twisted the hell out of the strap on her purse.

Clearly *not* OK. "All right. Out with it. What's bothering you, Carlie?"

"Other than my ex on the loose and wanting to *end* me and steal my son?" She shrugged. "My mom called today. She and my grandmother want me and Tyler to come home for Thanksgiving." Another mega-sigh filled his SUV.

"That's good, right?" He glanced at her. Hadn't she told him she'd lived with her mom and grandmother for a while before moving to Perfect? "Why do I get the feeling you're not happy about the invite?"

"My brother and his family will be there, too." She shrugged.

"You have a brother?" This was news to him. She hadn't mentioned a brother before.

She nodded. "He's older. I haven't seen Ron for years, and I've never even met his wife and kids." The corners of her mouth turned down. "I wasn't invited to their wedding."

Now that just made him mad. "Where was *he* while you were sliding into the dark side?"

"*He* was busy being a straight-A student and the perfect son." She let out a shaky laugh. "I guess we both reacted differently to my parents' divorce and everything. Ron became an uptight control freak and a judgmental perfectionist. I became an addict and a—"

"Don't say it, Carlie." Wes gripped the steering wheel. "He should've been looking out for you. That's a big brother's job."

"I get why you think that, Wes. You were expected to look after your younger brothers and sisters while your parents worked. I'm sure that message was drilled into you from day one, and with your nature, of course you took it to the *n*th degree." She shook her head.

"But that's not how it was in my world. My mom and grandma didn't put that on my brother. He had his own life. By the time we moved in with my grandparents, Ron was a senior in high school and getting ready to go off to college. The two of us were never what you'd call close, and once I got involved with drugs and ran away, he disowned me altogether." She kept her eyes fixed on her purse. "We haven't spoken since the day I was arrested for prostitution. I'm sure he was relieved to hear I'd changed my name, so there was no association between the two of us."

Anger on Carlie and Tyler's behalf exploded in his chest. No way was he going to let her face her brother without backup. "We're going."

"*We're* going?" Her eyes widened. "They don't know about . . . I mean, they know Jared escaped from prison. It's been on the news, but I didn't mention you or what's been going on in Perfect. I don't want them to worry."

She hadn't even mentioned him? That bit. "What *did* you say?"

"I told my mom I'd think about it and get back to her. I figured it would be best to hear what the sheriff and the marshals have to say before making a decision. I don't want to put anyone else in danger, and with Jared armed and on the loose, it might be better to stay put."

They'd reached the outskirts of Boonville, and Wes turned onto Indiana 62. With everything else going on, he'd completely forgotten Thanksgiving. He and whatever siblings and their families were around always gathered at his mom and dad's. Once all their children had grown and gone, his parents had bought a little two-bedroom bungalow in an older first-tier suburb of Evansville. "Jared isn't so stupid that he'd approach a houseful of witnesses, and he's not the only one armed. If the marshals won't let you leave town, you and Tyler will come to my parents' house for Thanksgiving."

"Is that an invitation or an order?" She scowled. "Thanksgiving is two weeks away. Hopefully, Jared will be behind bars by then, and you won't have to drag me and Tyler around with you wherever you go."

"It's not like that." He pulled into the parking lot of the Warrick County jail. The sheriff's offices and dispatch were housed on one side and the jail on the other. "I'd love to have you and Tyler there. I . . . we've . . ." Heat crept up his neck and filled his face. "You should know I've made a commitment to Tyler. He had a bad dream a few nights ago, and he and I—"

"A *commitment?*" Carlie's eyes flashed sparks. "What kind of commitment did you make to my son without talking to me about it first?"

He hadn't handled this well at all. "I promised to be there for him. We kind of adopted each other. Tyler is my little brother now, and—"

"You should have talked to me about this before saying anything to Ty. Did you give any thought to how that's going to affect him if I decide to move somewhere else?" Her voice rose. "Have you considered what it will do to him when he's disappointed by yet another man in his life?"

"Me disappointing Tyler is a foregone conclusion in your mind?" His chest ached where her words slammed against his sternum. "I'm not your dad, Carlie, and I'm not your ex or your brother. Just because the men in your life let you down doesn't mean every man on the planet is bound to do the same. This is about your mother's invitation to Thanksgiving, isn't it? Hearing your brother is going to be there has stirred up all kinds of sh—"

"You think you have me all figured out, don't you?" Her hands curled into fists on her lap, and anger flashed from her like the hazard lights on his SUV.

"Hell, no. I don't even have *me* all figured out." He barked out a mirthless laugh and pulled his SUV into a parking spot. Once he cut the engine, he cast her incredulous look. Did she not realize what a mess he was? "What makes you think that?"

Carlie crossed her arms in front of her, not making any move to leave. "Because you . . ." She bit her lip and clammed up.

"Would you mind expanding on that just a tad?"

"Because, Wes," she said, glancing at him for a fraction of a second. "You put two and two together and came up with *whore*."

"Carlie, I—"

"That's not all." Her voice broke, and his heart broke right along with it. "Sometimes you stare at me so hard, I swear I can feel you taking me apart bit by bit. It's as if you're studying each component part to find out what makes me tick." She searched his face. "You are, aren't you? You're figuring me out."

"Not exactly." He ran his hand over the back of his sweaty neck. Mostly he'd been undressing her in his mind and fantasizing about putting his hands all over her, along with his mouth and other parts of his anatomy. Should he tell her that? Probably not.

"Yeah. You are. And then you ferret out all of my secrets. You take them from me without my permission and rob me of the chance to share them with you. It's . . . intrusive."

OK. Maybe he did do that a little bit. "I have twenty years of military experience. I've been trained to process things a certain way and to analyze situations to my advantage. Add to that my PTSD, and . . . well . . . I *need* to understand the world around me. I can't turn that off." He reached for her hand, and when she tried to tug it free, he held on. "I didn't put two and two together and come up with whore, Carlie. I swear that's not at all how I see things."

"But you—"

"No, Carlie." He shook his head and gave her a hard look. "What I came up with is that somewhere along the road, your life took a wrong turn. The important part of that story is not what you did back then, but what and who you are today. You're an incredible mother, a strong, intelligent woman and beautiful from the inside out."

"Oh." A stunned expression suffused her features.

"I'm not going to let you or Tyler down." He rubbed the back of her hand with his thumb. "You *can't* leave Perfect. That would definitely lead to disappointment, and I wouldn't be the one responsible." She pulled her hand from his so fast he had no chance to hang on.

"Excuse me?" She blinked at him, her eyebrows raised. "Did you just tell me—"

"That didn't come out right." Or more likely it hadn't gone over well, because it was exactly what he'd meant. "Can we start this conversation over *after* we talk to the marshals?"

She made a growling noise and unbuckled her seat belt. Without a glance his way, she climbed out of his car.

Did she not know him at all? Why would she assume he'd let Ty down? That stung. Granted, she was angry and prickly at the moment, and at some level he understood her churned-up emotional state really didn't have that much to do with him. At least she trusted him enough to let her feelings show. After everything she'd gone through with her ex, that counted for something. As affronted as he was, knowing she trusted him caused a rush of pride.

Wesley hurried to catch up to her. "Carlie, what I meant to say is that I hope you decide to stay in Perfect after all of this trouble with Jared is behind you. You have friends here, and a job I know you love." She didn't respond. If he could string together enough words that made sense, maybe she'd come around to seeing things his way. He forged on.

"I swore to Tyler that I'd look after him, be there for him. He needs a positive male role model in his life. Surely you can't argue with that fact. He needs me, and I'm not about to turn my back on the vow I made to him. I can't be there for Tyler if the two you aren't in Perfect. Plus, you and I have gotten to know each other pretty well. Haven't we?"

She cast him a disgruntled look.

He placed his hand on her shoulder to stop her. "I was hoping we could continue to hang out, do stuff together." Heat filled his face. "We get along pretty well, don't we?"

Her eyes took on a challenging glint and drilled a hole through his hide to his soul. "Do you mean you want to date me, Wes?"

Gulp. He meant friends with benefits with an appropriate amount of distance between the two of them. Now was probably not the best time to bring up that suggestion. "You're the closest I've come to wanting that, but . . . I was thinking more along the lines of a . . . close friendship."

Again her eyes sparked. What had he said to upset her this time? He couldn't get any traction with her. Sucking in a breath, he searched his brain for a way out of the quagmire. "We had a discussion about this. Remember? We both agreed we carry a lot of baggage. You said you didn't think you could trust a man with your heart again. I have PTSD, and I—"

"Wait." She glared. "Do you not remember the photo I showed you? You know, the one where my jaw and ribs were broken by the one man I should've been able to trust the most? Do you really think veterans corner the market when it comes to PTSD?"

"No. That's not what I think. But it's different." *Shut up!* Every time he opened his mouth, he made things worse. He jammed his hands into his jacket pockets.

"*Close* friends, eh?" She aimed her gaze toward neutral territory, the building in front of them. "As I recall, we started a conversation Saturday night, and I asked whether or not we were going to risk getting involved." She gestured between the two of them. "As in dating. I guess you've answered *that* question." She turned away from him and started walking.

"No, I haven't. Not really." Was that a door closing in his face? "You issued an ultimatum—involvement or you'd find somewhere else to stay while Jared is still on the loose. You said we should both think about it before we decided. That's what I've *been* doing." Anger flared. Come to think of it, who was she to issue ultimatums to him? "My primary concern right now is your safety. L&L is the best place for you and Tyler, so leaving is off the table."

"First of all, you don't get to tell me what is off the table. I make my own decisions. Second, that's not what I said Saturday night. I didn't issue an ultimatum, and you know it. I was making an observation and stating the obvious." She lifted her chin. "So, you've been giving what I said some thought, and you came up with . . . what? When you say *close* friends, what exactly *do* you mean, Wes?" She canted her head and scrutinized him.

"Uh . . ." His mouth dried up, and his mind blanked. He caught the hurt lurking in her eyes before she turned away. He'd hurt her? How? Wasn't he trying his damnedest to come up with a plan that would work for both of them? Clearly she'd gotten the "benefits" intent behind his muddled spiel, and it hadn't pleased her. *Great. Note to self: I suck at the whole male-female dynamics thing.* Or maybe he just sucked at opening his mouth and letting words spew out.

"Let's go," he snapped. "Paul and the marshals are waiting." He tried to place his hand at the small of her back again, but she moved out of his reach. Her eyes were too shiny. Bright. Oh, God. Not tears. "I'm sorry, Carlie. Whatever it is I said or did to upset you, I'm sorry."

"Forget it. I've just been under a lot of strain lately, and I'm taking it out on you." Her eyes filled, and she ran her knuckles under them. "I'm sorry. You've done nothing to deserve the brunt of my bad mood." She sucked in a huge breath and let it out slowly. "I'm fine now."

Fine was not the vibe he was getting from her. Nope. She stiffened her spine and quickened her stride, and he trailed along behind her. Silently. They made their way through the heavy metal doors to the check-in point. Their IDs were inspected, and they went through the metal detectors. A deputy pointed them toward the sheriff's office.

Wes knocked, and the sheriff called for them to enter. Wes trailed through the door after Carlie, his temples throbbing. He needed sleep and space to think, and he wasn't going to get either of those things anytime soon.

Two men were seated in the chairs facing the sheriff's desk. Other than the handguns both marshals wore in shoulder harnesses, they could be anybody you'd meet on the street. Regular guys, able to blend into a crowd.

"Carlie, Wes." Paul perched on the front corner of his desk. "This is Bruce Murphy, and this is Andrew Pelletier."

The two men rose and offered their hands. Wes shook Murphy's first, and then Pelletier's. "I'm Wesley Holt, and this is Carlie Stewart." Carlie stood silently beside him, a pillar of prickly tension.

"Have a seat, you two." The sheriff gestured toward the faux-leather couch pushed up against the cinder-block wall. The marshals turned their chairs to face the couch.

Pelletier lifted a folder from Paul's desk before taking his seat. "Ms. Stewart, Sheriff Taylor has brought us up-to-date on everything that has happened so far. We've read through your file and your ex's."

Carlie nodded. Wes reached for her hand, and this time she didn't pull away. Hers was icy cold against his.

Murphy shifted in his chair and leaned toward them. "When we're after a fugitive, they generally leave a trail for us to follow. Debit or credit card use, cell phone use, something that gives us a pretty clear idea where they've been and where they're headed. Other than a withdrawal from a joint account with his brother in Indianapolis, we have nothing to go on where Jared Baumann is concerned."

"Your ex is not using debit or credit cards or a cell phone," Pelletier added. "And he's not staying in motels or with former associates. Baumann has gone underground, and that makes his connection to you and your son crucial to his capture."

"Great." Carlie blew out a shaky breath.

"It's true." Murphy smiled, his eyes filled with sympathy. "You and your son are the only reason we have any idea of his whereabouts today."

"We believe he fled the area after the manhunt," Paul said. "But not permanently."

"I agree with you." Carlie's gaze went from man to man. "Jared will wait until he thinks he's thrown all of you off, and then he'll come back. He's obsessive."

"We'd like you to resume life as normal," Murphy said. "Go about your daily routine as though you believe he's gone for good."

"Should I move back into my house?" She glanced sideways at Wes, and her lips compressed into a tight line.

"No." Wes shook his head. "Her place is not safe."

"We agree," Murphy said. "It's easier for us to blend in with the folks in town, and we'd prefer it if you remained where you are. We'll be undercover. You'll be aware of our presence, but it's best if you pay little to no attention to us. If one of us is at the diner where you work, greet us like you'd greet any other customer. No more, no less."

"You don't think he'll come into the diner, do you?" Carlie's grip on Wes's hand tightened.

"No, but we do think he might watch the diner from a distance." Murphy grinned. "And we do have to eat, Ms. Stewart."

"Oh." Carlie let out a nervous laugh. "Right."

"Carlie's family wants her to come home to Indianapolis for Thanksgiving," Wes said. "Would that be OK, or would you prefer we stay in Perfect for the holiday?" He included himself in her plans and held his breath to see if Carlie would raise a fuss. She didn't. He savored the fragile victory.

The two marshals shared a look. "Jared has family in Indianapolis," Pelletier said. He opened the file on his lap and studied the sheet of paper on top. "Besides his brother, he has his father and a few cousins, uncles and aunts there. We suspect the brother had a hand in Jared's escape. A sizable withdrawal of funds happened the afternoon before Jared's escape from FCC Terre Haute." He glanced at his partner again. "We have surveillance at his father's and his brother's residences in case our guy heads home. Sure. Go to Indianapolis for Thanksgiving if you want, Ms. Stewart. We'll follow."

"Won't that put my family in danger?" she asked, her voice strained. "What about during the hours we're out in the open and on the road?"

"I won't lie, there are risks, but if Baumann is in proximity to you, we'll do our best to get to him before he can cause any trouble."

"So, for the most part, act with caution, resume life as usual and go about our business." Traveling for the holiday was something they'd have to talk more about. None of them knew at this point if her ex had help on the outside or if he was acting alone. Wes squeezed Carlie's hand. "Anything else?"

Pelletier fixed him in his gaze. "We know a bit about your history as well, Mr. Holt. You're a decorated war hero and a retired major in the Marines. I don't need to tell you to be aware of your surroundings, but I do need to remind you to let us do our job. Don't interfere."

He had to bite back the retort he wanted to make, along with the outrage. Jared Baumann had managed to escape a federal prison and elude Evansville's SWAT team, K9s and law enforcement personnel from several counties. Maybe if he *had* interfered a little more, the bad guy would already *be* behind bars.

The marshals continued their discussion with Carlie, asking her for details about her ex and his previous associates—stuff he and Carlie had already discussed with the sheriff. Wes's mind turned to their earlier argument. He'd thought she'd be pleased that he wanted to be there for Ty. *Got that wrong.*

Why had his suggestion that they remain close friends hurt her so much? His brain ached. She'd managed to twist him into a knot so tight, he couldn't even find the loose ends to untie himself. Time to call in the reinforcements. He needed to talk to Noah and Ryan. Tonight's PTSD group couldn't come fast enough. Men were so much easier to deal with than women.

His gaze drifted to Carlie. Engrossed as she was in her conversation, he was free to stare at her. The thought of her leaving his life sent his poor heart scudding across the cold concrete floor. Her hand had warmed in his, and she leaned into him as she answered questions and shared what she knew about her ex.

He wanted to wrap his arms around her, hold onto her so tight she couldn't slip away from him. He'd come up with some kind of compromise to keep her and Ty in Perfect. What that might be, he had no clue.

🐏 🐏 🐏

After their PTSD group therapy, he and the guys always went out for a burger and a few beers, or in Ryan's case, coffee or a soft drink. Wes surveyed the dimly lit interior of the VFW. Their buddies had moved to the corner to play foosball. He asked Ryan and Noah to stay with him at their table. Swallowing his pride, Wes launched into his tale of woe where Carlie was concerned. Noah and Ryan listened, occasionally asking an all-too-perceptive question or two that set Wes's teeth on edge. "So, what do you think I should do?"

"Well," Ryan began, setting his elbows on the table. "Resistance is not only futile, it's foolhardy. We've both been where you are, Wes. We've both suffered the same doubts and fears, put up the same barricades and hidden behind the same wall of denial. It didn't work for either of us, and it's not going to work for you."

Noah smirked. "He's right, you know. Besides, when you do give in, you'll find surrender has its . . . perks."

Wesley took a fortifying swig of his beer. "I don't know if I'm capable of surrender, no matter what the perks might be. You know my history."

"We all have history, Wes." Noah cocked an eyebrow and leveled a look his way. "The question you have to ask yourself is this: is Carlie worth more or less than the baggage you insist on carrying around with you? At some point, you have to weigh the past against the possibility of a brighter future. Either you let go of the baggage and make the leap, or you hold on to the baggage and the opportunity moves on. The decision rests entirely with you."

One side of Noah's mouth quirked up. "But when you do make that decision? I'd appreciate it if you'd do it on the twenty-first or the twenty-third. Those are my squares in the pool."

Wesley groaned.

Ryan laughed. "I have the twentieth and the twenty-fifth. I'd appreciate it if you'd keep *those* dates in mind."

"I thought you two were my friends," he groused.

"We are." Ryan chuckled again. "We're friends who are way more objective than you are right now. That's all."

"I know Paige invited you and Carlie to the poker game tomorrow night." Noah pushed his empty plate aside and put his elbows on the table. "Since the US Marshals told the two of you to act like life is back to normal, you and Carlie should come to the Malloys'."

"That's not normal for either of us." Wes frowned. "I've never been to poker night, and neither has she."

"*We* know that, but Baumann doesn't. Going to a social gathering would appear normal to most people." Ryan flashed him a wry grin. "Carlie's ex doesn't know you aren't normal."

"Thanks." Wes huffed out a breath.

"No offense intended." Ryan waved his hand around the table. "None of us sitting here tonight are exactly what you'd call normal, Wes. That's what unifies us. My wife has already lined up a sitter to come to our place Friday night. Our kid is down for the count by seven thirty or eight, tops. The sitter can take care of Tyler, too. You'll be among friends, and the two of you could probably use an evening out. Put a little fun into your lives. See how the two of you do together in a social setting before you make any decisions."

Wes pinched the bridge of his nose. Weariness pressed into him from all sides. "I don't know. With everything that's going on, I haven't been getting much sleep lately. I probably wouldn't be good company. Besides, Carlie didn't seem too enthusiastic about the prospect when Paige brought it up with her the other night. She has to work at the diner early the next morning.

"Besides"—Wes shook his head—"she hates the idea that everyone in Perfect knows everyone else's business. Carlie has a past she doesn't want uncovered. You know what I mean?"

"Her past is safe with us, and anyway, it's her present that counts." Ryan turned his coffee mug around a few times. "Believe me, I know how she feels, but I also know that once her history is exposed to the light of day, she'll get over it." He met Wes's eyes. "I did."

Ryan had lost his fiancée in a tragic accident before he enlisted in the army, and he blamed himself for her death. He'd been suicidal when he arrived in Perfect, self-medicating with alcohol. Ryan had hidden the pain from everyone, playing a dangerous game of Russian roulette every night until Noah's sister, Paige, intervened.

Wes had heard the tale in group about how Paige had thrown Ryan's gun into the Ohio River the morning she found him passed out with the suicide note and a vintage revolver beside him. If anyone knew about hidden pasts, it was Ryan. Wes gave him a slight nod.

"Nothing could appear more normal than going to poker night with your friends," Noah said. "Am I right?"

"I guess." Wes pushed his chair back and stood up. "If I can talk her into it, we'll be there. I'll let you know tomorrow morning." He reached for his wallet. "Speaking of Carlie, I need to see her before I start my shift tonight if I'm going to ask her about tomorrow night's poker game." Glancing at the bill beside his plate, he pulled some cash from his wallet and set it down on top of the slip of paper. "You two have given me a lot to think about." He snatched his jacket from the back of the chair.

"Remember"—Ryan grinned—"I have the twentieth and the twenty-fifth."

"Screw you," Wes retorted. Laughter trailed him all the way to the door. He climbed into his SUV and headed toward Perfect. Surrender had its perks. Maybe, but he didn't know if he could surrender. Somewhere along the way, the betrayal and hurt he'd suffered at his ex-wife's hands had gotten tangled up with his combat PTSD until he could no longer decipher which was which. His head could still make the distinction, but not his gut. Neither could his heart.

Did he have to say out loud to Carlie that he wanted to get involved? Couldn't he just slip quietly into this whole relationship thing without a declaration on his part? At this point, he didn't even know if she'd agree to go out with him. He'd save face and leave himself an out if he kept quiet, kept it casual. Two friends hanging out, that he could manage. Slip a toe into the water, see how it went and back out if need be. No harm, no foul.

He'd start with poker night.

By the time he parked his SUV behind L&L, the palms of his hands and his forehead were damp with sweat. By the time he'd climbed the steps to the third floor, his legs shook and his heart had lodged itself in his throat.

He was a Marine, dammit. He sucked it up, unlocked the door and strode inside. Slipping out of his jacket, he looked around and listened in an effort to locate his target.

The apartment was quiet, but light shone from the living room. After he hung his jacket on a peg, he unlaced his boots, took them off and set them by the back door. He didn't want the sound of his strides on the hardwood floor to wake Tyler. Plus, doing so bought him a little time to get himself together.

Swiping his damp palms down the legs of his jeans, Wes walked toward the light. Things hadn't entirely unbent between him and Carlie since their argument at the sheriff's office. He had no idea how she'd respond. Still, he was willing to take the chance. If she said no, he could claim he'd just been suggesting an activity that would appear to the world that they were resuming life as usual.

When had he turned into such a chickenshit? He found Carlie curled up on the couch with some kind of craft project on her lap. Cross-stitch? "Carlie."

She raised her gaze to his. "Wes."

"Would you like to go to poker night with me tomorrow?" She didn't answer, and his heart pounded so hard he could hear it inside his head. "Paige has a sitter already lined up for Sean and Ty."

"Sure," she said, her voice hesitant. "Sounds like fun."

She smiled slightly, and the breath he'd been holding left him in a dizzying rush. "Good." He nodded like a bobblehead. "Good. Well . . ." He gestured with his thumb toward the kitchen. "I'm going to go fix something to eat during my break tonight at work." He'd moved into the babbling-fool stage. *Wonderful.*

"I already packed a meal for you—leftovers from the pot roast, potatoes and vegetables Ty and I had for supper." Her attention returned to her project.

"You did?" His chest filled with a tantalizing warmth. "Thank you. I appreciate your thoughtfulness, Carlie." OK, now he sounded like some kind of stiff tape-recorded phone message. *We appreciate your call. Leave your name and number and we will get back to you . . .*

Carlie eyed him, amusement lighting her pretty blue eyes. "Why, you're entirely welcome, Wesley. Thank you for noticing my thoughtfulness."

He swallowed the groan rising in his throat and backtracked to the kitchen. *Inhale. Exhale. Concentrate on bringing your heart rate back into the normal range.* Wes focused on making coffee.

He'd done it—made the first move. Shaking and sweaty, he felt as if he'd been through the spin cycle of an industrial-size washing machine. He placed his hands on the kitchen counter and closed his eyes. He'd slipped his big toe into the water, turned a corner in his life and taken a risk. He and Carlie had a date. Did she know it was a date? He hoped not.

CHAPTER EIGHT

"The Malloys' yard looks like a used-car lot for pickup trucks and SUVs." Carlie grinned. "With the occasional soccer-mom minivan thrown in for good measure." A couple of cars followed them down the long drive. The poker games would start in about twenty minutes, enough time to get Tyler settled with the sitter.

She held her covered bowl of pasta salad on her lap as Wes drove slowly over the bumpy ground in search of a place to park. They'd be safe, all right. It looked like half the town's population showed up for poker night. Thank heavens her black eye had completely healed. She didn't want to deal with the curious stares from those few who hadn't heard the gossip or come into the diner in the past couple of weeks.

Wes brought his SUV to a stop. "Ready?" He peered into his rear-view mirror at Tyler.

"Are Toby and Lucinda gonna be here?" Ty asked in a tight voice.

"Not this time, partner." Wes unbuckled his seat belt. "I'm afraid you're going to have to suffer through an evening with a toddler and a teenager."

"But . . . I'll be *upstairs*, and you'll be *downstairs*." Tyler repeated what Carlie had explained to him earlier. "Right?"

"That's right, and if you need anything, you can come find us," Wes told him. "Let's go."

Carlie waited while Wes got Tyler out of his booster seat. She was almost as nervous as her son. At least she'd gotten to know Paige, Cory and Ceejay a little better, so she wouldn't be completely surrounded by people she didn't know.

Wes held Tyler's hand as the three of them walked to the house toward the well-lit veranda. "The marshals are here, aren't they?" Lord, she sounded just like Tyler. She knew the marshals followed her everywhere, but she still needed reassurance.

"They'll be outside watching the house and yard, and the sheriff is also here. I saw his truck parked on the grass." He put his arm around her. "Everything is going to be fine. Let's relax and have some fun tonight."

Carlie nodded and bit her lip. Wes ushered her and Tyler through the front door into the foyer. Delicious smells from the kitchen washed over her from all the food people brought to share. A cheery fire burned in the fireplace in the great room, and the house was filled with warmth, light, conversation and laughter.

"There you are," Paige called as she approached. "I'm so glad you all decided to come tonight."

Ryan joined his wife. "Let me take your coats. We're putting them in the den." He pointed to the door just off the foyer.

"Wow, Paige." Carlie looked around. She handed Wes the bowl so she could get herself and Tyler out of their coats. "Your house is gorgeous."

"Thanks. We like it. The design is based on the old farmhouse that stood here before we bought the property."

Carlie traded the coats in her hand for the bowl, and Wes went off with Ryan to deposit their things in the den. "Where do you want me to put this?" she asked, holding up her offering for the snack table.

"In the kitchen." Paige leaned over and put her hands on her knees. "I'm glad you're here, Tyler. You, Sean and the sitter are going to have your own party upstairs."

"We are?" His eyes widened.

"Yep. Pizza and a movie." Paige straightened. "How does that sound?"

"Good." He smiled shyly. "I like pizza."

"Come on, you two. We'll drop the food off in the kitchen, and then I'll take you upstairs." Paige started down the hall toward the kitchen.

Carlie took her son's hand and followed. People milled around, and she noticed a number of card tables had been set up in the great room that served as the living and dining room.

"Hey, Carlie," Cory called and waved. Her fiancé, Ted Lovejoy, stood beside her, along with the town butcher, Denny Offermeyer. Paul Taylor was part of the group, too. Ted lifted a Solo cup of beer in greeting, and Paul tipped his head and smiled.

Carlie waved back. Once they got to the kitchen, her jaw dropped. The cozy room looked like something out of a country decor magazine. Antique kitchen tools hung on the walls, along with old-fashioned signs advertising fresh eggs, vegetables or farm equipment. Granite countertops, country-style cabinets, every modern amenity possible and the same gleaming oak floor covering the rest of the first level completed the perfect picture. "I *want* your kitchen, Paige. In fact, I want your whole house."

Paige's smile grew wider, and her eyes sparkled. "This is my favorite room." She sighed. "Ryan and I enjoy going to flea markets and antique stores, poking around and finding things we can use in our home. He's got such an artistic eye. His talent comes in handy when decorating. Wait till you see Sean's room." She greeted a group of people standing by the counter and introduced Carlie and Ty to them.

Paige set the pasta salad on the counter with all the other containers and slow cookers. "Ryan painted a mural in Sean's bedroom. Come on. Let's head upstairs, and I'll show you." She led them back to the front of the house and up the stairs to a baby gate at the top.

The second-floor landing opened into a large space the Malloys used like a family room. A sectional couch, TV and children's toys filled the space. Paige led her to the first door on the left.

Inside the cozy bedroom, Sean sat on the carpeted floor with a pretty blonde who appeared to be around fourteen or fifteen. She had the look of a Lovejoy and bore a strong resemblance to Ted. A pile of wooden blocks was strewn around in front of the toddler, and he was trying to stuff one of them into his mouth. As soon as Sean saw his mom, he dropped the now soggy block and grinned, then got up and toddled over to her with his arms outstretched.

Tyler moved to stand in front of the mural Paige had mentioned. Pasture, ponies and cherubic little cowboys wearing cowboy hats and boots and holding lassos filled the entire wall. "I have planets and stars that you can see in the dark in my room," Tyler said. "This is cool too, though."

Paige shared a grin with Carlie as she hoisted her son to her hip. "Tyler, Carlie, this is Allie. She's one of the many Lovejoy cousins in Perfect and Ted's niece. She'll be spending the evening with you and Sean. Allie, this is Carlie Stewart and her son, Tyler."

"Hi, Tyler. I'm glad you're here." Allie smiled. "You can help me keep Sean busy. We'll have our pizza soon, and once Sean is in bed, you and I can watch a movie."

"OK," Ty said. He sat down on the carpet and began building a tower with the blocks. "Does Sean have any Legos?"

"Not yet." Paige set her squirming son back down. "He's still too young for Legos. Sorry."

"That's OK." Tyler shot her another shy smile. "I like blocks. Come on, Sean. You can help me," he called to the toddler.

A grin lit the boy's face, and he squirmed until Paige set him on the carpet. He plopped himself down next to Tyler and promptly batted over the tower of blocks with a hearty sound of glee. Tyler laughed and began to gather the blocks together again. A frisson of pride in her son shot through Carlie. He was so sweet with Sean. Ty had a compassionate and loving nature with everyone, and he always stuck up for others in his class.

Somehow, despite all the bad decisions she'd made with her own life, she'd done something right by her son. Carlie started for the door. "Wes and I will be right downstairs, Ty. If you need us, you can come get us."

"I know, Mom." Tyler was already stacking the blocks again. He didn't even glance her way.

"Thanks for watching my son for me, Allie," Carlie said. "I'll have to get your name and number before I leave. I'm always looking for babysitters."

"I'll write them down for you, Ms. Stewart. I'd be happy to watch Tyler for you sometime."

Ten minutes later, everyone began to purchase their poker chips, signaling that it was time to begin the games. Groups drifted to the tables set up in the great room. She and Wes joined Noah, Ceejay, Ryan and Paige at the oval oak table in the dining room.

Noah handed Carlie a laminated piece of paper. "We made these up for newbies. It tells you what the different hands are, and what beats what."

"Oh, thanks." Carlie took it and started reading the list. "It's even in color." She held it out for Wes. "Do you already know how to play?"

"I do, but it's been a while." He arranged his chips in front of him. "If I need to take a look, I'll let you now."

"I'll keep it on the table between us." Carlie set it down.

"I should warn you." Wes glanced around the table. "I have a competitive streak."

THE TWISTED ROAD TO YOU

Noah laughed. "You haven't met competitive until you've played poker with my sister."

"Hey." Paige shot her brother a mock scowl. "Shush. You're pretty cutthroat yourself when it comes to winning."

The banter between Noah and his sister sent a pang of longing through her—and envy. The two were close, and Paige had told her how protective her older brother was toward her while they were growing up. Would she and her brother, Ron, ever reconcile? Carlie doubted it. Forcing her thoughts away from her dysfunctional family, she looked around. There had to be about twenty people here tonight, all talking and sharing laughter. Dammit, she was going to relax and enjoy herself. No more brooding. "Let's get started." She rubbed her hands together. "I'm looking forward to winning all your chips away from you."

"Oh?" Wes glanced sideways at her. "It's a game of strategy and wits, and you're a novice. Don't get your hopes up."

"Haven't you ever heard of beginner's luck?" She shot him a look of challenge. His answering smile melted her insides.

"We keep the stakes pretty simple." Ryan pointed to the chips in front of her. "The white chips are worth a nickel, the reds are a dime, blues are a quarter, greens are worth fifty cents and the black chips are a dollar. Everybody starts out with the same amount, and we tally up afterward. The value of the chips is printed on the back side of that sheet in case you forget."

Carlie turned the cheat sheet over to take a look.

"Tonight we're going to teach you how to play," Ryan told her. "But don't expect us to go easy on you."

"Oh, don't worry." Carlie shook her head. "I don't plan to go easy on the rest of you, either."

"That's my girl," Wes said with a chuckle.

His girl? His words settled around her like a soft, warm blanket. Did he mean it, or was he just taking part in the banter flying around the table? Her nerves sizzled and popped with awareness. Leaning slightly, she caught a whiff of the aftershave he used, mixed with the clean scent of soap and his natural smell. Delicious in a very masculine way—and familiar. She reveled in the rare sensation, the feeling of belonging rushing through her. Wes gave those feelings to her, and more.

A ping of guilt shot through her. She'd been so unfair to him the day the two of them had met the marshals. She'd dumped all her frustration and stress over his head like he'd been the cause. He hadn't raised his voice against her in anger, nor had he laid blame at her feet. Even though he'd done nothing wrong, Wes had apologized. For the past two weeks he'd stood by her side with a steadfastness she'd never known in her entire thirty-four years of existence.

She risked a glance his way and found his warm hazel eyes fixed on her. Her temperature shot up a few degrees. She smiled, and for once she didn't hide what she felt for him. The pulse in his neck quickened. Heat flared in his eyes, and her breath quickened.

"Hey, you two," Ceejay quipped. "Time to quit making eyes at each other and start playing poker."

Carlie studied the chips in front her, heat rising to her cheeks. "Then deal the cards already."

Ryan shuffled. "We'll start with something simple, five-card draw." As he dealt, he explained how to play.

By the fourth or fifth round, Carlie began to get the hang of it. After the last ante and draw, she compared her cards to the cheat sheet. Ryan opened with a dime. Everyone tossed in their chips, and it was her turn. She sat up straighter. Holding her cards close to her chest, she grinned. "I'll see your dime and raise you fifty cents."

Ryan groaned, shook his head and tossed his cards facedown onto the table. "*Somebody* needs to teach you about poker faces, Carlie. You won't win as much if you let everyone know you have a great hand." He rose from the table and stretched. "I fold. I'm going to go get something to eat."

"I fold, too." Ceejay stacked her cards neatly in front of her and stood up. "Anybody want a beer?"

"Sure," Noah said. "I'll have one, and can you bring me a few of those mini quiches, honey?"

"Sure, just don't lose all our money while I'm gone." Ceejay patted her husband's shoulder before walking away.

Wesley put his chip in. "I call, Ms. Stewart."

"So do I," Noah said, tossing in his green chip.

Paige tossed in her chip. "Let's see what you have, newbie."

Carlie turned her cards over with a flourish. "Four tens."

"Curse that beginner's luck," Wes huffed, throwing down his cards.

"You win." Paige turned her cards over. "I have two pairs."

"I only have a pair of twos." Noah grinned. "I only stayed in the game on the off chance you were bluffing."

"Bluffing." Carlie shot him a questioning look. "You'll have to explain how bluffing would be useful in poker."

"Nope. I don't think I will." Noah stood up and stretched. "I for one like it that you don't have a poker face."

"Let's all take a break," Paige said. "I'm almost out of chips anyway."

"Actually," Carlie said, glancing at the clock on the fireplace mantel. She was surprised to find it was already past ten. "I have to get up early tomorrow morning, and it's getting late. We should probably get going."

"Smart. Quit now while you have most of our chips." Noah shot her a wry look.

"I told you I would," she boasted. "I'm a firm believer in beginner's luck."

"We're not playing in December, since there's already so much going on," Paige told her. "But in January, we'll teach you a few new games, like Texas Hold'em. That's what most of the tables are playing tonight."

"I'm going to go see what became of my wife," Noah said, glancing around the room.

Carlie stacked her chips as Noah walked away to find Ceejay. Paige soon followed her brother, and Carlie's mind drifted. January seemed like a long way off, and her future was too uncertain to make plans that far away. Her stomach tightened. Would she be back in her rental house by then? The little white house she'd loved so much would never feel safe to her again. Jared had seen to that.

Oh, but she'd loved the peace and quiet of living in the country. The sounds of the birds, tree frogs and other creatures of the summer, accompanied by the occasional lowing of the McCurdys' cows at milking time, soothed her. Having space for Tyler to explore and play outside meant a lot to her. Plus, rush hour in her neighborhood consisted of a tractor or two and a few pickup trucks loaded down with hay or bags of feed moving along the lane at a sedate speed.

The things that gave her comfort, made her feel safe, had been ruined for her once again. Like Wes had said more than once, the house was too isolated. Even when her ex was back behind bars, he'd continue to obsess about her and Tyler. He didn't have a life sentence. Eventually he'd get out for good, and the terror would start all over. She'd never be free of him. Not really. She shook her head.

"What's the matter?" Wesley leaned close.

"January," she mumbled. "I can't even think about next week, much less a few months from now."

"Things will get better." Wes covered her hand with his.

"No, they won't. You have no idea what it's like. Even when my ex is caught and back behind bars, it'll only be a temporary reprieve." Frustration and anger surged. "I'll always be waiting for the next time he shows up—looking over my shoulder and jumping at shadows. Sometimes it feels like fear is the only thing constant in my life," she bit out.

"*Was* the only constant in your life." He placed a finger under her chin and turned her to face him, his eyes boring into hers. "You're not alone anymore, Carlie," he said, his voice gruff. "Whenever you need me, I'll be there for you. That's a promise and a constant."

She forgot how to breathe and had to swallow against the tightness banding her throat. As much as she longed to believe him, she just couldn't. Despite promises too numerous to count during her life, being able to rely on anyone other than herself had never panned out for her. Why would he be any different?

"I appreciate the thought, Wes, but who knows where either of us will be a year or two from now. You don't owe me anything. I'm the one indebted to you for all the help you've already given me. A few home-cooked meals and a little light housekeeping doesn't begin to cover it." Her eyes stinging, Carlie rose from her chair, grabbed her poker chips and walked away before he could say anything else.

She was losing it. The stress was getting to her, and once again she'd dumped all over Wes. Regret pinched at her already frazzled nerves. They'd been having such a good time, and she'd wrecked it. She found Ryan in the kitchen, talking with the sheriff and Denny Offermeyer.

Paul winked at her. "We hear you cleaned up tonight."

"I did." She lifted the stacks of chips she held in both hands.

"Glad you could make it tonight, Carlie," Denny said. "We hope you'll become a regular."

"Thanks, Denny. I'll think about it." She turned to Ryan. "We have to be going. Can you cash these chips in for me?"

"Sure." Ryan set his soda on the counter. He took her chips from her. "Wait here, and I'll be right back."

"How're you holding up?" Paul asked.

She shrugged. No reason to dump on him, too. "I'm all right."

"I think the stress is starting to work on her last nerve." Wes's deep voice so close behind her sent Carlie's heart racing. He placed his hands on her shoulders and squeezed. "I already cashed in my chips. I'll go get Tyler. What do we owe the sitter?"

"Paige said she and Ryan are paying Allie, and if I wanted to give her a little extra, it was up to me. Whatever you give her, I'll pay you back with my poker winnings." She glanced at him over her shoulder. "I'll meet you in the den to get our coats." She couldn't tear her eyes from him as he made his way to the front of the house. He stood a head above most people, and Lord, how she loved the way he moved.

"So, you and Wes are a couple now?" Paul asked.

"Huh?" Her attention shifted back to the sheriff. "A couple? No." She frowned. "Until Jared showed up, the only time I ever saw Wes was when he came to eat breakfast at the diner. We've never been on a date. He's . . ." She frowned. "We're . . ."

Paul chuckled. "Well, once you get it figured out, you let me know."

"Why?" she asked.

"Just curious." His eyes twinkled. "Haven't you heard about the wager going on at L&L?"

"A wager? No, I hadn't heard." She frowned. "What kind of wager?"

"Ask Wes." He grinned. "It's good to see you out and about, Carlie. I know the circumstances are less than ideal, but you have to admit, your ex's sudden appearance hasn't been all bad. I hear you're taking self-defense classes with a few of the local gals, and here you are playing poker with the rest of us. You've been in Perfect for a couple of years now. It's about time you joined the community."

Ryan returned, saving her from having to respond. He handed her some cash, and she folded the bills and stuffed them into a pocket. "Thanks so much for having us tonight, Ryan. I had a great time."

"We're glad you and Wes joined us," he said.

"Nice to see you, Paul, Denny. I'm sure we'll talk soon." Carlie set out for the den, stopping to say her good-byes along the way. By the time she got to the door, Wesley and Tyler were coming down the stairs.

Her son looked ready to fall asleep standing up. "Did you have a good time, sweetie?"

"I had a very good time," Wes answered, a lopsided grin lighting his face. "How about you, *darling?*"

She couldn't help but laugh. "What about you, *Tyler?* Did you have a good time?"

"Yeah. I like Allie." Tyler yawned. "She's pretty."

"But not as pretty as your mom, though. Right, partner?"

"I guess." Tyler shrugged his shoulders.

Wes walked into the den and fished through the pile of coats for their things. He handed her coat and purse to her.

"What's gotten into you?" Carlie asked, blinking at Wes.

"What? Hasn't anyone ever told you you're beautiful before?" He blinked back, imitating her look of confusion. Then he helped Tyler into his coat. "You were heading into a skid earlier, and I'm just trying to put us back in fun mode. Is it working?" He waggled his eyebrows at her.

She grinned. "It is." Did he really see her as beautiful? "I really did have a great time. Poker is fun."

"If you're winning." Wes slipped into his jacket. "You're just lucky I went easy on you tonight."

"Is that so?" she teased back. "I think I held my own pretty well."

"Yeah, well, if only you'd held your cards as well as you *held your own.*" He shot her a sheepish look. "I peeked. Next time, hold the cards closer."

She gasped. "You did?"

"I was sorely tempted. But no. I didn't." He scowled at her. "I can't believe you think I'd cheat."

This was a new side to Wesley, one she'd never seen before. Teasing, flirting—she didn't know what to make of it. She trailed Wes and her son outside. The gibbous moon illuminated the yard, giving the parked cars a silvery gleam. The night was clear, and the stars were especially bright. "Brrr. It's cold tonight." Taking Tyler's hand, she followed Wes to his SUV.

His cell phone chimed the moment they got to his car. He checked the texted message. "Bruce says no sign of your ex tonight." He texted back. "We're good to go."

Once they were headed down the Malloys' long drive, Carlie got to thinking. Wes had invited her to go to poker night *with* him. He'd been so nervous. Had he viewed tonight as a date? "You know, this is the first time we've ever done anything social together. Thanks for inviting me to go with you." She threw it out there and held her breath.

Wes glanced sideways at her. "I had a good time, too. No reason why we can't continue to do things together, is there?"

"No reason at all. So . . . you want to get . . . *social*?" Was that the same as involved? She peeked over her shoulder at her son. He'd fallen asleep the minute Wes had started his SUV.

"Didn't I just say that?" He frowned and kept his eyes on the road.

Clearly he was uncomfortable with the direction their conversation had taken, and she wasn't about to push. "The Malloys have a nice house, don't they?" All that got was a nod. She racked her brain for something to say to bring things back to the happy place they'd been. Nothing came to her. "I left my bowl there," she muttered.

"Paige will get it back to you." Wes shifted and reached for her hand. He meshed their fingers together. "I'm glad we did this. I really like seeing you relaxed and enjoying yourself. Seeing you happy makes me happy, Carlie." He glanced at her for a second, and then focused on the road again. "Is that OK with you?"

She sensed the vulnerability in his question, enough to cause her heart to skip a beat. "Sure." She nodded. He kept her hand in his and drove down the highway toward Perfect. Staring out the windshield, she thought about what the sheriff had said to her.

He was right. If Jared hadn't turned up the way he had, she and Wesley would still be virtual strangers, only seeing each other for the brief moments it took him to eat his breakfast at the diner each morning. She wouldn't have started taking self-defense classes or come to know the women she now counted as friends. What would Jared think if he knew about the good that had come out of his intrusion into her life? She smiled.

"What are you thinking about?" Wes gave her hand another squeeze.

She beamed at him. "I was just thinking about how sometimes plants grow best when their roots are buried in manure."

"OK." He snorted. "That was random."

They were on the main street of Perfect, and close to home. "Not really. Tonight Paul pointed out how my ex has forced me out of my comfort zone. I'm making friends and being *social*." This time, she did the hand squeezing. "When you get right down to it, I've gotten to know you because of Jared, and for that I'm truly grateful."

The pleased expression suffusing his face, and the vulnerability she'd glimpsed in him tonight, sent her spirits soaring. He turned into the alley, drove the half block to L&L and pulled into his parking spot. "*Dammit.*"

She sucked in an audible breath, and her soaring spirits tanked. The tires on her Ford had been slashed, and every bit of glass shattered. "He knows." Her mouth went dry, and she trembled. "Jared knows about the US Marshals. That's why he didn't follow us to the Malloys' house tonight. This is a message."

Dread lodged itself in her chest, and she could hardly breathe. Thank God Tyler was asleep. She didn't want him to see this. It was bad enough he'd seen Jared hit her. Worse, he'd heard his dad threaten to end her and take him away. Then Jared had backed up his threats with the attempted kidnapping. Her son was already having a tough enough time. He didn't need this reminder that his dad was still out there stalking them.

"I'm going to disable the alarm," Wes said, his voice low. "Stay right where you are. When I come back, I'll get Tyler out of his seat and carry him inside. You'll have to open the door for me." Wesley leaned over, unlocked his glove compartment, drew out his handgun and stuffed it into his belt.

Carlie waited while Wesley unlocked the back doors to L&L and slipped inside. Lights went on, and he returned for them. He opened the rear door of his SUV and lifted Tyler out.

Holding her sleeping son, Wesley nodded to her. She climbed out and hurried to open the door for him. Once inside, they secured the building and climbed the three flights of stairs to his apartment.

Carlie pulled her keys out to open the door into the kitchen. Her hand shook so badly, it took a couple of tries before she could fit the key into the lock. Wes placed a hand on her shoulder just as she managed to get the door open. They'd left a few lights on, wanting to give the impression that someone was home, and she was glad for the light now.

Rex met them at the door. He whined and stayed close to Wesley's side as they made their way to Ty's bedroom. Carlie turned the covers back on the bed, and Wes laid her son down on the mattress.

"I have to take Rex outside," he whispered. "I'll call the marshals and let them know what's happened."

Carlie followed him out of the room. She closed the door softly behind her. "I don't want you to go out there, Wes. Call the marshals first and wait for them to show up. Rex can wait a while longer." Fear choked her, and she still shook from head to toe. "Please don't go out there."

He pulled her into his arms. "I won't go to the alley. I'll take Rex out front." He rubbed her back. "Jared's not anywhere near here anymore, sweetheart. He did his bad deed for the night, and like the coward he is, he's long gone. I'll be all right."

She shook her head and gripped the front edges of his jacket. If she held on tight enough, he wouldn't be able to leave the safety of the third floor.

Wes gently pried her hands free. "Go take care of Ty. You don't want him sleeping in his jeans and sneakers, do you?" He kissed her forehead. "I'll be back in a few minutes. I promise."

"You *promise*? You can't say for sure Jared is gone, and you have no control over what he plans to do." She struggled to keep her tears at bay. "What if he's waiting for you to step outside? He's armed. Have you forgotten about the rifle he stole?"

"Trust me." He stepped away from her. "I'll be back in a few minutes."

"If you won't wait for the marshals, then let me come with you," she begged.

"Absolutely not." He closed the space between them. Giving her a little push, he sent her toward Ty's room. "Get Tyler tucked in, and I'll be back before you know it." He gave his dog a silent hand command, and Rex took his place by Wes's left side.

Desperation ate away at her as she watched him leave. She wanted to run after him. No. It wasn't a want. She *needed* to go after him, so she could place herself between Wes and any possible harm. The urge to do just that overwhelmed her, but Wes wouldn't allow it.

A ringing started up inside her head. Torn between running after him and staying put, Carlie forced herself to turn away. She went into Ty's room and got him undressed down to his T-shirt and briefs. As she pulled the covers up over him, her heart seized. If anything happened to Wesley or her son, it would be the end of her.

Running her fingers through Tyler's unruly hair, she worried. If anything happened to her, what would become of her son? She hadn't made any plans or drawn up a will. Whom did she trust enough to care for him? Her mom? No. Her mom couldn't protect Tyler from Jared. She leaned over and kissed his forehead. He made a sound and then turned to his side without waking. She'd have to come up with a plan. Maybe the Maurers would take Ty. She and Jenny were distantly related, after all.

She ached inside. She'd isolated herself for so long that she had no one. For far too long she'd cultivated acquaintances, but no real friends—until recently. Jared would find a way to ruin that for her, too.

A gaping, bleak emptiness gripped her. She wanted to run fast and far from the pain. Hadn't that been exactly what she'd done after her dad left? Running straight into trouble hadn't helped, and the drugs only numbed the hurt while permanently messing up her life. She knew that now. No matter how fast you run, your troubles stick with you like a shadow. Wanting to flee was her go-to response to emotional turmoil. Doing so in the past hadn't solved anything, and it wouldn't change anything now.

She was left with few options. What could she do? All she knew was that she wanted things with her ex over and done with for good. Sighing, she got up from her son's bed and walked out of his room, closing the door behind her. For tonight, at least, she and her son were safe and secure.

She walked to the living room and paced, as if moving would bring her some kind of solution. A key fit into the living room door, and she stopped. Wesley and his dog walked inside, sending relief flooding through her.

"I called the marshals. They're going to come take a look at your SUV, but I told them not to disturb us." He slid out of his jacket and hung it in the front closet. She caught a glimpse of the handgun tucked into the back of his belt. He pulled down a metal lockbox from the shelf in the closet and put the gun away.

"Go get ready for bed, Carlie. Then come back out here and hang out with me on the couch for a while." He glanced at her. "Unless you feel like you can sleep."

"I can't."

"Before you get any ideas about having your wicked way with me, forget it." He shoved one shoe off with the toe of the other.

"What?" She couldn't have heard him right.

He shot her a teasing look, his eyes filled with warmth. "You're in no shape to be alone right now. Stay with me until you're calmer, and I promise to behave myself. Comfort and company. That's it."

"OK," she said, raking her fingers through her hair. "You're right. I don't want to be alone. I'll be back in a few minutes." Her mind had stopped functioning. She'd gone from panicked to fuzzy headed. The tension she'd been living under had depleted her. After washing her face and brushing her teeth, she changed into flannel pajama pants, a sleep T-shirt and her extremely unsexy chenille robe. She slipped her bare feet into her slippers and padded to the living room.

Wes had his feet up on the coffee table. He held the remote for the TV in his hand. "I found a Christmas movie. It's not even Thanksgiving yet, and they're already showing Christmas movies." He patted the couch beside him. Once she curled up next to him, he spread the throw over her lap and put his arm around her shoulders. "I put Rex in with Ty. The both of them are out for the night."

"Good."

"Do you have comprehensive insurance coverage on your car?"

"No." Another worry to add to her list. "I only have the basics. The car is twelve years old, and I've been saving to buy a newer model."

"Ted and Kyle work on cars out at the Lovejoys' farm. The two of them do bodywork and mechanical stuff. I'll talk to them about your car tomorrow. I'm sure we can work out a deal to get it fixed. It's just a matter of throwing new tires on and replacing the windows and lights."

She nodded again, gratitude stealing her voice.

"You're wrong, you know," he said after a few moments of silence.

Puzzled, she glanced at him. "About what?"

"At the Malloys', you said I have no idea what it's like for you." He drew her closer. "I do understand, Carlie. When you're living in a militarized zone, you're always waiting for an IED to explode in your face, the next grenade to be launched into camp or the next raid. Every man, woman and child you meet on the street, you're sure, is going to pull out a gun and shoot you dead." He let out of huff of air and leaned his head back on the couch. "Shadows, rooftops, doorways and windows become a source of fear."

He ran his hand up and down her arm. "The friendlies don't look any different than the bad guys over there. Every pile of trash in the road or even mounded dirt could mean your death. It's not safe to drive under a bridge, or pass by a house, a ditch or a hill. You're surrounded by danger twenty-four-seven with no break, and you can't ever let down your guard or relax. As you pointed out, you too have suffered long-term, sustained trauma. I imagine the feeling of never being safe is the same for the both of us, even though the cause is completely different."

"I"—she cleared her throat—"I just get so tired of living under this dark cloud. The constant fear weighs a ton and drags me down. For a while there, I believed I was finally free of Jared, and I was beginning to trust my surroundings. Now I'm right back where I started, like I haven't made any progress at all."

He made a noise deep in his chest. "Wrong again, Carlie. You've made tremendous progress, and you have friends who care about you now."

That much was true, and she was grateful for her new friends. "I've been thinking a lot about Thanksgiving."

"And?"

"My brother didn't invite me. My mom and grandmother did, and as much as I'd love to see them, I don't want the added stress of coming face-to-face with my brother right now. I don't want to expose myself or Tyler to Ron's disapproval and judgment. Besides, I'm still hurting over the fact that he disowned me. If he wants to rekindle our relationship, he knows where to find me." She stared at her lap. "I guess I'm looking for permission to tell my mom not this year. What do you think?"

"It doesn't matter what I think. What matters is what you can and cannot handle. You have a son to think of, Carlie. The best thing you can do for Ty is to take care of yourself. If you feel going to your mom's for the holiday will only add to your stress, then don't do it."

"I'll call her tomorrow." She felt liberated somehow. Even though she knew she didn't need anyone's approval for her decision, Wes's words had been a balm. She had enough to deal with. She didn't need to put up with another load of tension.

Wes twisted around, leaned against the corner of the sectional and stretched his legs out on the couch so that they covered her knees. "Come here. Lie down and put your head on my shoulder. Try to get some rest, Carlie. I'll watch over you and Tyler."

Wes was such a good man, how could she help but love him. *I love him?* Oh, God. Was it true, or was she just reacting to his role as her savior? Once things settled down, she'd have time to sort it out. Wes had been the object of her fantasies for so long she couldn't be sure whether or not what she felt was real. Besides, objectivity was beyond her with him so close.

She stretched out, put her arm around his waist and snuggled up against him. "Do you know anything about a wager going on at L&L?" she mumbled through a yawn.

"Nope." He made another one of those grunting noises. "I try to stay out of the nonsense that goes on at work." Wesley kissed the top of her head and turned his attention to the Christmas movie.

Carlie peered at the TV. "Is that . . . are you watching the Hallmark Channel?"

"Don't you have to work early tomorrow morning?" He squeezed her gently. "Shouldn't you be sleeping?"

"It is the Hallmark Channel." She grinned. "You're a romantic."

"If you out me, I'll deny it," he said in a stern voice.

"I won't tell a soul." Sighing, she snuggled closer and fell asleep, safe in Wesley's arms.

CHAPTER NINE

WESLEY WOKE WITH A START. The arm he had wrapped around Carlie had gone numb. Lifting his head, he glanced at the clock on the shelves. Four in the morning. He'd slept five hours through the night without a single nightmare. How long had it been since he'd accomplished that feat? He couldn't remember. Must be the sleep deprivation catching up with him.

Carlie made soft chuffing noises in her sleep—probably what woke him. A wave of tenderness worked its way through him. Damn, she was pretty. He shifted, trying to get some circulation back into his arm. Sometime during the night, she'd flung a leg over him, and her arm rested across his chest. The scent of her shampoo filled his senses, and a soothing warmth spread where she pressed against him.

Bone-deep contentment filled him. The feeling was like nothing he'd ever experienced before. Possessiveness gripped him, and his throat tightened at the intensity of the emotions welling up inside him. Leaning close, he brushed his lips against her temple.

She didn't have to get up for another hour, and he was in no hurry to disentangle himself. Wes put his head back down and relished having Carlie stretched out beside him. The tension she was under was reaching a critical point, and she was showing the wear and tear. Jared had somehow managed to elude them all while continuing to stalk Carlie and Ty. Any day now the guy would make his move to get to them, and Wes wasn't about to sit around and wait.

Ken's suggestion that he and the guys perform their own special ops mission had been more and more on Wes's mind. Brushing his jaw against Carlie's silken hair, he thought about what needed to be done. If he and the guys did decide to pull their own mission, he'd have to talk to Paul and the marshals, get them on board. Keep it legal.

Half an hour before Carlie had to wake up, he slipped out of her hold and went to the kitchen to start a pot of coffee. Then he headed to his room for a quick shower and a change of clothes. By the time he returned to the living room, she was beginning to stir. He fixed them both mugs of coffee and returned to her. "I brought coffee. It's time to get up, sweetheart."

Carlie groaned, stretched and then pushed herself up to sitting. She brushed the hair from her face and reached for the coffee. "Mmm." She took a sip and sighed. "Just what I need. I can't believe I spent the whole night on your couch."

A crease had formed across her cheek where she'd pressed against the seam of his shirt. Adorable. "You seemed so content I didn't want to disturb you." He sat beside her.

"Thanks for keeping me company until I fell asleep last night, and for the coffee this morning." She put her mug down and folded the blanket he'd spread over them last night. "I need to shower, dress and get Tyler ready to go to Ceejay's."

"Why not leave Tyler here with me today? I'm sure the two of us can find something to do, and he could use a few more hours of rest."

"You sleep all day, Wes. How would you watch him?"

"I slept with you on the couch last night. I might stretch out again until he wakes, but I've had enough rest for today."

"We spent the night together?" She glanced at him in surprise.

He nodded, remembering how she fit so perfectly against him. "Once Tyler is up, I'll bring him to the diner for breakfast. He'd like that."

"That's asking a lot. You'd be giving up another Saturday. With Tyler and me staying here and underfoot all the time, don't you want the place to yourself for a while? Don't you have things you want to do?"

"Yes. I want to spend the day with Ty. He's a great kid, and I enjoy his company. I'll take him to the park in town. There are bound to be some kids there he'll know, and it'll do him good to get out in the fresh air and play. It's supposed to be a nice day. The temps are going to reach the sixties."

Her expression turned wary. "The park is too open. I don't want Tyler in a place where Jared can get to him."

"I'll call the guys. I have to talk to Kyle and Ted about your car today anyway. I wouldn't put Tyler in danger, Carlie. You know that." He'd also call Ken. Hopefully, all three would meet him at the park in the afternoon, and they could talk about putting a plan together—something to flush Jared out into the open.

"You really want to watch my six-year-old?" Doubt clouded her features.

"I do. Tyler and I are buddies, and buddies spend time together."

"All right. Have it your way. That means I have a little more time to drink my coffee before I have to shower. I'll call the Langfords and let them know Ty isn't coming over." The corners of her mouth turned up. "So, how was the rest of the Hallmark movie last night?"

"Beats me." He chuckled and reached for his mug. "I started to doze, so I turned it off and fell asleep." *With you wrapped in my arms.* Another wave of tenderness hit him square in the solar plexus, knocking the breath out of him. What would it be like to fall asleep each night with Carlie beside him, or to wake every morning tangled up with her?

"Sure you did." She laughed.

"Laugh all you want. It's true." Wes picked up his phone from the coffee table. "I'll text the marshals. Since I'm watching Ty, I won't be able to walk you to the diner, and I want them close to you."

"I hadn't thought about that." Carlie tensed. "I . . . I've gotten so used to having you there for me when I go to work . . ."

He couldn't help the rush of pride her words evoked. She'd come to rely on him, and whether they intended for it to happen or not, they were building trust. "I'll stand outside the front door and keep an eye on you." He texted his message, hoping one of the marshals was up. He got an immediate response. "Pelletier will be watching from across the street."

"I'll be so glad when this is over. It's going to take my nerves a year to settle down again." Carlie rose, put her arms over her head and stretched. Her robe had come untied, revealing a slice of bare skin where her shirt met her pajama pants.

Wesley's pulse raced, and it was no easy task keeping his hands where they belonged. He wanted to pull her close, nibble that bit of skin, kiss his way down to . . . He gripped his mug and steered his wayward thoughts—not to mention his eyes—in a different direction.

"I'm going to go shower," Carlie said, picking up her coffee.

New images flooded his mind—Carlie naked, slick with soap and standing under a stream of hot water. Not helping. He shifted, trying to ease the tightness of his jeans. Holding his mug above the obvious effect the visuals in his head were having on his anatomy, he hoped like hell she didn't notice. "I'll be here." She walked away from him, and he imagined himself in the shower with her. Forcing himself to stay put, he drank his coffee and waited.

Forty-five minutes later, Wes stood on the sidewalk in front of L&L and watched Carlie walk alone down the sidewalk. He searched the shadows and doorways for any sign of Jared. Pelletier sat in his vehicle across the street, and as soon as Carlie got a block down, the marshal started his car and followed. Wes waited until she disappeared through the door of the diner before he turned back into L&L, set the alarm and climbed the stairs to his apartment. He stretched out on the couch, keeping an ear open to his surroundings, and closed his eyes.

He must've nodded off again, because the sound of a door opening and Rex's nails clicking against the floor woke him. Wes glanced at the clock. He'd managed another couple of hours of sleep. Good. He needed to think clearly today.

Ty walked into the living room, his hair a tangled mess and sticking up all over. Wes couldn't keep from smiling at the sight. "Hey, partner, good morning."

"Morning." Tyler tied the belt of his bathrobe. "I'm supposed to be at the Langfords' house," he said as he climbed onto the couch.

"I talked your mom into letting the two of us hang out together today. Rex needs to go outside. Will you be all right on your own for a few minutes?"

"Yeah." Tyler picked up the remote and found a channel with cartoons.

"While I'm gone, go fill Rex's food bowl like I showed you. One full scoop."

Tyler grinned and slid off the couch. "OK."

Ty ran off to the kitchen, and Wes turned toward the door with Rex at his side. Once he was standing between the buildings, he sent a few texts. Ted and Kyle got back to him right away, agreeing to take a look at the damage to Carlie's Ford, and then they'd join him at the park. He didn't hear back from Ken, but that didn't surprise him. It was still early, and Ken might still be sleeping.

Rex finished taking care of business, and the two of them made their way back to the third floor. Tyler was on the couch watching cartoons again. "Hungry?" Wes asked.

Tyler nodded. A man of few words. Wes grinned. "I thought we'd head down to the diner to have breakfast with your mom. You in?"

That got another nod, this one more enthusiastic. Tyler shut off the TV and hopped down. "I'll go get dressed."

"Brush your teeth while you're at it—and that hair." That last part got an answering grumble. Wes chuckled, and then his phone chimed. He pulled it out of his pocket. Ken had texted:

```
About time, bro. See you in the park at
one.
```

Good. Taking the offensive felt good, gave him a sense of purpose and forward momentum. Ty returned, dressed, but with his hair still spiked and tangled. It looked as if he hadn't used a brush all month. Wes shook his head. "Go brush your hair, partner. Your mom will think I don't know how to look after you if you don't."

"I did!"

"Do it again. Wet it down a little this time."

Tyler stomped off, and Wes's grin turned into another chuckle. Tyler came back, his hair dampened, but not in any better shape. *Pick your battles.* He glanced at the shelf inside the closet and pulled down a baseball cap with a USMC patch on the front. He tightened it as far as it would go and plopped it backward onto Tyler's head. "Let's go. I'm starving." He held out Ty's jacket.

"Me, too." Tyler took off the cap, studied it for a minute and put it back on. "Can I keep it?" He peered hopefully at Wes.

"Sure." He squished the too-large cap down on the kid's head. "You'll grow into it eventually." Hand in hand, they made their way downstairs and out the front door, heading the two blocks down the street to the diner. Wes scanned the area and kept Tyler close to his side. Perfect was a quiet place on Saturday mornings, and not much in the way of traffic rolled through town this early in the day. "Would you like to head to the park this afternoon?"

"Yeah." Tyler bounced over a seam in the sidewalk. "Can Rex come, too?"

"Of course. He'd never forgive us if we left him at home while we're at the park."

"Can Toby come, too?"

"I hadn't thought of asking him, but we can call the Langfords after breakfast." Wes's stomach rumbled as they reached the door to the diner. He opened it and hustled Tyler inside. The delicious breakfast smells made his mouth water.

"Morning," Harlen greeted them from his customary place behind the cash register. "I like the hat, Ty, but it's a little large. Don't you think?"

"Hi, Mr. Maurer. Wes says I'll grow into it eventually." He beamed. "It's my hat now."

"Is that so?" Harlen's eyes widened, duly impressed. "Carlie reserved your regular table. You two can seat yourselves, and she'll be with you shortly."

"Thanks." Wes guided his charge by the shoulders toward their corner table. He could get used to this—Saturday mornings with his buddy Ty, having breakfast at the diner. He got that familiar jolt the moment he caught sight of Carlie. He could get used to that, too. Maybe.

"What's with the hat?" Carlie turned Wes's coffee cup over and filled it. A container of cream, a small box of crayons and a kid's place mat had already been set on their table.

"His hair isn't cooperating this morning." Wes snatched Ty's cap off for a second.

"You need a haircut, my boy." Carlie sighed.

"Can I get my hair cut like Wes's?" Tyler asked.

Wes couldn't keep the stupid grin off his face. Carlie's laughter washed over him, and once again the deep feeling of contentment filled him. *Dangerous. It won't last, and then what?*

"Sure. It'll be a lot easier to manage. I'll take you to the barber after school on Monday."

"I can clip his hair for him," Wes said. "I do mine all right. In fact, we'll take care of it right after breakfast."

"If you insist." Still grinning, Carlie pulled out her order pad and a pen from her apron. "Do you two know what you want this morning?" She gazed at her son, her face glowing with love.

He wanted that look turned his way, and if he were honest with himself, he'd admit that he wanted a lifetime of mornings like this. He could almost see it. Tyler grown and on break from college, the two of them heading to the diner together . . .

The e-mail his ex sent him flashed through his mind, followed by the stunned look on the young Marine's face as he collapsed on the desert road. The acrid stench rolling from the burning Humvee, and the grisly sight of charred bodies swamped him. Gunfire and the sound of RPGs detonating echoed inside his skull.

His heart pounded, and sweat beaded his forehead and dampened his palms. Bitterness at his screwed-up state rose like acid to burn him from the inside out. He took a deep breath and rode it out while Ty told his mom what he wanted.

Carlie turned to him, her expression filled with concern. "Are you OK? You're . . . a little pale."

"Yeah. Sure. I'm fine, just hungry." He studied the menu, like he didn't have the entire thing memorized. "I'll have a bacon, cheese and spinach omelet, a side of fresh fruit, and make the hash browns—"

"Extra crispy with onions," Carlie finished his sentence. "Got it." She scrutinized him for a second. "I've given it some thought, Wes, and I'm glad Tyler has you to look out for him. It's just that . . . I don't want to take advantage of you, and—"

"I know. We'll talk about it later." He gripped his coffee cup. "Kyle, Ted and Kenny are coming over this afternoon," he said. "Rex will be with us, too. Are you OK with Ty going to the park with three men and a dog to protect him?"

"Sure." She placed her hand on his shoulder for a second. "I trust you to watch over him." She patted his shoulder and walked away—with his battered heart in her apron pocket.

Tyler hummed while he colored the cartoon characters on the place mat, bringing Wes back to a calmer state of mind. Thanksgiving was this coming Thursday, and he wanted to execute the flush-out-Jared mission the week after—if the guy hadn't already been captured by then.

The bell over the door chimed, and the two marshals walked in. They took places at the counter, nodded a greeting and then ignored him. How would they react to whatever he and his men planned? What would he do if they didn't go along with it?

He'd go through with it anyway, that's what he'd do. He and the guys would hand Jared over to the marshals once they had him, and that would be that. Carlie would move back to her house, and maybe he'd risk asking her out again. Poker night had gone well, but thanks to her ex, it had ended badly. No. Not entirely true. He'd slept with her, holding her in his arms all night.

The sense of contentment he felt with Carlie only made the threat of loss worse. The closer they got, the more he had to lose. His gaze strayed to her, like it always did, like it had since the day he'd first laid eyes on her.

The guys were right. He couldn't undo what was already done and there was no middle ground. He only had two options: advance . . . or retreat.

After breakfast, he and Tyler walked back to L&L. Wes opened the front door, ushered Tyler through. He set the alarm, and they climbed the stairs to his apartment. "You ready for your haircut, Ty?" he asked as he opened the door to his living room.

Tyler nodded. "But I still get to keep the hat, right?"

"Of course you get to keep the hat," Wes said, hanging their jackets in the closet. Rex gave them both an enthusiastic tail-wag greeting and followed them into the living room. "You think I'm the kind of man who would give you a gift and then take it back?" He feigned a scowl. Tyler shook his head and grinned. "Good, because I wouldn't do that. I'm going to go get the clippers and a towel. Go to the kitchen and pull a chair to the middle of the room. I'll meet you there."

Tyler ran off with Rex at his side, and Wesley went to his bathroom to gather his cordless clipper and a towel to wrap around Tyler's shoulders. He made his way to the kitchen and found Tyler with a rope toy, playing tug-of-war with Rex. "Ready, Ty?"

"I guess." Tyler dropped the twisted rope.

Wesley lifted him into his booster seat and wrapped the towel around his shoulders. He ran his fingers through the kid's unruly hair and turned on the clipper.

"Is it going to hurt?" Ty asked in an alarmed tone.

"Not if I do it right." Wes studied the kid's head. "Hasn't the barber ever used a clipper on you?"

Ty shook his head.

"As long as you stay still, there shouldn't be any problems. Tuck your chin down to your chest."

The little guy tensed as he tilted his head down. "The man who used to be my daddy hurt my mommy," he whispered.

Wesley's heart squeezed. He shut off the clippers and set it on the table. "I know he did, Ty." He brought a chair around and sat in front of Tyler. "You want to talk about it?"

Ty shrugged, and his eyes filled.

Wes swallowed hard. Tricky territory, and he probably wasn't the best person to have this discussion with a six-year-old boy. As a Marine, Wesley had killed, so what could he say without sounding like a hypocrite? He sucked in a long breath and let it out slowly. "It was wrong for him to hurt your mom. You know that, right?"

Tyler nodded, his face a mask of misery and confusion.

"It's never OK to use violence . . ." *And here's the hypocritical part.* He'd certainly seen more than his share of violence. He racked his brain for the truth—the truth as he saw it, anyway. "OK, you're probably too young for this, but here goes." He placed his hands on Tyler's shoulders. "You know I'm a Marine. We talked about that, didn't we?"

"I'm gonna be a Marine, too." Ty nodded. "When I grow up."

"Well, that's a good goal to have, because Marines are all about protecting freedom, our country and the people who live here. What your dad did to your mom, that's unacceptable, partner. Totally unacceptable. If someone threatens to harm another person, like you or your mom, it might be necessary to use violence to protect them, but it's never OK to use violence as a means to control or coerce someone. Good people don't use violence just for the sake of hurting others. Does that make sense to you? Do you understand there's a difference?"

Tyler's eyes met his, and the look of fierce determination on the little guy's face brought a lump to Wes's throat. Tyler's chin came up. "I'm going to protect my mommy, like you do, Wes. We can protect her together, can't we? 'Cause we're brothers."

"Yeah," Wes managed to rasp out. He drew Tyler in for a tight hug. "We can do that, bro." He had to struggle to pull himself together. Shaving the kid's head with shaking hands was not a good idea. "You ready to have your hair clipped now?"

Tyler nodded against Wes's shoulder.

"Good. Let's do this, then." He stood up, unbunched his shoulders and went for the clippers. "Look down and hold the towel. I'm coming in." He turned the clipper back on, held Tyler's head forward and began.

Tyler shivered and giggled. "It tickles."

"Hold still, because if I nick you, that's not going to tickle." Blond hair fell to the kitchen floor and covered Ty's shoulders. Wesley changed the clipper length once he'd done the sides and back so he could leave it a little longer on top. A few more passes and he finished. "Let's clean up here, and then you can take a look."

"OK." Tyler ran his hands over his head. "Feels weird."

Wesley took the towel from Ty's shoulders and brushed his neck with it. "I'll sweep, and you hold the dustpan," he said, lifting the kid from his booster seat. They made quick work of cleaning up, and then the two of them headed for the bathroom down the hall. Wesley flipped on the light. His eyes were drawn to Carlie's things—the makeup sitting on the counter, her hairbrush and hair dryer. A couple of bras hung from the shower curtain rod. Plus, the room smelled like her. Whatever perfume or shampoo she used lingered in the air. He inhaled, liking that her presence filled the space.

"Ready?" He gripped Tyler around the waist.

"Yep."

Wesley lifted him to kneel on the edge of the sink so he could look into the mirror. "What do you think?"

Tyler turned his head back and forth, studying his reflection. "I like it!" He met Wesley's eyes in the mirror and grinned, his eyes shining. "I look just like you."

Another lump clogged his throat at the obvious adoration in the kid's eyes. "Yep. Practically twins." It was going to slay him when Tyler and Carlie moved back to their own place. He lifted Tyler back to the floor. "We have a while before it's time to go to the park. What do you say to a game of checkers?"

"I don't know how to play checkers." Tyler reached for Wes's hand. "Can we build a fort with my Legos?"

"Sure. We can do that." He let Tyler lead him to the living room, his heart full and aching at the same time.

🐏 🐏 🐏

Tyler had found a couple of friends from his school at the park, and they were playing on the monkey bars with Rex circling the playground equipment in an effort to keep the kids herded into a tight knot. Wesley kept an eye on Tyler, and he and Ken patrolled the perimeter of the playground.

"Here's what I'm thinking," Ken began, his tone eager. "We get a bunch of the guys together. You, me, Noah, Ryan, Kyle, Ted and maybe one or two others. We know Baumann is watching Carlie, and we can use that to our advantage. So, Kyle, Ted and Ryan head out of town to Carlie's house in the afternoon. Baumann won't take any notice, because only you, Carlie and the kid are on his radar. Have the guys hide their vehicle somewhere close, and then lie low in the brush behind Carlie's house." He glanced at Wes. "There *is* brush out there, right?"

"Sure. There's plenty of cover."

"Good. You, me and the kid leave town a little later. Hopefully Jared will see us leaving, so he'll know you're not with Carlie. We'll head toward Noah's place and drop Tyler off there. Then, we'll take a back route to Carlie's. We can ditch the car a half mile or so away, and we'll take the front of her house. Once it gets dark enough to ensure our presence will go unnoticed, Carlie will take off from your place in her Ford and head to her house. She'll go in the front door and leave immediately from the back." Ken used his hands to illustrate what he talked about. "Ted will be responsible for getting her away. He'll take her to Noah's house and stay there with her and her kid."

He shot Wes a determined look. "And then we wait. Jared will believe Carlie's alone inside her house. Her car will be parked out front, and she'll turn on a few lights inside. Once he shows up, we'll do a citizen's arrest on his ass and turn him over to the authorities. Done. Simple."

"Simple?" Wes shook his head. "He's armed."

"So? We'll be armed, too." Ken's eyes took on a feral gleam. "He'll be surrounded and outnumbered. We'll disarm him easily enough, and I'll bring some of those zip ties to cuff him."

"I intend to share the plan with the marshals and Sheriff Taylor. I'd rather they make the arrest."

"That's a big mistake." Ken jammed his hands into his jacket pockets. "They'll only muck it up." He shot Wes a pointed look. "Or worse, they'll tell us we can't get involved in police business."

"Still, I want to be on the up-and-up. A lot can go wrong."

Ken growled. "Don't do it, man."

"Have to." It wasn't so long ago that Wes had been the authority in command. "Do you miss it?" he asked, knowing Ken would understand what he meant.

"Hell, yeah, I miss it. I miss the adrenaline rush, and that feeling you get when your team executes a successful mission. I miss the brotherhood, knowing the guy next to me has my back, just like I have his." He kicked at a pebble, sending it skipping across the dry grass. "I'll tell you what I don't miss, though. I don't miss seeing my buddies going home in flag-draped coffins, and I don't miss IEDs, suicide bombers or the paranoia." He let out a bitter laugh. "Oh, wait. The paranoia's still with me."

"Would you have stayed in if you hadn't been injured?" Ken's hip had been shattered by an IED, and he'd also suffered traumatic brain injury when the IED detonated. His hip had been put back together with pins and an artificial joint, and he suffered with migraines and irritability from the TBI. Still, Ken was one of the lucky ones. He could still think clearly, still function fairly well.

"I doubt it. If I never see another Taliban insurgent or al-Qaeda again, that'll be just fine with me. And I'm over the whole primitive-desert-living scene." Ken stopped walking and scanned the area. "Anyway, it's a moot point, since I was given a medical disability discharge."

Kyle and Ted walked toward them across the park, the two of them deep in conversation. Wes and Ken moved closer to where Tyler played with his friends and waited for the two men to join them.

"Little prick sure did a number on Carlie's car." Kyle shook his head. "Thankfully, he only damaged the body. He didn't mess with the engine. It won't take much to fix it. New tires, glass, headlights and taillights. I can call a few friends still in the bodywork business and get what we need at wholesale."

"Carlie only has to pay for the parts," Ted added. "We're happy to help her out. And anyway, the job will only take a couple of hours max with the two of us working together."

"Thanks. I owe you." Wes scanned the area for anything suspicious, and then he and Ken went over their plan briefly with the two. "What do you think?"

"I'm in," Kyle said. "But I agree with Wes. It's better to bring in the sheriff and the marshals. I've got way too much going on right now to risk getting into trouble. I've just been accepted into Pacific University's PA program." Kyle straightened. "I start classes in May, and I'll be moving to Oregon in April."

"Good for you, man," Ken said, punching Kyle's shoulder.

"Does my sister know?" Everyone knew Kyle had been taking prerequisite classes for the past year so that he could get into a physician's assistant program. Why hadn't he found a program closer to home? Brenda's heart was going to break if she and Kyle were separated.

"Of course she knows. I'm hoping she'll come with me."

"Oh." More changes in his life. Great. He and his youngest sister had grown a lot closer since he'd retired and moved back home to Indiana. Would Brenda leave her home and family for Kyle? And what about her job? He'd miss her if she decided to follow Kyle.

Rex barked, bringing Wes's thoughts back to the issue at hand. "I'll arrange a meeting with Sheriff Taylor and the marshals." He checked

- 1 5 6 -

his watch. "Carlie's off work in ten minutes. I should run this by her first before talking to anyone else. She might not agree to take part."

"In that case, once it's dark enough, we could drive her car out to her place ourselves, turn on a few lights and hope Jared *thinks* she's there. If we're lucky, he won't be able to see who's driving the Ford." Ken rubbed his hands together. "We might not flush him out the first time. It'll probably take a few tries."

"You're way too eager." Kyle huffed out a laugh. "And it's making me nervous."

"Have you talked to Noah?" Ted asked.

"I did, and I mentioned something about it to Ryan, too. Noah had some stuff going on today and couldn't meet us, but he's in. So is Ryan." Wes glanced at the playground. "I've got to get going. Thanks, guys. I appreciate your help. When you know what the cost is going to be for Carlie's car, let us know."

"Will do," Kyle said. "Ted and I will tow her car to the farm today. We brought cables with us."

Wes turned back for a second. "Do you need the keys?"

"Nope. No windows," Ted reminded him. "We'll need the keys to drive it back, but not now."

"Later," Ken called as he too walked off toward his car.

Wes leashed Rex and called Tyler to him. "Your mom is going to be looking for us. We don't want to keep her waiting."

"OK." Tyler waved at the children he'd been playing with. He slipped his hand into Wes's and danced along beside him. Tyler never just walked. He bounced, hopped and skipped everywhere he went. He squeezed Ty's hand, and the boy looked up at him, his eyes full of trust. Wes's heart did its own hop, skip and bounce.

The longing for a family of his own slammed into him, blindsiding him. His eyes stung and he had trouble drawing breath. And here he thought he'd buried that dream deep enough that it couldn't resurface. He'd never questioned his choices before, but now he did. If he'd gone to college right out of high school instead of enlisting, he wouldn't be having nightmares. He'd sleep at night like everybody else, and he wouldn't need to sit with his back to the wall or constantly do surveillance checks wherever he went. He'd be whole.

The little boy holding his hand, causing his heart to stutter, would be his. There would be one or two other children besides, and trust wouldn't be an issue. He glanced down at Tyler, who still wore the cap he'd given him. Swamped with regret, tears blurred Wes's vision.

Tyler deserved a father who would love and protect him, and instead, he got the dad who beat his mom and terrorized them both. Not right. Not right at all. Wes's jaw clenched so tight it hurt.

They reached the diner, and Wes tied Rex's leash to a meter. He struggled to bring his emotions under control. Regret didn't do him any good. He couldn't change the past, and he couldn't deny that his years as a Marine filled him with a sense of accomplishment. He'd served his country as he was meant to do, and that was that. Tamping down on his roiling emotions, he opened the door. "Let's go get your mom, partner."

"What are we gonna do tonight, Wes?"

"I hadn't thought about it. Is there something you want to do?"

"Can we go see a movie?"

A darkened theater full of people Jared could easily blend in with, being exposed and vulnerable. Not a good idea. "Hmm. How about we make popcorn and hot chocolate and watch a movie at home? Your choice."

"Yeah." Tyler jumped over the threshold into the diner.

Carlie was waiting for them, and Wes's insides did that quivering thing they always did at the sight of her. Would he ever get over the impact she had on him? Probably not.

She already had on her coat, and she sat at the counter talking to an elderly man who had a newspaper laid out before him. Only a few customers remained in the diner, all of them regulars he recognized.

"I'm leaving, Jenny," Carlie called toward the back.

THE TWISTED ROAD TO YOU

"Hey, you two. I like your new haircut, Ty." Jenny waved at Wes and Tyler through the opening to the kitchen. "See you on Tuesday, Carlie. Enjoy your days off."

"Wow," Carlie said, running her hand over Ty's newly shorn scalp. "Looks great, kiddo."

"Where's Harlen?" Wes looked around the small diner.

"He's helping the cooks take the garbage to the dumpster," Jenny said. "Do you need to talk to him?"

"No, I just wondered. Thanks." Thinking the retired sheriff might not be there to look after things bothered him. "Tell him I said hello."

"I will, Wes. Take care." She disappeared from the window.

Wes brought Carlie up-to-date on her car as they left. "They towed it away already."

"What's wrong with our car, Mommy?" Tyler walked along between them.

"It's broken, and Mr. Lovejoy and Mr. Reeves are going to fix it for us."

Tyler nodded. "I went to the park today, and Rex came with us. Jonathan and Brian from my school were there, and we played."

Carlie's eyes met Wes's, and the warmth and tenderness her expression held sent his pulse racing.

"Sounds like you had a good time." She smiled at Wes and mouthed, "Thank you."

"I did, and do you know what?" Ty chattered on. "Wes says we can make popcorn and hot chocolate and have a movie night. Can we, Mommy?"

"Sure. After supper."

"What are we having tonight?" Wes asked. How easily the three of them had fallen into a routine, and he was the beneficiary in every way. Look at how he already took her for granted and assumed she'd cook. "I mean . . ."

- 1 5 9 -

She gifted him with another sweet smile. "I'm baking chicken tonight."

"Sounds good." She deserved to be taken out for dinner, somewhere fancy, expensive. It wouldn't be easy to pass it off as anything but a date, though, and he wasn't *there* yet. Social gatherings with people they knew in common were safer. "Are you going to self-defense class this coming Wednesday?"

"Yep. It's the last freebie. Cory and I have signed up to take kick-boxing. The class starts the second week of December on Tuesday evenings."

Would she be back in her own house by then? Part of him, most of him, hoped not. How long could he and the guys put off their plans to capture Jared? "My offer to go with you and watch Tyler still stands."

"Thanks, Wes. I'd like that."

Movement caught his eye, and the prickly sensation of being watched set his fine hairs on end. A man wearing a hooded sweatshirt walked along the opposite side of the street with his hands jammed into the pockets and his head down. Wes studied him. He was built like Jared, but . . .

Just then, the man lifted his head and stared. Baumann wore a full beard now, but there was no mistaking the look of hatred and rage coming at Wes. Pure malice pulsed off the guy. *Shit.* Had Jared been lurking around at the park, watching Ty, staying just out of sight?

Wesley's heart hammered against his ribs, and his hands curled into fists—every muscle tensed for a fight. He wanted at the guy, but not with Carlie and Tyler beside him. Not now. Plus, he wasn't armed, and Baumann might be. Memories of the combat knife the guy had used to threaten Carlie flashed through his mind.

Carlie hadn't noticed Baumann's presence, or his reaction. Tyler was jabbering away to her about his day, and her attention hadn't strayed from her son. Wes kept them blocked, out of Baumann's line of vision. He pulled his phone from his pocket and texted the marshals with a description and a location. By the time he was done and looked up again, Baumann was gone. His phone pinged, and he read the text from Bruce, letting Wes know he would search the area.

Carlie's ex was either becoming careless—making him even more dangerous—or more bold. Wes hustled Carlie and Ty into the safety of L&L, his blood still rushing through his veins. Things were about to escalate. They were running out of time to catch Baumann before he did something really stupid.

The marshals had gotten his message, and Bruce was after Jared by now, but would he get him? Doubtful. Baumann had a knack for disappearing like smoke into the shadows.

❧ ❧ ❧

Carlie returned from putting Tyler to bed and plopped down on the couch beside Wes. "Ty is worn out. His eyes closed the minute his head hit the pillow."

Wes leaned forward and propped his elbows on his knees. He'd been waiting all night for the chance to tell her about the plan, and now that Tyler was in bed, he didn't intend to wait another minute. "We need to talk."

"What is it?" Carlie's face went from happy to fearful. "What's wrong?"

"When we were walking home from the diner this afternoon, Baumann was across the street, watching." He glanced at her. "I suspect he may have been at the park while we were there as well."

She sucked in a breath. "Are you sure it was him?"

He nodded. "We made eye contact."

She groaned and covered her face with her hands. "Where were Andrew and Bruce? Aren't they supposed to be following us everywhere?"

"Andrew was sleeping. They're taking shifts now. Bruce was at the edge of town gassing up their car when I texted him. He did a search and got back to me while you and Ty were choosing a movie." He straightened and put an arm around her shoulders. "Jared managed to slip through our fingers. Again."

Carlie laid her head on his shoulder and let out a shaky breath. "I'm so tired of this. I'm sick to death of feeling afraid and angry all the time. Teach me how to shoot a gun, because I'm about ready to take matters into my own hands."

He chuckled at the steely tone in her voice and tightened his hold around her shoulders. "The guys and I were talking today, and we've come up with a plan. I wanted to run it by you before I discuss it with the sheriff and the marshals."

She studied his face. "Tell me."

He went through the plan with her in as much detail as they had at this point. "If you don't want to do this, just say the word. It's entirely up to you."

"You wouldn't allow the sheriff to use me as bait before, and now you're suggesting that I become the lure to flush Jared out of hiding?" She canted her head, her expression pensive. "What if he approaches the house from the back just as I'm slipping outside? There's a good possibility that's what will happen, since he's been camping out in the fields."

"We'll have men hiding there, Carlie. If Jared does appear, they'll be ready. They'll get him. Since he won't expect anyone else to be there, I'm hoping he won't have the rifle with him."

"You're hoping?" Her voice shook. "What if he does have the rifle with him?"

The last thing he wanted was to put Carlie into a hostage situation. *Unacceptable.* "Forget it. We'll do the whole thing without you. All Jared needs to see is your car there with the lights on inside the house. Hopefully, that will be enough to draw him out."

Carlie reached for the hand he had gripping his knee. She laced her fingers through his. "No. It's me he's watching. He'll know whether or not I'm driving my car." She bit her lip. "I'll do it on one condition.

If a few less L&L staff, and a few more law enforcement personnel are there, I'll be the bait. If things don't go according to plan, I don't believe Jared will kill me. At least not until he has Tyler in his grasp. He won't know where Tyler is, and I'll be his only link to his son. It's his son he wants." She swallowed. "Not me."

"*I* want you, Carlie." The words came out of his mouth before he even knew he was going to say them. He just couldn't stand what her ex had done to her, the way he'd made her feel so worthless and fearful.

"Speaking of *wanting*," she whispered, keeping her eyes on their twined fingers. "I've been doing a lot of thinking lately, and—"

He grunted, and one side of his mouth quirked up. "You certainly *have* been doing a lot of *thinking* lately. This is the second time you've opened with that sentence."

She flashed him a disgruntled look. "I've had more on my mind in this one month than I have in the entire past year. OK?"

"OK." He chuckled. "So, what have you been thinking about now?"

"I"—she bit her lip for a second—"I don't want to wait until we've made up our minds about getting involved, becoming a couple or any of that stuff. I want you, Wes. Can we agree to let the future take care of itself? We have all night, and neither of us work tomorrow. I just feel so safe in your arms, and . . . and it's been so long since I've wanted anybody." She glanced at him, her face flushed. "I've never wanted anyone the way I want you. There. I've said it."

The words *I feel safe in your arms* got stuck in his head and stayed there. His insides lit up like a bonfire, every inch of him on full alert and heating up fast. "Are you sure this is a good idea? Sleeping together is going to complicate things."

What the hell was he saying? How was it ever a good idea to talk a gorgeous woman out of going to bed with him? And this wasn't just any woman, this was Carlie—the woman he'd lusted after since the first day he'd watched her bustle around the Perfect Diner.

BARBARA LONGLEY

He held his breath and prayed, grateful as hell he'd had the foresight to pick up a box of condoms after that night on the couch when they'd come so close.

"Are you really going to force me to talk you into having sex with me?" She started to rise. "Because if that's the case, you can just—"

"Oh, no." He tugged her back down. "No convincing necessary."

CHAPTER TEN

CARLIE SNUGGLED CLOSER TO WES on the couch and placed her palm on his cheek. Was she crazy? Maybe, but ever since the words *I love you* had popped into her head, Carlie had done a 180-degree turn in her thinking. She wanted Wesley Holt—on any terms. If he couldn't offer more than what they had right now, then so be it. As long as he remained in her life, she'd take as much as he could give. "I want you, Wes."

He stood, reached for her hand and brought her up into his arms. "Carlie," he whispered, trailing kisses down her cheek to her neck. "This isn't just . . ." He cradled her face between his palms and stared into her eyes. "You and Ty . . . you two mean a lot to me. You know that, right? Things could never be just casual between you and me."

Placing her hands on his wrists, she nodded, too breathless to speak. His heated gaze roamed over her face, stopping at her mouth and then coming back to her eyes. The desire she glimpsed, coupled with tenderness, brought a sting to hers.

Without a word he led her to his room. The moment the door closed behind them, he drew her into his arms and kissed her deeply, sweeping his tongue into her mouth to dance with hers. He held her so tight she was completely enveloped in his strength. Never before had she felt so protected or safe. For most of her life, she'd felt as if she was an outsider, looking in, never fitting in anywhere. With Wes she experienced a sense of belonging she'd never had before. With Wes, her past didn't matter. The kiss consumed her, and the sounds of his labored breathing sent waves of need cascading to the very center of her being.

He slid his hands under her shirt to caress the bare skin at her waist, and shivers of pleasure surged from her head to her toes. She wanted more and pressed herself closer, letting him know what she needed. He groaned and moved his hands down over her bottom. Suddenly, she found herself lifted into his arms. With a gasp, she wrapped her legs around his waist, and he strode over to his bed.

Wesley sank down to the edge of the mattress with her straddling his lap. He tugged at her shirt at the same time she tugged at his, their hands getting in each other's way. She stifled her nervous laughter at their clumsy efforts and stilled his hands.

She was over thirty, and she'd nursed her son. A jolt of insecurity hit her. She had stretch marks and certainly couldn't claim to be as perky as she had been a decade ago. And what about the poochiness from pregnancy that never seemed to go away completely? Plus, she hadn't planned this. If she had, she might have chosen a sexier bra, something lacy and revealing in red or black—with matching panties.

Carlie kept her eyes on his and pulled her T-shirt over her head. Embarrassed by her standard issue, no-lace-not-sexy plain white bra, she gauged his reaction, glancing at him through her lashes. The sudden intake of his breath, the slight tremor in his hands as he reached for her, made her feel like the sexiest woman in the world. She unhooked her bra and took it off slowly.

"You're so beautiful, Carlie." Wes's voice came out a hoarse rasp. He ran his hands over her shoulders, down her arms and back up to cup her breasts in both hands. "So damned perfect."

I'm perfect? Insecurity...gone. Electric heat shot straight to her sex as he rubbed his thumbs over her hardened nipples. Carlie worked his shirt off and did a little heavy breathing of her own. She ran her hands over his well-defined torso, broad muscled shoulders and biceps. A dusting of hair covered his chest, forming a path that led down into his jeans. She traced that path with her knuckles, barely skimming over his bare skin. His stomach muscles twitched and jumped under her touch.

His erection pressed into her where she straddled him, and she rocked against the hard length. There was nothing small about Wesley Holt. He was all male, muscled and magnificent. His skin was smooth and hot to the touch, his hooded gaze even hotter. She stared, feasting on the sight of his bare torso.

Could a woman have an orgasm just by looking at the man she loved? Because she was close—damn close.

Carlie wrapped her arms around his neck, reveling at the feel of his bare skin against hers, at the way his chest hair tickled. She kissed him, and he fell back, taking her with him. In a matter of seconds, they both managed to tear off the rest of their clothing. Wes moved her to the center of his bed. Lying beside her, he slid a hand over her, his eyes traveling along the path of his palm. He leaned in and thoroughly ravished her mouth. She was lost to everything but sensation, to everything but Wesley.

His hands were everywhere, leaving heat waves and arcs of pleasure in their wake. Aching with her need for release, Carlie pressed against his erection and explored his body as he did hers. She was on a journey of discovery, encompassing hard planes and smooth skin over firm muscle. His breaths against her skin, the thickness of his arousal, brought her to a fever pitch. She reached for him, running her hand over his hard length.

He went still for a second, sucked in an audible breath and held it. Then he thrust against her, and she tightened her hold. His hand came to her center, and his marvelous fingers delved and toyed with her most sensitive places.

Groaning, he dropped his forehead to hers. "I'm not going to last long at this rate," he choked out. "You're so . . . I haven't . . . it's been—"

"Me, either," she said on a sigh. Lifting her hips, she urged him to increase the pressure of his strokes. "I don't care how long it lasts, Wes. All I know is that I want you. Now."

His chuckle reverberated through her. "Yes, ma'am." He rolled over to the edge of the bed and opened the drawer to his nightstand. He pulled out a condom and sheathed himself. She watched, and an answering throb and a surge of wetness had her pressing her thighs together. Wes came back to her side and kissed her deeply, his hands taking up right where he'd left off.

Trailing kisses down her throat, he drew a nipple into his mouth, rolling the hardened bud with his tongue and nipping at it lightly. She arched into him, waves of pleasure washing through her. Once more he stroked her, growling low in his throat as he plunged his fingers into her slick heat.

Thrusting into her with his fingers while circling her clit with his thumb, he drove her mad, coming closer and closer to sending her over the edge. "Wes . . ." she cried out. He increased the speed of his strokes. Her toes curled and her eyes shut tight. Shuddering in his arms, she came undone, pulse after pulse of pleasure taking her away.

He lifted himself to cover her and nudged her knees apart. "Look at me, sweetheart."

Aftershocks from her climax still raced along her nerves. She stared into his eyes as he entered her. *This* was what she'd fantasized about for more than a year, this soul-to-soul connection. His eyes conveyed so much—tenderness, passion and caring. He kissed her, his tongue dominating hers. He rocked into her, and the pleasure built again. She matched his rhythm, lifting her hips to meet his.

"Carlie," he whispered, nuzzling her neck. "You feel so . . . so good." He growled deep in his throat, his movements faster, harder. She gave herself up to the intimacy of being one with the object of her fantasies. Her insides coiled, catching on the edge of release and hovering for a painfully sweet moment.

Wesley drew her knees up, deepening his thrusts, and the change in position sent her careening into another orgasm, this one stronger than the first. A second later, he joined her. Collapsing, he pressed her into the mattress with his full weight. She wrapped her arms around him, willing him to stay right where he was.

It took a few moments for their breathing to come back to normal. When it did, he rolled to his side, taking her with him. He cradled her, running his fingers through her hair and kissing her temples and eyelids. "Don't go anywhere," he said before rising from the bed. "I'll be right back." Sated, she caught a glimpse of his equally impressive backside as he crossed the floor to the master bathroom.

Being with Wes had far surpassed her fantasies, and she couldn't deny that what she felt for him was real and lasting. She could accept things as they were. Couldn't she? A niggling doubt crept out from the deepest recesses of her mind. Had she once again fallen for the wrong man? Could she be happy living parallel lives, never fully meshing into the family she longed to have?

Taking a deep breath, she caught his scent on the bedding, and her heart fluttered. Uncertainty clogged her brain when all she wanted to do was bask in the afterglow of their lovemaking. Hadn't she been the one to suggest they let the future take care of itself?

Wes returned and stretched out beside her. "Stay with me tonight," he said, drawing her against his chest. "I want to fall asleep with my arms around you."

How could she refuse? Nodding, she forced her concerns away and relaxed against him, savoring his warmth. If her past was any indication, all she might ever have with Wesley were nights like this one, each of them going their separate ways come morning.

Forcing her thoughts in another direction, she placed her hand on his chest. His heart beat strong and steady beneath her palm. "I've been thinking—"

"Again?" He chuckled. "Is that what you were doing while I was making love to you? Thinking?"

"No." She pulled back to scowl at him. "This occurred to me earlier when we were talking about the plan to draw Jared out into the open."

"What about it?" Wes went back to playing with her hair, wrapping the curls around his fingers.

"The first day we met with the marshals, you ordered me to go to Thanksgiving at your parents' house. Remember?"

He grunted. "I remember having my ears blistered that day."

"You deserved it," she huffed against his throat. "Jared is becoming bolder. He showed himself to you, and that worries me. I'd love to go to your parents' house for the holiday, but I don't want to expose their whereabouts to my ex. I wouldn't put it past him to vandalize their property just because you brought me there. Also, we also have a lot to discuss with the marshals and the sheriff."

"I'm not following where you're going with this, other than to say no to Thanksgiving with the Holt clan. But then, the blood hasn't fully returned to my brain yet." He squeezed her close. "Your fault."

She smiled and kissed his chest. "I'd like to cook a Thanksgiving meal here, and we could invite the marshals and the sheriff to join us. Andrew and Bruce . . . I don't know if either of them has a family, but holidays with nowhere to go must be hard on them both. The sheriff does have family nearby, but with his recent divorce and all, I don't know if he has plans. And maybe we could talk Brenda, Kyle and Ken into joining us. Would it upset your parents if you and your sister didn't come to their house this year?"

"Hmm. I'm sure they'd understand, given the circumstances, and with four other siblings and their families, it's not like their house will be empty without us." He ran his hand up and down her back. "Are you sure you want to go to all that trouble?"

"I love to cook." She propped herself up on her elbow. "What do you think? Can we have the holiday here in your apartment? We can move the kitchen table into the dining room, and with a card table and folding chairs, we'd have plenty of space for everyone. After dinner we can discuss the plan and see what the marshals and Paul have to say."

"All right. Tomorrow I'll call my parents and run it by them, and then I'll talk to everyone else." He reached for the drawer of his nightstand and pulled out another condom. "In the meantime . . ." He raised his brow, his expression hopeful. "Whatever shall we do for the rest of the evening? I'm not ready to sleep yet. Are you?"

Laughing, she threw her arms around him and drew him close for a kiss. Wes took his time with her, as she did with him. Taking turns tasting and touching, they discovered what the other liked and needed. Sighing, lingering, they made love until they lay panting in each other's arms. Carlie couldn't remember a time when she'd felt this completely at ease and replete. Her gentle giant's touch was so tender she turned to mush in his arms.

Wes was not a man who took without giving in equal measure. He wasn't one to see that his own needs were met, turning away once he reached the finish line. No. Wesley seemed to crave her touch as much as she craved his. He snuggled up to her, wrapped her in his arms and tucked her head under his chin before falling asleep.

Carlie remained awake long after he succumbed to exhaustion. Listening to the deep, even sound of his breathing, she committed the moment to memory. Her fantasy had turned to reality, and she'd never be the same. No matter what the future brought, being with Wesley Holt tonight far outweighed the risk of heartbreak.

❦ ❦ ❦

While Wes and Tyler were playing, Carlie slipped into her room to make the call she dreaded. Her grip tight on her cell phone, she entered her mom's number. She picked up on the third ring. "Hi, Mom. It's Carlie."

"*Kara,*" her mother corrected. "I've been waiting to hear back. When are you and Tyler planning to get here for Thanksgiving?"

Her mother had never accepted or approved of her name change, saying it didn't alter anything from her past, no matter how much *Kara* wished it did. She'd tried to explain the name change was to prevent Jared from finding her and Ty, but her mother only grew more adamant in her disapproval. Carlie's heart squeezed painfully. "Well, that's the thing." She raked her fingers through her hair. "We aren't coming." Seconds of silence filled her ear.

"Are you basing your decision on what's happening with your low-life ex, or because your brother and his family are going to be here as well? Because if—"

"Both." She should've e-mailed. Talking to her mother reduced her to the emotionally wrecked adolescent she'd been so long ago. "I'm under enough stress as it is right now and—"

"Don't you think it's about time you made peace with your brother?"

Her mother's plaintive tone sliced right through her—all the way to the wounds deep inside that never seemed to heal. "Mom . . ." She struggled to pull herself together. "I'm not the one who disowned him. He turned his back on me. I know he's your perfect son and all, but why are you putting it on me to mend anything between the two of us?"

"I'm not putting it just on you. I've had the same conversation with Ron, and why you believe I see him as perfect is beyond me. I've never said that."

No, you didn't have to. I felt it every single day. "My choosing not to come home for the holiday has a lot more to do with keeping myself and Tyler safe than it does with our dysfunctional family dynamics. I have a support network here. I'm never without protection. Plus, I'm hosting a Thanksgiving dinner for my friends and for the US Marshals who are stuck in Perfect while Jared is on the loose."

"I'm disappointed."

Of course you are. When haven't I disappointed you? "So am I."

"Your grandmother is going to be heartbroken," her mother said, heaping more guilt over her head. "She's not going to be around forever, you know."

Dammit, she could not let herself be dragged into the deep well of guilt her mother seemed determined to plunge her into. "I'm sorry, but I'm doing what is best for me and Tyler. Besides, if we did come, Jared would follow, and I don't want to put the rest of you in danger." In her mind, Carlie counted her blessings and ticked off all of her accomplishments, determined not to let this conversation undermine her hard-earned self-esteem. "Once Jared is back behind bars, Tyler and I will drive up for a weekend, or you could always come to Perfect. I'm sure Gran would enjoy a visit with her cousins."

"I suppose . . ."

"I have to go, Mom. Some friends and I are taking self-defense classes, and my ride should be here any minute. Tell Gran I love her, and I'll see her soon."

"I will. I'm holding you to the soon part, Kara. It's been too long since we've seen you and Tyler."

"It's Carlie, Mom. That's my name now, whether you like it or not. I'll call again once Jared has been captured, and we'll make plans then." Heaving a sigh, she put her phone away and squared her shoulders, relieved that the call had been made.

She strode out of her room toward the front closet, past Wes and Ty, who were wrestling on the rug in the living room. The sight of the two of them having such a great time went a long way toward lightening her mood. Knowing she'd spend the evening with her friends helped her as well.

"Are we about ready to go?" Carlie asked, taking jackets out of the closet. "Brenda is going to be here any minute, and I don't want to be late for my last self-defense class." Tyler giggled and shrieked. He and Wes were roughhousing with each other in the living room, with Rex running circles around them.

She shook her head. Neither one had heard a word she'd said. How could they, what with her son being held upside down by his waist and laughing as he was. "Hey," she called. "Put my kid down, and let's get ready to go."

Wes's phone rang. He set Tyler on the rug and pulled his cell from his pocket. "Brenda and Kyle are on their way up."

"Kyle?"

"I gave him your car keys this morning while you were at work, and he drove your car back. Brenda followed in his truck."

"My car is done already?"

"Yeah. I paid the guys for the parts. You can write me a check when you have a minute."

"Oh, thanks. I'll take care of it as soon as we get home tonight." Carlie handed Tyler his jacket, and then she slid her arms into hers. As soon as she heard footsteps in the hall, she opened the living room door.

Beaming, Brenda entered, holding both hands behind her back. "Guess what."

Carlie grinned. "What?"

Brenda brought her left hand forward and held it up. She waved her hand, and the diamond on her ring finger sparkled under the light. "We're engaged! Kyle and I are moving to Oregon this April, and he starts his physician's assistant program in May." Grinning, Brenda admired the ring on her finger.

"I'm so happy for you both." Carlie gave her friend a quick hug. "Congratulations!"

"You'd better take care of my baby sister," Wesley warned, his tone half teasing. "Or you'll answer to me."

"You know I will, bro." Kyle and Wes did that shoulder-bumping, back-slapping thing men do. Rex barked, and his tail wagged furiously as he picked up on the excitement.

Jealousy, sharp and quick, sliced through Carlie. All her mistakes, all the bad decisions she'd made, robbing her and her son of any chance at a happily-ever-after, piled up on her. Self-recrimination only added to the load. She forced the smile to remain fixed on her face and kept her eyes on the happy couple. She couldn't bear to look at Wes right now or she'd lose it.

Kyle handed Carlie her car keys. "I parked your Ford out front. Less chance of a repeat performance if you keep your car under the streetlights and on the main road."

"I will. Thanks so much for fixing my car." She tossed her keys into her purse. "And congratulations on your engagement. I'm excited for you both."

"We were going to make the announcement at Mom and Dad's on Thanksgiving," Brenda gushed. "But since we're going to be here, we stopped by and told them today."

"What's *engaged* mean?" Tyler's gaze went from one adult to another.

"It means that Brenda and Kyle are going to get married." Wes ran his hand over Ty's head.

Tyler's face scrunched, but he didn't ask any more questions. Carlie slung her purse over her shoulder. "We'd better get going."

"Are you joining me and Ty?" Wes asked Kyle. "We're dropping the ladies off, and then we're heading to McDonald's for a Happy Meal."

"There's a playground there," Ty said with a hop.

"Sure." Kyle grinned. "I could go for a Happy Meal."

Once they were on the road to the Warriors' Den, Brenda launched into the plans she and Kyle had made. "We're having a small courthouse wedding in March to save money, and then we're heading to Oregon for our honeymoon at a B&B near the Columbia River Gorge. It's supposed to be really beautiful. While we're there, we'll look for a place to live near campus, and I'll keep an eye out for a salon where I can work. The two of us have enough money saved to get us started."

"It sounds wonderful. You two are going to have such an adventure." Carlie tried to infuse her voice with as much enthusiasm as possible. She was thrilled for Kyle and Brenda, and she wished them all the best. Still, the envy lingered and the self-recrimination squatted like a toad on her shoulders.

"It's going to be a tough couple of years." Kyle draped his arm across the back of the backseat of Wes's SUV and rested his hand on Brenda's shoulder. "One year of intense classes and exams, and the second year I'll be on clinical rotations. I know I'm asking a lot of Brenda, but I just couldn't face the future without her, and I didn't want to risk losing her to some other guy while I'm away."

"Aww." Brenda let out a happy sigh. "I would've waited, but I'm glad we're going together."

The pride and love shining from their eyes as they gazed at each other across her son's car seat caused a fresh rift in Carlie's heart. She glanced at Tyler. He seemed to be deep in thought, too somber for a six-year-old. "You OK, Ty?" He nodded, his expression still solemn.

The rest of the drive to the Warriors' Den, Carlie and Brenda talked about Thanksgiving, the menu and who would bring what. By the time they reached their destination, they were a few minutes late. "Mind Wesley at McDonald's, Ty," Carlie told her son as she and Brenda scrambled out of the SUV.

The two of them hurried inside. Most of the women were already warming up, and the instructor spared the latecomers a harried glance. As they hurried to the locker room, Brenda flashed her hand, the one with the diamond, at Ceejay, Paige and Cory. *That* elicited squeals of glee, and the three trailed after them into the locker room.

"Oh, my God, Brenda, let me see." Cory grabbed her best friend's hand. "When did this happen, and why didn't you call me immediately?"

Ceejay took Brenda's hand from Cory. "How did he propose?"

Brenda launched into the story of how and when Kyle had proposed. Paige moved to Carlie's side as Cory and Ceejay lapped up the romantic details. "You OK, Carlie?"

"Of course I'm OK. I'm thrilled for Kyle and Brenda. They're great together, and I'm sure they're going to be deliriously happy." She bit her lip and stuffed her purse and jacket into the nearest locker.

"Umm . . . no doubt. They will be happy together." Paige moved closer, scrutinizing her. "I was referring to the situation with your ex, but . . . sure, let's talk about—"

"Oh. That." Heat rushed to her cheeks. "The whole thing is making me edgy. Obviously. Did Ryan tell you about the plan?"

"Yes, he—" A loud knock on the door stopped all conversation.

"Ladies, let's go!" Lee Greenwood called through the door. "We're waiting on you before we begin."

The five of them filed out of the room like guilty schoolgirls caught smoking in the lavatory. Carlie and her friends took their places in line. A chorus of congratulations aimed at Brenda ensued from the others in the class, and then they settled down to business.

Carlie threw herself into the exercises. She did her kicks, lunges, rolls and yells. She blocked and jabbed and practiced all the ways she'd learned to free herself from a multitude of holds, with the instructor pretending to be her attacker. If anyone ever attempted to use her as a punching bag again, she wanted to be ready.

They'd only been at the lessons for three weeks, but already her muscle tone had improved. By the time the class wrapped up, Carlie was drenched in sweat and infused with the calm she always got out of the physical exertion. Another benefit to add to the list. She couldn't wait to start kickboxing. Grinning, she followed her friends into the locker room.

"We should do something to celebrate your engagement, Bren," Cory remarked.

"After your wedding." Brenda wiped her face with a hand towel. "One wedding at a time. I don't want to steal any attention from your day, and there's plenty of time to plan something after. Kyle and I don't want a lot of fuss. We're keeping things simple. Moving is going to be expensive enough."

Ceejay raised her hand. "I'll host a wedding shower in February at our place. Get a list of guests ready for me."

"I'd like to help with the shower, Ceejay," Carlie added.

"Great." Ceejay flashed her a grin.

"I'm going to miss you, Bren," Cory blurted.

"I'll miss you, too, all of you, but Kyle and I will be back." Brenda pulled her stuff out of the locker. "Both of our families are here, and this is where we want to settle and raise a family. Kyle is hoping to get a job at the VA hospital in Evansville."

"What's it going to be tonight, ladies?" Paige asked. "Ice cream or pie?"

"Pie *with* ice cream," Carlie said, flexing her biceps. "We've earned a treat." Ever since Brenda had shared her exciting news, self-pity had wreaked havoc on her mood. She would not allow her own petty problems to detract from the happiness of the moment. No more self-pity, and no more recrimination. She had her health, her sobriety, her wonderful son and friends. If that's all she ever owned, it would be more than enough, and way more than she'd ever hoped for.

❦ ❦ ❦

Carlie filled bowls with the side dishes for their Thanksgiving dinner while Wesley carved the turkey. He kept snatching pieces and popping them into his mouth as he loaded the platter.

"If you keep that up, we won't have enough left for everyone else." She shook her head at him.

"Can't help it. I love turkey right from the oven, and this one is so good." He sneaked another morsel. "Mmm, tender and tasty." He leaned close, circled her waist with one arm and nuzzled her neck. "Just like—"

"What can I take to the dining room next?" Ken appeared, a smug look on his face as he caught them midnuzzle.

Carlie's face flamed, and she handed him the mashed potatoes and roasted vegetables. "Take these. I'll bring the gravy and corn bread." She narrowed her eyes at Wes as she passed him. Grinning, he followed her with the platter of sliced turkey.

"This looks and smells amazing," Bruce said, taking a seat. "Again, I can't tell you how much I appreciate the invitation, Carlie."

"Me, too," Andrew said, rubbing his hands together. "It's too bad Sheriff Taylor couldn't make it."

"Just leaves more for the rest of us," Ken said, his speculative gaze roaming from Carlie to Wes. "Let me see, it's the twenty-eighth today, right?"

Wes glared, and Kyle burst out laughing.

What was that all about? She ignored it and glanced toward her son. "Did you wash your hands, Ty?" He nodded and took his place. Wesley said grace, and then the offerings were passed around the table. Wes helped Tyler fill his plate and cut his meat. Carlie's chest filled with warmth at the sight of their heads bent together, both with identical buzz cuts. She couldn't ask for a better mentor and role model for her son. She did indeed have a lot to be thankful for, even with her ex on the loose.

Not much in the way of conversation took place during the meal—
a few questions put to the marshals about where they came from and
how they became US Marshals, talk about Brenda and Kyle's recent
engagement—mostly everyone just ate.

"Carlie, everything is delicious," Kyle said between mouthfuls. "My
compliments to the cook."

More compliments flew around the table, and warmth filled her.
"I'm glad everything turned out. Brenda made the desserts. We have
pecan and pumpkin pies."

Brenda groaned and put her hand on her stomach. "I don't have
room for pie."

"I do," Tyler chimed in. "Can I have pie now, Mommy?"

"Sure you can, Ty. What kind do you want?" Carlie stood up and
grabbed a couple of dishes.

"Pumpkin, please, with whipped cream."

"The rest of us can wait to have dessert a little later," Wesley said.
"I'll make coffee and clear the table."

"I'll help." Kyle stood up and took the dishes from her hands. "Carlie,
you sit. We'll take care of clearing and putting the leftovers away."

"I'll get Tyler his pie." Ken followed Kyle and Wes.

"With whipped cream," Tyler called after them. "Don't forget."

By the time the kitchen had been cleaned and dessert served, Tyler
had fallen asleep on the couch. Wesley covered him with a throw while
Carlie refilled everyone's coffee. She set the thermal pot in the center of
the table and took her seat.

"One of the reasons we asked you two to join us tonight is because
we want to run something by you," Wesley told the marshals. "We've
come up with a plan to flush Baumann out of hiding."

"Oh?" Bruce leaned in and placed his elbows on the table. "Let's
hear it."

As Wesley and Ken described what they had in mind, Carlie kept an eye on the marshals. A couple of times they exchanged glances, but she couldn't tell what the silent communication meant.

"We were going to suggest something similar, though without involving civilians other than Carlie," Andrew told him.

"We're not just civilians." Wesley crossed his arms in front of his chest. "We all have combat experience. We're trained soldiers . . . veterans with several deployments under our belts."

"We've faced stuff you can't imagine and lived to tell about it." Ken's jaw tightened. "It's our plan—we *will* be there."

"Wait." Brenda frowned. "Won't Carlie's ex be suspicious? She hasn't gone anywhere alone all month, and now she's suddenly going to head out to her place by herself?" She shook her head. "He's going to know something is up."

"What if you, me and whoever else are willing make it look like we're having a girls' night out?" Carlie turned to Brenda. "I wouldn't be alone to start with. We can go to the bar and grill at the edge of town. Jared doesn't know I still don't drink. If he thinks I've had a few beers and then I head out to my place alone, he'll chalk it up to lowered inhibitions and see it as an opportunity."

"Perhaps." Bruce shrugged. "The entire plan depends upon whether or not he's watching you at that particular moment in time. A stakeout like this will likely take longer than you think. As far as being suspicious goes, it's been our experience that the longer these things drag on, the more frustrated and desperate the criminal becomes."

"When that happens," Andrew continued for his partner, "most of these idiots lose what little judgment they had to begin with, and they do something stupid. That's when we catch most of them. Baumann showed himself to you on the street. He's close, real close to the point where he's going to lose control."

"That makes him more dangerous." Wes's eyes fixed on her. "What if he tries something while Carlie's on the road? He already took a shot at her once. I don't want to put her in that position again, especially when she's alone and vulnerable."

Everyone went quiet, and all eyes turned to her. "He wants his son, and Jared won't know where Tyler is. His previous attempt to kidnap him failed. Jared will want me in a position where he can force me into leading him to his son. He's not going to take a chance on the road, not when anyone could drive by and see what he's up to." Carlie's head ached, and the food in her stomach turned into a hard lump as more scenarios, all bad, were discussed. "Is he still stealing cars?"

"He is." Bruce stood up. "We'll talk to Sheriff Taylor. He'll want his agency involved."

"It's late, and we should get going." Kyle stood up next. "We're agreed that we'll execute the first attempt next Tuesday evening?"

Wes nodded. "That will give us a chance to go over everything with the rest of the guys while we're at work."

Everyone nodded, and Carlie's breath caught in her throat. Lord, she hoped the plan worked. More than anything, she wanted Jared back behind bars and out of her life. She was making her stand here. No more backing down or running away. She had friends in Perfect, a good life and a support network. No way was she giving all of that up. Surely, once Jared was in prison again, he'd be forced to abandon any further notions about targeting her and Tyler ever again. She was no longer alone and defenseless.

Ken was the last to leave. "Thanks for a fantastic dinner, Carlie. You two enjoy the rest of the long weekend. I'll see you Sunday night, Wes," he said with a grin. "You, me and the guys have lots to discuss."

"See you. Set the alarm on your way out."

Ken nodded and waved. Wes nudged the door shut with his foot and dragged her into his arms. "I've been waiting all day to do this," he said, raining kisses down her neck to her collarbone. "You smell so good." He nipped at the tender place where her neck met her shoulder and fondled a breast. "Like turkey, gravy and potatoes. Mmm, yum. My very own Thanksgiving feast. Take me to bed, woman."

She laughed and tilted her head as his mouth sent shivers down her spine. "I have to get Tyler into bed first. Let's leave the dessert dishes until tomorrow."

"Done. I'll clear the table and put the pies away." He patted her bottom. "You take care of Tyler. Last one in bed has to submit to the whims of the other."

"Deal." She pushed out of his arms and hurried to where Tyler lay sleeping on the couch. She loved this side of Wes: playful, teasing, with no hint of the trauma he'd suffered clouding his gorgeous hazel eyes. If only things could always be like this between them.

She decided to allow him to beat her to bed, more than happy to let him take charge of their lovemaking. After all, Wesley Holt had always been her wildest fantasy.

CHAPTER ELEVEN

DESSERT DISHES AND FORKS IN hand, Wesley hurried to the kitchen and placed them in the sink. He fully intended to be the first to reach his bedroom. Images played through his mind, so many things he wanted to do with Carlie. Where to begin? Grinning, he wrapped up the pies and tossed them into the fridge, and then he strode to his room—the first to get there. *Yes!*

Already hard and aching with anticipation, he stripped, stretched out on his bed and tucked his arms behind his head to wait. What was taking her so long? Finally, Carlie walked into the room, closed the door behind her and leaned against it. Her eyes widened for an instant as she gave him the once-over. Then a seductive smile lit her pretty face.

"I win," he said, still grinning.

She laughed low in her throat. Sexy. "Is that what you think?"

He patted the place beside him. "Oh, yeah. Come here, woman." Tonight he didn't want to think about the future or what would become of the two of them. He just wanted to be with her.

"Your wish is my command." Walking slowly across the room, she unbuttoned her blouse, shrugged out of it and let it drop to the floor.

His gaze riveted on the lacy little bra she wore. Red. He gulped, and whatever blood remained above his waist rushed south.

Stopping at the edge of the bed, she canted her head. "More?"

He managed a nod.

Just as slowly, her movements sensuous, she undid her slacks and slid them down, stepping out of them one leg at a time before tossing them aside. Her panties—what little there was of them—matched the lacy red bra, leaving little to the imagination. He lost his ability to think.

"Turn around so I can see all of you," he managed to rasp out. "And touch yourself while you're at it." She did as he asked, skimming her palms over her breasts, her hips and shapely bottom. Then she put one of her hands down her panties and stroked herself. She groaned, and he went rock hard. "Take everything off, lie on the bed next to me and make yourself come. I want to watch you have an orgasm, Carlie."

"All right," she said with a sexy little grin. Hooking her thumbs under the elastic of her panties, she shimmied out of them. Next she unfastened the front clasp of the wispy bit of lace covering her breasts and let it fall to the floor with the rest of her clothing.

He lost his breath at the sight of her. What was this gorgeous woman doing with him when she could have anybody she wanted? He'd seen the way other men looked at her, and it drove him crazy. She crawled onto the bed, her gaze on his face, and laid herself out next to him like some kind of pagan offering, a feast for his eyes. "Look at me while you stroke yourself, baby."

Again she did as he commanded, and it was the single most erotic thing he'd ever beheld in his entire thirty-eight years. Carlie writhed beside him, her eyes staring into his, arching her back as she masturbated.

"Ahh," she sighed, her eyes closing as her release hit her.

Wes wanted his mouth where her hand had been. He couldn't keep from touching her for a second longer. Drawing her into his arms, he kissed her, plunging his tongue into her sweet mouth, demanding her passion in return. Her skin, so soft under his callused hands, the feel of her small body in his arms, sent all kinds of possessive and protective urges chasing through him.

He took one of her hardened nipples into his mouth, suckled and nipped, reveling in the sudden gasp his touch brought forth from her. Moving to give her other breast attention, he slid his hand lower to her cleft. So slick. Hot. He nearly went out of his mind with wanting her. He kissed and nibbled his way down her curvy body, making his way down the bed until he was right where he wanted to be. His hands shaking, he spread her thighs wide and looked his fill. "I am one lucky son of a bitch."

He leaned forward and ran the tip of his tongue around her swollen clit. Her hips came up to meet him, and he was lost. "Mmm . . . taste so good." He put his hands under her bottom and lifted her, burying his face in her heat until she cried out for mercy.

"Too much! I want you inside me, Wes."

Lifting his head, he raked his gaze over her. Her eyelids at half-mast, lips swollen and her hair mussed, she looked as if she'd been thoroughly loved. He'd done that to her. A swell of masculine pride filled him. "We're just getting started, sweetheart." He moved across the bed to his nightstand and pulled out a condom. Lying down beside her, he ordered, "I want you to put this on me."

"With pleasure." Carlie took the foil packet from him, tore it open with her teeth and rose to her knees. She ran a hand down his chest, tracing circles around his nipples, down his torso and then around his navel. She took him in her hand and stroked him from his balls to his head. He sucked in a breath, his hips coming up off the mattress. Slow torture, that's what she was about as she continued to touch and tease.

"Now, woman. Put it on."

She laughed and slowly sheathed him. He sat up, grabbed her around the waist and lifted her to straddle him. Moving them back so he could lean against the headboard, he positioned himself and lowered her to impale himself deep within her welcoming heat. He moved his hips and rocked into her while cupping her breasts.

Carlie rested her hands on his shoulders, matching his rhythm. "So good," he whispered. He wanted to make it last, a slow burn building in intensity, but his body had other ideas, and soon he needed more. Groaning, he flipped them so he covered her and nudged her thighs wider apart. He gave in to the need to thrust harder and faster.

Her scent was all over his face, and her taste lingered in his mouth. He kissed her deeply, wanting her to taste herself on his tongue. His senses roared with the primitive need to brand her. *Mine.* Carlie shuddered and spasmed around him with her release. He came with explosive force, continuing to thrust into her slick heat until every last shudder rocked through him. Spent, he rolled to his side, took her into his arms and crushed her to him.

The sound of their ragged breathing filled his bedroom. He breathed deeply, inhaling her essence deep into his lungs. "We're not done yet."

She chuckled against his throat. "I don't think I can move."

"That's OK. I'll carry you."

She blinked. "Carry me where?"

"To the shower. I want to slide my hands all over your soapy body."

She ran her hand over his chest. "Then what?"

He sighed, contentment settling deep into his bones. "Then I plan to wrap you in my arms—we'll be naked, of course—and fall asleep."

She ran her knuckles down along his jaw. "Tell me again who won?"

Wes placed the new end table on his workstation and settled into sanding the oak with fine-grade sandpaper. All the restlessness that had been plaguing him for weeks? Gone. He rolled his shoulders . . . loose, more at ease than he had been in years, and all because of Carlie. Images of the two of them in his shower, his hands and mouth all over her gorgeous body, flashed into his head. He couldn't wait to get naked with her again. A smile of supreme satisfaction broke free.

"How was your Thanksgiving, Wes?" Miguel asked, coming to stand beside him. "Must've been good, because you sure do seem . . . relaxed." He rubbed his chin and studied Wes. "Almost like—"

"Almost like he got laid?" Ken quipped. "Oh, Carlie, you're as tender and tasty as this turkey," he mimicked, pretending to fondle a pair of breasts and french kissing the air. "I love turkey right out of the oven . . . mmm."

The rest of the crew stopped working and turned to stare—first at Ken's antics and then at Wes. His face heated.

"Caught him nibbling on her neck with his arm around her waist." Ken spread a meaningful look around the room. "Where there's nibbling, there's—"

"Knock it off." Protectiveness for Carlie flared. "Every one of you has work to do. I suggest you focus on furniture and not on my personal life."

"Sure, but we're gifted and talented, boss. We can talk *and* work with our hands at the same time. Give us the date," David pleaded. "I've got fifteen dollars riding on this."

"I'm not giving you anything." Wes scowled. "It's none of your business, and there's no way I'd pull a kiss-and-tell on Carlie."

Miguel went back to his workstation. "Good for you, Wes. I wouldn't do that to Celia, either. None of their business. Idiots," he muttered. "It's no wonder you're all still single." He cast the crew a disapproving look.

"You didn't buy any squares in Ken's stupid pool?" Wes's brow rose.

"Hell, no. I was raised to respect women. My mama would smack me silly if I got involved in something like that, and my wife would banish me to the garage." Miguel shook his finger at the others. "What goes on between a man and his lady is nobody's business. I never let my wife send me sexy pictures while I was deployed, either. Didn't like the way the guys acted—like they had a right to drool all over someone else's woman, even if they were just pictures."

Ken snorted. "I suppose you never drooled over any of those sexy shots being passed around?"

"I didn't. How do you think those wives and girlfriends would feel if they knew the pictures meant only for their lover's eyes were being passed around to an entire platoon of horny fools?" Miguel asked. "Get your head outta your butt, Ken, before it's too late for you. Find a nice girl and settle down. Once you do, you'll understand."

"Not gonna happen," Ken bit out.

Wesley caught the flash of pain in Ken's eyes. His heart wrenched for the guy. He knew his story only too well. After his fourth deployment, Ken's wife had given him an ultimatum: leave the military or she'd leave him. When Ken reenlisted, his wife kicked him to the curb. And it was during that fifth deployment that he'd been injured. "Time for a change of subject."

"How about some rock 'n' roll?" David moved to the sound system.

"Sounds good," TreVonne added. "And for the record, not all of us are single. I've been seeing someone for about six months now. In fact," he said, strutting to the work order basket, "we're looking for a place to live together. If everything goes as planned, I'm going to put a ring on her finger 'bout this time next year."

"Good for you." Miguel high-fived him as he passed by.

"How'd you meet this woman you're seeing, Tre?" David asked. "I don't even know how to meet women these days."

"A friend fixed us up," TreVonne answered. "Cheryl is a biology teacher at Central High School in Evansville, where a buddy of mine works. She's smart, educated, and she doesn't put up with any of my shit. No, sir. She keeps me honest and on the straight and narrow."

Skepticism clouded Ken's face. "And that's a good thing?"

"Hell, yes. Any woman who makes me want to be a better man is a keeper in my book. That's the kind of woman you want raising your children. Isn't that right, Miguel?"

"It is," Miguel agreed. "Women civilize us. I like being *civilized*, especially since regular sex and home-cooked meals are included in the package."

Ken snorted. "What I hear you saying is that it's really the regular sex civilizing you, and not necessarily the woman."

"Naw, bro." Miguel shot Ken a pitying look. "It's the love. It's having a family and a place to call home. Try it. You might like it."

"I *did* try it," Ken mumbled. "Didn't work out for me."

Being around Carlie and Ty made Wes want to be a better man. Had his ex ever made him feel that way? Nope. Mostly Tina had made him feel inadequate. He'd never been able to please her, no matter what he did or how hard he tried. "Did you guys hear about Kyle and my sister Brenda?"

"No," David said. "What about them?"

"They're getting hitched." He told them about the rest of Brenda and Kyle's plans.

"That's great," TreVonne said. "I did hear Kyle got accepted into grad school, and I wondered what would become of the two of them."

His crew settled into work, and Wes let his mind drift. When he and Carlie argued in the sheriff's parking lot, Wes had told her he wasn't her father, brother or ex, and just because the those men in her life had let her down, it didn't mean he would. Carlie wasn't anything like his ex, either. Just because Tina betrayed him and broke his heart didn't mean Carlie would do the same.

Could it be that their troubled pasts made them perfect for each other? Who better than he to understand and deal with Carlie's issues? Who better than Carlie to understand and deal with his?

Surrendering to whatever it was between them—diving headfirst into an uncertain future—just might be his greatest challenge yet. If only he could manage to untangle his relationship issues from his combat PTSD. He had miles of obstacle course to get through before he could straighten himself out. What came after decathlons? Was there such a thing as a dodecathlon? Because that's what he faced, and he hadn't been in training for years.

He checked the wall clock. Ryan and Kyle had agreed to come in early so they could go over the details of Tuesday's mission one final time. He and Ken had taken Tuesday night off, and they'd settled on the four of them for that night: Ken, Ryan, Kyle and himself. All veterans. Ted had been willing, but in the end, they all agreed it would be safer to stick with guys who had seen active combat. Plus, Cory, also a veteran, had stepped up for girls'-night-out duty.

With the marshals, that put them at a team of six. Six against one punk. Paul and his deputies had agreed to discreetly cover the roads leading into and out of town, so Baumann couldn't escape by that route should he slip by the stakeout team somehow.

"Hey, Wes?" David called over the music.

"Yeah?"

"You got any other single sisters? Maybe one who looks like Brenda?"

"Sorry." Wes grinned. "My other sisters are married. Brenda's the baby of the family."

"Figures," David muttered, turning back to his work. "How about the rest of you? Sisters? Friends? Friends of friends? Fix me *up*, guys. I'm begging you."

"If I did have a single sister, I wouldn't set her up with your sorry self," TreVonne teased.

"I can ask my wife if she has any single friends," Miguel offered. "But it'll cost you."

David frowned. "*Cost* me? Like, what are we talkin' here. A six-pack?"

"More like a truckload." Miguel chuckled. "And it would have to be the good stuff, imported."

The music and the buzz of conversation went on without Wes. He checked out, his mind turning to Tuesday night's mission. Camping out in the cold and coming up empty-handed had to be working on Baumann's nerves. The marshals were right. Carlie's ex was about to pop, and they'd be there to catch him when he did. Deep in his gut he knew—Baumann would take the bait on the first stakeout. In fact, he was counting on it.

❦   ❦   ❦

Carlie returned from Tyler's room to the living room and began to pace. She'd been fidgety all afternoon, and her constant motion put Wes on edge. He strode across the room and drew her into his arms to stop her perpetual motion. "Kyle and Ryan are already in place, and the marshals should be arriving at your house about now. We'll have the house completely surrounded," he reminded her in a reassuring tone.

"Once you and the girls head to the bar and grill, Ken and I will set out for the Langfords' with Tyler. We've covered every possibility, every escape route. Things are going to work out fine. You'll see." Carlie trembled in his arms. If anything happened to her . . . Wes tightened his hold. "I won't let Jared hurt you, sweetheart, I swear, and—"

"And I can take that to the bank?" She huffed out a tremulous breath. Tilting her head back, she met his gaze. "I believe you, Wes. I just . . . I'll be glad when this is behind us. I'm nervous but not afraid."

"That's my girl." He brushed his lips across her forehead before letting her go. Footsteps approached from the hallway. "That'll be Cory and my sister," he said, crossing the room to open the door. The two women walked in.

"Ready?" Brenda asked.

"Not really." Carlie reached into the closet for her jacket. "But I'll go anyway."

"I'm riding with you to the bar and grill, and Brenda is following in her car." Cory leaned against the doorjamb. "Do you have your pepper spray with you?"

Carlie reached into her purse and pulled out the small leather-clad canister. "I do."

"Keep it handy," Wes said, pulling her close for a quick hug. "See you later."

Carlie nodded and followed the other two women out the door. They'd told Tyler his mom was going out with friends and Wes was taking him to play with Toby at the Langfords'. It would be another twenty minutes or so before Ken showed up.

Wes took his Beretta out of the lockbox and loaded it. He made sure the safety was on before shoving it into the back of his belt. Tugging his sweater down, he covered the gun, hiding it from view. If Tyler saw it, he would pester Wes with questions he didn't want to answer.

Speaking of Tyler, Wes decided to see what his little buddy was up to. He headed toward his room and peered inside. Rex lay flat on his back sound asleep, and Tyler sat on the floor surrounded by action figures and Legos. "What are you building there, Ty?"

"A fort." He grinned at Wes. "Is it time to go to Toby's house?"

"Not quite." Wes walked in and sat on the corner of the bed. "I just thought I'd come see what you and Rex were up to." At the mention of his name, Rex's tail dusted the floor, and his eyes opened. He shifted from his back to his side but stayed put.

Ty's face scrunched, and he kept his eyes on the Legos he held in his hands. "Do you like my mommy, Wes?"

"Of course I do. You and your mom mean a lot to me. Why do you ask?"

Ty's gaze met his for a fraction of a second before returning to his toys. He shrugged his narrow shoulders. "If you and Mommy got *engaged*, you could get married. Then you'd be my daddy." Another quick glance flitted to Wes and darted away just at quickly. "You *said* you'd be proud to have a son like me."

"I didn't lie," Wes rasped out. He could barely talk past the lump in his throat, not to mention the vise squeezing the blood from his thudding heart. "I . . . It's . . ." He ran his palm over his buzz cut. What could he say? *It's complicated, and I'm scared shitless?*

A six-year-old boy longing for a father's love, longing for what his friends had . . . Tyler wouldn't care about *complicated*, and he sure as hell deserved better than *Well, kid, you see, I'm afraid to let myself love you and your mother, because my heart might get stomped into the dirt again.*

Nothing like a child to strip a man's soul bare, revealing him for the chickenshit he really was. He sucked in a fortifying breath. "I don't know what's going to happen in the future, Ty, but no matter what, we're brothers. That makes us family."

Tyler's chin quivered, and he nodded. Wes could hardly breathe through the ache in his chest. His dog's ears pricked, and he sat up at attention. Saved by a knock on the door, Wes shot up. "That'll be Ken. Put your shoes on, and let's go. Rex is going to the Langfords' with you."

By the time they got himself, Tyler and his dog loaded into Ken's pickup, Wes had managed to check his roiling emotions. He had to focus on the task ahead. It wouldn't do anybody any good if he arrived at Carlie's house still bent from his conversation with Tyler.

"You excited about Christmas, little dude?" Ken asked once he pulled onto Perfect's main road out of town.

"Yeah, but we don't got a tree yet," Ty said.

"Are you going to go see Santa?" Stopped at Perfect's one traffic light, Ken turned to glance at Ty. "I remember how excited I always got when it was time to put in my request to the fat man in red."

"I don't know," Ty answered, his tone uncertain. "How many days is it till Christmas, Wes?"

"Today is the second of December, partner. Christmas is on the twenty-fifth. There's time." Wes hadn't given Christmas a thought. He scanned the street, noticing the decorations for the first time. The streetlights had been wrapped in red plastic ribbon, making them look like candy canes. Greenery adorned with shiny ornaments sprouted from large pottery urns on the street corners, and Christmas lights had been strung on all the boulevard trees. He'd never decorated his apartment. Since it was just him, he hadn't seen the point.

At the end of town, they passed a roped-off lot selling Christmas trees, and Wes had to bite his tongue to keep from suggesting he, Carlie and Ty buy one sometime this week. After tonight, chances were good that Baumann would once again be in custody. Carlie and Tyler would return to their own house, because he hadn't asked them to stay. His insides twisted. So much for putting a stopper in the cracked bottle leaking his emotions.

Cory's wedding was only seventeen days away as well. In two weeks, he'd pick up the new suit he was having altered, and there was the rehearsal and groom's dinner to attend. He hadn't asked Carlie to be his date. *Coward.* She deserved so much better than what he had to offer. He swallowed hard and stared out at the late-afternoon landscape. Bare trees, tangled brush, fields of stalks from last fall's harvest and dry grass all formed a stark pattern passing by his eyes.

Ken turned into the Langfords' long driveway, and the truck bounced along the ruts toward the house. Noah and his son waited for them on the porch. Tyler started to squirm when he spied his friend. "Am I going to eat supper at Toby's house?"

"Yep. And you'll have all evening to play." Wes climbed out. "Your mom and I will pick you up later, after your bedtime. If you want to sack out on the Langfords' couch, go ahead." He helped Tyler out of his seat belt, and the kid launched himself at him, wrapping his arms around his neck. Wes hugged the little boy hard against his chest, the lump back in his throat. "Ken, get my dog out of the truck, would you?"

"Sure."

"You OK, partner?" Wes patted Ty's back. Tyler nodded and laid his head on Wes's shoulder.

"Tyler, you know what? My daddy is grilling burgers and hot dogs for us," Toby chirped. "And Mommy made brownies for dessert. Do you like brownies? 'Cause if you don't, we got ice cream, too."

Ty raised his head from Wes's shoulder and grinned at his friend. "Yeah, I like all of that." Rex appeared at their side, his tail wagging like he was all in for burgers and brownies.

"All set?" Noah widened his stance on the porch.

"Of course." Wes set Tyler down. "Be good and mind the Langfords, Ty."

"I will," he called before running inside with his friend.

Noah moved to the railing. "Be careful tonight."

"Always." He grinned. "What could go wrong? We have six armed men, and Baumann's just one punk." He waved and started back toward Ken's pickup. "We'll let you know how it all turns out."

"Finally we can get this show on the road," Ken huffed once Wes climbed back into the truck. Ken checked his watch before putting his truck in gear, and his fingers tapped away at the steering wheel as they bounced down the driveway.

"Anxious?" Wes asked.

"Wound up. I always get this way before a mission." Ken cleared his throat. "Listen, man. I owe you an apology."

Wes flashed him a questioning look.

"The wager about you and Carlie." Ken shrugged and glanced at Wes. "I gave everyone their money back. The two of you . . . that's a good thing. Didn't mean any disrespect."

"Forget it." Wes went back to perusing the landscape. "I wasn't going to give anybody a date anyway."

"I figured that out," Ken said with a grunt. "I was just rattling your cage."

Wes shifted in his seat, tugging at the seat belt across his chest. "The marshals got permission from the neighboring farm to park our vehicles behind their barn or the silo. It's about a mile from Carlie's. We can hike through the wheat field to get to her house."

"Got it."

An hour later, Wes, Ken and Andrew hunkered down in the brush surrounding Carlie's front yard. Wes positioned himself off to the side so he had a cross view. All cell phones had been set to vibrate, with the lights dimmed. On the verge of disappearing, the sun cast streaks of dark orange across the gray-and-purple horizon. Wes's phone vibrated. Ken texted:

```
Piece of cake. Easiest mission we've
ever been on. Yes?
```

Wes snorted and peered across the darkening yard where Ken hid in the shrubbery. Just as the sun sank out of sight, headlights appeared on the two-lane toward the house. His phone vibrated again.

```
Go time!
```

Andrew texted to all of them, alerting the guys guarding the back-yard.

Wes drew in a long breath and watched the approaching vehicle. Carlie's Ford turned in to the driveway and pulled up to the house. Soon she would walk through the house and out the back door. Ryan would whisk her away to safety, and she'd wait at the Langfords' for him to come get her and Ty. He let out the breath he'd been holding and settled in for the long vigil.

❧   ❧   ❧

Carlie parked her car in the yard, not too close to the house, though. The men hiding in the brush would need a clear, unobstructed view of her front door if they were going to stop Jared before he could get inside. She gripped the steering wheel for a few moments. Her nerves were stretched taut, almost to the snapping point.

Shivering, she climbed out with her keys in her hand and walked to the front door. It was already so dark she couldn't see the keyhole to unlock the door and had to use the little flashlight she kept on the ring holding her keys. Once inside, she turned on the front floodlights so the guys could see the yard, and then she flipped the on switch to her living room.

There. Her job was done. Relieved, she headed toward the kitchen and the back door. Just as she was passing the hallway leading to the bedrooms, a form emerged from the shadows. Her heart stopped. Her worst nightmare stood before her, holding the hunting rifle he'd stolen.

Jared grabbed her by the arm and slammed her against the wall. "Well, well, well, what do we have here?" he snarled. "Finally."

She gasped, adrenaline and panic scrambling her brain. "H-how—"

"You come here alone?" He pressed his forearm across her neck. She nodded.

"'Bout time you came home, bitch. Where's my boy?"

"H-he's with friends," she stammered. Jared backed off, kept the rifle aimed at her and glared. Her heart pounding, she sneaked her hand into her purse, searching for the small leather-clad canister of pepper spray.

Jared slammed the butt of the rifle into her ribs. "Ahh." She bent over, the wall behind her the only thing keeping her upright. Pain radiated through her side, and she couldn't breathe. Her purse slipped to the floor, and he kicked it out of her reach.

"Where's your bodyguard now? Huh?" He laughed, and the sound cut through her like fingernails on slate. "Damn, Kara. I've been waiting for this for far too long. Wasn't nice of you to make me wait. I knew you'd have to come home eventually, knew you'd need more of Ty's stuff . . . or yours."

"Wh-what . . ." God, she had to pull it together. She wasn't alone, and she wasn't without skills of her own. "What do you want, Jared?"

"I told you. I'm not leaving this hellhole without my son. He belongs to me, and you had no right to take him. A boy needs his father." He put a hand around her neck and slammed her head against the Sheetrock. "That big goon. You sleeping with him?" He squeezed her throat, then he suddenly let her go and paced before her like a zoo animal in a concrete cage. "Of course you are. Once a whore, always a whore. I'm gonna *kill* that fucker."

No! Her eyes stung, and panic choked the air from her lungs. *Dammit, think.* She forced herself to take a deep breath, letting it out slowly. Wes was a Marine. He was armed, and he'd know how to deal with a lunatic. Plus, two US Marshals and three combat veterans had his back. No way Jared could get past them to hurt Wesley.

What were the men in her yard doing right now? She should've left the house immediately, and they had to know something had gone wrong. She needed time, and she didn't want to tip Jared off that her house was surrounded. Things would get really ugly if she became trapped inside between the marshals and Jared. *Think.*

She knew Jared. He had an ego. The idiot had always believed he was smarter than everyone else, and the man loved to brag. If she could keep him talking, she could buy some time to pull herself together and make a plan. "How did you get inside my house?"

"Easy." He stopped pacing, pointed the rifle at her and puffed out his chest. "The day that big dumb lug of yours broke down the door,

I hid in the woods and waited until you all left." He shot her a look of disdain. "We were married for five years, Kara. I know your habits."

He started pacing again, as if he couldn't stay still. Was he high? She tried to catch a glimpse of his eyes, but the light in the hall was too dim for her to see them clearly. If he was high . . . *Oh, God.*

"I pried the broken door open, slipped in and went through your kitchen drawers." A look of triumph suffused his face. He pulled her spare set of keys from his back pocket and dangled them in front of her. "You're so dumb. Predictable." His burst of frenetic laughter sent shivers down her spine. His lips curled into a sneer. "You're so stupid, you made it easy. You always kept our spare keys in a kitchen drawer. Remember? All I had to do was get inside and look for them."

She knew that manic laugh. Jared was high on something. Meth or crack. Her heart slammed against her aching ribs. That made him ten times as unstable and unpredictable.

"Once I had the keys, I put the door back and hammered the nails in place with a rock. Then I made sure to destroy any signs that I'd been there." He swiped his sleeve across his forehead, his eyes darting around the house and back to her. "You came alone, right?"

"You already asked me that. If somebody was here with me, you'd know by now." She swallowed the fear lodged in her throat and forced herself to get air into her lungs. "You managed to elude an entire SWAT team, the sheriff's department and a heat-detecting helicopter," she said, stroking his ego. "How'd you do that?"

Jared wanted his son. He wouldn't kill her until she led him to Tyler—unless the men outside stormed the house. *God, don't let them do that!* A plan began to take shape. Pretend defeat, go along with him and get him outside. She was no longer the defenseless victim she'd once been. She knew a few moves. Once they got to her car . . .

"Too smart for those idiots." Jared tapped his temple. "The second I heard the helicopter, I knew what was up. I took off, went across the river to Louisville and laid low for a few days until the heat let up." He smirked. "Of course, I knew better than to move in here right away. Nope. I waited and watched. Once I was sure nobody was keeping an eye on your place, I made myself at home. By the way, we're out of groceries, honey. Sorry 'bout that." He laughed at his own joke, sniffed and swiped his sleeve over his forehead again.

"You're smart, all right," she lied, wrapping her arms around the throbbing ache in her middle. "So what's the plan? I'm not going to fight you anymore."

"Bullshit." His eyes narrowed. "But it doesn't matter. You either cooperate, or I'll put a bullet in your head and dump your body in a ditch." He snorted. "Not until I get what I came for, though." He pressed the barrel of the rifle under her jaw again. "If you behave, maybe I'll let you live."

Anger freed her from the stranglehold of fear and panic. No way was she going to let this lowlife scumbag get anywhere near her son. She knew what she had to do. "OK, OK. I want to live," she cried, feigning submissiveness. "Please, let me live." She poured on the pleading tone. "Tyler needs me. If you take him, take me, too. You know you can't take care of him by yourself."

Jared straightened. "Here's what we're going to do." He yanked her away from the wall by her jacket. "We're going outside to your car, and we're going to drive to wherever it is that these friends of yours have my boy." He wrapped his arm around her neck and forced her toward the front door. "You're going to walk up to their house like everything is all hunky-dory and you're just there to pick up our son." He squeezed her neck. "If you don't act like everything is fine," he whispered in her ear, "I'll have to shoot you . . . and your friends, too. You understand?"

Seething, she nodded. Thanks to the Warriors' Den, she knew how to get out of the hold he had on her. She must have practiced the technique at least a thousand times. She just had to wait until the time was right, and then she'd make her move.

She said a prayer that everything would go the way she hoped and that Wesley would know what she was up to. She had to come up with a way to show him that she had things under control. If he didn't get it, he'd do something rash, putting himself at risk. If only she could text him.

Trust me, Wes, and wait until I'm out of the way before you do anything.

❦ ❦ ❦

Wes shivered and drew his collar tighter around his neck. Minutes went by, and silence blanketed the area—the kind of quiet that only happened in rural areas. The moon rising on the horizon peeked out from between the clouds, its silver light casting ghostly shadows in the surrounding fields. An owl hooted, and then a cow mooed from the farm down the road before everything once again went still.

His phone vibrated in his breast pocket. "Dammit, Ken," he muttered under his breath. He pulled it out, ready to order his friend to knock it off. He hit the message icon, and his blood turned to ice in his veins as he read Bruce's text.

```
Ms. Stewart did not come out of the
back door as planned. Repeat, Carlie
has not exited the house.
```

Wes shot up and drew his gun, his blood going from ice-cold dread to fiery rage in an instant. Baumann was inside the house with her. How? Wes would tear the place down with his bare hands to get to her. He took a step, the need to protect Carlie overriding good sense.

"Get *down*," Andrew hissed. The marshal grabbed Wes's arm and yanked him to the ground.

"He's in there with her," Wes hissed back. His heart pounded so hard, he was sure Baumann would hear it from all the way inside the house.

"Maybe." Andrew kept hold of Wes's arm. "But that doesn't necessarily mean the guy knows we're outside. Baumann wants his son, and he knows no one is going to hand the kid over to him. Carlie's the only one who can get to Tyler. If Baumann is in there, he'll come out . . . with Carlie." The marshal drew out his phone and texted to everyone to stay put.

When? Baumann could keep Carlie prisoner for hours, torturing her into compliance. The thought of that asshole's hands on her turned Wes inside out. Fear and rage arced along his nerves, alternately setting him on fire, then chilling him with dread. "Fuck, fucking fuck!" he huffed out under his breath.

"Pull it together." Andrew gripped Wes's shoulder. "Or back away. You're no good to Carlie if you lose it."

Wes sucked in a breath and nodded. Andrew slipped away into the darkness. Seething, Wes undid the safety on his gun and stared at Carlie's front door. Time crept by, each minute a century. Wes tried to flip the Off switch to his roiling emotions—and failed. *Dammit!*

Letting Carlie down was *not* an option. If she had a single bruise on her, not even the marshals would be able to stop him from tearing Baumann apart. He'd fucking eviscerate the guy. How the hell did Baumann get into the house? They'd all checked. No one saw any signs of a break-in, or they would've alerted the team before Carlie went inside.

The front door opened, and Wes's full attention centered on the two emerging figures. Carlie and her ex walked out and down the concrete steps to the yard. Baumann had his arm wrapped around her neck, and he held the stolen hunting rifle loosely slung over his left arm. Carlie held her arms around her middle like she was in pain.

Wes saw red—murderous red. Carlie scanned the yard, her expression determined, calm. He knew that look. She was planning something. He only hoped the marshal saw what he did.

Once she and Baumann got to her Ford, Carlie twisted out of her ex's hold and shoved him away from her. Then she dove to the ground and scrambled under her SUV.

"Goddamned bitch!" Baumann shouted, bringing the rifle to his hands. He started to go after Carlie.

Dammit! He had to do something. Wes shot up with his gun raised and ready. If he needed to kill the bastard, he would, and the consequences be damned. "You're surrounded, Baumann. Give it up."

"US Marshal," Andrew shouted at the same time. "Drop your weapon." He leaned out from behind his cover with his gun aimed at Baumann.

"You!" Baumann straightened and swung the rifle in Wes's direction. Glaring, he lifted the barrel and fired.

The impact sent Wesley staggering back. His left side stung, then burned like holy hell.

"Get down, Wes!" Ken shouted.

Wes dropped, all right. Not because he'd been ordered to, but because the searing pain brought him to the ground. He fell flat on his back, writhing in agony, unable to get breath into his lungs. Shouts and three more shots filled the air. Liquid warmth spread along his side. Somehow he managed to get his jacket unzipped. He pressed against the wound, and his hand came away covered in blood. His vision began to narrow, and he felt himself slipping out of consciousness. "No," he groaned. "Not now . . ." Not when he had so much to live for.

Everything about his life came into sharp focus then. He loved Carlie and Ty, dammit, and he wanted a lifetime with them. He wanted to grow old with Carlie and watch Ty turn into the fine young man he knew he would become. *I'm a fool.*

He'd been too stubborn and afraid to grab the gift he'd been given, refusing to surrender completely, heart and soul. What he and Carlie had was worth far more than his fear and his stupid pride, and yet he'd refused to set aside his baggage for her.

His breaths came in shallow, pain-filled gasps. *Don't let it be too late. Please, God, don't let me bleed out before I tell Carlie I love her! She needs to know.*

CHAPTER TWELVE

Carlie's heart pummeled her bruised ribs. She hugged the dirt under her car as the rifle Jared held went off, sending shock waves through her. Someone shouted, and she peered out from between the rear tires. Horrified, she watched helplessly as Wesley fell. More shouts and gunshots reverberated through the air, and her ex thudded to the ground a few feet from where she hid.

"Wesley!" Carlie cried, scrambling out from under her car. *Let him be alive. Please let him be alive!* She grimaced as she stood. Shoving the pain aside, she took off toward the spot where Wes had disappeared behind the brush.

Kyle grabbed her by the arm as she ran by him. "Let me go!" She tried to twist out of his hold, desperation to get to Wes clawing at her.

"Wes needs our help, Carlie." He gave her a shake. "Go get clean towels and a blanket." He pushed her in the direction of the house, and then he took off at a run. "Now!" he shouted over his shoulder.

In a haze of shock, she dashed back to the house, hurried to the linen closet and snatched an armload of towels and a thick woolen blanket. Racing back outside, she hardly spared a glance at Jared's still form sprawled out in the dirt. Bruce Murphy was checking him for a pulse. Was he dead? She didn't know or care. Both marshals were there. Let them deal with her ex. Nothing else mattered but getting to Wesley.

Kyle took the towels and blanket from her trembling hands. She dropped to her knees behind Wes and cradled his head between her palms. "Wesley," she sobbed. "Oh, Wes . . ."

Turning him on his side, Kyle probed around his back, eliciting a wince and a sudden indrawn breath from Wes. Kyle unbuckled Wesley's belt and yanked it out of the loops of his pants, laying it out under him. "The bullet went straight through. Hang on, buddy. I've got you." Kyle pressed a towel to the wound on his back and laid him down gently on top of the leather belt. Then he placed a folded hand towel over the entrance wound and brought the belt around to fasten the make-shift bandages in place. "Damn, should've brought a medical kit," Kyle muttered.

"Ambulance is on the way," Ryan said, hovering over them with Ken coming up fast behind him.

Kyle nodded. "Cover him with the blanket, and prop his feet up on a few of the towels." He glanced at Carlie. "The bleeding is slowing."

She kept Wes's face cradled between her hands, needing the contact. If only she could will her strength into him through her palms, or somehow take the injury from him, she would.

Wesley's eyes flickered open, and he brought a hand up to grip hers. "Carlie . . . want to . . . need to tell you . . . I . . . I want to . . . surrender . . ."

Surrender? What the hell did that mean? Surrender to death? She gripped his large hand with both of hers. "Don't you dare," she commanded, but her words were wasted. His eyes rolled back in his head, and he went slack. A wrenching sob tore through her, and she brought his hand to her face, pressing it against her cheek.

"Wes has lost a lot of blood." Kyle placed two fingers over the artery under Wes's jaw. "But he's got a pulse and he's breathing. He's just fainted."

Relief swept through her. Sirens approaching grew louder by the second, splitting the air with their shrill warning. *Let the ambulance get here in time. God, please let them get Wesley to the hospital in time!* A few minutes later, the ambulance and the sheriff's vehicles turned her yard into a light show of pulsing red, amber and blue. The EMTs wheeled a gurney over. The two attendants started working on Wes even as they lifted him onto the gurney. They checked his vitals and slipped an oxygen mask over his face as they wheeled him to the waiting ambulance.

Carlie hurried after them. "I want to ride with him to the hospital."

"Sorry." The closest EMT shook his head; the two of them hoisted the gurney into the back, jumping in after it. "Can't let you, not in a trauma situation."

"Where are you taking him?" she asked as he began to close the doors.

"Trauma center at St. Mary's in Boonville." The double doors shut, and the ambulance took off with the siren slicing through the air again.

Carlie stood in the yard, her gaze fixed on the ambulance taking Wesley away. Her world crumbled around her. This was all her fault. She'd allowed him to get involved in her problems, and look where it led. Hot tears streaked down her cheeks. She lifted her hands to swipe them away. They were covered in blood. Wes's blood. Raw, aching grief tore her heart in two, and bile rose to the back of her throat.

"Hey." Ken laid his hands on her shoulders gently, turning her toward the house. "Let's get you cleaned up, and then I'll drive you to the hospital."

"I . . . I can't go back into that house. Not ever." She glanced at Jared's prone form. He hadn't moved. The sheriff and the marshals stood around him, talking and making notes. Two deputies were putting up yellow plastic tape all around the yard. One of them walked over and sprayed a white outline around Jared. The shaking started up again.

"OK." Ken patted her shoulder. "You wait here, and I'll see what I can put together." He took off at a trot toward the house.

She didn't want to be left alone, but she didn't want to get any closer to her ex's corpse, either. She was free, free from the terror for good, but at what cost? *Wesley.* The price of her freedom was far too great. She choked on a sob and wrapped her arms around her aching rib cage. The group conferring around her ex broke up, and Andrew and the sheriff walked over to her.

"How are you holding up?" Andrew asked.

She shook her head, swallowing convulsively.

"Maybe you should sit down." Paul took her by the elbow. "Is your car unlocked?"

"I . . . I want to get away from here." Crime scene tape surrounded her house and yard, a stark reminder of the terror the night held. "I have to get to the hospital. Ken offered to drive me there." Speaking of Ken, he strode toward her with the plastic dish tub she kept in her sink, a couple of dish towels draped over one shoulder and her purse slung over his wrist. "Can I leave?" she asked.

"Sure, but we'll need to talk to you soon. We need to get your statement," Andrew told her. "Tomorrow afternoon OK?"

She nodded. Ken set the dish tub on the hood of her car, along with her purse. He led her to the Ford, dipped a dish towel into the steaming water and began to wash the blood from her face. Kyle and Ryan joined them, and the three men, Wesley's friends, surrounded her. Their protectiveness and care penetrated the shock that held her in its grip. "Thank you for . . . for—"

"Everything's going to be OK, Carlie." Kyle put his arm around her shoulders. "Wes is tough. He'll survive."

"Do you know that for certain?" she asked. Kyle's mouth tightened, and he turned away. Her stomach dropped. "W-why did he do that?" Carlie searched the faces of the men around her. "Why did Wes expose himself to Jared like he did? He should've stayed hidden."

Ken raked his fingers through his dark brown hair. "I'm sure he wanted to distract Baumann from going under the car after you. *That* was a brilliant move, by the way." He patted her face dry with a towel. "I don't think he expected the guy to fire on him. A sane person would've dropped the weapon and put his hands up where we could see them. I guess Baumann wasn't sane."

"He was high on something," she choked out. "Definitely not sane."

"Doesn't surprise me, and I don't think Wes thought it through," Kyle remarked. "He acted on instinct. In case you haven't noticed, Wesley is pretty protective when it comes to you and your son."

Kenneth finished washing her face and took her shaking hands in his. He dipped them into the warm sudsy water and gently scrubbed the blood away. "Not much I can do about your clothes," he told her. "Do you want to stop by L&L and change on our way to Boonville?"

"No." She stared down at the blood smeared across the front of her jacket and the dirt and grass stains on her jeans. "I . . . I just want to get to the hospital as soon as possible."

"I called Noah and let him know what happened," Ryan told her. "They said to tell you they'll keep Tyler and the dog for as long as you need them to, and they also said not to worry. Tyler and Toby are having a great time."

Oh, God! I'm the worst mother ever. She bit her lip. Tyler hadn't even entered her mind since the moment she'd seen Wesley fall. "Th-thank you for calling them for me."

"Ken and I are going to stick with you tonight." Kyle squeezed her shoulders again and let her go. "Brenda is on her way to St. Mary's, and we'll meet her there."

"I'm going to stay with the marshals until things are buttoned up here, and then I'm heading home," Ryan said.

Carlie nodded again. She'd moved into the numbed-out stage of shock, with the same image circling around in her head over and over: Wesley, the man she loved with everything she had, falling to the ground, shot by her ex. Her fault. She hiccupped, and fresh tears flooded her eyes. She couldn't get a grip on her emotions.

Ken handed her a towel to dry her hands. He dumped the water and placed the tub on her front steps.

"Ready?" Kyle grabbed her purse from the hood and opened the front passenger door of her Escape. "I'll follow in my car. Give me your keys. Ken came with me tonight, so he'll drive your Escape."

She drew her car keys out of her jacket pocket and handed them over. Grimacing, she clutched her middle as she bent into the front seat of her car.

"You're hurt." Kyle placed her purse on the floor by her feet.

"Jared struck me with the butt of the rifle when I tried to get the pepper spray out of my purse." She settled gingerly into the seat. "I should've had it in my hand when I went inside."

"We're going to get you checked out while we're at the hospital." Kyle reached in and helped her get her seat belt buckled.

"I don't think anything is broken." She leaned back and sucked in a breath. "I've had broken ribs before, and I know what that feels like."

"Regardless of what you think, I'm taking you to the emergency room." Kyle patted her knee before handing Ken her keys.

"Wes is going to be fine," Ken said as he slid behind the wheel of her car. "Kyle was a corpsman and a med tech in the army. He'd know."

God, she hoped they were right. Nodding, she stared out the window at nothing.

"I'm sorry," Ken muttered. "Seems like I've done nothing but mess things up lately."

"What are you talking about?" Carlie turned away from the window, frowning.

"The stakeout was my idea, and so was the wager."

"First of all, the stakeout was a good idea. It sure beat waiting for something to happen. None of us could have known that Jared has been camping out in that house." She shuddered, remembering the terror of discovering him inside. "And . . . the wager?"

Ken's brown eyes met hers for a second before turning back to the road. "Wes didn't tell you?"

"No, but the sheriff mentioned something to me about a pool. When I asked Wes, he said he doesn't get involved in the nonsense that goes on at L&L."

"That's the truth. He doesn't get involved in that stuff. The pool was entirely my idea, and the whole thing was in poor taste. We were wagering on when the two of you . . . er . . ."

"Really, Ken?" She flashed him an incredulous look. "Seriously? Wes would never share that with anyone, and neither would I."

"I know. Immature, right?" He shrugged, his expression sheepish. "I apologized to Wes, but Carlie . . ."

"What?"

"When it comes to you, the guy is clueless. I just wanted to shake a few of his brain cells loose." He glanced at her again. "We all know he's crazy about you. Everybody can see the way that thickheaded Marine looks at you."

"How he looks at me?"

"Sure. Even before your ex showed up, I saw the look. You know, the few times I went to the diner with him for breakfast." Ken grunted. "He looks at you like you're the reason the Earth spins on its axis."

She'd seen the desire in Wes's eyes, but she'd also been the one to run into the concrete bunker he'd built around his heart. She ached, and not just from her bruised ribs. They'd both put up walls around themselves, not trusting, afraid of being let down again. Despite what she'd seen in the movies and read in romance novels, sometimes love just wasn't enough. She sighed.

"I witnessed what happened tonight. Wes stood up because your ex had that rifle in his hands, and it was clear the guy was going after you under the car. Wes did what he did to distract Baumann. He took a bullet for you, Carlie, and if that doesn't say—"

"I didn't *want* him to take a bullet for me." Her voice broke. "I wanted him to stay safely hidden in the brush." Ken's words, meant to reassure, only brought a fresh wave of heartache. "It's my fault he was shot. Not yours. I never should have let him get involved."

"Like you could've stopped him." A wry grin lit his face. He pulled into the parking lot at St. Mary's hospital and followed the signs to the main entrance.

She hadn't been any good for Wesley Holt, that's for sure. After everything she'd been and done, she didn't deserve him. *Oh, God.* What if his friends were wrong and Wes didn't make it? Her throat closed up, and she couldn't breathe. He had to make it. How could she bear it if he didn't?

Ken took her by the elbow and led her into the hospital lobby. She stood silently behind him as he asked for information from a silver-haired woman sitting behind the reception desk. The woman's fingers flew over the computer keyboard in front of her. "Mr. Holt is just leaving the trauma center and going into surgery now," she told them. She produced a printed map of the facilities and proceeded to show Ken where they would find the waiting room within the surgical center.

"Thank you," Ken said, taking the map from the receptionist. Once again he took Carlie's arm and led her through the hospital corridor. "I'll get you settled in the waiting room, and then I'll go rustle us up a couple of cups of decent coffee." He studied her face. "How does that sound?"

"I'd like that." She bit her lower lip. "Everyone at L&L has been so great. I . . . I don't know how to thank all of you. I don't even know why you've all rallied around us the way you have. Tyler and I are . . . *were* strangers to all of you a month ago."

"Noah Langford has a knack for bringing good people together at L&L, and the crew always rallies when one of us needs a hand. Wes is one of us. When he took you in, you became one of us. When he told us you needed our help, we were happy to step up. That's just the way it is in the military, and it's the way we do things at L&L." Ken's voice came out a little hoarse. "I have no idea how I managed to get a job there. I really don't."

"You're a good guy, Ken." She glanced at him, only to have him turn away. "Don't sell yourself short."

They reached a carpeted waiting room with couches, chairs and a counter area where a lone staff person wearing scrubs sat on a tall stool behind a computer. Carlie caught sight of Wes's sister Brenda, huddled over a clipboard, filling out paperwork with Wes's wallet open wide on her lap. An older couple sat beside her, a tall, lanky man with salt-and-pepper hair and a beard, and a petite woman with short blonde hair streaked with silver. The man had his arm around the woman, whose eyes were puffy and red rimmed. She clutched her purse and rested her head on his shoulder.

"Oh, God," Carlie whispered. "Wesley's parents." How could she face them? Her feet planted themselves on the threshold, refusing to budge. Brenda raised her eyes from the clipboard, catching sight of her before she could turn around and flee. Her eyes were also red rimmed and puffy.

Brenda's hands shook as she set the clipboard and wallet aside. She gestured toward the couch across from the one she and her parents occupied. "Oh, Carlie, are you OK? Kyle texted to let me know what happened."

"I'm all right." The older couple's eyes were on her now. She would have bolted for the nearest exit, except Ken still had her by the elbow. Her palms grew moist, and her poor heart took off at a gallop. Ken started her toward the couch. Carlie tried to swallow the lump of guilt clogging her throat.

Brenda rose from her place. "Carlie, Ken, this is my mom, Maggie, and my dad, John. Mom, Dad, this is Carlie Stewart and Ken Johnson."

Maggie's gaze went to the smear of blood on Carlie's jacket, and the woman's eyes filled. Carlie took it off, wadded it up so the blood wouldn't show and tossed it on the couch. "Mr. and Mrs. Holt, I'm so sorry about Wes, I—"

"I worried about that boy day and night for twenty years while he was in the Marines." Maggie shook her head, tears rolling down her cheeks. "I thought . . . I thought my worrying days were over now that he was home."

"Now, Maggie, he's going to be fine." John patted his wife's shoulder. "He's going to be just fine," he repeated, as if to convince himself. "It's nice to meet you two. Have a seat."

Another wave of recrimination knocked into her as Carlie sank down to the couch. She couldn't look Wes's mother in the eye.

"I'm going to make a coffee run." Ken gestured toward the exit. "Can I bring any of you a cup?"

"Sure," Brenda said. "Cream and two sugars for me. Mom, Dad?"

"Thank you, son. I'd love a cup. Black is fine, but my wife isn't a coffee drinker."

"Tea, Mrs. Holt?" Ken glanced at Wes's mom.

"Thank you; that would be nice. I like honey in my tea if they have it, otherwise plain is fine."

"Carlie?" Ken's hands were clenching and unclenching at his sides.

"Black with a couple of sugars, thanks." She reached for the wallet in her purse.

"I've got it." Ken strode out of the room before she could even get her wallet out, leaving her alone with Wes's family—and her all-consuming shame and blame. She didn't know where to look or what to say, and her mouth had turned into a spit-free zone.

"Wes had a bunch of scans and tests done in the trauma center. They gave him blood and made sure he was stabilized before they sent him to surgery," Brenda said, her voice quavering.

"Did they say . . . did the doctors give you any idea . . ." Carlie bit her lip. "How is he?"

"They didn't say." Brenda went back to the forms on her lap.

"We don't blame you for what happened, Ms. Stewart," Mr. Holt said, his voice hoarse. "We want you to know that right up front. Our son . . . well, he's always been . . ." He cleared his throat a couple of times. "Brenda told us about your . . . situation, and we're glad he stepped up to help you and your boy." He glanced at his wife. "Isn't that right, Maggie, honey?"

Mrs. Holt sniffed and nodded. "So . . . we hear you and your little boy are living with our son? Are the two of you—"

"Oh, I'm . . . we're friends." Heat flooded her face. "Wes offered to let us stay with him in his apartment until my ex could be apprehended, because he believed we'd be safer there. I'm staying in one of the extra bedrooms, and my son is in the other."

Brenda's brow rose slightly, and one side of her mouth quirked up for a second. Did she know? Was it obvious that she and Wes were sleeping together? "Wesley is incredible," Carlie stammered. "I'm sure you know how amazing he is. I want you to know how very thankful I am to . . . to have him in my life. My son absolutely idolizes him, and the two of them share such a bond," she babbled on. "Wes is great with Tyler. He's so patient and . . . and caring." The Holts sat up a little straighter at her praise.

"He's always been that way," Maggie said, her voice tinged with pride. "Wesley has always looked out for others, including his siblings. It'll be good to have him home for a while." She fidgeted with her purse. "Since he can't be on his own after the surgery, we'll bring him home to stay with us while he recovers."

"No!" The word escaped before she could stop herself. Mr. and Mrs. Holt stared in surprise at her outburst, and she noticed Mr. Holt's eyes were hazel, just like Wes's. Her heart flipped, and more heat rose to her face. "I mean . . . Wesley has done so much for me and Tyler. I want to repay his kindness. Tyler and I are already living in his apartment, and I have tons of vacation time saved up. I want to take care of him. Please,

Mr. and Mrs. Holt, let me do this for Wesley. I . . . I need to. I want to take care of him the way he's taken care of us."

His parents shared a look, as if discussing the matter. Mr. Holt nodded. "All right, young lady. I guess we ought to be on a first-name basis then, don't you? We'll be around if you need us. Wes has never been good at being the one who needs help. If he gets too ornery, you just give us a call, and we'll set him straight."

"I will. I promise." All the air left her lungs, and she slumped against the back of the couch. She didn't want to leave Wes, and she really didn't want to move back into the scene of the crime. That's all the house was to her now, a crime scene. Her lease was up in four more months, and she intended to talk her landlord into letting her out of it early. She'd start looking for a new place to live immediately, somewhere in town and not so isolated this time. Closer to work . . . nearer to Wesley.

Her chest tightened. She'd miss living with him, and so would Tyler. What would become of her relationship with Wes now that the danger had passed? Would the two of them go back to leading their separate lives? Being nothing more than friends with sex on the side would devastate her. She knew that now.

Kyle strode into the room, and Brenda got up and hurried to him, her eyes filling with tears. He wrapped his arms around his fiancée and held her tight, uttering soothing words and rocking her back and forth. "John, Maggie," he greeted Wes's parents. "Any word?"

"He's in surgery. That's all we know," Wes's dad said. "Now it's just a matter of waiting."

With his arm around Brenda's waist, Kyle moved her back to the couch. He picked up the clipboard, scanned it and asked, "Are you done with this, Bren?"

"I think so." Brenda sat back down.

"I'll take it to the desk, and then I need to get Carlie to the emergency room."

Carlie opened her mouth to protest, but Kyle shook his head, his expression stern. "I ran into Ken in the hall on his way to get coffee. Once he's back and you have your coffee, you and I are heading down-stairs to have your ribs X-rayed just to be sure."

Brenda's eyes filled with concern. "What happened, Carlie?"

She glanced at Wes's parents, and mortification sent heat rushing to her face. What would they think of her if they knew her history? They'd probably insist that Wesley recover with them.

"If you don't mind, you can tell us," Maggie urged. "We know some of the story. Brenda told us, and sometimes talking about things helps."

"All right." She took a minute to gather her wits, and she explained how her ex had injured her and how he'd tried to force her into taking him to Tyler. Finally, she described how she'd gotten free.

"Did you use something we learned in our self-dense class?" Brenda asked, her eyes wide.

She nodded, and a tiny flare of pride lit within her. "Once I got out his hold, I rolled under my car, so I'd be out of the way and whoever was closest would have a clean shot at him."

"How did Jared get inside the house?" Kyle perched on the edge of the couch beside Brenda. "None of us saw any signs of a break-in, and believe me, we looked."

"He didn't have to break in." She shared with them what Jared had told her about how he'd pried the broken door free. She raked her fingers through her hair. "I should've figured he'd do something like that."

"Our son broke down your door?" John's eyes narrowed.

"The day my ex showed up," Carlie told them. "Wes saved my life that day, and my son's." Memories of the past month played through her mind, especially the way Wes had raced through her house with his gun drawn.

Every tender moment they'd shared since that day flashed before her: their first kiss, the way he protected her and Ty, his quirky sense of humor when he turned playful . . . Oh, God, she'd never told him she loved him. Her eyes filled, and she stared at Kyle helplessly.

"OK." He rose. "Ken will be back soon. I'm going to take these forms to the nice lady behind the counter, and then we're heading to the emergency room."

She accepted the tissue Brenda handed her. Once Kyle returned, the two of them made their way to the emergency room, where she had to fill out forms of her own. Luckily, the waiting room was pretty much empty, and it didn't take long before she was examined, X-rayed and declared bruised, not broken. She walked back to the waiting room and found Kyle reading a magazine. "Told you," she said. "No broken ribs."

"Good. Now I don't have to worry anymore." He tossed the magazine back on the end table, rose and stretched. "Ready to head back to the surgical center?"

"Yes." She followed him to the elevator. "How much longer do you think it will be before we hear something about Wes?"

"It's hard to say." Kyle hit the Up button. "It depends on what kind of damage the bullet did to him. Judging by the entry and exit wounds, his spleen, splenic artery, a kidney or renal artery could've suffered a hit or a nick. Then there's the transverse and descending colon—possible damage to the lower ribs and diaphragmatic injury." He glanced at her. "Which would explain why he was having difficulty breathing."

"Oh. Are any of those things life threatening?" She studied his face. He wasn't giving anything away. "Brenda said Wesley was stabilized in the trauma center. That's a good sign, isn't it?"

"Hard to say. We're going to have to wait to hear from the surgeon."

Not at all what she wanted to hear. Needing distraction, she grasped at something else to talk about. "Ken said you were an emergency medical technician in the army. Is that why you decided to become a physician's assistant?"

The elevator door opened, and he gestured for her to exit first. "I do have a lot of experience, and being a PA makes sense. It's good money and the hours are decent."

"Did you think about medical school at all?"

"Nope. The time commitment for medical school is extremely intense. I'm thirty already. I want a family and a relatively normal life with time off for vacations." He guided her toward the surgical waiting room. "Being a PA is the perfect job for me."

A normal life, family and vacations sounded like heaven to her, and just as far out of her reach. Once again envy reared its ugly head, and she immediately tamped it down. "I'm so excited for you and Brenda."

"Thanks. Me, too." Kyle's attention shifted to Brenda as they walked into the waiting room. He sank down on the couch next to her and reached for her hand. "Any news?"

Wes's dad shook his head. "Nothing yet."

Kenny lifted a cardboard holder from the end table and held it out to Carlie. It held the last cup of coffee. Hers. She reached for the to-go cup. "Thanks." Taking a sip of the now tepid brew, she settled on the couch next to him.

"That's been sitting awhile. There's a microwave over there," Ken said, pointing to a table next to a vending machine in the corner. "Want me to warm it up for you?"

"No. It's fine." She took another swallow and set it on the table. Then she leaned back and closed her eyes. All the tension she'd been under had taken a toll, and exhaustion closed in. She must've dozed off, because hearing Wesley's name being called woke her.

The Holts were standing. Carlie looked around, but she didn't see a doctor.

"Are you here for Wesley Holt?" the nurse behind the counter asked. Carlie stood up with everyone else, her stomach lurching.

"Yes, ma'am," Wes's dad said with a nod.

"Mr. Holt is out of surgery, and he's being moved to his room now." She checked the computer and wrote something down on a sheet of paper. "This is his room number. The surgeon will meet you in the reception area to go over everything with you."

"Thank you." Kyle stepped forward and took the paper from her.

"Take the hall to your left and follow the signs," she told them.

All six of them filed out of the waiting room, and Carlie took up the rear. What if nonfamily members weren't allowed? Ken dropped back to walk beside her, and she shot him a grateful smile. She wasn't the only outsider.

They came to a busy hub staffed with nurses, with doors to rooms surrounding the circular counter like spokes in a bicycle wheel. A tall man in scrubs leaned against the counter with a chart in his hands. A surgical mask hung around his neck and paper slippers covered his shoes. "Holt family?" he asked, surveying the lot of them.

"Yes." John stepped forward. "I'm Wesley's father, and this is his mother." He put his arm around Maggie.

The surgeon held out his hand. "I'm Dr. Sunderman." He shook John's hand. "Follow me, and we'll go over everything." The doctor led them to yet another waiting room, and they huddled around him.

"Mr. Holt came through the surgery very well, and we expect him to make a full recovery," the surgeon said. "We had to repair damage to an artery and a tear to his spleen, his diaphragm and a section of his colon. We're keeping him until Friday morning. I'll have directions for his aftercare, and prescriptions for antibiotics and something for pain to send home with him. Who will be picking him up?" Dr. Sunderman looked around their huddle.

"I will." Carlie stepped forward, her heart leaping around inside her chest. Wes would make a full recovery.

Brenda moved to her side. "Here's my brother's wallet. His insurance card is behind his driver's license, along with the card for prescription medications." She handed the worn brown leather to her, and then she fished around in her purse. "Here's his phone, keys and watch, too. I'm glad you're going to take care of him, Carlie."

Carlie took Wes's things, feeling like she'd been handed the keys to the kingdom or something. "I'll take good care of him."

"We know you will," John said.

"Mr. Holt is still under the anesthesia, but if you'd like to stop into his room to see him, that would fine." Dr. Sunderman gestured toward the door. "His vitals are good, and he's resting well. If you have any questions, you can call the number at the top of this sheet." He took a paper from the clipboard he held. "His room is the second door on the right. I'll leave you now. I know you're anxious to go see him."

Once the surgeon left, Carlie let out a huge sigh, and she wasn't the only one. "He's going to be fine."

"We should go check on him," Brenda said. "Then I suggest we all go home and get some rest. It's midnight, and I know some of us have to work tomorrow."

"We'll stay for a while. The rest of you go on home." Wes's dad and mom led the way to their son's room, which was the size of a large closet—there was hardly enough space to accommodate the six of them crowding in together. Wes was hooked up to monitors and intravenous fluids. Her heart wrenched at the sight of her big, strong Marine so still, pale and incapacitated.

"Oh, he's not going to take this well at *all*." Ken frowned, looking down at the side of the bed.

"Being helpless, you mean?" Carlie asked, puzzled.

"Hell, no. I'm talking about the Foley catheter stuck up his you-know-what." Ken shuddered. "Worst part of the whole ordeal, and I speak from experience."

Carlie giggled, a nervous reaction, no doubt, mixed with the heady knowledge that Wesley would be OK. Then Brenda let out a snort like she was trying hard not to laugh, and soon everyone was smiling. All the anxiety and fear dissipated. She swiped at her eyes, but this time her tears were tears of relief. Friday morning she'd bring him home, and she'd be the one to take care of him for a change.

🐏 🐏 🐏

Carlie yawned as she stuffed clean clothes and Tyler's toothpaste and toothbrush into a plastic shopping bag. How she was going to make it through her day at the diner on four hours of sleep was beyond her, but first she had to head out to the Langfords' and get her son off to school. She grabbed Ty's backpack, her jacket, and purse and hurried downstairs.

Miguel met her at the bottom of the stairs. David and TreVonne looked up from their work. "How're you holding up?" Miguel scrutinized her. "Kenny texted this morning with the news."

"Wesley is going to be fine," she mumbled. "He came through the surgery well, and he'll be home on Friday."

"We know all that." Miguel's eyes zeroed in on her. "How are *you* holding up, Carlie?"

"I don't know." It had to be exhaustion and the aftermath of everything that had happened, but the need to purge had her in its grip. "Last night . . ." Her jaw clenched for a second. "Last night I was held at gunpoint by my ex, who swore he would put a bullet in my head and dump my body in a ditch if I didn't go along with his plan to take Tyler. Then I saw Wesley fall to the ground after my ex shot him."

She gripped the plastic bag holding her son's things with both hands. "My yard is now wrapped in yellow crime-scene tape, with a white outline of Jared Baumann's body right where he dropped. Can I get back to you on that question? I . . . I have to get these clean clothes to my son. He spent the night at the Langfords', and I need to make sure he gets off to school in clean clothes." She shook her head. "I don't know what to tell Tyler about . . . about Wes and . . ."

Miguel shared a look with the other two men. "You'll let Noah know I left a little early to look after Carlie?"

"Course we will." TreVonne nodded. "Go. We'll put your tools away."

"Come on." Miguel crossed the room and grabbed his jacket. "I'll take you to the Langfords'. I don't think you should be driving today."

"I appreciate the help." She blinked against the sting in her eyes. "I don't think anyone is safe with me on the road right now. Only got a few hours of sleep last night." She followed him out the back door, and for once, she didn't check the shadows for a threat. Miguel opened the passenger side of his car for her, and she slid into the leather seat. "Thanks, Miguel," she said as he started the car down the alley.

"No problem. You need anything, you just let me and the guys know. Wesley . . . well, he's important to us. You know?"

"I do know. He's important to me and Tyler, too." She sighed, making a mental list of everything she had to do to get through today.

"Me and the guys are going to head out to Boonville to visit Wes this morning."

"He'll like that." She smiled. "Tell him I'll be by later, after I meet with the marshals." Giving her statement would finally give her closure where Jared Baumann was concerned. It hadn't completely sunk in yet. No more worrying about when or where he'd show up to wreck her life anymore. His reign of terror was over. Still, the cloud casting a shadow over her life in Perfect lingered, and the only way to free herself was to expose her past to the light of day. Only then could she move forward, free of shadowy secrets.

🐏 🐏 🐏

Carlie glanced at Tyler, who was sitting next to the babysitter on Wes's couch. Brenda and Cory stood by the door, waiting for her. "We're going to go visit Wes at the hospital. I'll be home in a few hours, Ty. You be on your best behavior for Allison, all right?" Ty nodded, not taking his eyes from the pretty teen. "You have my number, Allison. Call if you need anything. Make sure Tyler brushes his teeth before he goes to bed."

"I will, Ms. Stewart." Allison smiled. "Bedtime at eight." She lifted the sheet of paper with the instructions Carlie had written for her. "Got it."

Satisfied, Carlie walked out of the apartment with her friends. "I think my son has his first crush."

Cory laughed. "I think you're right."

Ceejay and Paige were parked out front in the Langfords' van. She and the other two women climbed into the back. Ceejay pulled onto the road toward Boonville. Carlie sucked in a fortifying breath. The women in the van had come to mean a lot to her. She had to trust that they'd accept her despite the things she'd done when she was a teen, and if they didn't . . . well, then they weren't the friends she'd thought they were. "I asked all of you to join me tonight because there's something I need to talk to you about."

"You're in love with my brother?" Brenda asked, grinning at her.

"No . . . well, yes, but that's not what I wanted to tell you."

"Ha!" Brenda laughed. "Knew it."

"We all know she's in love, Bren." Cory looked askance at her friend. "Let the woman speak."

Carlie's gut clenched. So they knew she was in love. That didn't mean Wes would ever allow himself to feel the same for her. "OK. Here goes. There are things I want you to know about my past, and it's not pretty." It took her the entire drive to St. Mary's to tell her story, and she didn't leave any of the ugliness out.

Ceejay found a parking space, pulled the van into it and shut off the engine. Carlie held her breath, waiting for a reaction. Silence filled the van, and her heart sank.

"You didn't have to tell us, but I'm glad you did, Carlie." Cory patted her hand. "For your sake."

"Wow," Brenda said. "I think you ought to write a book about your experiences."

"You should," Cory added. "Just think of the women you could help by sharing your experiences. You are an inspiration."

"So are you." Carlie's eyes widened. Cory had been sexually assaulted by her staff sergeant, and the army had given her a dishonorable discharge rather than deal with the issue. "You fought the entire US Army and won. All I did was—"

"You're both amazing, strong, intelligent women." Ceejay unbuckled her seat belt. "Maybe the two of you should write a book together."

Paige twisted around to grin at both of them. "I'm proud to know you both. In fact, I'm proud to count all of you as my friends."

"Aw, shucks." Brenda sniffed dramatically. "We're having a bonding moment here, aren't we?"

Laughter filled the van, and they all got out. Carlie floated to the hospital entrance, her heart and soul unburdened and free. No more running. She'd found her permanent place. She and Tyler would put down roots and build a life in Perfect. She had friends. Glancing at the women around her, her chest swelled. Good friends who accepted her for who she was. She had a job she loved, and a community where she belonged. And when the situation arose, she'd be there for her friends the way they'd been there for her.

Now, if only she could find a way through the labyrinth of Wesley Holt's PTSD and trust issues. If only she could find the way to unlock his heart. . . . Her breath caught and her insides fluttered. He'd told her he wasn't partner material, that he no longer had it in him to give his love. He was wrong, but could she convince him?

They reached Wes's room, and she heard the hospital TV flipping from channel to channel. Brenda led the way, and she was next as they all entered the tiny room.

Wes frowned. "It's been like Grand Central station all day in this closet they call a room."

Brenda kissed his forehead and fluffed his pillow. "A little surly, are we?"

"A lot restless." Wes rearranged the blankets, covering the plastic bag of urine hanging from the rails of the bed. "I'm ready to go home, and the doctors won't let me."

"Aw, poor baby." Cory grinned.

"Your color is much better than it was yesterday." Carlie wanted to throw her arms around him, kiss him all better, like she did with Tyler when he had a scraped knee or elbow. She moved to his side. "Surly or not, it's good to see you alive and breathing."

His gaze sought hers and held. "It's good to be alive and breathing." One side of his mouth turned up. "How did it go with the marshals today?"

"Fine. They took my statement at the diner before I picked Tyler up from school."

Wes laid his head back on his pillow. "I hear they stopped by the hospital, but I was out. Don't know when they'll be back." The stand holding plastic bags of fluid next to him made a whirring sound, probably sending a dose of painkiller into his vein.

Cory stood at the end of the bed. "Does it hurt much?"

"Only when I'm awake." Wes nodded toward the bags hanging from the stand. "I'm on some pretty powerful painkillers." He yawned. "Can't wait to get out of here. I have twenty staples in my side. Damned uncomfortable." He peered at Carlie, his eyelids drooping. "They tell me to rest, but then they won't let me. Every four hours some sadistic soul in scrubs comes in and starts poking, prodding and sticking me with needles."

"Friday." Carlie straightened his blankets. "I'm coming to pick you up Friday morning."

"Not soon enough," he groused. "I'm tired. Drugged. Not good company." His eyes drifted shut.

She took the remote control from his hand and set it on the table next to his bed. Carlie brushed her lips across his forehead and straightened. "What he means is . . . thank you all for coming to visit." She smiled, gazing down at her wounded Marine.

"He's going to be a bear to take care of once he's home. Whiny, churlish and demanding." Brenda snorted. "You are a brave woman, Carlie Stewart, and I don't envy you."

"I can handle it." In fact, she couldn't wait. He'd nurtured and protected her for more than a month. Hell, he'd taken a bullet for her. Now it was her turn to take care of him. Wesley would have to learn to trust and rely on her for a change.

CHAPTER THIRTEEN

THE HOSPITAL ORDERLY SET A covered bowl and yet another plastic container of green Jell-O on the wheeled tray, raised the back half of Wes's bed and positioned the tray in front of him.

"How the hell is my body supposed to heal when all you people give me to eat is clear liquids and Jell-O?" Wesley grumbled. "I'm starving to death here."

The orderly pointed to the small whiteboard hanging on the wall. "Says clear liquids only. We can't bring you anything else until those orders are changed by your doctor."

He wanted to hurl the bowl out the window, but then he'd have nothing at all—not to mention the act would be childish. But dammit, he hurt all over, hated the invasive needles and tubes with a passion, and he was hungry. Really hungry. If doctors truly wanted their patients to heal, they'd let them eat, and they would set them free to sleep in their own homes in their own beds. He heaved a loud, unhappy breath.

A nurse in purple scrubs, carrying a tray with a tiny paper cup and a syringe, strolled in just as the orderly left. She set the tray on the end table, took the dry-erase marker from the ledge of the whiteboard and erased the day nurse's name. Then she wrote hers in its place. "My name is Sarah, and I'll be your night nurse." She moved his supper tray to the side and wheeled the blood pressure machine closer.

He nodded as she came at him with the blood pressure cuff. What was there to say? *Nice to meet you? I so appreciate the constant torture and the lack of peace you'll be providing for the next ten hours?*

"Have you passed gas or had a bowel movement, Mr. Holt?" she asked.

"Yes to the gas. No to the other." His face heated. The ridiculous question probably caused his blood pressure to spike. He glanced at the digital numbers displayed on the machine's screen to see if his theory proved true. "When can I get this needle out of the back of my hand and all these tubes out?"

"When your doctor gives the order. Dr. Sunderman or his PA will be by during rounds tomorrow morning. You can ask them then." His blood pressure checked and the cuff removed, she picked up the syringe filled with whatever she meant to stick into him.

His gut clenched. "What is that?"

"It's heparin to prevent blood clots while you're bedridden." Nurse Sarah pulled his blankets down—without permission—and his hospital gown up to reveal his abdomen, which already held several bruises from previous needle pokes. She pinched his skin and stuck him. "Once you're up and walking around, we can stop giving it to you if you'd like."

He grimaced at the burning sting. "I'll get up now if it means I don't have to have the belly shots anymore. I swear they're worse than the gunshot wound, even though the bullet went clear through me."

She smiled and handed him an orange capsule and a glass of water. "I'll just check your dressing, and then I'll leave you to your supper."

He downed the pill, deciding against asking what it might be for. "This is not supper." He gestured toward the tray. "Broth and Jell-O are cruel and unusual punishment. When can I have something real to eat, and what do I have to do to get a real cup of coffee around here?"

"You've had an invasive surgery, plus you've been flat on your back for twenty-four hours. Your digestive system can't handle solids for a while. You can ask your doctor about your diet tomorrow." She spared him a sympathetic glance. "Would you like me to see if you can have some ice cream?"

"Yes, please." He leaned his head back on the pillow and closed his eyes. His churlish tirade had worn him out. Being so weak didn't sit well. Not at all well, and he didn't care much for being in pain, either.

"In the meantime, try to get the broth and the Jell-O down. I'll have an orderly come by later to help you stand up and walk around for a bit."

"Yes, ma'am. Thank you. I apologize for being such a pain. Maybe I'll manage to pass gas or poop while I'm up and around."

"Let's hope so." Nurse Sarah smiled again as she checked his incision, covered him back up and wheeled his poor excuse for a meal back over his lap. "If you need anything, just press the button." She made sure the cord with the call button at the end was wrapped around the guardrail of his bed and within reach, and then she left him. The door swung closed after her. It took a tremendous amount of energy to position himself so he could drink the broth, and he was sweaty and shaking from the effort. Just as he reached for the bowl, someone knocked on his door.

"Come in," Wes called, hoping against hope Carlie had returned. He knew better. It had only been a couple of hours or so since he'd fallen asleep right in the middle of her visit. He hadn't even gotten a kiss, what with his sister and the other women crowding his space. He wanted Carlie's kisses and her arms around him, dammit.

Bruce Murphy and Andrew Pelletier strode in. "Hey, Wesley." Bruce reached out and shook his hand. "How're you feeling?"

"Like I was shot with a semiautomatic hunting rifle," Wes quipped, shaking his hand, then Andrew's. "I suppose you two need my statement."

"Yep." Andrew pulled the single chair up to the bed and took out a laptop from the briefcase he carried. Bruce settled himself on the deep windowsill.

"After I went down, I was pretty much out of it. I didn't ask Carlie, didn't want to upset her, but what about Baumann?" Wes asked.

"He's dead." Andrew opened the laptop.

"Your shot or Kenneth's?"

"Mine."

"Good. You'd have a tough time explaining why a civilian was involved." Wes grinned. "Makes the paperwork so much easier."

"Indeed it does, Major Holt. Indeed it does." Andrew spared him a brief look, his fingers tapping away at the keyboard. "I guess having been a commander in the military, you'd know a bit about paperwork."

For the next twenty minutes, the two marshals grilled him with questions about what happened that night. Then they had him sign a few forms before packing everything back into the briefcase.

"We have one final question for you." Bruce came to stand by his bed.

"What's that?" Exhaustion tugged Wes back to the edge of drug-induced slumber.

Bruce stared down at him, his expression guarded. "We need to know if you intend to sue."

That woke him up. "Sue?" He blinked.

"You were caught in the middle of a crime scene, which resulted in an injury," Andrew added. "Of course, we didn't authorize your presence there, but . . ."

"Ahh." Wesley nodded. "No. I definitely do not intend to sue. You two can relax."

"Didn't think you would." Andrew grinned. "We managed to keep your presence there out of the news. As far as the associated press knows, only US Marshals and the Warrick County sheriff's department were involved in the incident leading to fugitive Baumann's death. Have you ever considered a career as a US Marshal? We're always looking for good agents, and with your military background, you'd be a shoo-in."

Wes chuckled and then grimaced. Laughing hurt. "No, but thanks. I like my job at L&L, and I like living in Perfect. I'm staying right where I am." *With Carlie and Tyler.* The thought no longer caused him any trepidation. Nothing like getting shot to put things into perspective. Now all he had to do was convince Carlie he wasn't like the men in her past. He wouldn't let her or Tyler down.

🐏 🐏 🐏

Wes walked around the central hub of the hospital floor, wheeling along the stupid stand holding the bag of fluid dripping into his veins. At least he'd managed to get rid of the catheter and put an end to the belly shots. It was only Thursday. How was he going to make it to Friday without going bat-guano crazy in this place?

He glanced at the wall clock behind the counter. Almost time for rounds, and today he hoped to convince Dr. Sunderman or his PA to cut him loose early.

"Good morning, Mr. Holt," one of the nurses behind the counter called. "It's good to see you up and about."

"Morning. Yeah, it's good to be out of that bed for a while." He pulled the edges of his flimsy hospital gown together in front. He wore two. One to cover his bare backside and the other to cover his front. Still, the fabric was . . . thin. The elevator door beyond the nurse's station opened, and Noah, Kyle and Ryan poured out.

"Hey, Wes." Kyle lifted a cardboard carrier filled with covered cups. "We brought real coffee."

Wes smiled his first genuine smile in two days. "Thank God. You have no idea how much I've been craving a decent cup of coffee. All they serve here is hot water with just enough grounds to give it color . . . I think it's called wa-fee." He glanced toward the nurses' station. A couple of them smiled, which was a good thing, because he was pretty sure he already had a reputation for being a whiner.

"I've walked around the hall enough for now." He led them to his room, arranged the tube and the wheeled stand and tried to get comfortable on the hospital bed. Major fail. Hospitals were not conducive to comfort.

Kyle passed the coffees around. "Before I forget, we have your handgun. You dropped it on the ground Tuesday night, and I picked it up. It's locked away in Noah's office for now."

"Good. Thanks, Kyle. I wondered what happened to my Beretta." Wes took his coffee from the tray, held it up and took a sip, savoring the strong, rich brew. "Mmm, that's good. Aren't you guys supposed to be working?"

"We're on a coffee break." Noah lifted his cup. "Figured you could use a little diversion. Ryan and I know what being in the hospital is like. Without distractions, it'll drive you nuts."

Noah had lost his leg when a suicide bomber drove his truck into their convoy in Iraq, and Ryan had been hurt in the same bombing. Wes's wound seemed insignificant when compared to what the two of them had gone through. Both had suffered burns along with their other injuries. "No doubt you do."

"We brought you a couple of magazines we thought you might like." Ryan set a plastic bag on the rolling tray. "So, how're you feeling?"

"Weak and dizzy mostly, but that's because they won't give me any real food." Wes sucked down another swallow of the strong brew, savoring the taste. "How's my crew doing without me?"

"Fine. Miguel is keeping the guys in line."

"Can't wait to get back to work," he muttered. "Back to my own bed . . . Say, will you guys stick around until Dr. Sunderman stops by on his rounds and help me talk him into letting me out today?"

"I don't think so, Wes. Don't want to cause a setback in your recovery." Noah chuckled and shook his head. "Besides, everything is already arranged for tomorrow morning. Carlie starts her vacation then, although I don't see taking care of a wounded Marine as any kind of vacation."

At the mention of Carlie's name, a shiver of anticipation shot through him. Images of sponge baths leading to more than just getting clean danced through his mind. A stupid grin covered his face. "I'll have to make it up to her, take her on a real vacation soon. Maybe a romantic weekend away."

"Giving in, are we?" Ryan shot him a smug look.

Wes shrugged and took another swig of the delicious coffee. "It was inevitable and resistance is futile."

"Not to mention surrendering has its perks." Noah laughed.

"Take my advice, and plan something special for the moment you tell her how you feel," Kyle said. "Women love to be romanced. You might want to wait until you're well enough to take her out."

Wes nodded. A shard of doubt wedged itself into his brain. What if Carlie didn't feel the same, or she didn't want the same things he did? Sure, they were sleeping together, but she hadn't said anything about her feelings for him. In fact, she'd said more than once she didn't think she could trust another man with her heart.

Didn't matter.

If it was the last thing he ever did, he'd convince her he was a safe bet. He'd never let her down. Resolve and a feeling of certainty filled him. He had a goal in his sights, and he intended to reach for the dream he'd thought long dead.

Every two minutes Wes checked the clock and fought the urge to climb the hospital walls or pace the confines of the tiny room. Dr.

Sunderman's PA was due to arrive any minute with discharge papers, and Carlie would be here to take him home.

A light rap on his door sent his pulse racing. "Come in." Carlie swept in, and her presence and scent filled the small room. His system flooded with a host of emotions, elation being topmost.

"Ready to go home?" she asked, setting a canvas tote on the narrow bed.

"You'd better believe it."

"I'll help you get dressed."

"Uh . . . no. I think I can manage." How helpless did she think he was? He pushed himself to standing, only suffering a little light-headedness and a few sharp twinges of pain. "If you'd just take the clothes out of the bag and set them in the bathroom for me."

Carlie opened the bag and pulled out a pair of boxers and a T-shirt. "Modest all of a sudden?"

"Somebody might walk in," he muttered.

"Like your doctor or nurse?" she asked, her expression incredulous. "Because they haven't already seen everything? How easy is it for you to bend with all those staples in your side?"

"All right, all right." He flashed her a look of resignation. "Point taken. Yes, please, Nurse Carlie, help me get dressed."

"I'd be glad to." Boxers and a T-shirt in hand, she came to him. "Let's get the boxers on while you're still in the gown." She crouched down and held the elastic waistband open. "Lift one foot at a time, and I'll slide these on for you."

Wes had to brace himself with a hand on the wall, and a rush of embarrassment flooded through him. How was he supposed to tell Carlie he loved her when he couldn't even put on his own underwear? "I feel like I'm eighty," he groused, more heat filling his face as she tugged his boxers up over his hips and settled them around his waist.

She patted his cheek. "You'll be back to your old self before you know it."

"I hope so." Kyle was right. He needed to wait until he could do for himself before making a grand declaration to her. *I love you. Could you please help me get off the toilet? I'm feeling a little dizzy.* Nope. That wouldn't do at all. Talk about the antithesis to romance.

"Lose the hospital gown," Carlie ordered, rolling the hem of the T-shirt.

He reached back, undid the ties and took off the gown, tossing it on the chair. "I can manage shirts. It's pants, socks and shoes that are challenging." He took the T-shirt from her.

She gasped. "Oh, Wes." She covered her mouth and stared at the line of staples holding him together. "I . . . I'm so sorry. Actually seeing your incision . . . it's different than just knowing you were shot and had surgery."

He glanced down. The edges of the skin held together with metal staples were still an angry red, and where the bullet had entered, a greenish-purple stain spread around from his front to his back. His injury was swollen, puckered and ugly. "You didn't shoot me. Whatever it is you have running around in your head, let it go. You didn't cause Baumann to pull the trigger, and you didn't force me to take part in the stakeout. We did what we had to do, and now it's over." Wes put the shirt on and tugged it down to cover his side.

"It's just that . . ." She lifted tear-filled eyes to his. "I . . . I can't bear seeing you hurt."

He drew her close, held her in his arms and inhaled her sweet essence. She wrapped her arms lightly around him, and they just stood there. He hadn't had the chance to do that Tuesday night after he'd been shot, and it was about time he got to savor the comfort of having her in his arms. "I'm so proud of you, woman. What you did, the way you kept your cool and timed your escape . . . pure genius." He kissed her forehead. "You were amazing."

"And you were an idiot." She pressed her hands against his chest and her pretty blue eyes roamed over his face. "Why didn't you stay hidden, Wes? The marshal had a clear shot. You didn't have to—"

A brisk knock on the door interrupted any reply he might have made. Dr. Sunderman's PA, Richard, strode into the tiny room in his usual efficient, businesslike manner. "Ah." He swept his gaze over the two of them still embracing. "Feeling better, I see." A grin flickered to life, eradicating his usual professional mien, and disappeared just as quickly. He held a folder and a clipboard in his hand. "I have some discharge papers for you to sign, and we need to go over your aftercare instructions."

Richard glanced at Carlie. "Are you his caregiver?"

Carlie nodded and took the folder from him.

"Soft food only for the next two weeks. Anything that can be thrown into a blender or a food processor is fine." He scrutinized Wesley. "Understand?"

"Yep. Soft food. Two weeks." Could a nice, medium-rare rib eye steak be pureed, because he craved red meat something fierce. Probably because they'd been starving him at the hospital.

"Make an appointment for about ten days from today to have the staples removed. There's a card in the folder with the number and location of the clinic where Dr. Sunderman and I see patients. You'll also find a prescription for pain meds and another for antibiotics there. Take all of the antibiotics. While you're at the pharmacy, pick up some stool softeners and a mild laxative. Constipation is a common problem following surgery." He glanced at him. "That reminds me. Have you—"

"Yes. Thank you for asking. I have pooped." He would not miss everyone's preoccupation with the movement, or lack thereof, of his bowels.

Another grin flickered across Richard's face. "Keep the area of your incision clean and dry. Showers only, no baths, hot tubs or swimming pools until you're completely healed." He handed him the clipboard and a pen. "All the instructions for aftercare are in the folder, should you forget. If you notice any sign of infection or unusual pain, contact us immediately. Read these forms, then sign, and you're free to go."

Wes quickly scanned the forms, signed where he had to, and gave the clipboard and pen back to the PA. "Thank you."

"You're welcome. Wait here for an orderly with a wheelchair to take you downstairs."

Richard nodded and left.

Carlie reached into the tote bag. "Sweatpants next."

Wes let her help him get dressed, and then he eased himself down to sit on the bed to wait for the orderly with the wheelchair. "You're on vacation?"

Carlie nodded, a small smile lighting her features. "After everything you've done for me and Tyler, I'm glad I have the chance to repay the favor. I took two weeks off to take care of you. It's the least I can do since—"

"Let's get something straight between us right now," he said, his voice gruff. "You and I"—he ran his hand over the back of his neck—"we both have a tendency to take on blame where we don't need to. I believe it's my fault you walked into that house without checking it first for your ex, and you think it's your fault I was shot." He shook his head. "We're not going to do that anymore, Carlie."

"We aren't?" Her eyes widened and grew bright.

Wes reached for her hands and drew her to stand between his knees. "No, we are not. The fault lies with Baumann. Period. From this day forward, we're going to let it go." He lifted her hands and kissed one palm and then the other. "Deal?"

She nodded, put her arms around his neck and held him against her chest. God, he'd wanted to feel her arms around him since the moment he'd arrived at the hospital. Home. She was home to him.

"Knock, knock," the orderly called from the doorway. "Got a wheelchair with your name on it. You about ready to bust loose?" He left the chair in the hall and came in to scan the bar code on Wes's wristband.

"Hell, yes."

"I'll let you wheel him to the main entrance." Carlie pulled a jacket he didn't recognize from the tote bag and helped him into it. Then she gathered her things. "I'm going to go get my car and pull it up to the main entrance. I'll pick you up there." She leaned down, kissed him and left.

What seemed like an eternity later, Wes was in the front passenger seat of Carlie's Ford and heading home. "Whose jacket am I wearing?" He ran his hand over the navy-blue outer shell.

"Yours." Carlie glanced at him. "I picked that up to replace the one that . . ." She bit her lip. "The marshals took your old jacket as evidence, and besides, it was pretty much ruined."

"Ah. Thanks. I like this one." He glanced at her, studying her profile. "I miss Tyler. Can't wait to see him. What did you tell him?"

"Only that you were hurt in an accident." She sighed. "I don't really know how to deal with telling him his biological father shot you and that Jared is . . . I have an appointment set up with a child therapist. I don't want to tell him what really happened without providing him with professional support. He's already been through so much."

Wes reached for her hand. "You're a good mom, Carlie. The best." Then he closed his eyes and rested.

"We're here, Wes," Carlie said, nudging him while unfastening his seat belt.

"Mmm, good." He stretched. "So glad to be home." Carlie came around and helped him out of his seat. He put his arm around her shoulders to steady himself. "I think I'm ready for a long nap. It's the painkillers. They knock me out."

They entered through the loading dock doors to find all the staff gathered. A handmade banner that said **WELCOME HOME, WESLEY!** hung over his workstation. His eyes stung. "Man, it's good to be back."

"Oh, Bunny," Cory cried before giving him a hug. "We're all so glad to see you."

A round of greetings, handshakes and pats on the back sapped the last bit of energy out of him. He needed to get off his feet. "Thanks for the warm welcome, but I think I need to get upstairs and lie down." He wiped the sweat from his face.

Kyle came to his side and propped him up, and Ted opened the freight elevator. Carlie got on last and moved to his other side. With his friend's help, Wes shuffled into the small space.

The elevator jerked into motion and started the ascent to the third floor. "Being injured bites." He leaned against the padded wall, hoping he wouldn't pass out before making it to his bed.

"I hear you," Kyle said. "Carlie, I'll help you get Wes situated, and if you need any help, just text me. I'll be right downstairs."

"I will, thanks."

They reached the third floor, and Kyle opened the metal gate. Wes pushed himself off the wall. The scent of pine or spruce wafted over him in the hallway. A Christmas wreath hung on the door. Nice. Carlie unlocked the door to the living room and swung it open. Kyle once again offered his support. "Wow," Wes said, surveying his apartment.

A Christmas tree, decorated with a dazzling array of colorful ornaments, had been set up in the dining room, with a red-and-green velvet patchwork tree skirt spread out underneath. The buffet held a row of glass candleholders with winter scenes etched on the outside and greenery decorating the base. A number of holiday figurines had been placed on end tables and the bookshelves. "Looks like the Christmas elves have been busy."

"I hope it's OK." Carlie took his jacket and opened the closet door. "Do you like it? I have a six-year-old, and—"

"I love it, Carlie." His throat closed up. "Smells good in here, like sugar cookies and evergreens. Smells like Christmas." All the fantasies and dreams he'd had for a loving wife and children of his own washed through him, weakening his knees even more. His apartment had always been nothing more than a place to live, but Carlie and Tyler had transformed the place, turning it into a cozy home. He didn't want to lose that warmth or the sense of family. Not now. Not ever.

He couldn't look at Carlie for fear he couldn't hide the intensity of his roiling emotions. Blinking against the sting in his eyes, he kept his gaze fixed upon his surroundings.

"Tyler and I made cookies. We figured you'd have a lot of visitors now that you're home, and we wanted something to offer your guests."

All he could manage was a nod in response.

"A few of the guys and I went out to Carlie's old place and helped her bring more of her stuff here, including the Christmas decorations." Kyle started him forward. "Do you want to be out here on the couch or in your bedroom?"

"Here on the couch would be good." Wes looked around the room at all the festive decorations, and a surge of hope filled him. Maybe his dreams weren't dead after all. "I'll have access to the TV and books."

By the time Kyle and Carlie helped him get comfortable on the couch, his eyes were drooping. Weariness mixed with utter contentment swept him away. Carlie covered him with a blanket and kissed his forehead before he drifted off to sleep. He was a happy man, and if being shot was what got him to this place, then he'd gladly do it all over again.

Noise in the hallway woke Wes—Tyler's chatter and multiple sets of footsteps. He pushed himself up, anticipation revving his pulse. Amazing how much he'd missed his little buddy. The apartment door opened, and Tyler ran in, followed by Carlie, Brenda and Wes's parents. His mom held a pan of something, and he caught the scent of her famous lasagna. Brenda held a covered plastic bowl with a foil-wrapped loaf of garlic bread on top. His mouth watered. Real food at last.

"Look who I ran into downstairs." Carlie grinned.

"Hey, good to see all of you, and that lasagna smells wonderful." Wes kept his gaze on Tyler, and his eyes stung. Had to be because of his current weakened state.

The women headed for the kitchen, and Tyler bounced over to him. "John says he's your daddy."

"That's right. He is." Wes smiled at his father. "Have a seat, Dad."

"How you feeling?" His father took a seat.

"Better now that I'm home, and I have my little buddy here to cheer me up." He ran his hand over Tyler's buzz cut.

Tyler put his hands on Wes's knees and stared at him. "Mommy said you got hurt in a accident."

Wes grinned and blinked at the sting in his eyes. "That's right, and the doctors stapled me back together."

"They *stapled* you?" Tyler giggled. "My teacher has a stapler on her desk, but she won't let us use it by ourselves. Can I see?"

"Sure." Rex came into the room, stretched and yawned. Once the old dog had figured out he was free to sleep on Ty's bed, he spent most of his time there. He ambled over to nudge Wes's hand in greeting. It was almost too much, and he ached from the fullness of his life, seeing everything through a new light. Carlie and Tyler, his family . . . he truly was a wealthy man. He lifted his T-shirt, revealing the staples.

"Like Frankenstein," his dad said, chuckling.

"Cool." Tyler's eyes went as wide as saucers.

Brenda walked back into the living room. "Kyle will be up once his shift is over, and we're all staying for supper. Come on, Tyler. You and I need to take Rex outside."

"OK, and then I get to feed him. It's my job," Tyler announced. He followed Brenda toward the kitchen, where Rex's leash hung beside the door.

Wes sighed, basking in the good feelings of being surrounded by people he loved.

"Great kid," his dad said.

Wes nodded. "And smart as a whip, too."

"Good woman."

Glancing at his dad, he nodded again. "Absolutely."

"We like Carlie. You serious about her?"

He had to swallow the sudden lump in his throat before he could answer. "Yes. Very."

His dad reached over and placed his hand on Wes's shoulder, giving him a squeeze. "That's good, Wes." His voice hitched. "Your mother and I want to see you happy."

All he could manage was another nod. Laughter drifted from the kitchen, followed by the high buzzing hum of the blender turning his meal into baby food. "Sounds like Carlie and Mom are getting along well."

"I'm sure Maggie is telling Carlie about some of your exploits as a youngster." He snorted.

"Dad, do you still get a jolt to the heart when you see Mom, or did that stop after you two got used to each other and settled down?" The sensation disappeared pretty quickly with his ex, and their relationship had become more habit than love story. He and Tina had been so young when they married. They'd never talked about what each of them wanted out of the deal, either. He suspected what they'd felt for each other had been more hormonal than emotional.

The way he felt about Carlie? Something different altogether—soul-deep, growing by the day. He had no prior experience with the depths he now plumbed.

"Your mom still sends my pulse racing, son. Even more so now that we're done raising the six of you kids, and it's just us again. We didn't get nearly enough of that when we were first married. You came along that first year." He grinned. "I don't think it's like this for most couples, though. Your mom and I . . . well, we're just lucky in love, I guess. Nobody makes me laugh like my Maggie. She's the best part of me."

"I want that with Carlie." He'd have to ask around, find a romantic place to take her out to dinner. Candlelight and linen tablecloths, and he'd buy her flowers. Once he'd healed up a little more, he'd take her on a real date and tell her how much he loved her and Tyler. He had plenty of time. His heart tripped. How would she react? Just because he dreamed of becoming a family with her and Ty didn't mean she wanted the same thing.

CHAPTER FOURTEEN

By the time Carlie saw the Holt family out the door after dinner, Wesley's lips were compressed into a straight line and he kept shifting his position on the couch. She hurried to the kitchen for his pain pills, an antibiotic and a glass of water. Poor guy, he must be so uncomfortable. She headed back to the living room and glanced at her son, who hadn't left Wesley's side all evening. "Go get ready for bed, Tyler, and I'll be there in a few minutes to tuck you in." She set the glass of water on the table.

Tyler slid off the couch, his expression uncertain.

Wes studied him. "What is it, partner?"

"Are you gonna get all better?" Eyes wide, he stared up at Wes.

"Sure I am, but it will take some time."

"You said we never get too big for a hug," Tyler reminded him, his voice quavering. "Remember?"

"Of course I remember, and I could sure use one right now." Wes's Adam's apple bobbed, and he opened his arms. "How about you, partner?"

Tyler rushed toward him. "Whoa." Carlie caught him by the shoulder before he could slam into Wes's injury. "Take it easy. Wes is sore."

"Sorry," Tyler said, glancing up her. "I forgot to be careful."

"It's OK." Wes drew her son into a hug. "No harm done." Wes's eyes were bright as he caught her gaze. Then Tyler moved in his arms, and Wes grimaced.

"Come on, Ty. After I get you to bed, I need to help Wes, so I can tuck him in, too."

Grinning now, Tyler backed out of Wes's arms. "You gotta be tucked into bed just like me?"

"That's right, and I'm not complaining about it, either. It's nice to have your mom take care of us, isn't it?"

"Yeah," Tyler agreed before bouncing down the hall to his room.

She handed Wesley his pain pill and slid the water closer before following her son.

Once she had Tyler down for the night, with Rex in his customary place stretched out on the end of the bed, she returned to find Wes leaning back on the couch with his eyes closed. His color had definitely improved, and his appetite was good. Overcome with relief and gratitude, she stayed where she was just to stare at him, her heart full.

He opened one eye, catching her midstare. "It's been a long day. I need to get to bed pretty quick here. I'm beat, which is pathetic." He ran his hand over his forehead. "I'm going to be completely out of shape by the time I can start exercising again."

"It won't take you long to recover your strength. Talk to Dr. Sunderman when you get the staples out, and ask him when you can start exercising." Moving to his side, she held out her hands to help him up. "Let's go."

His breath hitched in the transition from sitting to standing, and she positioned herself beside him when he swayed on his feet.

Carlie stood nearby while he got himself ready for bed—in case he needed to lean on her. She turned down the blankets on his bed and offered support as he eased himself down. "Good night, Wes. Sleep well." She pulled the covers up around his shoulders and kissed his forehead.

Wesley reached for her hand as she straightened to leave. "Stay with me."

"It's only been few a days since your surgery. I don't want to risk bumping into your incision while I'm asleep."

"What if I need you during the night?" He yawned.

"I'll hear if you call out for me."

"Want . . . arms . . ."

"I'll stay with you until you fall asleep." Her words were wasted. He was already out. Still, she stretched out beside him, placed her head on his shoulder and her arm around his chest. He rubbed his cheek against the top of her head and sighed.

His familiar warmth and scent seeped into her very bones, filling her with a sense of completion. She placed her hand over his heart, just to feel the reassuring steady beat. Her own heart beat in sync with his, and it always would. Once he was feeling stronger, she'd tell him how she felt. Her insides fluttered at the thought. How would he react to the news that she'd fallen in love with him?

She'd experienced the way he shut down and withdrew into himself when the two of them got too close, or whenever relationship issues came up. He'd already told her he didn't have it in him to give his heart again, and maybe that hadn't changed. All he'd ever offered was close friendship, and he only suggested that they could continue to hang out together. Nothing more.

Regardless, she was determined to tell him, even if he didn't return her feelings. He deserved her honesty, and besides, no risk, no gain. Just . . . not today. *Still a coward.*

"Make yourselves comfortable." Carlie set the tray of coffee and cookies on the coffee table. "Help yourselves," she added. David and Miguel had made a point of stopping by each night for a visit before their shift, and, while grateful for their thoughtfulness, she longed for company-free downtime.

"Thanks, Carlie." David helped himself to coffee and a cookie. "Where's Tyler?"

"In bed already," she said, taking a seat on the couch.

"You're lookin' a lot better today, Wes." Miguel reached for a cookie.

"Thanks. I'm feeling better." Wes shifted and glanced at the clock.

Wes might last another hour before she'd need to dose him with pain meds and see him off to bed. It had been five days since she'd brought him home from the hospital, and each day he did more for himself. He was well on the way to regaining his health, but he still tired out quickly, and he still suffered a lot of discomfort.

"When are you coming back to work?" David asked around a mouthful of sugar cookie.

"Soon, I hope," Wes told him. "The staples are being taken out in a couple of days, and I'm going to work a few short shifts next week and see how it goes."

"Good," David said. "It's not that we miss you or anything. It's just that you're the only one who can keep Ken's whining to a minimum. He's the crankiest guy I've ever known."

"He can't help it. He's the way he is because of the traumatic brain injury," Miguel chided. "Irritability and mood swings are symptoms. Cut him some slack."

"Well, thank you for the heads-up, Dr. Garcia," David quipped. "I didn't know, and even now that I do, I'm telling you, it doesn't make him any easier to be around."

"Ken's a good guy," Wes said with a pointed look. "*All* of us get cranky from time to time, and it's a good thing we're surrounded by coworkers who understand. Isn't that right?"

David looked like he was about to argue. Carlie shot up from the couch and grabbed the thermal pot from the coffee table. "Anyone want more coffee?" She circulated around the living room as if she were at the diner, filling coffees, offering more cookies—diffusing tension.

Wes set his mug aside. "No more for me, thanks."

A constant stream of visitors had been invading their privacy at all hours every day since he'd come home from the hospital, and Carlie could see Wes had reached his saturation point. He wasn't alone on that score. Exhaustion wore her thin. She'd need a vacation to recover from her vacation if things didn't improve.

Between playing hostess to Wes's visitors—which had included his siblings, their spouses and children, his parents—and being caregiver to her son, the dog and Wes, the two of them had barely spent two minutes alone together all week. And when they were alone, Wes mostly napped or groused.

She sorely missed the closeness they'd shared before he'd been shot—not to mention how much she missed sleeping with him in his bed. "It's time for your pain pill." Carlie opened the plastic bottle, dropped a pill into her palm and handed it to him. "Not too many left."

"That's OK. I don't need them nearly as much as I did a week ago." He turned to the guys. "One good thing about the painkillers, I sleep the sleep of the drugged, without dreams or nightmares. No wonder so many veterans develop a dependence on the things." He glanced pointedly David's way at that last remark, and the guy's face turned red.

"I'll be ready for bed in about ten minutes. The pain meds knock me out," Wes hinted to the two men lounging in the living room. "Thanks for coming by. Sitting around all day is boring as hell."

"No problem, Wes." Miguel stood up. "Come on, David. Let's go grab a burger before our shift starts. Thanks for the cookies and coffee, Carlie. We'll let ourselves out."

"You're welcome," she said, gathering napkins and the thermal coffeepot.

Wes got up to help her clear the table and bunched the mugs together by their handles and set them on the tray. "Let's put a Do Not Disturb sign on the doors."

"They mean well." She glanced at him over her shoulder as she headed for the kitchen. "Your friends are glad you're home and on the mend. We all are."

"You're right, and I'm grateful, but I need a break from all the company." He placed the coffee cups in the sink.

"Did David have a problem with pain pills?"

"He did, but thankfully he's drug-free now." Wes stretched and yawned. "I'm going to go get ready for bed. Will you come tuck me in, Nurse Carlie?"

"Once I get everything squared away here I will." She put the remaining cookies into the plastic container. "Go on. I'll check on you in a minute."

"Check on me, eh? Be still my racing heart." He let out a long-suffering sigh. "Sounds sexy as hell."

"You're in no shape for sexy, and I don't want to cause you any pain." That got her a disgruntled look and a humph in response before he strode off in the direction of his room.

She shook her head at his surly tone. Taking care of him was like having a two-hundred-pound toddler, right down to pureeing three meals a day until his food had the consistency of a jar of Gerber's best.

By the time Carlie went to look in on Wes, he was sound asleep. She got clean clothes ready for him to wear the next day and placed them on the bathroom counter within easy reach. Before she headed for her own room, she stretched out beside him, as she had every night.

"Stay," he whispered, putting his arms around her. "I need to have you in my arms. Nothing more."

He had no idea how much she longed to do just that. He'd been healing well and gaining strength. Still, he was a long way from being out of pain, and she was a restless sleeper. "Not until the staples are out, but I'll stay until you're asleep."

He growled low in her ear, tightened his hold around her as if he meant to keep her there no matter what, and then he fell sound asleep. When she was certain he wouldn't wake up again, she slipped away, regretting the loss of his arms around her the moment she left them.

❦   ❦   ❦

Carlie returned to Wes's apartment after dropping Tyler off at school. Slipping through the back door into the kitchen, she listened for signs that he was still sleeping. Everything was quiet, which meant she had some time to herself. She hung her jacket up and dropped her purse and the newspaper on the table. Today she intended to start looking for a new place to live, another house to rent or an apartment. It didn't matter which, so long as the place was in town.

Her gut wrenched at the thought of leaving. She loved living with Wes, and moving was going to tear her apart. Still, the two of them hadn't talked about a future. She hadn't found the courage to tell him she loved him. Mostly it was fear that held her back. Things were great with Wes, and she hovered on the edge of not wanting to wreck what they had and needing to tell him. Besides, he hadn't asked her to stay. She had to have a plan B in the works.

She started a pot of coffee brewing, grabbed the newspaper and set out for her room to gather her laptop, a notebook and a pen. By the time she placed her things on the table in the living room, the apartment smelled of fresh coffee.

Her laptop open and everything she needed beside her, she began her search. The blinds were open, and the bright sunlight pouring in warmed her as she scanned the housing ads in the paper. The sound of Wes's shower alerted her to the fact that he was up, which meant she had a good twenty minutes before he'd need attention. She jotted down telephone numbers and addresses of a few places that looked promising.

Rex lay at her feet in a pool of sunshine on the rug. His tail flapped a greeting. Carlie glanced up to find Wes staring her way. Her heart flipped at the sight of him. His large frame was bathed in sunlight, making him look like some ancient warrior god. All he needed to complete the picture was a broadsword. She couldn't suppress the grin that image provoked. His eyes widened a fraction at her smile, and the way his gaze roamed over her caused a rush of heat. Sleeping apart was becoming more and more challenging. "Good morning."

"Morning. I smell coffee. Do you want some?"

"Sure." She went back to scrolling on her laptop. "It's fresh. I just started the pot a couple of minutes ago."

"What are you up to there?" He scrutinized the things surrounding her, and his brow furrowed.

"I'm looking for a new place to live." She bit her lip. "I can hardly make myself walk inside my old place, and I refuse to go there by myself. I can't move back into that house, Wes. I just can't." She turned back to her laptop, not wanting to see the relief he might feel at the notion of her vacating his space.

"You don't have to."

"I know I don't, and it's a good thing. I talked to my landlord, and he's letting me out of my lease early."

"You can stay here."

Forever? Her heart pounded and her palms grew moist. He couldn't mean forever. More than likely he was doing what he always did, being a compassionate hero in light of her circumstances. "I appreciate the offer, because I'll have to stay until I find a new place."

She glanced at him, and the look of panic clouding his features brought a sting to her eyes. Even the thought of continuing to live under the same roof with her gave him the shakes? *And now comes the heartbreak.* She swallowed and averted her gaze.

"Don't leave, Carlie," he blurted, his voice barely audible.

What? Her eyes flew to his. "I'm not leaving Perfect, Wes. I'm just looking for a house or an apartment closer to town. It'll be a few months before I'll be able to move, and I won't go anywhere until you're completely healed."

"That's not what I meant." He wiped his palms on his sweatpants. "This isn't how I planned . . . things," he rasped out.

"Things?" She'd never seen her big, strong Marine look so unhinged. The corners of his mouth turned down, and his jaw muscles twitched. Adrenaline pulsed through her veins. "What *things* were you planning?"

He ran his hand over the back of his neck. "I had it all worked out in my head. Once I was healed up some, I was going to ask you out on a real date, somewhere fancy for a nice dinner." He walked toward the couch. "Then, over candlelight and a very expensive meal, I planned to tell you what ran through my mind when I thought I was going to bleed out in your backyard."

Images from that night filled her mind. She heard the gunshot, saw the man she loved drop . . . "I was so afraid for you." She stifled a sob, not entirely successfully. "What . . . uh . . . what ran through your mind?"

"Mostly I realized what a fool I've been, and how I let my pride and fear get in the way of the best thing that has ever happened to me." His gaze held hers. "That would be you and Tyler, by the way. Everyone knew the truth about what I was feeling long before I caught on. It took a bullet to knock some sense into me."

Wesley eased himself down beside her. "Carlie, after I was shot, I prayed like hell that I'd live long enough to tell you how much I love you and Tyler. I don't want you to ever leave me. I can't imagine spending another day without the two of you in my life. Stay here. Let's give us a shot, go all in, get involved . . . socialize." He reached for her hand. "Let's be a couple. What do you say?"

She burst into tears. Not the silent kind, either, but the noisy, sloppy-wet kind of weeping. Relief, elation, disbelief and love swirled through her with such intensity, she couldn't speak, much less breathe. *He loves me!* She could hardly take it in. The object of her fantasies, the best man she'd ever known her entire life . . . Wesley loved her. She swiped at the tears flooding her cheeks with her shirtsleeve and sniffed a couple of times, trying to pull herself together enough to tell him what was in her heart.

"I'm sorry. I didn't mean to upset you." He let go of her hand and pushed himself up.

"No!" Carlie gripped his wrist and tugged him back down.

He hissed out a breath. "Ouch."

"I'm sorry. I . . . I didn't mean to jar your side, but . . . but don't go. Just give me a minute." Inhaling deep breaths, she reached for calm. "Don't you want to know what ran through my head that night?" She hiccupped. "I mean besides being angry with you for putting yourself in front of a bullet."

"I don't know . . ." He glanced at her askance, his expression battened down tight. "Not if it's going to cause more crying."

"I can't help the tears, Wes, so you're just going to have to deal," she said, her voice shaking. "When I saw you fall, my entire world came crashing down. I didn't know whether you were dead or alive, and . . . and it felt like my heart was being ripped right out of my chest." She sniffed again.

"All I could think was that I hadn't had the chance to tell you how much I love *you.*" She tightened her grip on his wrist. "While you were lying there, you said you wanted to surrender. Do you remember? What did you mean?" She turned tear-filled eyes to him. "I thought you were telling me you wanted to give up . . . that you wanted to die!"

"No, Carlie, oh, baby. That's not what I meant at all." He put his arms around her and lifted her to his lap, grunting from the effort. "I meant I wanted to give up all the baggage I've been carrying around, all the stuff from my past that was keeping us apart. I was trying to tell you that I'm ready to give you my heart—completely, no reservations, doubts or fears. That's a good thing, isn't it?" Wes rubbed her back.

Carlie nodded against him. "It is. I never believed something as wonderful as this could ever happen to me. You . . . you took a bullet for me, Wes. Why did you do that?" she asked, putting her arms around his neck, clinging to him for all she was worth.

"I swore I wouldn't let Baumann hurt you, and I keep my promises. I only meant to distract him from going after you. I didn't think the guy would shoot me." He kissed his way down her temple to the place where her shoulder met her neck. "I'm sorry I put you through such a fright. Next time I'll stay hidden, I promise."

A sloppy laugh broke free. "I'd rather you promise there will never *be* a next time. How many women can say their boyfriend took a bullet for them?" She shivered and tilted her head for more of his kisses. "I never thought a man like you could ever—"

"Hold it right there," he ordered, his voice gruff. "We're not going to do *that* anymore, either."

"Do what?"

"The whole I-don't-deserve-you thing. We both have a tendency—"

"To take on blame we don't deserve and to feel unworthy?" She let out a shaky sigh.

"Exactly." He held her close. "I love you, Carlie, and it's the kind of love that grows stronger every day. What I feel for you is a forever kind of thing, and you can take that to the bank."

"I love you, too," she said on a sob.

"Good. It's settled." He kissed her.

Her insides nearly exploded with desire and a giddy joy. Wesley ran his fingers through her hair, melting her bones and sending shivers of pleasure down her spine. Without a doubt, she could place her trust, heart and future in his hands. He'd never let her down. Wes was not a man who broke his promises, and he'd never hurt or abandon her.

He broke the kiss and cradled her head against his shoulder. She placed her palm over his pounding heart. He simply held her, giving her time to take it all in. They were a couple. Wesley Holt loved her! Never in a million years could she have foreseen her life taking such an incredible twist. If it hadn't been for her ex . . .

Her gut wrenched at the thought of all she'd been through with Jared. The pain, terror and heartache from her past gripped her. *No. Let it go—look what it led to. Look who it led to.* Wes ran his hands up and down her back and nuzzled her temple. His warmth and strength, the steadfastness that made him who he was, seeped into her, filled her. In that instant, Carlie forgave her ex. Holding on to the anger and hurt would only pollute what she had with Wes, and she wouldn't let that happen.

"Carlie, would you be my date for Cory and Ted's wedding?" Wes murmured into her ear.

Happiness welled. She had friends in Perfect, the love of a good man, a job she enjoyed, a community and a place to set down roots for her and Tyler. "I'd love to be your date for their wedding."

"And tonight . . . will you *finally* move back into our room? Please?"

Another shaky sigh escaped. "I will, yes."

"Good." He held her away from him, a lopsided grin on his beloved face. "I could really use a sponge bath about now, Nurse Carlie."

She blinked at him through her tears. "You just showered."

He waggled his eyebrows. "But I'm still . . . *dirty.*"

She laughed, stood and reached out a hand to help him up. Would he always turn her insides to molten lava with just a look? Lord, she hoped so. "Well, then, I just might have to lick you clean."

"Yes, please. Do that, Nurse Carlie."

She led him to his room—correction, their room—and stripped him bare, teasing with barely there skin-on-skin brushes. He played the helpless patient while she played the caregiving nurse. She helped him stretch out on their bed, touching and caressing him as she did. Then she stood back and did a little striptease for him.

"You have no idea what you do to me, woman." His gaze raked over her, leaving her breathless and wanting.

She crawled across the bed to reach him, ran her tongue over one of his nipples and nibbled her way up to his mouth. "Tell me, Wes. What do I do to you?"

He wrapped his arms around her, pulled her to him and ravaged her mouth with a kiss. When he finally came up for air, he stared into her eyes. "Since the first day I laid eyes on you at the diner, you've held the starring role in a whole bunch of sexy dreams—a year and a half's worth, in fact." He nuzzled the tender spot behind her ear. "I'll bet you had no idea, did you?"

She trembled in his arms, overcome with love for her big Marine with his gentle ways and quiet nature. "I didn't. I thought I was the only one fantasizing about us. Your visits to the diner were the high point of my days, Wes. I'll bet you had no idea, either." She drew back to study him. "Did you?" She slid her hand down to stroke him, gratified by the sudden intake of his breath.

"Nope. But I like the sound of that."

"Tell me what you dreamed about, Wes."

"I'd rather show you."

He put an end to their conversation as he showed her what she did to him and what she meant to him. Their lovemaking took on a depth and intimacy she'd never before experienced, and she knew she'd cherish these memories for the rest of her life. Opening herself up, she gave him all of her trust and all of her heart. He'd earned them, and deep in her soul she knew their love would only grow stronger with each passing day.

Together, they'd make a lifetime of memories to savor. Wesley was her dream and her greatest fantasy, and she planned to spend the rest of her life showing him just how much she loved him.

❧ ❧ ❧

The wedding march began, and everyone stood and turned to watch the procession. Carlie had a place of honor in the turn-of-the-century redbrick church. She sat in the front pew next to the bride's mother, because Wesley would walk Cory down the aisle, and *she* was his date. A frisson of pleasure at the thought brought a smile to her face.

The bridesmaids appeared. Brenda, the maid of honor, led the way on Noah Langford's arm. Paige and Ryan were next, and then Ceejay with one of Ted's brothers. Then the bride appeared, a vision of loveliness in her long white gown and veil. Cory was absolutely luminous and radiating joy.

Everyone's eyes went to the bride, while Carlie's were riveted to the handsome man escorting her. She'd never seen him dressed in anything but jeans before, and man, did he wear that charcoal-gray suit well. The red rose pinned to his lapel added just the right touch of dashing elegance. If he ever got tired of being a furniture finisher, he could easily turn to modeling. Carlie's breath hitched at the sight of him.

The two made their way up the aisle toward the altar, where Ted, the eager groom, waited, a look of stunned awe suffusing his face and a reverent love shining from his eyes. Once Wes reached Carlie's pew, he caught her eye and winked, sending her heart leaping for joy. Ever since the day they'd decided to become a couple, he never let an opportunity pass to let the world know she was his and he was hers. She grinned, letting everything she felt for him shine through.

As Cory and Ted said their vows, binding their lives together, not a single eye remained dry. The moment they were introduced as Mr. and Mrs. Lovejoy, a cheer filled the picturesque church. Grabbing her coat, Carlie followed the wedding party outside to mingle with the rest of the guests waiting on the steps out front to throw birdseed over the newly married couple. The bells pealed as the couple appeared, took their birdseed pelting and climbed into the limo waiting to whisk them off to the reception.

Wes found her. Taking her hand in his, they headed to his SUV. "I'm starving. I hope the food at this shindig will be decent."

Ever since his recovery, his appetite had been huge, and he'd started working out again. They often went to Boonville together. She'd go off to her kickboxing class, and he'd head to his gym, then they'd go have dinner together afterward. Now that no threat hung over them, they made sure to get a sitter a couple of times a week so they could go out on dates.

"I'm sure the food will be great. I've heard nothing but good things about the country club where the reception is being held." She pulled out the directions to get there from her coat pocket and unfolded the map. "I'll copilot."

"Have I mentioned how gorgeous you look in that dress? Can't wait to get you home tonight, so I can take it off you."

"You have, thank you. Have I told you how hot you look in that suit?" She glanced at him through her lashes. "And the feeling is mutual. Can't wait to get you naked."

Wes gave her a quick kiss as he opened the door of his SUV for her. "Let's not stay too late."

"Good idea." Carlie sighed and settled herself against the leather seat as Wes turned his SUV onto the road toward the country club. The day had been clear and sunny, not too cold, and the rural two-lane meandering along the river, with the brilliant sunset as a backdrop, painted a lovely picture. "I'm so glad Ted and Cory's day was so perfect. Even the weather cooperated."

"Mmm. We've never danced together before." He glanced at her. "I don't even know if you like to dance. Do you?"

"With the right partner, I do." She smiled. "How about you?"

"It's been a while, but sure. I'll get out there and move around the floor with you tonight."

The country club and golf course were situated on a stretch of rolling hills on the banks of the Ohio River. Wes pulled his SUV around the circular drive to the front entrance, got out and handed his keys to the valet parking attendant. He tucked the ticket into his pocket and once again reached for Carlie's hand.

She loved that he liked to hold her hand or put his arm around her wherever they went. They passed through the opulent lobby and followed the signs pointing to the Lovejoy reception.

Carlie gasped as they entered the ballroom. Everything was so gorgeous and elegant. Round, linen-draped tables held red glass candleholders all aglow with the soft golden light. Ted and Cory's wedding cake sat majestically on a table off to the side, adorned in rich red buttercream roses and green leaves, with the traditional plastic bride and groom standing proudly at the top. Equipment for the disc jockey had already been set up at the edge of the large dance floor.

Other guests began to drift into the room, and soft classical music played through the speakers in the ceiling. "Come on, let's find our table."

She and Wes were seated with the parents of the bride and groom, along with two of Ted's siblings and their spouses. She hadn't been wrong about the food, which was delicious. Once the tables were cleared, coffee poured and the cake cut by the bride and groom and served, the lights dimmed and the party began in earnest.

In honor of Cory's father, Wesley led the bride out onto the dance floor for the first dance. Carlie's eyes stung as he spoke into a microphone about Cory's father, a fallen Marine, and how proud he was that he could step up for his brother in arms on this momentous occasion in Cory's life.

"Wesley reminds me so much of my husband," Cory's mom whispered, her eyes filling. "He's a good man."

Carlie fished a couple of tissues from her purse and handed one to her, keeping one for herself. "I'm so sorry your husband isn't here today, Mrs. Marcel."

"He is here, honey. He is." Mrs. Marcel dabbed at her eyes.

Carlie hoped so, but she didn't know what to say to that, so she focused on Cory and Wesley waltzing around the dance floor. The man could dance, and she couldn't wait for her turn.

Finally, it was her turn, and Wes led her out on the dance floor. He took her into his arms and swept her around to a slow song. They chatted and laughed with their friends as they danced, and happiness lit her up inside. She'd found acceptance and a place where she belonged.

"I love you, Carlie," Wes whispered into her ear.

Closing her eyes, Carlie laid her head on his shoulder and snuggled closer, savoring the moment. "I love you back."

"Get a room, you two," Ryan Malloy teased as he and Paige came up beside them.

Carlie laughed as Wesley winked. "We intend to," he drawled before whisking her away from the Malloys. "As I was saying . . . I love you, and you love me. That's not going to change."

"Nope, it's not," she agreed.

"Have you ever given any thought to having more children?"

She nodded, her throat tightening. "I've always hoped for more. I'd love for Tyler to have a sibling." Glancing up at him, her breath caught at the intensity of his gaze. "Or two."

"Two would be good. I think we both agree about where we're heading, and here's the thing . . ." He cleared his throat. "I don't want to wait, Carlie. Seems like I've been waiting for you my entire life, and I don't want to wait any longer. We're not getting any younger, and we both want a family. How'd you like to go pick out rings with me this week? Let's get married . . . soon."

The hope and love shining in his eyes made her weak in the knees and breathless. "OK," she squeaked, her eyes tearing again. "Let's go ring shopping and plan a wedding, a small wedding with just our friends and family."

"Don't cry, sweetheart. It makes me crazy when you cry."

"I'm not crying," she huffed out, tears spilling down her cheeks.

He chuckled, his expression filled with tenderness. "Did you know that Noah adopted Ceejay's daughter, Lucinda?"

"No." She brushed the tears away. "I thought Lucinda was Noah and Ceejay's."

"Luce was around four when Ceejay and Noah got together. Her dad was Noah's stepbrother, and he died before ever bothering to meet his daughter. It's a long story, and not the point." The music stopped, but he didn't let go of her. He leaned down and pressed his forehead against hers. "How would you feel about me adopting Tyler? I couldn't love him anymore than I already do, even though I'm not his biological father. You know that, don't you?"

"Oh, Wes," she cried. "I'd love nothing more. Tyler adores you, and you've been so good to him." She swallowed a few times. "He's going to go nuts when we tell him."

Another slow song started, and Wesley took her hand, twirled her around in a spin, and drew in her back into his arms to move her around with some fancy footwork. "You're really good at this dancing thing. We might have to start doing this on a regular basis," she said, smiling.

He twirled her again. "Deal."

"My dance partner for life," she whispered as he held her close. "Ted and Cory's wedding today, Brenda and Kyle's in March—are you sure you're not just caught up in the moment, swept away by the wedding fever?" She stared into his wonderful hazel eyes, so filled with love as he gazed back.

"Nope. I'm sure." He brushed his lips against hers. "Well, maybe a little influenced tonight by our surroundings. I had it all worked out in my head. I planned to have a ring for you under the Christmas tree, and when you opened it, I was going to propose." He glanced around the ballroom, a look of utter contentment settling over his features. "But I like the idea of picking out our wedding rings together. I want you to have something that you'll be happy wearing for the rest of our lives.

"Carlie, you rekindled my dream for a family of my own, a dream I buried so deep I didn't believe it could find its way to the surface again." His voice broke. "You humble me with your courage and loyalty—your heart. As far as I'm concerned, the wedding can't happen fast enough."

"I feel exactly the same, Wes. You're my hero, and you always will be." She stopped dancing. "Let's go home."

"If you insist." Grinning, he led her from the dance floor. "Speaking of home, I was thinking this coming summer we should start looking for a house to buy, something with a nice yard for a dog and our kids."

She laughed, unable to contain the elation coursing through her. "I'm convinced. If you've done all this thinking, tonight's proposal couldn't have sprung from the current wedding vibe."

"Like I said, you've held the starring role in my dreams since I first laid eyes on you. May as well make it official." He handed the plastic coat check chip to the attendant, and then he held her coat for her while she slipped her arms into the sleeves. He leaned in close and spoke low into her ear. "I'm going to get lucky tonight, aren't I?"

"Why, yes. *We* are going to get lucky—tonight, tomorrow, and for the rest of our lives."

ACKNOWLEDGMENTS

A BIG THANK-YOU TO PHILLIP Mohs, a veteran in the military police and a military dog handler. First, for his service to our country, and second, for his willingness to answer all of my questions about commands for military working dogs and their training.

Another big thank-you goes out to my wonderful son-in-law, Thomas Menton, who graciously answers all of my questions about law enforcement, different law enforcement agencies and how they all work together. Also, I want to thank Tom for hooking me up with the Warrior's Cove and their self-defense classes for women. You rock, Thomas!

To my wonderful critique partners, Tamara Hughes and Wyndemere Coffee. Thank you. I am so very fortunate and grateful to have the both of you in my life.

To my wonderful agent, Nalini Akolekar, and the amazing crew at Montlake Romance, a big fat thank-you for making it possible for me to do what I love best—tell stories!

A NEW SERIES BY BARBARA LONGLEY

Don't miss *This Handyman's Heart,* the first book in the Haney Family series by Barbara Longley

Fall 2016

CHAPTER ONE

Brrr. Sam huffed out a breath, and a cloud of steam formed in front of his face. Minnesota winters were frigid, and the frigid had started early this year. They'd already had a couple of below-zero nights, and it wasn't even the middle of November yet. If it weren't for hockey, snowmobiling and ice fishing, he'd move south.

Of course, he'd miss Grandpa Joe and Grandma Maggie, along with his younger brother and sister. His siblings might be willing to make the move with him, but his grandparents would never leave St. Paul. All of their kids, grandkids and great-grandkids were here. *Guess I'm stuck.*

He circled to the driver's side and climbed into his old Ford work van. Turning the key in the ignition produced nothing but a reluctant *Rrrr-rrrr-rrrr*. "Come on, buddy. I don't like the cold or Monday mornings, either, but you don't see me staying in bed." He patted the dashboard, like that would somehow encourage the van to start. Shivering, he tried again and got the same refusal. "I'll let you think about it for minute, and then you have to crank. We have work to do." He waited a minute and tried again. The engine turned over, earning another pat to the dashboard.

Content to sit while the engine warmed up, Sam sipped his coffee and turned on the radio. He had plenty of time before he needed to set out for his first job of the day, and his favorite morning talk show was about to begin. He tuned the radio to "Loaded Question" and leaned forward to adjust the volume so he could hear the radio over the fan. Cheesy music announced the morning show was about to begin. Sam grinned. They always posed some outrageous question. Last week's had been, "What's the worst first date you've ever been on?"

Another time the hosts had asked, "What's the weirdest thing you've ever eaten?" Hilarious.

"Good morning, Twin Cities! You're listening to the wake-up crew, Dianna Barstow and Russell Lund, and it's time for . . . da, da daaaah, 'Loaded Question!'" the male counterpart of the duo announced. "What's our question for today, Dianna?"

"Well, Russ, I think we have a winner here this morning. Today's question is: What's the sluttiest thing you've ever done?"

This ought to be good for a few laughs. Sam adjusted the fan so it blew on the windshield. He could get out and scrape off the ice, but why bother? It would just frost up again by the time he was back inside. Better to let the van warm up and defrost on its own. Grandpa Joe always said there are two kinds of lazy, smart lazy and dumb lazy. If you're smart lazy, you do things right the first time, so you don't have to do them over. That's how Sam saw himself. Smart lazy.

"Whoa! Good one! What is the sluttiest thing you've ever done, Dianna?"

"Ahh." She laughed. "Good question. Spring break five years ago. No details."

Their banter went on for another few minutes before the DJs announced their telephone number and turned it over to the listening audience. Since the talk show hosts often gave out some pretty sweet prizes—like hard-to-get concert tickets or cash—Sam had the number in his speed dial. He hadn't won anything yet, but he wasn't about to give up. For the next few minutes he listened to one outrageous story after another, choking on his coffee when laughter sent it down the wrong pipe.

A husky, feminine voice came over the air. "Hi, my name is Yvonne."

"Hello, Yvonne," Dianna and Russ said in unison. "What's the sluttiest thing you've ever done?"

"Well," she began, hesitating slightly.

Her voice sounded familiar, and her name . . . "Naw. Couldn't be."

"I'm recently divorced, and I kept the house," Yvonne finally blurted.

"OK. Go on," Russ prodded.

"It had been a while since I'd . . . you know . . ."

"Had sex?" Dianna chortled. "We're listening. We're all listening."

"I had a few things that needed to be done around the house, and a couple of my girlfriends kept telling me I should hire this handyman named Sam. So I did."

Sam froze, and not from the cold. "Cripes!" It *was* her. He'd done some work for Yvonne two weeks ago. He thunked his head against the steering wheel and groaned. "Great. *I'm* the sluttiest thing she's ever done. I wonder if there's an award for that."

He imagined what his plaque might look like hanging on the wall of his tiny office. Polished brass mounted on an oval piece of oak, and the engraving would read, "Sluttiest Carpenter Award of Excellence"—for going above and beyond the call of duty.

"OK, Sam the handyman," Russ teased. "Tell me. Just how handy was he?"

"My, oh my. Let me tell you. He was plenty handy and incredibly hot. After he did the job, I did him." She sighed. "It was wonderful."

Yvonne's happy sigh over the air brought a smile to his face. He liked to leave his customers completely satisfied. Oh, right. That bit would have to be added to his award. He sat back up. "You were plenty hot yourself, Yvonne."

Maybe she'd have another job for him to do soon. He shook his head. Not a good idea. Women got ideas when he came around a second time—*relationship* ideas.

He shuddered at the thought. His life was exactly the way he wanted it. Who needed all the drama, all the demands and upheaval that came with the whole relationship package? Who needed the heartache? Not him. Strings-free, protected sex and the bachelor life suited him. He had his buddies, his brother, sister, grandparents and a great extended family. He lived la dolce vita—the sweet life. *Why fix it if it ain't broken?*

Listeners were weighing in about Yvonne. About him.

"It would bother me knowing my partner had probably done it with half the women in the Twin Cities," one listener commented. "He's the slut. Yvonne was just a lonely divorcée, and Sam took advantage of her. Maybe he's a sex addict. For all we know, she was just one of a dozen he did that day."

"Sex addict?" Sam scowled at the radio. "Slut? Wait just a doggone minute. I've done nothing wrong." Before he realized what he was doing, he'd grabbed his phone from the cup holder and hit speed dial. His outrage grew with each passing second. He was a good guy, honest and up front. He never led anyone on. Plus, his moral compass worked just fine, thank you very much. His call was answered on the fifth ring.

"This is Russ, and you're on the air. What's the sluttiest thing you've ever done?"

"Yeah. This is Sam Haney. I'm Yvonne's handyman, and—"

"Whoa! No last names here, Sam Haney. We like to protect the innocent, Handyman Haney. Did you get that, ladies? Sam Haney, the handsiest handyman in the Twin Cities."

"Hands-On Haney the Handyman!" Dianna chortled with glee, and the two of them laughed. "Get his number for me, would you, Russ?" Dianna chimed. "As a matter of fact, Sam, why don't you share your number with all of us?"

Aww, cripes. Idiot. Their jokes were stupid, and he didn't appreciate being the punch line. "Listen, you wouldn't believe how women throw themselves at me on the job. I can show up for work scruffy as all get-out, raggedy flannel shirt, faded, torn jeans, unshaved and hair a mess, and they're still all over me. Women love me."

"I'm sure they do," Russ said, and both hosts sniggered lewdly.

The word *cliché* popped into his brain. He shoved it aside. There was nothing cliché about him. He just needed to find a different morning talk show, that's all. "Look, I don't mess with married women, or women who are involved with someone, and it's not me who comes on to them. It's the other way around. We're consenting adults, enjoying a little safe, recreational sex. That's all there is to it. No addiction. No taking advantage. Nobody is getting hurt. I'm unattached, clean, healthy and a decent guy. Can I help it if women want me?"

Trudy laughed out loud, delighted by the latest installment of "Loaded Question." She turned the bacon frying in the skillet and headed to the fridge for eggs. She liked to send her husband off to work with a good, hot breakfast in his stomach. Returning to the kitchen counter, she set the eggs down and turned up the radio.

She gasped, hardly believing Yvonne's handyman had the audacity to come on the air. Pulling her iPhone out of her apron pocket, she called her sister's number. Nanci picked up right away.

"Is that you, Trudy?"

"Are you hearing this?" Trudy demanded. "Are you listening to 'Loaded Question'?"

"I am. I already looked up Handyman Haney's place of business on the Internet. Haney & Sons Construction and Handyman Service. No job is too big or too small, according to their website. Might have him do a few jobs for me." They both giggled like teenagers.

Trudy sighed. "I know it's wrong, but I wish my Haley would have an encounter like Yvonne's. She needs something like that to bolster her self-esteem since you-know-who did you-know-what to her."

"Still can't believe that little twerp bolted like he did, and only two weeks before their wedding." Nanci huffed. "Who does that? Who just up and suddenly decides they *have* to live in Indonesia—without the high school sweetheart they've been engaged to for two whole years?"

"I think there may have been another woman involved." Trudy forked the bacon out of the pan and set it on a stack of paper towels to drain. Cradling the phone between her ear and shoulder, she moved the pan, replacing it with a smaller one for the eggs. "Don't you think so?"

"Not for one single minute," her sister snapped. "I think he had a *man* waiting for him over there. I can't imagine any heterosexual male walking away from my gorgeous niece for any other reason."

"Aww. That's sweet—in a warped kind of way." Trudy melted a little butter in the pan, pushed the toast down in the toaster, and cracked the eggs over the skillet. "Haley is really down in the dumps, and it's been months. She needs something other than remodeling projects to shake her out of her slump. Have you seen what a disaster she's made out of her house?"

"I have, and it's frightening."

Frank Cooper, Trudy's own high school sweetheart, walked into the kitchen and kissed her cheek before helping himself to coffee and meandering into the dining room with his newspaper tucked under his arm. Trudy transferred her phone to her hand. "Can I call you back after breakfast?"

"Sure. Later."

Trudy put her phone back in her pocket and focused on flipping the eggs so they were over easy just the way she and Frank liked them. The toast popped up. While she buttered the lightly toasted whole-grain bread, a plan began to coalesce in her mind. She loaded two plates, cut a banana in half, adding them to their fare, and carried their breakfasts to the dining room. As usual, Frank had his nose buried in his newspaper.

She set his plate in front of him. "Frank, Haley's birthday is coming up."

He lowered the edge of his paper to send her an indulgent smile. "If I'm not mistaken, our daughter's birthday is in May. This is November." Setting aside the news, he put a napkin on his lap and reached for the salt.

"I know when her birthday is. *I'm* the one who carried her for nine months and went through seventy-two hours of labor bringing her into this world." She lifted her chin. "Excruciating labor, I might add."

"Seems to me the number of hours you were in labor grows with each telling." He raised an eyebrow and cut an egg with the edge of his fork.

She blew out a breath. "Her birthday *is* coming up—"

"I can't argue with that, sweetheart. Birthdays do come around once a year. They're always coming up. Even for you, though to me you're still as beautiful as you were the day we met."

"Oh, Frank, and you're still the sweetest man in the world." She slid her palm over his arm, warmth for her husband of almost thirty years filling her with gratitude. He'd given her two amazing children and a very comfortable life. She wanted the same for her only daughter.

"Well . . . I was thinking maybe we could give Haley an early birthday present this year." She squirmed in her seat just a tiny bit. "She's had such a rough time of it, and I just want to help her out. Don't you want to help her out, honey?"

"Mmm-mm," he agreed around a mouthful.

"Her house is a disaster area, what with all the home improvement projects she starts and never finishes. I'm afraid she's going to bring the place tumbling down around her ears, or worse. It's going to go up in smoke."

Frank frowned and nodded.

"What if we pay a handyman to help her put things back together so that her house is livable again? I want my little girl to be safe. Don't you want our little girl to be safe, Frank?"

Her husband's eyes twinkled as he swallowed his mouthful. "Haley isn't a little girl anymore, Trudy. She's twenty-six, with a well-established career and a home of her own. Still, it's an excellent idea. Take care of it, would you, sweetheart? Hire somebody, but check for references on Angie's List first."

"Oh, I will." *No, I won't.* She crossed her fingers in her lap against the small white lie, knowing exactly whom to hire. She rose from her chair. "More coffee?"

ABOUT THE AUTHOR

As a child, Barbara Longley moved frequently, learning early on how to entertain herself with stories. Adulthood didn't tame her peripatetic ways: she has lived on an Appalachian commune, taught on an Indian reservation and traveled the country from coast to coast. After having children of her own, she decided to try staying put, choosing Minnesota as her home. By day, she puts her master's degree in special education to use teaching elementary school. By night, she explores all things mythical, paranormal and newsworthy, channelling what she learns into her writing.

Ms. Longley loves to hear from readers and can be reached through her website, barbaralongley.com, on Twitter @barbaralongley, or on Facebook—facebook.com/barlongley.